HOLES
IN THE
PLAN

KATE PETTY

ISBN-13: 978-0692423769 (Kate Petty Productions)
ISBN-10: 0692423761

This book is dedicated to the members of the Rho Tau Epsilon fraternal order

CHAPTER 1 - TAYLOR

Whoever invented dubsteb obviously never listened to it when they were drunk or they would have seriously reconsidered what they were about to unleash on the world. I think anyone slumped in the corner of their friend's bathroom trying to sync the banging thrums of a turbulent remix with the crippling pulses in their brain would be ready for murder.

That's about where I was when my brother Daniel half-stumbled by the open bathroom door in Haleigh's parents' house. The fact that he noticed me at all meant he was probably faring better than I, but you can't be too hasty with those sorts of assessments.

"Taylor?" He did a double take at my less-than-dignified position on the floor.

"Present," I mumbled, wondering whether I needed to throw up.

He knitted his brow in a way normally reserved for debating politics rather than whether the rumpled mess of sequins propped against the bathtub was his sister.

"You okay?"

"Fabulous."

He pushed in and reached a hand towards me. "Here."

"No, leave me to rot."

Grabbing both wrists, he managed to pull me to my feet without either of us ending up on the ground. He held on to my arm for a moment either to stabilize me or himself, I'm not sure which.

I caught my reflection in the mirror. "Could be worse." I tried to smooth down my haystack of long, unruly hair. My efforts to straighten it earlier in the evening were beginning to wear off, and the dull brown strands had loosened into limp waves. "What time is it?"

He dug in his pocket for his phone, "One fifty-four."

I leaned heavily onto the counter, wanting to sit down again. "Can we go home?"

"Uhm," he pushed back his hair, the same light brown as mine, and knit his brow again. "Yes. We need a ride..." He checked his phone again, as if it'd provide some sort of solution.

"Rachel still here?"

"Yes!" He looked truly astounded to remember his girlfriend was somewhere around the house. "Yes. Where did I see her..."

Maybe he'd had more to drink than I thought. I followed him out of the bathroom, the music growing louder as we wove through circles of people standing and talking. We picked our way down a sleek, narrowly railed flight of stairs, more terrifying than I remembered them being on the way up. Daniel paused at the bottom, looking across the living room through the masses of people shouting over the deafening music and dancing with each other. When we found Rachel perched on a stool, watching a game of beer pong, Daniel made a straight shot through the crowd towards her.

"Are you good to drive?" He asked as we approached.

"Sure."

"How much have you had?" I asked.

She picked up her bottle of Shiner and squinted to see the fill line. "Beer and a half."

"Perfect," Daniel said. He gave her his keys and she took a final swig before standing to smooth her unwrinkled skirt. I glanced down at my now-crinkled dress, the sequins bent and unraveling in places. I felt a little judgment from Rachel as she smirked past us to lead the way outside. She and Daniel were three years beyond college graduation parties so I guess she had the right to judge me. I asked Haleigh for permission to invite them to hers because I hadn't known many people going and wanted Daniel as a social crutch but, as with most events these days, he and Rachel came as a package deal.

We were almost to the door when Daniel stopped us. "Should you go say 'bye' to Haleigh?"

I shot him a look but turned and scanned the crowd. Haleigh's dress, a blinding shade of hot pink, and her white-blond hair made her easy to find. "Don't leave," I warned Daniel as I stalked across the room to where she stood, laughing with a group of guys near the massive speakers egging on my headache. Even with the high heels Haleigh wore, she barely came up to my chin. I put a hand on her shoulder to get her attention.

"Hey, I'm leaving," I shouted over the music.

"What?" She shouted back, the smell of beer heavy on her breath.

I placed a hand on my chest. "I. Am," I pointed at the door. "Leaving."

"Oh. Okay." She turned back to the guys. I'm not sure why I bothered

I shuffled back to Daniel and Rachel and followed them outside. When Rachel eased the car up to the curb outside our house, well, our parents' house, I said a fast goodbye and slid out quickly, giving them a moment to do their goodnight thing. In my haste to get out of the way, I caught the mailbox with my hip, nearly knocking off the wooden 'The Bryant's' sign. It probably should have hurt like hell but I don't remember feeling anything. I just hoped Daniel and Rachel didn't see.

"Front or garage?" Daniel asked when he caught up to me a moment later.

"Garage. Quieter."

He nodded in agreement and punched in the code. I followed him inside until we split ways at the top of the stairs, neither of us bothering to say goodnight. I flopped onto my bed without undressing and tried to visualize sturdy things to offset the slow spinning inside my head.

Either the smell of coffee or the neighbor's lawn mower woke me the next morning. In the spirit of optimism, I credited the coffee and rolled out of bed to get some. A nasty headache started coming on with the movement and my mouth felt parched and dry. I made a straight shot down the stairs, chugged a bottle of water and bee-lined to the coffee pot in the kitchen.

I pulled a mug out of the cabinet and felt the spot on my hip where I'd run into the mailbox. It felt sore but I couldn't see a bruise yet. "Idiot," I mumbled to myself as I poured the coffee. At least I didn't drink enough to make me sick. The previous weekend's parties left me with a forty-eight hour hangover so, really, the bruise was an improvement. I lifted the mug to my lips and took a long, soothing sip.

"I thought I heard you come in last night, but then I didn't see Daniel's car this morning."

At the suddenness of Mom's voice, my throat clenched and I choked on the coffee I'd been in the process of swallowing. I hadn't noticed her sitting in the adjoining sun room.

"We left it at Haleigh's," I told her between coughs. "Rachel offered to drive us home."

"That was nice of her," she replied neutrally, playing along with the pretense that we left it there out of convenience and nothing more.

I took my coffee and sat in the chair next to hers, glad for her willingness to overlook the obvious. I shouldn't bother trying to hide the details from her, she knew I drank. I was long past the legal drinking age but I was still adjusting to living at home again and wasn't used to sharing my social life with Mom.

She sat in her usual morning position, coffee in one hand, book in the other, sock-clad feet propped on the coffee table in front of her and sandy blond hair twirled into a messy bun on top of her head. With the sweatshirt and long pajama bottoms she wore, you'd never guess it was the middle of May in Texas.

"Was the party fun?"

I shrugged, "Not bad."

"Did anyone end up bringing gifts?"

"A few, but I think most of them were from her family. I told you, people don't do the gift thing as much for college graduation parties."

"See, it'll be better to just have your graduation celebration with the family," she reasoned. "Everyone's had enough of the party thing."

Even with the headache, I wasn't quite on that page yet. The long string of parties over the past couple of weeks was perfect for ignoring everything I didn't want to think about regarding post-college life. The idea of a quiet, sophisticated dinner with the family toasting to the last four years probably seemed appealing to people graduating with useful degrees and launching into respectable sounding careers. With my studio art degree, however, I was gearing up to join the vast ranks of unemployment and gladly welcomed any distractions.

"Good morning," Dad greeted me, coming into the sun room, cup of coffee in hand.

"Morning."

"Did you hear back from JCH?" he asked, referring to an advertising company I'd grudgingly submitted my portfolio to over a week ago.

"Nope." My unsuccessful job hunt wasn't on the list of things I wanted to discuss in the morning. Really, I didn't ever want to discuss it, but especially not then.

"Did the Tinley Group contact you?"

"Nope." That was a lie. They'd respectfully denied my application they day before via a nicely written, automated email, which may or may not have had something to do with the general trajectory of last night.

"Where else are you looking into?"

"I don't know, Dad."

But of course he wasn't going to drop it. "You need to make that your project for today. The longer you wait the less likely it is companies are going to hire you."

"Can we not talk about this first thing in the morning?"

"It's almost eleven o'clock."

"I just woke up."

"I understand you've had lots of parties and fun lately," he started, condescension edging into his tone. "But you can't put things off forever."

"It's been *three weeks*," I said, unable to keep my voice from rising. "Give me a break."

"Hey, hey," Mom warned, jumping in to mediate.

I looked at both of them darkly.

"How about I make breakfast?" she offered, not waiting for an answer before heading to the kitchen. Dad stood to follow her.

"Do you need some more coffee?" He asked.

"No. Thank you." I did, but accepting felt like letting him win.

He left me brooding with my empty cup. Eventually, the scent of fresh beignets, yeasty and sugary, drew me to the kitchen table, and we managed to eat with civility, but I declined their offer to go run errands together. Dad asked too many questions and the idea of a family errand day felt too much like high school. I stayed at the table until Daniel showed up, shirtless with his hair sticking out in every direction.

"Morning," he said sleepily.

I nodded in his direction. Following the family routine, he pulled a cup out of the cabinet and filled it with coffee.

"Need a refill?" he asked, raising the coffee pot.

I accepted gratefully and he came to join me at the table, wasting no time stuffing large bites of airy beignet into his mouth.

"Dad started the job thing again," I told him.

He shook his head in sympathetic annoyance.

"You know what the really sucky part is?"

"What?"

"I don't even want these jobs I'm applying for."

It felt like an enormous confession, but he only shrugged. "Work sucks," he said.

"It shouldn't have to. I thought that was the whole reason you're supposed to go to college. Study things you like, get a job you're passionate about."

He gave me an amused look. "It's not like I love analyzing financial charts all day long," he said, finishing a bite. "But I do it."

"You have powdered sugar on your chin," I pointed out flatly.

He brushed his hand across his chin and managed to get most of the sugar off. "At least you're not locked into a job yet."

"Yeah, but I'm supposed to be. I can't even get off square one, and worse, I don't really want to. There's nothing I want to do."

"Tough. Find something. Can't sit around and not do anything all day."

He had a point. "Maybe I should live out my childhood dreams and start a bakery," I mused, poking at a beignet.

"Make beignets!" he suggested excitedly.

"No, too Creole."

He poked his fork through the last beignet on the plate between us, making a hole in the middle of it. "Doughnuts?"

I pulled off the beignet and took a bite. "You're useless."

He smiled and took the beignet back before I could eat any more.

CHAPTER 2 - DANIEL

After breakfast, Taylor drove me to get my car from Taylor's friend's house. It was still parked at the end of the street where we'd left it the night before. When we got back home, I left it in the driveway instead of pulling into the garage to wash it since it was the fourth Saturday of the month. I always wash my car on the fourth Saturday of the month. I unwound the garden hose from the side of the house and got a bucket from the garage to hold the soapy water. A couple of sponges were inside the bucket, right where I left them the last time I washed my car. The afternoon sun burned the concrete of the driveway, so I stood on the grass and used the hose to water the ground around my car until I could actually walk on it. I crossed the drive to where I'd left the bucket, poured in some soap, filled the bucket, gave my car a quick rinse, and then got to work.

The air was hot and my shoulders ached from sitting at my desk all week but it felt good to be outside and working with my hands. I'd been at it for about fifteen minutes when I heard a car door slam. I looked over the top of my car and saw Haleigh walking up the drive. She gave a little wave when she saw me.

"Hey, Haleigh," I said, continuing to scrub at the doors.

"Hey," she stopped a few feet away. "Nice car."

"Thanks." I guess she'd never seen it before. I looked at my car, trying to picture it from her perspective. She was brand new when I bought her a little over two years ago. Her graphite colored exterior and chrome trim, still scratch-free, sparkled blindingly in the sun. I hadn't started on the wheels yet, but the chrome rims gave a sharp impression even with the layer of dirt covering them. It was a good looking car. But all I saw was two doors when four would have been more convenient and a tight, compact frame that looked cool but barely had enough trunk space for a case of beer.

Taylor came outside, keys in hand, and started for her car on the other side of the driveway. Sometimes I started to feel bad about getting to park my car in the garage with Mom and Dad's while she had to leave hers outside. Normally I ignored the guilt but she'd seemed so bummed at breakfast that morning.

"Hey," I said as she unlocked the door. "If you leave your car I'll wash it for you."

She stopped with her hand on the car door and glanced at Haleigh.

"I don't mind driving," Haleigh said.

"Okay," Taylor agreed. "Thanks."

She pulled back her arm to toss me the keys over my car and my breath caught, knowing that I was about to see the first scratches mark the exterior. Yet somehow she'd managed to not throw like a girl for once in her life - the keys sailed smoothly over the roof and I caught them easily.

"Nice throw."

She gave a ridiculous bow before turning with Haleigh to leave. I rinsed off the doors and continued working my way around to the bumper and then the other side. I finished my car, pulled it back in the garage, and started on Taylor's. Her normal parking spot was at the far edge of the driveway, flush against a row of prickly holly bushes, so I reversed the car and parked it in the middle of the driveway. I was still working on it when Mom and Dad pulled up, forcing them to park at the base of the driveway.

"When are we ever going to teach that girl how to park a car?" Dad grinned, his arms full of groceries.

"Sorry, I'm almost done."

"Not a problem," Mom said cheerfully. "That's nice of you to wash your sister's car."

"Wish I knew how to get on that list," Dad said. His tone was light and joking but you could tell he kind of meant it.

"I can wash yours too," I said. "Just leave me the keys." I would have been happy stopping my charity at Taylor's car - the ache from my shoulders had worked its way through the rest of my back, but it wouldn't have been right not to offer.

"Thanks," Dad said, handing me his keys. "I owe you a rent discount."

9

My jaw tightened reflexively. I took the keys. Recently, I couldn't stand anything that brought attention to living at home. Taylor moving back in made the situation feel like high school again which, in turn, made me feel even more pathetic than before. Nothing to be done about my living situation for the time being though.

I put his keys in my pocket and glanced at my car, sitting arrogantly in the garage. I scrubbed at some tree sap on Taylor's windshield. Without the car payments, moving out might have been a possibility by now. At the beginning, living at home was a temporary fix while I put a little money in the bank and took care of the upkeep I'd been doing on my old car. At the time, it was fifteen years old and the repairs were running me several hundred dollars every few months. It adds up.

I tried looking at new cars before I got officially hired on with Colson Caldwell, but it was pretty depressing. My intern's salary gave me no hope of being able to afford anything more than a small step above the piece of junk I already owned.

But then one day Tom, the regional VP of Finance, called me to his office and offered me the full time junior analyst position, with benefits, two weeks of paid vacation, and a signing bonus. Tom promised a promotion within the year, so I started shopping for different cars. I used my signing bonus as a down payment and bought a little more than I could afford, counting on the promotion to offset the costs in a few months. The months turned into two years and there I was, still sitting at the same desk, in the same office, with the same job title.

Buying the car had been glorious though. When I thought I found the one, I brought Rachel to the dealership with me. We'd only been dating a couple of months at the time but she openly balked at the price of the one I had my eye on.

"Daniel," Rachel hissed when the car salesman went inside to get the keys for a test drive. "This is way too expensive."

"I'm just looking."

"You're tempting yourself," she insisted. "What happened to looking at used cars?"

I glanced at the spec sheet taped to the corner of the window. "This one has forty-two miles on it," I grinned.

She shot me a look but the car salesman was approaching so she didn't say anything else. I saw her face when we took it for a drive though. She slid onto the black leather seat and took her time adjusting it in every direction. Her deep green eyes swept over the interior, taking in the moon roof, the controls for heating and cooling the seats, the window that rolled up and down without protest. The window on the passenger side of my old car got stuck at half mast unless you hit the door in the right spot.

Car salesmen always talked about "seeing" myself in whatever car they were pushing on me but the thing was, seeing Rachel is what won me over. I drove us through quiet, tree lined neighborhoods and kept glancing over at her as the breeze blew through the open window, swirling her long black hair around her shoulders. She looked so beautiful and content. It sounds dumb, but I loved that moment and I wanted to live it again with her next week and next month and five years from then. It was perfect. And then the car salesman spoke up from the back seat, telling me to pull into a cul-de-sac so I could see how tight the car could turn. It was hard to forget he was there after that, but I already had my moment.

I bought the car when we returned to the dealership. I rode the high of owning the new car right up until the time for my promised promotion came and passed. The bills from the bank were a monthly reminder to not make the same mistake again.

Mistake or not, I took a lot of effort in caring for the car, something I bitterly thought to suggest Mom and Dad try with their own. Their hulking SUV, covered with more dirt than I thought possible, took the longest out of the three. When I finally finished, I returned the bucket with my car washing supplies to the shelf in the garage next to Dad's toolbox and recoiled the hose. I went inside to shower and then made a sandwich and ate alone in front of the TV. The Rangers were playing the Mariners but it was already the bottom of the ninth and the Rangers were down, 8-1. I turned off the TV as soon as I finished eating.

Because it was the last Saturday of the month, I went back to my room after lunch to run through my budget. The last Saturday didn't always fall on my car washing day but I kind of liked when it did. The balance of the two worked nicely. I sat down at my desk, a heavy, wooden thing I'd picked up at a garage sale after graduating, and turned on my laptop.

Growing up, I'd only used my room for sleeping. When I'd traded my college apartment for my room back home, I'd tried to rearrange things more sensibly since I was used to having distinct spaces to work, sleep, and relax. Hence the garage sale desk, crammed into a corner with my laptop and a few books I'd kept from college.

I'd shoved my ancient twin bed in the opposite corner. The comforter and pillows were a hideous orange and white for the university I'd been obsessed with at the beginning of high school. They were on my list of things to go as soon as I had some extra money to throw around.

Another corner of the room was taken up by the doors for the hallway and the bathroom, which left the remaining corner for a TV and an old futon I bought my freshman year of college. The futon lacked some of the comfort it initially offered, but I thought the stray springs, faded cover, and lumpy cushions gave it character.

When my laptop booted up I opened the spreadsheets I used to track and budget my finances. Every so often Rachel told me about some new budgeting software, each one more dynamic and innovative than the last, but I held tight to my spreadsheets. I created them when I got my first job in high school and they worked as well as they always had. I saw no reason to move to a new system when mine worked just fine.

I pulled a stack of receipts from my wallet and added them into their respective categories. When I finished, the numbers looked a little rough. The amount left in my discretionary spending column had fallen into the double digits, but I needed to make it stretch five more days. Rachel and I had been debating going to a concert that night but after seeing the spreadsheet, I decided we'd have to just do dinner instead. The concert could wait.

CHAPTER 3 - TAYLOR

"How many books can they write about studying for the LSAT?" Haleigh asked, her round blue eyes widening in disbelief at the shelves of books displayed before us.

"A lot, apparently." My attention wandered to more interesting sections of the bookstore. With her over-the-top graduation party out of the way, Haleigh was laser-focused on her upcoming LSAT and managed to mention it in nearly every conversation. I could happily kill a lot of time browsing through books, but I drew the line with the law school prep genre. If I could just go over an aisle or two... I stood on my tiptoes – Fiction & Literature wasn't too far away and I saw the cooking section only a little further.

"Taylor."

I whipped back around, "What?"

"I asked which one you thought I should pick." She held two nearly identical volumes in her hand.

I pretended to study them both critically, as if I actually knew which book would be better. Surely she knew I was the last person she should be asking?

"The one on the left," I said. It had a prettier cover.

She nodded, her eyes narrowed as she scrutinized the books. "I think you're right."

"Ready?" I asked, hopeful.

"I want to read through it a little, just to make sure." She stepped towards a small group of tables and chairs. "Is that okay?"

"Absolutely," I said, grateful to be released. "Just come find me when you're ready."

Remembering I already had too many novels at home to read, I skipped the Fiction & Literature and went on to Cooking. Apparently it'd been too long since I'd been in an actual bookstore. The selection overwhelmed me; Baking, Canning & Preserving, Drinks & Beverages, Gastronomy, Natural Foods, Organic Cooking, Professional Cooking. How such a wide variety of books was still being published with everything available on the Internet was beyond me, but I wasn't complaining. I reached for a cheerful, yellow book of gourmet cupcake recipes. The pages were bright and lively, filled with short, concise instructions and large, beautifully clear photographs of impeccably decorated cupcakes. I could already smell the toasted coconut sprinkled on top of the piña colada cupcakes but, before I could even make a dent in the book, Haleigh appeared at the end of the aisle.

"There you are." She walked toward me quickly, her ponytail swishing behind her. "I knew I should have looked here first."

"What on earth were you thinking?" I teased, wondering whether she really should have known to look here. Haleigh and I were decent friends but we tended to spend time together out of convenience more than anything else. We'd been part of the same group of friends in college but it wasn't until recent weeks, after everyone had graduated and moved elsewhere, that we began spending more time with each other.

"I started in studio art and graphic design of all places," she said with heavy sarcasm.

I made a face. "Ew."

"Are you getting that?" She nodded at the cupcake book.

I gave the price on the back a quick glance. "Yeah, why not?"

"I call dibs on the first recipe you try out."

"Deal."

I purchased the book and on the way home I read the list of recipes to Haleigh, letting her vote on which one sounded best.

"Red velvet."

"Yes."

"Salted caramel."

"Wait, no. I pick those."

"Pink champagne."

"You can put champagne in cupcakes?" She asked, turning onto my street.

"Evidently so." I skimmed the ingredients list. "Yep. A cup and a half."

"Ooh, I pick those." She pulled up to the curb in front of my house and frowned a little. "Does it, like, completely suck living at home again?"

"Um, it's fine I guess."

She shook her head, unconvinced. "I would die."

I figured it was a good thing her parents agreed to continue paying the lease on her apartment then.

"What are you doing later?" She asked.

"I don't know, probably just ignoring major life decisions waiting to be made."

She rolled her eyes, "Call me if you want to go out or something."

"I will," I told her, closing the door behind me.

I walked up the driveway, debating which cupcake recipe to start on. I flipped open the cookbook again but didn't even make it to the kitchen before I heard Mom calling from some other part of the house.

I stopped to yell back, "What?"

Her reply was just low enough that I couldn't make out a single word. I set down the book and walked back towards the living room.

"What?" I called again.

She repeated herself but I still couldn't understand what she was saying or figure out which part of the house she was in. She spoke slower with longer pauses between words, as if that would help.

"Still can't hear you!"

Annoyed, I sank onto the arm of a chair to wait. I had no idea why she thought it was a good idea to start a conversation from the opposite end of the house, but I refused to participate. She could play her absurd Marco-Polo game by herself.

Eventually she came into the room holding an old pair of running shoes, looking cheerful and unperturbed by our yelling match.

"Did you hear any of what I said?"

"Nope."

"Don't sit on the arm, you'll ruin the furniture."

I gave her a look before sliding down the arm of the chair onto the seat. She sat opposite me and bent down to put on her shoes.

"Ms. Cuartela came by a little bit ago," she started. Our neighbor had been living next door as long as I could remember but we never saw much of her. I only knew she had a thing for bright colors, a tidbit I gleaned from her turquoise front door - a DIY project which had earned her several letters of protest from the Homeowner's Association - and a wardrobe of silky lounge pants in the most garish shades of the rainbow. Every time I saw her going to get the mail or out in her front garden, she was sporting a new pair of those pants in some loud, eye-catching pattern.

"She's going to Florida to visit her grandchildren for a week and —"

"She has *grand*children?" I interrupted. "I thought she was, like, forty."

"Sixty-one last month."

I raised my eyebrows. For all her eccentric clothing choices, Ms. Cuartela was kind of a knock-out. Her black hair fell long below her shoulders and looked much softer and healthier than mine. Her olive skin didn't even have any noticeable wrinkles. Granted, I'd never been close enough to make a serious assessment, but from afar she looked fine.

"She asked if you'd look after her house while she's gone," Mom continued. "Just watering the plants and getting the mail."

"*Just* water the plants?" Her front porch was on par with a plant nursery. I'd never been in her backyard, but from the glimpses I'd seen through the leafy bamboo plants bordering her yard, the place looked like a jungle. If she'd told me I'd have to take care of a flock of peacocks too, I wouldn't have been surprised.

"There's not too much," Mom said finishing the knot on her shoe and standing. "And I'm sure she'll pay you very generously."

That certainly made things sound more attractive. "I take it you already told her I would?"

"I said you'd go over to pick up a key as soon as you were home." She walked past me to go water our own yard's plants. "You can thank me for getting you the job later," she added, closing the door behind her. Extra money would be nice, but I made a face at her anyway before going for the door. The cupcakes would have to wait.

Ms. Cuartela's front yard looked as wild as always. A winding graveled path cut through the tangled mass of plants, forcing me to walk to the end of our drive and across to the front hers before I could enter the yard. On either side of the path a sea of crawling, flowered plants and taller, leafy greenery covered the yard. I noted a few patches of golden yellow black-eyed Susans and a handful of blush colored peonies stretching above their surrounding greenery, but most of the plants were unfamiliar to me.

The path extended to three wooden steps which led to the aforementioned plant nursery, or front porch, depending on who's talking. I knocked on the turquoise door and watched a butterfly floating between a large stone container of yellow roses and a weathered window planter brimming with orange petunias.

She came to the door wearing a pair of those pants – pink and green and yellow swirled together in some sort of mod pattern reminiscent of the sixties.

"Hello, Taylor," she said warmly. You couldn't really say she had an accent, that was too extreme, but she spoke with the slightest lilt on her words, as if she took effort to pronounce every syllable correctly. It made everything she said sound important, like she hand-picked each word before speaking, instead of blurting out whatever came to mind.

"Hello, Ms. Cuartela."

"No more of the Ms. Cuartela. You're a college graduate now."

I guess no one filled her in on how little graduating actually changed things.

"Please," she said. "Call me, Lola."

"Okay," I agreed, thinking how odd it was - not knowing her name before, and also how perfectly the name matched her. Lola.

"Would you like anything to drink?" she asked over her shoulder, leading the way into her kitchen.

"I'm alright, thank you."

Like the rest of her home, Lola's kitchen felt warm, cheerful, and completely out of place in our cookie-cutter suburban neighborhood. A large L-shaped island counter filled most of the room. The cabinets below the counters were painted the same turquoise blue as the front door, but the counters, walls, and upper-cabinets were different stains of smooth, polished wood. In contrast to the front garden which, although beautiful, felt borderline chaotic, the kitchen was neat and organized. The only disorder was a pile of long-stemmed sunflowers scattered on the counter, but somehow they also fit perfectly in the scene.

From the refrigerator, Lola took out a large pitcher of iced tea – the only evidence we were still in the South, not in a summer home off the coast of Spain.

"Are you sure?" She started to pour a glass. "I cannot promise our tour will be very quick."

I have a personal rule of never accepting anything on the first offer - drinks, food, rides, whatever - and generally not on the second unless it's an emergency, but there are few things in the world I love as much as iced tea. "Okay, you convinced me."

She smiled and poured another glass, handing it to me across the counter. The flowers caught her attention then. "Give me a moment to put these in some water," she said, and bent down behind the counter to look through the cabinets below.

I sipped my tea. It was unusual, but delicious. I took another sip. It was only a little sweet and tasted lightly of fruit and some sort of spice, almost like a toned-down, slightly citrusy version of chai tea.

"This is really good," I told her when she resurfaced holding a large vase.

"Thank you." She brushed back a lock of hair, fallen out of place from her search, and moved to the sink to fill the vase with water. "I haven't quite mastered Southern cooking and baking, but I can make iced tea." She quickly and precisely arranged the sunflowers in the vase, turning them so each burst of golden petals faced out and up. "Does it still count as Southern sweet tea if I only added half a cup of sugar for the whole batch?"

"Probably not," I laughed. "But I love it."

"Then you can have the recipe," she smiled. She stepped back from the vase. "Let's go have a look at the yard, yes?"

She took her tea and led me out through the back door. The yard was every bit of the jungle I'd imagined. Occasional palm trees grew among the bamboo skirting the fence, and throughout the yard there were six shorter trees with the most beautiful spray of magenta flowers I'd ever seen. I knew too little about gardening to estimate how many different plants were out there, but it was more than I could count.

The magenta flowered trees roughly divided the yard into sections, like a flagstaff to mark the alcove of plants extending behind them. Four of the alcoves were just half circles of grass bordered by plants, but one had a tiny bistro table tucked behind its leaves and another held a rustic, wrought iron bench. A graveled path wound around the trees, kind of in the shape of a giant, sideways ampersand, connecting the back porch to each of the alcoves.

My eyes moved slowly, taking in the yard. I looked from one end to the other, taking in a pair of hummingbirds zig-zagging above sage bushes, a beautiful pond with a serenely dripping waterfall and –

"Oh my gosh. Is that a flamingo?"

"Yes, that is Balboa," she replied matter-of-factly.

I looked at her. She only smiled peacefully, continuing to survey her yard.

"There's a flamingo," I said.

She laughed, "Yes."

"Is he on loan from the zoo?"

"No, this is his home."

I couldn't figure out why she didn't think this needed an explanation. "Is that legal?"

"Probably not, but you'll keep the secret, I am sure."

"Where did it come from?" I was determined to get to the bottom of this.

"I'm not sure. Perhaps somewhere exciting," she suggested, her eyes widening excitedly. "Like, Argentina or Peru."

"No, no," I tried again. "How did you get a flamingo? In your yard. Here. In Texas."

She threw her head back and laughed hard. I waited, less than thrilled she found this so amusing. Finally she caught her breath and answered, "I had a lover who sold exotic pets. Balboa was a birthday present."

Maybe I should have seen that coming. Regardless, it shocked me, both the fact that she had lovers and, much more, the kind who gave zoo animals as birthday presents. Doubtless, the surprise covered my face because she added, "Don't worry, he doesn't bite."

Ah, yes. My chief concern.

"You'll need to feed him only once every afternoon." Just a couple of handfuls of shrimp. I keep them in the freezer."

At least they weren't alive. By then, it wouldn't have surprised me if she'd taken me down to see the shrimp farm in the basement. In comparison, the rest of our tour was uneventful. She described the plants in groups according to how frequently they needed water; some every evening, most only every three days, and a couple not at all unless the weather was unreasonably hot for the better part of the week.

"I leave tomorrow morning," she said when we came back inside. "I'll return a week from Wednesday."

As we approached the door, she took my empty glass and handed over a brightly colored, spotted house key.

"I chose the design with the flowers when I had the copy made," she grinned. "I thought it was fitting since you're my new gardener."

Looking closer, I could see the spots were actually tiny flowers. I felt kind of touched to see she'd put actual thought into the design of the key.

"It's perfect," I agreed, putting the key in my pocket. I gave her a little wave as I started down the path and returned home to my new cupcake book. After reading the entire book cover to cover, I picked out a recipe and started baking. Later that afternoon, Daniel bounded down the stairs in a cloud of cologne to where I stood, peering into the oven.

"Whoa," I teased, doubling over and faking a choking cough.

"Shut up." He punched my arm just hard enough to hurt a little.

"Watch it or you don't get to sample."

He squinted into the oven. "What flavor are they?"

"Chocolate."

"Frosting?"

"Blood orange."

He watched the oven for another moment. "Okay." He retreated to take a seat on the counter.

"Where are you going?"

"Dinner with Rachel," he answered, unbuttoning the cuffs on his shirt and rolling the sleeves back.

I'd forgotten it was Saturday. I tried not to care that the only plans I had were with the Kitchen-Aid. Mom came in through the back door, her face tanned and a little red from being out in the sun. Judging by the thin layer of dirt dusting her knees and shoes, I guessed she'd spent the entire afternoon in the garden. Though not nearly as impressive as Lola's, our yard managed to stay green and lush despite the summer heat, thanks to Mom's countless hours spent pruning, weeding, and watering the flower beds.

"Hey," she said, seeing me. "Did you go get the key?"

"Yep."

"What key?" Daniel asked.

"Ms. Cuartela's," Mom said.

"Hiring yourself out as a maid since you can't find a job?"

I decided not to acknowledge him.

"Taylor is going to take care of Ms. Cuartela's house while she's out of town," Mom explained, as if I were undertaking some great work of charity.

"This could be the start of a promising career for you," Daniel smirked.

Ignoring him I turned back to my cupcakes. The tops had lost their sheen so I reached in with a toothpick to test the center.

"You could call it Taylor's Tidying Service."

Only a few crumbs stuck to the toothpick. I went to remove the pan while trying to remind myself I was twenty-three and therefore old enough to stay above Daniel's teasing.

"Nothing wrong with embracing the domestic life you're destined to have anyways."

"Great," I smiled icily at him. "I can clean your house if you ever manage to move out."

"You're still living at home too."

"I just moved back in - you've got three years on me."

"Enough," Mom cut in.

"What? I'm just trying to give Daniel a little hope for the future." I faked a confused look. "Or were you planning on just converting your bedroom into an efficiency apartment when you get married?"

His face darkened – I'd hit a nerve. Pushing off the counter, he stormed out of the kitchen, slamming the front door a moment later. Mom looked at me and I felt every bit of her disapproval, but I just shrugged. "He started it."

I flipped the cupcakes out of their pan and picked up the cookbook to read the instructions for the frosting.

Mom started arranging the cupcakes into neat little rows. "Dad said he sent you some job listings he found."

I kept my eyes on the page. "Cool."

"If you need any help with a cover letter, he'd be happy to sit down with you."

"Okay." I avoided eye contact as I walked by her to get powdered sugar from the cabinet.

"He's probably still in his office," she continued, putting the cupcake pan in the sink.

"Kind of busy right now," I said, unable to keep the edge from my voice.

She turned on the faucet to rinse the pan. "I know this isn't what you want to hear right now, but you have to stay on the ball. You're not on summer vacation."

I could not, for the life of me, figure out why this conversation was happening for the second time that day. "Mom, it's Saturday."

"Your brother had his job three months before he graduated," she countered.

"He was an intern! It took them eight months to officially hire him!"

Refusing to raise her voice to meet mine, she said, "He had a job."

She left the room. I wasn't in the mood to bake anymore, but I knifed a blood orange and squeezed the pulp into a bowl. I mixed and whipped and frosted until I had twelve perfectly topped cupcakes. I felt hollow looking at them though. Baking normally offered me some sense of accomplishment. I loved starting with all of the ingredients, most of them raw and unpalatable by themselves. You blended and cooked and then a couple of hours later you had something beautiful and delicious.

But just then I felt nothing. I did the dishes and wiped down the counters before trudging up the stairs to my room, leaving all twelve cupcakes on the counter.

CHAPTER 4 - DANIEL

"What's the matter?" Rachel asked as soon as she climbed into my car.

"Nothing." I yanked the car into reverse and backed out of parking lot of her apartment complex. I threw the gear back into drive and tore down the street. We remained silent until we came to a red light a few minutes later. She reached over and ran her hand through the back of my hair, gently scratching up and down without saying a word. It calmed me down. She knew me too well.

"Argument with Taylor," I sighed.

"About?"

"Living at home. She was being a bitch."

"Hey," she warned.

"Sorry. She was though." The stoplight changed and Rachel gave my head a final pet. I felt like a puppy whenever she did that but I wasn't complaining.

"What did she say?"

"I don't know. It doesn't matter. That's just, like, the last thing I need, you know?"

"I know." She was silent for a moment and then asked, "Did you start it or did she?"

I glanced at her. Her expression seemed neutral but I knew she thought I provoked Taylor most of the time. "She did."

Rachel looked at me.

"Okay," I said. "I may have made a harmless joke about her not having a job yet."

She shook her head and sighed.

"The kid needs to learn to take a joke," I said.

"Maybe she's feeling a little sensitive about jobs like you are about living at home."

"I'm not being sensitive."

She gave me that look again.

I wanted to hold my ground but after a few moments I said, "You're right. I shouldn't have made fun of her." I kissed the back of her hand and held it as I drove.

"How about Adeline's for dinner?" I asked. When I'd called her earlier to suggest the change of plans she'd gone along easily, saying she wasn't really in the mood for a concert anyway. I think she lied a little bit but Adeline's, a French restaurant I knew was one of her favorites, always fixed things. The place fell a little on the expensive side but still came in cheaper than the concert.

"Why don't we go to The Tavern instead?" She asked, referring to a decrepit pub a few minutes down the road from her apartment. Inside, the place looked more than a little run down and was always dark no matter what time of day you went. I'm not sure they even had windows. The food was alright, just a bunch of burgers and sandwiches. Nothing to get too excited about. The main draw was the two dollar drafts available before eight o'clock every night. Show up at the right time and two people could eat and drink for under twenty dollars. We went there every other week or so. Her suggestion wasn't entirely out of the blue, but I strongly suspected she was just trying to keep things cheap.

"Do you not want Adeline's?" I couldn't read her tone.

"The Tavern sounds fine."

Dropping from the concert to Adeline's was acceptable. Dropping from the concert to the Tavern felt like a sharp kick to my pride. "Let's go to Adeline's."

"Okay," she finally said. "I'm really okay with The Tavern though."

"We're going to Adeline's." She could act indifferent all day long but I knew it was what she wanted.

I hadn't thought to call ahead but thankfully we only had to wait fifteen minutes for a table. The hostess ended up seating us at our favorite spot in the back corner. Most of the tables in the restaurant forced you to sit uncomfortably close to neighboring tables, but in the back corner there were a few unfinished cedar columns to provide a natural divider between the tables. It was still crowded, I could probably reach out and touch the couple at the table next to us, but you could talk without feeling like the people next to you were listening to your conversation.

"You never told me how work was yesterday," Rachel said as I poured water into our glasses from a carafe on the table.

"It was good, nothing exciting."

"Did you talk to Bhavesh about taking on some bigger projects?"

"No," I said a little too sharply. I make one comment, *one comment*, about hypothetically asking Bhavesh, the guy over me at work, about stepping up my responsibilities in the hopes of bettering my chance at a promotion and Rachel latches onto it like her cat when it tries to climb the curtains. "I found out I'm going to the conference in a few weeks though."

"Where is it again?"

"Vegas."

The waiter came and took our orders. We ordered our usuals, bolognese for me and steak tartare for Rachel. I tried not to gag at the mention of her order but when the waiter came back with her plate all bets were off.

"Think anything will come of the conference?" She asked when the waiter left.

"Does anything ever come of conferences?" I appreciated her hopefulness, sometimes I felt hopeful with her, but we'd been sharing frequent disappointments about my job for the last two years. It got old. "How was work for you?"

"Good," she said simply, studying her water glass. Rachel worked in the marketing department of an electronic commerce company. For weeks she'd been prepping for a presentation to the board on a major rebranding.

"Did the presentation go well?"

"Yeah."

Normally things like this didn't need to be dragged out of her. "And?"

"They really liked it."

I waited.

She shrugged. "They gave me a little salary bump."

"Yeah? How much of a bump?"

She gave me the number. It brought her salary a little shy of six figures.

"Wow," I said. "That's amazing. Congratulations."

"It's not a big deal."

"No," I insisted, trying to be genuinely happy for her. "That's huge. I'm so proud of you."

"Thanks," she said, her smile a little thin.

"What's wrong?"

"Nothing." She tried to look genuine.

"Seriously, what's your deal?"

She started to say something and stopped. She tried again, choosing her words carefully. "It's just… I know that maybe it's a little annoying having to be happy for me when your situation still sucks."

"My 'situation' doesn't suck," I said coldly. We both knew it did.

Her eyes widened but the waiter was back, distributing our plates and offering fresh cracked pepper. I knew I was on edge and being overly defensive but by the time he left I didn't know what else to say. And then I caught the scent of Rachel's steak tartare and I didn't even want to open my mouth. A meal of raw meat with a raw egg yolk on top seemed wrong on so many levels. I forced a bite of bolognese and tried to focus on the taste of cooked meat.

"I've been lucky with my job," she said after a moment. "Almost every win has been handed to me. But you go into your job every day and work harder than anyone I know for less reward than anyone I know." Her eyes were bright and serious as she spoke. "Maybe no one there notices but I do and I respect you a lot for it. The way you work even when there's no immediate pay off is a way better measure of the kind of man you are than the salary you make or your job title."

I held her gaze and we just kind of looked at each other. My heart hammered in my chest and wished we were alone so I could kiss her and try to explain how much I needed to hear what she'd said. But she'd already started eating the steak tartare so maybe it's okay I couldn't kiss her. I think she knew what it meant to me. I nodded and we went back to our meal. The rest of dinner continued perfectly until the waiter brought the bill.

"Here," she said, pushing her credit card at me.

"I've got it."

"No, really, take my card," she waved it impatiently.

"I've got it, Rachel."

"Let me pay for my half at least." She reached for the bill and tried to pull it from my hand.

"Stop it," I hissed, imagining the stares of the couple at the table next to us. She frowned but finally put her card back in her wallet.

The entire drive home, Rachel stayed silent. I got out when I pulled into her apartment complex and walked with her to the door. "I'm sorry." I said, pulling her into a hug.

She resisted for a moment before putting her arms around my waist and leaning her head against my chest. "It's okay. It's not that big of a deal if you let me pay every now and then though."

She *did* pay every now and then, that wasn't the issue. "I don't want your money, Rachel. I want a better job."

She sighed heavily. "I know."

I rested my chin on top of her head and tried to quit thinking about work. I couldn't though. Once I got hung up on the topic it took a solid day or two to get back out of the funk it put me in.

"Do you want to come inside?"

"Not tonight," I kissed her forehead. "I've got some stuff I need to work on." I didn't really, but I wished I did. Regardless, I wanted to be alone and there's not exactly a nice way to say that.

"Okay." She smiled a little sadly, probably knowing what I'd left unsaid. She kissed me goodnight and went inside.

By the time I got home I felt exhausted and raw from the up and down of our night. In the kitchen I found the cupcakes Taylor was working on earlier. She'd taken the time to pipe on the orange icing in tall spirals and topped them with little curls of orange zest. I couldn't understand why she would go to so much trouble on the decoration when no one but our family was going to see them but she'd always been like that. I took one and bit into it, leaning against the counter as I ate. The blood orange flavor sounded weird earlier but somehow the citrus and the chocolate thing worked. It tasted amazing. I washed it down with a glass of milk and started on another.

Standing there, eating the cupcakes she'd made, I thought of Taylor again and felt a twitch of remorse for how I'd acted earlier. She'd tried to hide her annoyance when I made the comment about her unemployment, but I could see it in the way she'd stood taller and held her shoulders back, refusing to yield. I don't know why I kept going.

I glanced up the stairs to see if her light was still on. Her door was near the top of the stairs, mostly visible from the kitchen, but I couldn't see anything but darkness. It was only ten o'clock though, no way could she already be sleeping. I put my glass in the dishwasher, flipped off the light in the kitchen, and worked on an apology in my head as I trudged up the stairs.

CHAPTER 5 - TAYLOR

At a loss for anything else to do, I turned off my light long before I was actually tired. I laid there half-sleeping for an ungodly amount of time until I heard what most would call a soft tapping on my door but, at the time, sounded like an ax murderer breaking into my bedroom and sent me jolting into the headboard.

Daniel eased the door open a few inches, "Taylor?" he whispered. "You awake?"

"*Ugh.*"

He took the noise for a 'yes' and came in, walking through the darkness to sit down in the arm chair a few feet away from my bed. By then the fear had subsided enough for me to remember I was supposed to still be mad at him. I wasn't really, but one has to keep up appearances.

"What do you want?"

"Sorry for earlier," he said quietly. "I was a jerk."

"It's fine," I said, sounding like it wasn't. But I meant it.

We sat there for a moment in the dark until I pushed myself into a sitting position and switched on the lamp next to my bed, making both of us squint uncomfortably. I waited for him to say something because he had this look he gets when he's been inside his head too long and needs a sounding board.

I got tired of waiting. "So. What's up?"

"I don't know," he said, pushing his hand through his hair. "Work. Rachel."

"Separately? Or are they related?"

"Both." It always takes a while getting to the point with Daniel. "I've got a trash job. I know I should be thankful, but I'm not."

"Why is it trash?" I asked, knowing the answer but trying to draw the issue out of him.

"Because it sucks. It's not hard, it's just boring, like they're trying to keep me busy." He paused for a moment before adding, "Did you know Rachel's making more than twice as much as I am?"

"Geez," my eyes widened. "How much are you even making?"

I felt bad for making fun of him before, but after he told me I felt worse. "Rachel graduated before you though, right? So she's been working longer?"

"One semester."

"Oh."

He slouched back in the chair, look every bit as weary as he sounded. "What am I doing with my life?"

"I try to avoid asking myself the same question every day."

"Maybe I should just try what you do and ignore reality."

"Hey."

"Sorry," he smiled, leaning forward onto his knees. "What are we gonna do with ourselves?"

"I don't know," I replied, slouching back under the covers. "You can be my assistant when I start my bakery."

"Wonderful," he said sarcastically. "I did try one of the cupcakes though. Amazing."

"Thanks. At least I can succeed at something," I said bitterly.

He frowned, misinterpreting my words.

"I didn't mean that you can't succeed at anything," I said. "I just feel like I never do."

"What am I good at? Math? Finances, save for the bottomless pit of a car I'm throwing my money into?"

"Better than baking and art."

"You get to connect with people though," he said. "You get to actually interact with someone when you bake, or when you talk to someone about their vision for a project and then you make it come to life on a canvas or a computer or whatever."

"I guess."

He rested his elbows on his knees and ran a hand through his hair again. Eventually he stood and went for the door, pausing with his hand on the doorknob.

"Sorry again for earlier," he said.

"No worries."

He left and when I turned out the light, I immediately fell asleep.

The next morning, Mom, Dad, and I went to church together. By nature Daniel wasn't much of an early riser, but he usually managed to appear in time for church. No one noticed he was still asleep until it was almost time to go and, since no one wanted to risk losing a limb for waking him last minute, we left without him.

After coming back home, I tiptoed carefully upstairs, not wanting to be the first to encounter him. If he hadn't been awake long enough, I'd have to deal with his foul attitude for not waking him. Daniel acted particularly unreasonable when it came to the lose-lose situation of waking or not waking him. I'd almost made it to my room when he came around the corner.

"Oh, good. You're back," he said.

I stopped. "Yeah," I said as apologetically as possible. I should have walked faster.

"I must have missed my alarm," he said simply.

"Oh." I wasn't used to such a mild exchange before noon.

I started to pass him, but he continued, "I did some research."

I noticed a thin stack of papers in his hand. "About?"

"Bakeries."

I sighed, waiting to hear some depressing statistic about their rate of failure or general lack of success. Daniel gets a weird kick out of finding those sorts of things.

"Development, infrastructure, permits, all of it."

I waited again for the cynicism.

He paused and squinted at his papers. "They're not as difficult to get up and running as I'd originally thought."

"I mean, you're looking at a month or so getting all your paperwork and financials together," he turned to another page in the stack. "Two months getting a building together, assuming you've got a space already outfitted for what you're trying to do," he looked at my face and mistook it for confusion about the building. "You know, commercial kitchen, zoned for retail."

I took a subtle sniff as he spoke. I couldn't smell any alcohol.

"But the beauty of those numbers," he smiled, really getting excited. "They don't account for the proprietors being a very capable financial analyst-prodigious baker, brother-sister, dream team."

"I already forgave you for being a jerk yesterday, if that's what this is about."

His face fell a little, "I'm serious."

"I don't doubt your research." I walked into my room, Daniel following closely behind. He stayed by the door while I sat on the edge of the bed to take off my shoes.

"Most failed bakeries and restaurants don't specialize enough," he explained.

"I could see that."

"Which is why," he continued excitedly again, taking my reply as encouragement. "We have to know what our niche is."

"How can we have a niche? You don't even know how to bake."

"Beside the point."

"Okay then, do tell. What," I asked, humoring him, "will be our niche?"

"Doughnuts."

I blinked at him.

"Gourmet doughnuts," he clarified.

"Sounds like an oxymoron."

"That's the beauty of it." He crossed the room to sit down next to me. Flipping through the papers, he pulled out two pages of doughnut diagrams, depicting hand-drawn doughnuts with a breakdown of ingredients. "It's fresh, innovative. You hear about them getting crazy with doughnuts – there's a mess of shops throwing bacon or cereal on top but this," he waggled the diagram around, "is classy."

The drawing did look very high-end. For a doughnut, anyway. I studied one of the pages with a golden-colored doughnut, topped with thick white frosting and wisps of light-brown below the title "Piña Colada."

"I borrowed your cupcake book and then looked up basic doughnut recipes. So this one," he pointed at the page, "is a basic vanilla cake doughnut. Except you add fresh pineapple to the batter and then make the frosting with coconut milk and a little coconut extract."

"What's the brown stuff?"

"Toasted coconut."

All of this coming from the guy who doesn't even know how to turn on the oven. "You have a job," I reminded him.

"A sucky job with an intern's salary."

I turned to look at him straight on. "Are you serious?"

He gave the papers a little wave in response. I just looked at him.

"Yes, I'm serious."

I exhaled heavily, not knowing what to think. "I have to go water Ms. Cuartela's plants." I stood up to leave.

"Think about it," he said unnecessarily. Of course I would think about it. What I didn't want to do was hope.

He left the room and I dug through a pile of clothes in my closet for the pair of shorts I'd been wearing the other day. I picked Lola's house key out of the pocket, smiling again at the little flower design, and went next door. I fit the key in the lock and eased open the turquoise door a little apprehensively. Something about being alone in other people's houses makes me kind of twitchy. Walking to the kitchen, I realized how large the house was, with high ceilings and wide doorways into each expansive room. The space felt oddly empty without Lola.

The refrigerator was one of those hulking chrome things with the giant drawer of a freezer. After awkwardly pulling the wrong way once or twice, the drawer opened with a spaceship-quality *kssshhh* noise. I found the unmarked plastic bag of tiny pink shrimp and let the drawer close with another *kssshhh*.

On the counter sat a legal pad with Lola's instructions, handwritten with elegant flourishes. I skimmed the page to verify the amount I was supposed to feed Balboa. She'd told me several times, but I wouldn't know the first thing to do with a dead flamingo. A dead, illegal flamingo. But I'd continue to overlook the illegality detail.

I toted the bag outside and approached the pond where Balboa stood, slowly bending and straightening one of his spindly legs. I'd never noticed how odd flamingo's legs are. They have those weak excuses for knees, bending their legs in the opposite direction of every other living creature. It doesn't seem very efficient.

When only a few feet remained between me and the water, Balboa craned his neck around and looked pointedly at me.

"Hey there," I greeted him, coming to a stop. "How's it going?"

I didn't expect him to reply or anything, but sometimes animals make me nervous in an awkward first date sort of way, where the silence would be far more awkward than rambling on about nothing.

"Good day so far?" I edged forward a little and he straightened, his chest puffing up and feathers ruffling, making my heart seize up for a moment.

"No, sorry. I agree. This is close enough." I waited to see if he would move again. "Guess you probably want your food then."

Slowly I reached into the bag and grabbed an icy handful. Per Lola's instructions, I tossed them into the water, letting them scatter down to the bottom. I waited to see if Balboa would do anything. When he didn't, I took my cue to leave and backed away from the pond.

"Enjoy, then." I gave him a tentative wave before jogging back inside to return the shrimp to the freezer.

While I navigated around the yard watering the plants, I kept an eye on Balboa. He strolled around his pond, taking long pauses to rest or think or something, but I didn't see him eat any of the food. Half an hour later I recoiled the water hose and left, hoping I hadn't done something wrong with the shrimp. Maybe it made him nervous to eat in front of a girl he'd just met.

CHAPTER 6 - DANIEL

Monday mornings generally moved slowly around the office. I filled my coffee cup from the break room and sat down at my desk a few minutes before eight. I couldn't remember the last time I'd come so close to being late, but the desks surrounding mine were still empty.

Last year the office managers petitioned for an interior redesign to get rid of our circa 1985 cubicles in favor of something more "open." Somehow they managed to get the go ahead and my desk, once situated within the comfortably high walls of a cube, now stood as part of a four-desk unit. Translucent pieces of glass about eighteen inches tall extended above the desks, dividing the space. The height of the dividers infuriated me more than the loss of my cube. When seated normally, you could only see the foreheads of the people across from you. The office managers insisted the whole point of an open office was to encourage "collaboration" and "teamwork," but every time you wanted to have a conversation with someone, you either had to stand up or crane your neck at a ridiculous angle unless you enjoyed talking at a piece of glass.

Right at eight o'clock, Kevin arrived and sat down at his desk, diagonal from mine. He didn't say anything as he approached, while he unpacked his bag, or when he sat down.

"Morning," I said.

"Morning," he mumbled without looking up.

I get it - no one wants to talk first thing in the morning, but I thought we should at least be courteous to each other. Something always seemed a little off with Kevin though. His white-blond comb over always looked wet, even at the end of the day, and his mouth and nose kind of pinched together in a way that made him look pissed off about something. He didn't say much but whenever he opened his mouth, he started his statement with, "I think." Every single time, I swear.

Also, the frames on his glasses changed every four months or so. At first I thought he broke them a lot but every now and then he recycled an old pair. I'd been working with him all of my two years at Colson Caldwell so, by my count, he was on pair six or seven now.

A couple months ago, my buddy Dax, who sits at the desk across from me, took Kevin's glasses and ran around the office wearing them and yelling a bunch of random statements, all of them starting with, "I think."

"I think the water cooler contains water," Dax said, easily dodging Kevin's grasping hand.

Unable to reach Dax across the desk, Kevin started to move around the side. Dax shuffled in the opposite direction, putting me between them. Not only is Dax at least a head taller than Kevin, he's a hell of a lot quicker.

"I think the quarterly reports should be given quarterly." Dax pushed my desk chair, with me on it, at Kevin and kept moving the other direction. Kevin stopped, his face reddening, hoping Dax would get bored.

"I think I need another pair of glasses." Dax worked his hair into something resembling Kevin's comb over. "I think —"

Kevin lunged again, sending Dax running in circles around our group of desks. Eventually, after Dax gave the glasses back and Kevin left to take an early lunch, he told me the lenses were plain glass. No prescription.

I thought of that as I watched Kevin take off his glasses and clean them with a cloth he kept in his desk. A few minutes later, Bhavesh, our team leader, arrived. Dax shuffled in last, as always, with his face unshaven and his dark blond hair going ten different directions. He was thirty minutes late but Bhavesh never said anything to Dax about it. He didn't get too worked up about anything as long as you did your work on time.

"Bryant," Dax nodded at me and turned to the others. "Bhavi. Kev-O."

"Good morning," Bhavesh said. Kevin glared.

I started the routine of updating my earnings calendars, even though they wouldn't be due until the end of day roundup. Not much else was said until Bhavesh stood up to go to his weekly management meeting.

"Did one of you do the finance reports?" Bhavesh looked between Kevin and me. Kevin's eyes widened beneath the dark red frames of his glasses.

"Yeah, I got them," I said, reaching for the folder containing the stack of papers I printed before leaving work on Friday.

He nodded, unsurprised and looked to Dax. "Client reports?"

Dax dug around in his desk drawer and finally came up with a slightly crumpled stack of papers. "Sorry."

Bhavesh sighed at the crumpled papers before finally taking them, shaking his head as he left for the conference room.

"Thanks," Kevin said, straightening in his chair to make eye contact with me.

"No problem."

Kevin and I were supposed to do the finance reports on Monday mornings and then update the earnings calendars for our clients afterwards. The details in our finance reports fell under the same umbrella of information, so Kevin and I normally took turns submitting them. The system worked fine until Kevin forgot one Monday and neither of us had a report to turn in. Bhavesh was less than pleased. I started running the reports every week, regardless of whose turn it was.

Management meetings never lasted less than half an hour so I put aside the completed earnings calendars and opened a new window on my computer to continue my doughnut shop research. Putting recipe ideas in front of Taylor would be enough to spark some imagination on her end, leaving me free to turn my attention back to our next steps.

Dax took Bhavesh's absence as an opportunity to do anything but work. "What'd you do this weekend, Danny?"

He tossed a stress ball at me. I caught it and set it down on my desk. "Nothing." No way in hell was I telling him about going to a college graduation party with my sister.

"Lame." He turned to Kevin. "What'd you do, Kev-O?"

"Nothing."

"Do any shopping for new glasses?"

I glanced up and saw Kevin's mouth twitch a little. Sometimes I felt sorry for him when he tried and failed to dodge Dax, but he made himself too easy of a target.

"Why don't you tell us what you did," Kevin said as coldly as he could manage.

"Well," Dax leaned back and folded his arms behind his head. "If you must know."

He started at the end, describing some girl he'd hooked up with, and then went back to the beginning to recount the details of his night. Kevin, for his part, actually seemed kind of interested. I went back to the doughnuts.

Ideally, we needed to avoid taking out a loan but it didn't seem possible to shoulder the costs of food supplies, marketing, and leasing a space. Time also presented an issue. Once we nailed down our goals and the steps we needed to reach them, working full-time would cease to be an option.

"What are you —" Kevin appeared behind me, eyeing the computer screen filled with pages of information on starting businesses and owning a bakery. I hit a button on my keyboard and all the windows closed.

"Nothing," I said, spinning my chair to face him.

"Obviously it was something," Kevin said accusingly.

Dax grinned from his desk. "Whatcha got over there, Danny?"

"Just doing work, unlike some people."

Dax looked at me seriously. "If you figured out a way around the company's website blocker, you'd tell me right?"

I turned back to Kevin. "What do you want?"

"I think we should discuss the Vegas conference." He took off his fake glasses and polished them with a little square of cloth he pulled from his pocket. "Unless you're too busy."

"What is there to discuss?"

"Schedule, logistics, meeting distribution, etcetera."

"Now?" We had nearly three weeks before the conference.

"I think we need to make sure we're proficient at maximizing our time while we're there."

I glanced at Dax to see if he thought Kevin was being as stupid as I did. He rolled his eyes as he got up to go to the water cooler behind Kevin.

"Why don't we talk about it later this week," I said evenly.

"I have meetings all day Wednesday and Thursday."

"Friday, then."

"I'll be out of the office."

"Dude." I wondered why I bothered trying to be nice him. "Fine - talk."

"I think we should go to one of the conference rooms," Kevin said.

Behind Kevin, Dax grabbed the water cooler at waist-level and started thrusting his hips back and forth.

"Okay, whatever." I grabbed a legal pad and pen so I could entertain myself while Kevin listened to himself talk. "Fifteen minutes," I warned him. I didn't get my stuff done ahead of time so I could listen to Kevin test out his business vocabulary. He could initiate pointless meetings with other people all he wanted but I had work to do.

CHAPTER 7 - TAYLOR

I spent the better part of my Monday morning preparing for an interview. A former colleague of Dad's co-worker's sister-in-law, or something like that, owned a small advertising firm called HRG. I'm pretty sure the first two letters are someone's initials and the 'G' stands for 'group', but every time I looked at the name it reminded me of a noise you'd make if you stubbed your toe. *Hrg.*

The company's claim to fame was a handful of commercial ad spots for a chain of state-wide water parks. Having recently been granted the privilege of managing the park's print and web advertisements in addition to the commercials, the company was looking for a new graphic designer. Cue the cheap-for-hire recent college grad, which is how I found myself clicking to the car in blister-inducing heels for a hastily arranged interview the same afternoon I'd made the call. I'd done a little research on the company, but still couldn't tell if it'd be a good fit.

"You don't know until you try," Dad chirped when I mentioned my misgivings. I tried to appreciate his wisdom, but his motivational poster quips always set me on edge.

Just the same, I tried repeating his mantra during the drive — *You don't know until you try* — but my thoughts quickly wandered back to Daniel. His bakery, excuse me, doughnut shop, scheme kept lingering on the edge of my mind. You don't just start a doughnut shop. Not when you're our age. I could admit the idea sounded appealing and exciting, but it was also one long step from practical. Hence the interview.

I found the office easily enough. Plain, dilapidated gray stone covered the exterior but inside, bright orange walls with a subtle scent of fresh paint lit up the room. A bored looking woman sat behind a thin computer monitor atop a frosted glass desk.

"Hello," I said, walking up to the desk. "I'm Taylor Bryant."

Her eyes looked half-closed in a mix between boredom and sleep, and her mouth turned down at the corners in a perpetual frown. She lifted a manicured hand to sweep her bangs to the side of her face and shamelessly flicked a glance over my outfit before making eye contact. "Who?"

"Taylor Bryant." She looked at me blankly so I added, "I'm here for an interview with Bill Lenthan."

Her eyes narrowed a little. Did she not know Bill Lenthan, or did she think it was odd I came to interview with him? She looked back to the computer monitor and clicked around a little bit.

"I don't see anything on his calendar," she said.

I waited, hoping she would suggest a solution. When a few moments passed and she still hadn't said anything I dug for my phone. "Um, he sent me an email." I swiped frantically through my inbox trying to find our email thread. "Hold on."

"I'll just let him know you're here," she said, reaching for a phone on her desk. "You can wait over there."

I put my phone back in my bag and took a seat on a hard, fluorescent green couch taking up more than half of the waiting area. The secretary spoke quietly into the phone and hung up.

"He'll be out in a minute."

"Thank you," I said, but her attention was already focused back on her computer. She didn't respond.

Eventually a tall man with black jeans, shiny black cowboy boots, and a crisp white oxford shirt stretching over an expansive gut strutted into the room. He wiped a napkin across his white mutton chops and hastily shoved it into the pocket of his jeans before extending his hand to me.

"Sorry to keep you waiting, just wrapped up lunch," he explained with an awkwardly loose shake of my hand. "I'm Bill."

"Not a problem," I smiled, trying not to guess what he'd eaten by the gust of breath across my face. It smelled spicy.

He led me back to a small office with a long desk extending across most of the length of the room. Someone should really explain to them the beauty of buying furniture more proportional to room size. One side of the desk guarded three large computer screens and an oversized desk chair. The other side was crowded by two smaller chairs, one occupied by a slight man with chunky black glasses, tapping away on a cell phone. Bill took a seat behind the desk, neglecting to invite me to sit as well, so I stood for a few awkward seconds before taking the remaining seat.

No immediate introduction was made so I turned to the guy sitting next to me and offered him an oddly angled handshake. He made an attempt to face me and introduced himself as Rand, not clarifying if that was a first name or a last name. Bill started clicking around on the computer and Rand turned his attention back to the cell phone. I waited, glancing between them. Maybe this was a test to see how comfortable I'd be to have around all the time. I crossed one leg over the other and leaned back a little. The legs uncrossed probably looked more casual, but I didn't want to look fidgety.

I studied Rand, trying to guess his age. It was hard to tell from the angle but he didn't look any older than thirty. Dark stubble covered his jaw and his short hair was pushed back from his face. He gave off that extremely technical, highly intelligent, computer hacker vibe, until his phone tilted a little and I saw he was playing Candy Crush. It kind of killed the illusion.

"So you just graduated," Bill said to the computer screen.

"Yes," I answered his non-question. "Two weeks ago."

"Fantastic."

He remained focused on the computer and Rand kept to himself. I forbade myself from filling the empty space. Another minute passed before Bill remembered me again.

"Done much commercial design?"

There we go, a real interview question. "Yes, actually," I reached into my bag for my tablet. "Would you like to see some of my work?"

He dragged his eyes away from the computer and took the tablet. His beefy fingers swept quickly across the screen, breezing through my meticulously organized work samples.

"I'm impressed," he said, sounding anything but. "Rand, how about you give her a tour of the office?"

Rand shoved the phone in his pocket and stood, waiting for me to exit since there was no room for him to walk around me. Out of the room, I matched his lazy walk from a half-step behind.

"So what do you do here?" I ventured.

He jumped a little, as if he forgot I was following him, before answering, "I manage our inbound marketing and am in the process of taking our CRM tools off of Bill's plate so he can have more bandwidth to meet with clients."

"Sounds like a party," I said sarcastically, without thinking. I cringed but Rand didn't seem to notice.

Once Rand got going, he proved to be more attentive than Bill and we sustained something resembling a conversation for most of the so-called tour. There wasn't much to see, but Rand showed me nearly every room anyway. *Over there is so-and-so's office, this is where we store such-and-such, and here's where we keep this-and-that.* Some rooms we passed by, others we peeked inside. No one was in any of the offices, so we admired the décor and kept moving.

"Here's a storage closet," Rand said, flipping on a light in a small room, nestled in the farthest corner of the building. It was empty except for a large, blank dry-erase board standing on wheels against the wall.

"Guess you guys don't have much stuff to store," I commented.

Rand stepped inside without answering and extended an arm toward the corner of the room. I followed and saw a large plastic container overflowing with neon, plastic guns and foam darts.

"Oh." I didn't know if I should act impressed or if a toy arsenal was a workplace norm I wasn't aware of.

Rand crossed the space and spun around the dry-erase board, revealing hand-drawn outlines of a person, a circle target, and a bird, each with a bullseye drawn on them.

"Want to give it a go?" He asked, not waiting for an answer before handing me a gun and loading one for himself.

I glanced in the hall to see if Bill or anyone else might see us. Unconcerned, Rand fired off a round, striking the bird three out of five times. I checked the hallway again and then fired my round, missing all but the last one.

"Come on, you can do better than that," Rand insisted. "Try again."

My palms were sweating. I didn't *want* to try again. Again, I glanced at the hallway before firing, but this time I managed to hit the bird four out of five times. Thankfully, the round satisfied Rand. He gathered up the darts, pushed the dry-erase board back into place, and we continued on our tour.

Down the hall, Rand pushed open a door to What's-His-Face's office and, to both of our surprises, found someone sitting at a desk, their back facing the door.

"Hey," Rand stepped inside as What's-His-Face turned around. *What's-His-Very-Attractive-Face.*

"Taylor, this is Ryan. He's a graphic designer."

"The best graphic designer," Ryan added.

"He's our only one at the moment," Rand said. "Taylor's interviewing for the new position."

"So you're my competition," he said with a grin.

"No, no," I said quickly but then, worried about sounding like I didn't want to work there, added, "Not yet anyway."

It ended up sounding flirty. I wanted to punch myself. Ryan smiled again and, turning to Rand, said, "I like her."

"She'll probably put you out of a job," Rand countered smugly before leading me out of the office. I looked over my shoulder in time to see Ryan give me an indecent wink and lip-bite. Oblivious, Rand closed the door, separating my horrified face and Ryan's laughter.

Rand deposited me back in Bill's office before continuing on his way. Bill asked a few pointless questions about my "design style" and "work routines" before spending the better part of thirty minutes talking about the company's clients, none so impressive as the water park, and the company's project schedule, none so demanding as the water park. He mentioned nothing about salary or hiring but promised to call by the end of the week.

Walking back to my car, I felt mostly confused, sure of neither their opinion of me nor my opinion of them. At the very least, Mom and Dad might consider this progress and ease up for a little while.

Mom met me in the driveway, on her way to the mailbox as I pulled in.

"How did it go?" She asked.

"Fine."

"Do you think they liked you?"

"I'm not sure."

Her attention diverted to the mailbox for a moment as she noticed our wooden 'The Bryant's' sign, dangling from a singe nail after my run-in with it the other night. She frowned and tried to push it back into place. "Did they seem interested in hiring you?"

"Kind of?"

"Were you dressed appropriately?" She looked at my outfit with visible concern.

I made a pathetic attempt at answering without annoyance and then retreated inside just as Dad was emerging from his home office for a coffee break. He sternly spouted off a similar barrage of questions.

"Don't forget to send a thank-you note," he warned.

"No one does that anymore."

"The people who get jobs do."

I tried to imagine Rand, Ryan or Shea writing a gracious note to Bill for getting to interview at their magnificent company. Miraculously resisting an eye-roll, I turned to go upstairs.

"Let's talk about your next steps at dinner," he added. "I'd like to see some sort of game plan for your next week or two."

I paused mid-step. To translate — a new batch of cover letters, lists of places to apply, resumés tailored for each company, and a big, all-encompassing *Goal* to tie it all together.

"Can I have until tomorrow night?" I kept my back turned. "I need a little more time to do some research."

"Sure," he said. "We'll talk then."

CHAPTER 8 - DANIEL

"I think I'm renting today," Dad said.

I scanned the selection of guns in the rental case. The shooting range mostly sold their stuff, but they also maintained an impressive stock for rentals - Kimber, Glock, Ruger, Beretta, Colt. Black velvet shelves held thirty or forty guns masked by the fluorescent glare of the ceiling lights. Dad leaned over the glass case, dropping his arm to stop the motion of the little duffel bag slung over his shoulder containing the two guns, ammo, and the ear and eye protection he'd brought from home.

Dad looked at me. "You?"

"Are you paying?" Dad's guns were free, rentals were more fun.

His eyes hinted at a smile. "Depends how well you shoot."

I nodded, knowing he'd end up paying regardless. Tripp, a guy with bigger jowls than anyone I ever saw on my side of fifty, stood behind the counter, fiddling with the cash register. If you heard him and Dad talking, you'd think they were lifelong friends, but they only knew each other from Dad's frequent visits to the range. Tripp made his way over as soon as Dad started inspecting the rentals.

"Whatcha thinking today, Glenn?"

Dad narrowed his eyes at the selection. "Not sure. Any suggestions?"

"You tried the new 22/45 Lite?"

Inwardly, I laughed a little. Dad always pushed the Ruger 22/45 Lite on Taylor whenever he talked her into coming to the range. He thought he could tempt her with the gun's flashy gold lamé upper. As far as guns went,

Dad considered it a "pretty" one, well-suited for any gun-shy daughter. But the pistol Tripp pulled out of the case was all black and no nonsense. He handed the gun to Dad to inspect.

"Looks more like the standard," Dad commented, turning the gun over and examining the exposed barrel.

"It's a little more traditional," Tripp agreed.

I followed their assessment of the grip, chamber, lock, and mag just fine, but didn't know nearly enough to contribute. Dad first took me to the shooting range on my eighteenth birthday and we'd continued going fairly regularly since then, save for the years I was away at college, but I'd yet to develop much of a passion for the whole thing. Going to the range was more about having something to do with Dad than kindling my love for firearms.

Tripp succeeded at talking Dad into trying the 22/45 Lite. He gave one to me as well and we pushed through the back door to the shooting range. We paused in the antechamber and Dad passed me a pair of shooting glasses and earmuffs from his bag.

"Pretty empty today," I said, looking through the windows to the rest of the indoor range.

Dad pushed his muffs off of one ear. "What?"

"There aren't many people here."

He looked down the line of target bays as he zipped up the duffel bag. From our vantage point we couldn't see any people, but only three of the bays had the paper targets pulled forward. "I guess Monday's aren't a big day for shooting."

We exited the antechamber and went down the row to a pair of bays at the end of the line. Dad passed me a box of ammo and we separated to our bays, divided by a concrete barrier about four feet tall. On the counter in front of me, I flipped the switch to reel the target hanger in. I waved at Dad and pointed to the empty hanger clips. He handed me one of the large pieces of paper featuring five circular targets, each about eight inches in diameter. I clipped in the target and flipped the switch to it down range.

I fired off a few shots. None of them missed the paper but a few missed the target circles altogether. I glanced at Dad's paper, hanging five yards farther down range than mine. Each of his first five shots hit their targets, one directly through the bullseye and the others on the next ring out. I focused on my target and finished the magazine, determined to get at least one bullseye. We ran out of bullets about the same time and pulled the targets back in. Dad leaned over the concrete divider between us to examine my target paper.

"Not bad," he said.

"I guess I'm a little out of practice." I eyed his target paper. Not a single shot strayed from the target circles. "Have you been coming here without me?"

"Never." He studied the paper. "What do you think of the Lite?"

"Front of the sight was a little hard to see," I said. Dad nodded in agreement but he hadn't seemed to have the same difficulties I did. "I feel like I'm firing a toy gun."

"Pretty easy to handle though." He gave me back the target paper. "Seems a little more reliable than the old model. I bet Taylor would like it."

"Maybe." If I were him, I would have given up on her liking guns by then. She tolerated the shooting range about once a year or so, but Dad persisted on trying to rope her into our routine. Part of me wondered why he couldn't be satisfied with the range being our thing but I tried not to dwell on it.

Dad started reloading the magazine and handed me the box of ammo to reload mine. "Did you hear about her interview today?"

"No, I didn't know she had one." Going to a job interview didn't sound like something someone starting a doughnut shop would do.

He nodded. "With Bill Lenthan's agency. I think it went well. She could go far at a place like that."

I shoved the magazine back in the gun. Some guy shuffled into the bay next to me and started loading up a twelve gauge shotgun. Happy to put an end to our conversation, I turned up the sensitivity on my earmuffs right before he started firing off the characteristically eardrum-shattering rounds. I didn't want to talk about Taylor's achievements or how far she would go with some damn agency when she was supposed to be thinking about our doughnut shop.

On the way home, I tried picking Dad's brain about the doughnut shop as inadvertently as possible.

"Do you know anyone who's started a restaurant or a bakery or anything?" I asked while he drove.

His thumb tapped the steering wheel as he thought for a moment. "I had a cousin who started a little café a few years back."

"Which one?"

"Rick. Do you remember him?"

"The tall guy with the beady eyes who played for the Dolphins?"

Dad smiled at my description. "I think 'played' is being generous but, yes, he was on the team."

"And *he* started a café?"

He nodded. "A little breakfast and lunch joint."

I met this guy, Rick, one time at a funeral seven or eight years ago. He looked like a Hardy boy and didn't know how to talk about anything but his football days which, I eventually found out, were relatively short. I never got the details straight but the story went something like Rick being picked in the seventh round of the draft, allegedly injuring himself in practice, and never actually playing in the regular season or playoffs. Basically he was the last person you'd expect to start a café.

"How did it go?"

"Went out of business in the first year."

I laughed, unsurprised. "Did he try again?"

"No. Your Aunt Karen told me he closed shop and disappeared. She thinks he knew things weren't working out, so he closed the doors, took the remaining funds from the investors and split. All of the employees' last paychecks bounced, it was all over the local news. No one's seen him since."

"Are you serious?" I couldn't believe this was the first time I was hearing about this.

"Yeah, I guess you were off at school back when it happened," he said.

My second cousin committed a federal offense and no one felt the need to tell me. "So I guess you're not a huge proponent of that kind of business," I ventured.

"I think it's a pretty poor career choice."

"Not everyone's as dumb as Rick."

"Maybe not, but restaurants are risky even for people with experience in the industry."

I cut a glance at him. He could make factual sounding statements all he wanted but I suspected him of being overly pessimistic. "I mean, if you

49

know your market, know what customers want, and have a good product, that kind of takes the guess work out of it, right?"

He shrugged. "Some. But there's a big difference between *you* believing in your product and making someone else, like investors, believe in your product."

He turned onto our street and I frowned, not wanting to end on that note. "But what if you came up with a business model that didn't require investors?"

"What, like a lemonade stand?"

I gave up. He could keep his pessimism to himself. I still had faith in the success of this doughnut idea but Dad made it abundantly clear how it would sound to a group of investors. Like a lemonade stand.

CHAPTER 9 - TAYLOR

Whenever I spend unnatural amounts of time gathering information about some random topic or another, I call it 'Pulling a Dan.' See: his aforementioned stack of research on hypothetical doughnut shops. That evening, I pulled a Dan to the tune of four uninterrupted hours before Mom's voice rang up the stairs.

"Taylor, dinner's ready."

How many times had the same words interrupted the hours spent studying in my same room at my same desk during high school? The memory both startled and depressed me but, unlike then, I didn't have to stick around. I jogged downstairs and, not wanting to explain what I'd been researching all afternoon, I told my parents I had plans with Haleigh, which was really only a half-lie. I hadn't made the plans yet, but I fully intended to make them. I probably didn't need to lie at all. Mom and Dad may not have even asked what I'd been doing all day but something about living at home makes you revert back to a lot of adolescent nonsense.

I started for the front door and then remembered my laptop. To my knowledge, neither Mom nor Dad ever snooped through my room when I wasn't there, much less my computer, but I felt an extra kick of paranoia. I ran back up the stairs, slid my laptop in a backpack, and took it out to the car with me. After settling into my car, backpack encased laptop safely removed from prying eyes, I pulled out my cell. Haleigh waited to answer until right before the call went to voicemail.

"What are you doing?"

"Watching 'Friends' reruns."

"Why did it take you so long to answer?"

"It's a really good episode."

"Have you eaten yet?"

"Nope."

"Want to go out? I can pick you up." I neglected to mention I was already on the way to her house. Haleigh also grew up in the city we went to college in and was living with her parents. Her living situation, however, was temporary. She planned on staying home just until she could find a new apartment for when law school started in the fall.

"I've already eaten out, like, five times in the past three days," she protested.

"*Live a little.*"

"I'm not wearing makeup."

"Put some on then."

"I don't feel like it."

"I'll bring over Chinese food."

There was a pause on her end. "Okay, fine."

Twenty minutes later I laid out the spread of food on her coffee table and we settled onto the couch to eat.

"How was your day?" she asked, prying the top off of her orange chicken.

A neutral enough question, but I guiltily blurted, "Dan and I want to start a bakery and I spent all afternoon researching it and I think it can work."

She stopped, holding her first bite of chicken in midair. "You what?"

"Well, a doughnut shop, I guess. Not a bakery." She didn't say anything so I added, "A gourmet doughnut shop."

She let out a short, little burst of a laugh before trying to match my seriousness. Placing her food on the coffee table, she readjusted her position to face me. "Okay, start over."

I began at the cupcake book and then followed with Daniel's wild proposal, my increasingly bleak job prospects, the interview, and then stopped to take a breath.

"Did that guy at HRG really bite his lip?"

"Definitely not the main point of the story, but yes. So what do you think?"

Haleigh looked at me, trying to decide something, and then laughed lightly. "Nice," she picked back up her orange chicken.

"Nice?"

She took a bite and waved her fork at my frown, "What?"

I waited.

"You can't be serious," she said.

Punishment for twenty-three years of sarcasm – no one takes me seriously anymore.

"Tay, you can't just start a bakery."

I hated when she called me "Tay." "Doughnut shop," I reminded her.

"Whatever," she shook her head dismissively, her tone becoming tender and syrupy as she attempted to reassure me about eventually finding a job. As if that was what this was all about.

"You'll land on your feet," she cooed. "Getting a job is really hard but wishing for something out of reach isn't going to help anything."

I wanted to argue, but instead I nodded my head, pretending to take her words to heart. Normally Haleigh's opinion didn't matter too much to me, but when I glanced at my backpack, hiding my laptop, I felt embarrassed for my enthusiasm.

"HRG might make an offer and you need to take the opportunity given to you, not go searching for something you think will make you happy."

I shrugged my shoulders and turned back to the TV. "You're right," I said, wanting to believe it and forget I'd ever entertained the idea. I eyed a stack of cardboard boxes by the door, still packed from her move back home.

Haleigh followed my gaze. "Have you given any more thought to moving in together?"

We'd talked about it briefly once or twice. She'd made it easy enough by already picking out a place and getting the papers ready to sign.

"I just can't commit until I know if I'll have a job," I said. "And more importantly what I'll be making at said job."

She nodded, doing a poor job of hiding her annoyance.

"I don't want to live at home any more than you want a studio apartment," I reminded her.

"I know," she said, not looking at me as she searched for the TV remote.

She un-paused the show and we let 'Friends' fill the silence as we finished our dinner. I left Haleigh's house feeling like a child for even thinking of starting a doughnut shop. I probably should have been pissed off about her condescension and general lack of support, but instead I moped around the house in a funk for the next few days.

Haleigh started spending most of her daylight hours either studying for the LSAT or attending LSAT prep classes. In the evenings, she went out with people from her class for drinks or additional study sessions. The last of my friends who stuck around for a little while after graduation, taking their time to pack up and move out, had finally left. Only Haleigh remained but, after our dinner, I felt content not seeing her for a while. I waited apprehensively for a call from Bill, or any other company for that matter, and distracted myself by taking as long as possible to tend to Lola's garden each day.

"How do you feel about having a full time caretaker?" I asked Balboa one afternoon.

Though he no longer acted like he was plotting my murder, we were still a few more pounds of shrimp away from being friends. I'd yet to see him actually eat in front of me, but every time I came by, the previous day's food was gone. He must be eating them or I'm guessing he would have keeled over already.

I finished watering the plants, returned the hose to its stand, and sat on the back porch steps. The late afternoon sun burned the air, but in the shade it was almost comfortable. At the very least, it was slightly better than home, which consisted of little more than prodding conversations by my parents about work and, if Daniel was around, conspiratorial winks, hinting at the plan I'd already given up on.

No other companies came calling but on Thursday an email arrived from HRG and sat unopened in my inbox. I pulled my phone out of my pocket and eyed the email for the fifth or sixth time that day. I knew what it said. The first few lines displayed in the preview betrayed the remaining contents of the message. The job was mine if I wanted it, but did I? Loaded question. Hence, my offer to Balboa.

When I grew too hot to sit outside any longer I heaved myself off the steps and ambled back home. I poured a glass of iced tea but couldn't appreciate it as much as I used to. Lola's tea tasted much better. I thought of trying to make some myself, but I'd have to make a trip to the store for at least half of the ingredients. It sounded like too much effort. I wandered through the house looking for Mom and eventually found her, sitting at a stool in front of her vanity, curling her hair.

"Where are you going?" I asked, sitting on the long counter stretching the length of the bathroom.

"Cathy Klinger is hosting one of those jewelry parties tonight," she said, rolling her eyes.

"Ew," I sympathized.

She switched the curling iron to her other hand and checked her watch. "Could I talk you into doing a huge favor for me?"

"What?" I warily sipped my tea, imagining dusting blinds or scrubbing mop boards.

"I'm supposed to bring a dessert, do you feel like making one for me?"

"Oh, sure. What'd you have in mind?"

"I'm not picky." She studied her reflection in the mirror. "Can you pass me the hairspray?"

I nudged the can towards her with my foot.

"It doesn't need to be anything elaborate, just..." She pursed her lips, searching for a word.

"Slightly frilly?" I offered. "Pleasing to a group of forty and fifty-something women looking for an excuse to get out of the house and drink wine?"

"Yes," she smiled.

"Cupcakes?" I scooted off the counter.

"Perfect, thank you, darling."

I accepted her gratitude like the martyr she was making me out to be, but we both know she was doing me the favor. It was one of those, Mommy's-Got-A-Big-Job-For-You tasks to make you feel important and needed. Childish or not, I happily thumbed through my cupcake book, which was proving to be more useful than I'd expected. I settled on lemon cupcakes with a toasted meringue frosting. If those don't scream housewife soirée then I don't know what does.

Mom excessively praised the cupcakes as she swept out the door holding the tray in her arms. After she'd left I tried to stave off boredom by cleaning the kitchen. When I finished cleaning, I swallowed my pride long enough to call Haleigh but she didn't answer. I trudged up the stairs to my room and after watching two back-to-back documentaries on my tablet tried turning out the light and closing my eyes.

Sleep refused to cooperate. I laid in the dark feeling acutely alone. Where the hell were all of my friends? Was I the only one completely failing at the post-college thing? Even if I did take the job with HRG, I couldn't imagine becoming actual friends with any of my would-be coworkers. When would this get better? When would the lonely, unproductive, inadequate part of this life stage end? I wanted to curl into a ball and never get out from under the covers but more than anything I just wanted to stop thinking.

When I heard Mom come home I pulled myself out of bed, mildly interested in hearing all the empty-nester gossip, but mostly desperate for any sort of reprieve from my thoughts. I went down the stairs to her room. All of the lights were off already, so I carefully shuffled through the dark hallway, touching the frames of photos and diplomas and other wall hangings to keep myself from bumping into the wall. My eyes adjusted by the time I reached the door to my parents room, but through the door I could hear Mom talking to Dad. Something in her tone made me stop short. I waited wondering if I should just go back upstairs. I held my breath and tried to listen through the layers of wall and door, only catching every few words.

"...asked what she got her degree in," Mom explained. "...generous of us...such a prestigious university...for *that*."

The timbre of Dad's muffled reply lifted at the end - it was a question.

"Could see...absurd they thought it...embarrassing...have to agree."

I glanced at my diploma, the closest wall hanging to Mom and Dad's door, newly framed with *Graphic Design* written in the traditional calligraphy, just like any other degree.

"...admit it's disappointing..."

I drew back from the door, mechanically retreating up the stairs and debating, only for a moment, if there could be any other interpretation to what I'd heard. I wanted there to be some other possible meaning.

Disappointed. In me. I wanted to break something, and then I wanted to cry. They were talking about my degree but wasn't that also me, by some extension? They were ashamed of what I'd studied for the last four years of my life — the thing meant to determine my trajectory for the next forty years. The anger returned. The whole time I was in school, they never made a single, negative comment about my major. Now it was too late to change anything.

I crawled back into bed and pulled up the covers, suddenly feeling exhausted. My mind reeled, trying to understand how so few words could make me feel so profoundly worthless and ashamed. But then feeling ashamed about their opinion made me feel even more ashamed. My eyes watered and I felt more pathetic than I had in my entire life. How many times had I cried in the past couple of weeks? I could think of at least five occasions.

"Oh for six," I whispered to myself. I laid there, crying silently until I fell asleep.

CHAPTER 10 - DANIEL

The icy air conditioning blasting through the vents in my car barely competed with the sun beating through the windshield. In hindsight, parking my car to face away from the sun would have kept things cooler, but I was trying to keep an eye on the entrance to the parking lot of the Tavern.

Initially I intended to wait for Rachel before going inside, but she still hadn't shown up and now I was just wasting gas. I turned off the car and started across the parking lot. Gravel crunched and I turned to see Rachel giving a little wave as she drove past and pulled into a parking spot. Of course. Now it seemed rude to go in without her.

I waited by the door to the Tavern while she took her sweet time doing whatever she was doing in her car. Big mistake choosing black dress pants over slacks for work that morning. I tried to stand in the thin shadow cast by the building. Even in the shade it was hotter than fried hell. By the time she got to the door the collar of my shirt was damp with sweat.

"Hey you," she said cheerfully as she approached.

"Hi." I opened the door without hugging her, anxious for the cool darkness of the Tavern. Pleasantries could wait until my body temperature returned to normal. Before my eyes even adjusted to the lack of light, Rachel had picked her way over to the bar and ordered two Shiners.

"Bless you," I said, sitting on the cracked leather stool next to her and taking a long sip of beer.

"Are you getting food?" She asked, looking at the menu.

"Hell no. It's too hot to eat." When the bartender circled back, Rachel ordered two burgers. I shot her a look.

"You'll cool down," she said, reaching over to rub my shoulder. I shrugged it off - her hand was hot. But when our food came I ended up eating all of my burger and part of hers. Sometimes I wonder why she puts up with me.

We ordered another beer after our plates were cleared and watched part of a reality show on the TV mounted above the end of the bar. There was a girl who kind of looked like Taylor singing for a panel of judges.

"Taylor and I are thinking about starting a business," I told Rachel, my eyes still on the TV.

"Really? Doing what?"

I looked at her. "Don't laugh."

She worked to hold back a smile. "I will not laugh."

"Doughnuts."

Her brow lifted a little. "Like, you're going to buy a doughnut shop?"

"No, we're going to start one."

She stared at me for moment, her eyes narrowed. "I really don't want to sound negative, please don't take this the wrong way, but isn't there already, like, a doughnut shop on every corner?"

"Gourmet doughnuts."

"Sorry?"

I sighed. Rachel could be incredibly slow sometimes. "Gourmet doughnuts," I said again.

"Isn't that kind of an oxymoron?"

Taylor's exact words. "Why does everyone keep saying that? It's a real thing."

She cocked her head to the side. "Can you give me an example?"

I sighed again and extended my leg so I could get my phone out of my pocket. I scrolled through my inbox to find an email I'd sent myself from work the other day with some doughnut research. I opened the link to a doughnut shop I'd come across out of New York and passed the phone to Rachel.

"Ah." She tapped the screen to zoom in on a photo of a vanilla frosted doughnut with some type of crumbled candy bar on top. After studying it for a moment she swiped to the next photo of a doughnut covered with kids' cereal. "I'm not exactly sure I'd call those 'gourmet' doughnuts."

"Well, no," I took the phone back from her. "They look kind of gross, but it's the same idea. I'm proposing we do something better. Here," I grabbed a paper napkin from a dispenser on the bar. "Do you have a pen?"

She reached down for her purse and dug through the contents until she found a pen and then passed it to me. I started sketching a rough version of the doughnut I showed to Taylor.

"You bake pineapple into the dough, frost it, and sprinkle it with toasted coconut," I explained as I tried to draw little wisps of coconut. The pen wasn't working so well on the napkin and I kept tearing little holes when I pressed too heard.

"Like a piña colada," Rachel said.

"Exactly." I set down the pen and took a sip of beer. "The problem is figuring out how to the fund the thing."

"Do you think your parents would lend you money?"

"Maybe." I recalled the amusement on Dad's face when he made the lemonade stand analogy. "Probably not."

"It doesn't hurt to ask."

"I want to sort out our product first. I need Taylor for that part but apparently she's looking for jobs now."

"I'm sure she can do both," Rachel said.

"Not if we're serious about this. But God forbid she miss an opportunity to maintain the favorite child status."

Rachel tried to look sympathetic and patted my knee but said, "You know it's not a competition."

As the only girl with three brothers, Rachel held a unique position in her family. Taylor and I were kind of on equal footing in that regard, but Rachel got to be "the only girl," which made her entirely unqualified to pass judgment on the situation. "Mom and Dad haven't stopped talking about all the places she's applying and how far she's going to go with her career. No one seems to doubt *her* ability to climb the corporate ladder."

Rachel really did look sympathetic after that. We sat in silence for a few moments, sipping our beers until she said, "Maybe this doughnut shop is something you and Taylor were meant to do. If you'd already been promoted you wouldn't even be entertaining this idea."

It was nice to think about, but I couldn't shake the familiar inadequacy weighing down on me. We turned our attention back to the TV until we finished our beers, tabbed out, and left. At home, I changed out of my work clothes and laid back on my bed, feeling more tired than usual. I stared at the ceiling fan and focused in on a blade, following it with my eyes as it whirred around in circles. At most, I could follow the blade for seven revolutions before I blinked or I lost track of its place, but it was peaceful in a mind-numbing sort of way.

Rachel seemed pretty optimistic about the doughnut shop but she would probably rather I just be better at the job I already had. We'd talked a couple of times about eventually getting married but there was no way I'd be able to support a family on my current salary and some part of me needed to be able to do that. Meanwhile, Rachel already managed to pay off her college loans and could have paid off her car too, but kept the loan going to build her credit. She wasn't super materialistic and didn't spend a ton of money on clothes or anything, but I didn't want to go into marriage barely scraping by. I wanted to be able to give her everything she wanted.

I shut my eyes. The ceiling fan was giving me a headache. Even if they promoted me at work the salary wouldn't be enough to raise a family on. I still had a long way to go on the finance career track and my time at Colson Caldwell made it abundantly clear how slow of a journey it was going to be. Plus, I really couldn't go very far in the company without going back to school to get my masters.

Starting a business though — *that* held infinite possibilities. Initially it might be slow going, sure, but after the first year or two we could see some serious growth. This could work.

I sat up in bed and crossed the room to my desk. Taylor needed to understand the kind of success we could have. It was my fault for not visually laying out the logic for her. If I could help her really *see* the plan, she'd get excited about it and throw herself into the project. Showing her the doughnut shop in New York would be a good start. She was just competitive enough for something like that to piss her off. I'd show her how we could make doughnuts better than the shop in New York and then she'd be hooked.

CHAPTER 11 - TAYLOR

Over the next few days, Mom and Dad all but stopped asking about my job search. If they had continued to nag like before, maybe I could have held out a little longer. Instead, they avoided the topic altogether with a subtle awkwardness, as if simply facing the facts. I worried they might start accepting Jobless Taylor as the new normal, which held a particular shame I refused to allow.

I threw my finicky misgivings about HRG out the window and starting filling out a W-4. Maybe Mom and Dad wouldn't be exactly proud of my new job, I sensed it was too late for any of that, but perhaps they'd toss some sort of kudos in my direction. At the very least, I would be getting a paycheck and show everyone that, in spite of my "useless" degree, I could be a financially independent member of society, just like everyone else.

Entering the office on my first morning, the first Monday of June, the secretary showed me to an empty desk, surrounded by three and a half faux-wood walls a little taller than my head.

"Enjoy," the secretary said dully and started back down the hall.

"I don't think I caught your name the other day," I said.

She paused before stopping to turn, as if she debated not stopping at all. "It's Shay."

"Nice to meet you." I forced a smile, determined to win her over. She couldn't have been more than five years older than me. It seemed perfectly sensible that we should be friends. "Thanks for showing me my cubicle."

The permanent frown on her mouth deepened. "*Cubicles* are for the blue collar pencil pushers at accounting firms," she said with conviction. "At HRG, we have workspaces."

"Oh. Sorry."

Genuine irritation masked her face as she turned again and swished back down the hallway to the front of the office. About three seconds after Shay's departure from my humble workspace, Mr. Not-As-Attractive-Anymore appeared.

"Remember me?" Ryan grinned.

"Sure. You're Ryan."

He frowned a little, almost unnoticeably.

"You don't remember my name, do you?"

He narrowed his eyes, trying to dredge up the name.

"Starts with a 'T'," I offered charitably after a few seconds.

"Theresa."

"No."

"Tara."

I shook my head and he looked at me blankly, already out of ideas. I left him on the spot for a moment. "Taylor."

"Yes!" he snapped his fingers, as if it'd been on the tip of his tongue all along. "Taylor."

When he didn't make any motion to leave I hinted, "Well, I should probably get to work then."

"Right," he thumped the feeble wall of my workspace, causing it to wobble alarmingly. "Tequila shots at two o'clock in the break room."

"What?"

"To celebrate your first day." He started to leave.

"Are you serious?"

"No, but I can make the suggestion on your behalf if you're interested." He winked again. I wondered if anybody ever found the gesture charming rather than creepy.

"I'm okay, thanks."

"Let me know if you change your mind," he called over his shoulder as he disappeared down the hallway.

I half-shuddered at the wink and turned back to survey my workspace. Contained within the walls stood a card-table of a desk and an uncomfortable-looking chair, probably from Ikea - all angles, fake wood, and metal-colored plastic. Just because I needed a win, I knelt down to look underneath the chair. Sure enough, a giant Ikea sticker clung to the underside of the seat. I smirked to myself as a booming, 'Hey' startled me. My head whacked the underside of the desk and, I swear, the top almost came off the legs.

"Hey," I answered, scrambling to my feet and trying to focus on Bill's face through the glitter of stars in my vision.

"Lose something?"

"No, I, uhm... yes. Well I thought I dropped something but, uh, I didn't."

"Got a project," he said, disinterested in my attempted explanation. "Bring your notebook."

I nodded and gave the desk a punishing kick before catching up to Bill, already several paces down the hallway. He led me to a conference room where a sharp looking woman sat wielding a leather-bound notebook.

"Carol Mellinger," he said as I entered, introducing her as the Chief Something-Or-Other at our prized water park, Fiji Falls.

I reached across the table to shake her hand. I should have taken the crush of her bony grip clamping down on mine as a warning. I debated which of the six available chairs to sit in for only a moment until Ryan entered and, after shaking Carol's hand like they were old friends, sat decisively next to where I stood. He gave me a mocking look as he pulled the neighboring chair out, not far enough to call a chivalrous gesture, but enough for me to get the point. I sat.

Bill gave a brief introduction to our topic, the new Fiji Falls website, and then Carol launched into her own diatribe detailing the company's thoughts regarding the current website and their desires for the new one. She finished with a definitive statement and then stared at me, coldly expectant. I glanced at Ryan to find him immersed with doodling on his paper - freakish monsters climbing buildings and high-tech planes shooting at them. He kept sketching away so I looked at Bill. He tilted his chin down, looking at me with questioning eyes.

"What do you think?" Bill prompted.

What did I think of what? Death Grip prattled on for ten minutes about why Fiji Falls dislikes their website and she expects me to whip out a solution? I didn't know the first thing about web design. I was a graphic designer.

"Well," I began, getting ready to attempt an intelligent reply. Carol's eyes bore into me. She knew I had nothing,

"What about completely revamping the layout to make the site more interactive while also simplifying the interface?" Ryan said.

Apparently deeming his artwork complete, Ryan turned the page to a typed, bullet-pointed outline of – I squinted my eyes – a new website plan. Clearly one of us had been told about this project beforehand. For the rest of the meeting I sat silently, trying to look engaged while inwardly attempting to convince myself it was okay I couldn't contribute. They'd blindsided me and Ryan dominated the conversation anyway, spouting off intelligent sounding quips of web jargon peppered with impressive sounding design lingo. At one point, after finishing a particularly long description of some HTML or CSS technique, Ryan looked at me with one of his smirks before directing his attention to Bill. I wondered if he had planned the doodling and the hesitation before launching into his pitch just to screw with me.

When Mellinger nodded with a smile, her first of the day, we stood and shook hands again. Ryan jetted off to "get started on some mock-ups" and Bill led Mellinger out to the front. I retreated to my cubicle and slumped into the plastic Ikea chair, taking deep breathes to calm myself. *Not a big deal, breathe in. The next one will go better, breathe out. You're still learning, breathe in. It's only your –*

"Taylor?" Bill interrupted. "My office, please."

My heart dropped to my feet and went through the floor. I meekly followed him to his office and stood by the door, my palms already damp with sweat. He dropped into his chair and spun to face me directly.

"What was that about?" He leaned back, folding his arms across his gut. I didn't know how to answer.

"Sir?"

He closed his eyes and pinched the bridge of his nose. "I understand you are new here. What I do not understand, is why you might think it's acceptable to go into a Client Strategy Meeting and not contribute a single piece of input the entire time."

I opened my mouth to speak, but he stood and cut me off.

"If Ryan could handle all of the graphic work we received, I wouldn't have hired you." He stood and was pacing now. A swell of fear washed over me. "I agreed to the addition of a second designer because I understood it could provide a significant benefit to the company, provided," he wheeled to face me again. "Provided, said additional designer were to actually participate, and not rely on their Co-Creative to carry the entire work load." He took a breath and slowly sat again. "Does that make sense?"

I nodded, though I was still hung up on "Co-Creative." HRG and their titles, I swear.

"Can we establish you are actually capable of speaking?"

A string of unpleasant words filled my mind, but I held them there, only answering with a, "Yes, sir," and a neutral face.

"It's a miracle," he muttered and turned to his computer, dismissing me.

I made it through the rest of the day, but I fumed for the entire car ride. I didn't scream, or yell, or curse, I just drove with my jaw clenched all the way home. I whipped my car into the driveway and then stormed straight to Lola's to cool down before I had to deal with my parents. I slammed the front door behind me and kicked off my heels, enjoying the sound as they clattered against the door.

"It is not the door's fault."

My chest seized as I whirled to see Lola leaning against the door frame to the connecting room with an amused look on her face.

"Sorry?" It was both a question and an apology.

"Whatever it is that has you so angry," she grinned, "I do not think the door deserves to be punished."

My cheeks flamed. "I'm really, really sorry." Sheepishly, I bent to retrieve my shoes. "I'll go ahead and get out of your way."

"Would you like to stay and chat?"

"No, no," I stammered, still trying to salvage some shred of my dignity. "Thank you, but I should go."

"You already have your shoes off." Her eyes danced, watching as I tried to come up with a reason to leave. "Come on," she continued when I didn't reply. "I have iced tea."

She didn't wait for an answer before starting towards the kitchen. I let out a resigned breath and put my shoes back down, this time placing them neatly upright by the door. After pouring a generous glass of tea, Lola led me back to the front room where she'd been sitting before my performance with the door. Her own glass of tea sat on a dark wood and wrought iron coffee table next to an opened magazine. It looked like *Cosmo* but I reminded myself Lola was sixty-one, after all.

She sat in a vibrantly colored, batik patterned arm chair and tucked her bare feet underneath her. Following my gaze she asked, "Do you read it?" She picked up the magazine and flashed the cover at me. *Cosmopolitan*.

"Not usually." I sat on the edge of the couch near her chair.

"It is not very good," she said with a frown. "But it helps me with my English."

I tried very hard not to imagine what kind of English she would be learning from *Cosmo* and why she found it necessary to know.

"Would you like to tell me why you are angry?"

Though thankful for the topic change, I wasn't sold on explaining the situation to her. I took a breath and readjusted on the couch. There wasn't exactly a polite way to say no, especially since I abused her door, and the more I thought about it, the more appealing it sounded. Unlike Mom and Dad, she didn't know Bill and hadn't been a part of the job hunting saga, which kind of made her an unbiased third party. After steeling myself with a sip of tea, I gave a short recap of my day.

When I finished, she looked at me thoughtfully and asked, "Why did you take the job?"

"I needed to."

"Why?"

Wasn't that explanation enough? I didn't really know what to tell her other than the obvious - I didn't have a job and my career clock was ticking.

"But a better job could come?"

"I guess, but then there's my parents." I hedged for a moment, wondering how much detail to go into. "They started nagging me about finding a job before I even graduated. Daniel had an internship when he was still in school and the company ended up hiring him after he graduated, so I guess that's what they thought I should be doing."

Lola nodded thoughtfully. "College is very different now than when your parents were there."

"You can imagine their horror when I graduated without any job prospects."

"But you have a degree. Why should they be concerned?"

I sighed. "Because it isn't a good degree."

She lifted an eyebrow. "I do not understand."

"I studied graphic design. Art isn't really the most financially rewarding thing to study."

"But it is what you love, I am sure they are proud of you."

"Not exactly." I thought of the conversation from the other night. "I, um, I overheard my mom and dad talking about it after my mom went to a party the other day. She was talking with someone there and I guess they made a comment about it being 'generous' of my parents to pay for me to study something like graphic design, and —" My voice caught. I cleared my throat and tried to blink back tears because I did *not* need to cry right then. "She said she was embarrassed."

Lola's look of sympathy only made it worse. When I started to speak again, my voice sounded high and flat, like it did when I was about to cry, but the words kept tumbling out. "My dad agreed, he said it was disappointing. But I really like graphic design, it's what I'm, like, trying to do as a career. It's who I am. So if they're disappointed and embarrassed of my degree, that means they're embarrassed of *me*."

I'm not sure when they started but by then there were a lot of tears. Lola passed me a tissue and I fixed my gaze on a painting hanging from the opposite wall. I forced myself to note the details to take my mind off of the conversation; there was a field, a large tree in the field, a woman walking, the woman wore a red shirt. It looked warm in the painting, like late September when the sun is still hot but the air starts to cool. When the tears stopped I looked back to Lola.

"They love you. Do you know that?"

I nodded. There wasn't anything else to say. The silence settled for another moment before I thought to apologize again for my earlier intrusion. "I didn't think you were supposed to come home until tomorrow," I added.

"Correct."

"Oh." I took a sip of my tea, wondering if she would elaborate or if I should ask. Maybe I hadn't watered the plants properly and someone reported back to her or perhaps I hadn't fed Balboa correctly after all. It might have been my imagination, but I thought he looked a little thinner. A few moments later she still made no reply. I caved and asked why.

"There was a last minute booking for a private lesson."

"A lesson?" My mind ran wild with possibilities. I mean, after the *Cosmo*...

"Yes, I teach dancing. Mostly salsa."

Of course. My sixty-one year old neighbor manages to teach salsa dancing on top of maintaining a modest jungle and caring for a finicky flamingo. Meanwhile, I'm failing at the job I've had for one day.

"Also traditional ballroom dancing," she continued. "For me the ballroom is a little..." she searched for the word. "Dull. But many couples want to learn for their wedding. Or I should say," she leaned in conspiratorially, "the brides want to learn." She leaned back and took a punctuating sip of tea. "I think the grooms would prefer salsa, it is more exciting," she said.

"Wow. Is that what you've always done? Taught dancing?"

"No," she scrunched her nose. "I used to work in a bank."

For the life of me, I could not imagine Lola trading her bright flimsy pants for a suit to sit behind a desk at a bank.

"The bank was even more dull than the ballroom dancing, but it served a purpose." She smiled, lost in thought for a moment. "How much better to have taught dancing all along." She shook her head, dismissing the moment of regret, and glanced at her watch. "I should start preparing for the lesson."

I downed the rest of my tea and stood to leave. "Thank you for everything. The tea was great as always."

"It is nothing," she said, following me to the door. "If you come by tomorrow, I will teach you how to make it."

I'm not sure if everyone could appreciate her offer as much as I did. Women in the South, maybe women everywhere for all I know, do not share their recipes. If it's one they're not particularly fond of you might get a copy. And you will definitely be promised recipes if they like you enough, but actually receiving the full-fledged instructions never happens.

"I can come by after work," I offered.

"Perfect," she smiled, waiting until I'd reached the sidewalk to shut the door softly behind me.

I went back to the house in search of Daniel. I found him in his room, playing a video game.

"Did you just get home?" He asked with only a quick glance away from the game as I flopped onto the futon next to him.

"Just about." Much calmer than I'd been an hour ago, I only let out a half-hearted laugh when he asked how the first day went. He misinterpreted my reaction.

"Easy?"

"Not exactly."

On the TV, a barrage of gun fire started and the cowboy he was moving around slumped in it's saddle. Daniel jolted, as if he was the one who took the bullet, and tossed the controller aside. After an exasperated sigh he turned and said, "I have something for you."

"Yeah?"

He stood and grabbed his laptop from his desk. After clicking between a bunch of open web sites, he came to a news article and passed the computer to me. Below an amazing, close-enough-to-taste photograph of three doughnuts, a reporter detailed the opening of a "cutting edge" shop in New York. The owners cranked out hundreds of doughnuts a day with all sorts of "innovative" flavor combinations. Local favorites included a maple-bacon creation and the "Salty Nip," whatever the heck that was.

"Buncha weirdos," I remarked.

"This is what I've been telling you about though. We can do this."

"But they already are."

"Doesn't matter. They're on the other side of the country and it's more of that weird stuff, not the gourmet thing we're going for."

I sighed heavily as we fell into the same pattern of argument. "It's not practical," "Practical doesn't matter," and back and forth again.

"I don't have the kind of money it takes to start a business." I paused before adding, "I barely have any money at all."

"I have some," he persisted.

I arched an eyebrow and asked for his definition of "some." I scoffed when he answered. It wasn't enough.

"It's a start. It's enough to get us going and then we'll trust God with the rest."

"You're naïve," I spat back, annoyed at having the God card pulled on me.

"I'm tired," he corrected. "I'm tired of doing work that isn't helpful or purposeful. I'm tired of feeling like I'm waiting for something to happen, and then realizing it's not, or rather, it is. Life is happening and I don't think I'm doing it right. I have this handful of talents I've been given and I'm barely even using them. When I do, it's with a computer – not with people or anything that even impacts people. And people are what matter. Relationships matter."

I just stared at him. I had no comeback. *Me too? Welcome to life? Isn't that all that's here?*

"Do you like your job?" He asked.

"No." Not much reason to lie at this point.

"Why not do something better then?"

"No one likes their first job," I argued as if I knew this for a fact. I tried to sound casual but it sounded fake and dim. "It's only my first day."

"Okay," he shifted on the futon, causing a stray spring to dig into my leg. I tried to ignore it, feeling more concerned with which angle he was going to try coming at me from. "Where do you want to be in five years?"

"Gee, Dan," I said with a mocking tone. "I don't know."

He ignored me and continued, "How about this – do you see your current job leading you somewhere you'd like to be?"

I gave the idea some thought. There didn't seem to be anywhere to go within HRG, it was such a small company after all. I could jump to bigger and better companies, but wouldn't I always be doing the same sort of work?

He backed off, knowing he'd caught me. "It's your life," he said gently. "Just let me know what you come up with."

He picked up the controller and started a new game. Dismissed, I left his room and trudged down the hall to mine, not sure what to do with myself. I hated these conversations about idyllic non-realities where money wasn't the goal and people had enjoyable sounding jobs and the important things in life didn't get brushed aside. Nothing ever came of them. No one actually lives that way. It must not be possible or more people would be doing it instead of just talking about it.

CHAPTER 12 - DANIEL

Rachel isn't better at computer stuff than me, but she has an incredible knack for dredging up the most obscure yet useful apps and websites. My favorite to date is a website that lets me access my e-books from the Internet, so I can read on my computer at work and look like I'm actually working. I'd been in the middle of reading an e-book about how some bakery tycoon got his start when a stress ball clocked my ear. In a flash I pressed a key to close the Internet window, an instinct now, and sat up to see Dax focused in on his computer, trying not to smile.

"You're an idiot," I told him.

He grinned unapologetically. "Me?"

From his desk, Bhavesh shook his head, trying not to smile. Dax was bad enough without any additional encouragement.

"Are you ready to go?" Dax asked.

Once a month the company held an office-wide happy hour in the bar on the first floor of the building. The clock on my computer screen showed it was a little after four.

"I guess so," I said. Kevin had already started packing up his bag and Bhavesh clicked off his computer screen. Together we headed for the elevators but once we got downstairs Bhavesh and Kevin would go their own ways and Dax and I would go another. The monthly happy hour wasn't an unwelcome event, it got us out of the office an hour early, but we already spent most of our waking hours together. At a certain point you run out of things to talk about.

Like the rest of the building, the bar had dark walnut paneled walls with glass and chrome fixtures. They used the luxurious atmosphere as an excuse to charge way too much for drinks and, as a result, the place normally stayed empty. The company picked up the tab for the monthly happy hours though. People already stood shoulder to shoulder at the bar even though we arrived only a few minutes after the start time. Dax and I pushed through the crowd to order and then took our beers back to a high top table near the floor to ceiling windows bordering two sides of the room. It gave us a good view of everyone else in the bar without seeming too antisocial, unlike Kevin, who stood off in the far corner, awkwardly holding a beer and texting on his phone.

"How did he even get hired here?" I asked Dax, not expecting an answer. He followed my gaze to look over his shoulder at Kevin. He was still texting on his phone but he kept glancing up at a group of execs standing a few feet away, probably debating whether or not to force himself into their conversation.

Just watching him irritated me, but Dax turned back around with an amused smirk. In a weak attempt at a British accent he said, "I believe they call that 'nepotism,' Danny."

My eyes widened. "No."

He nodded, grinning at my surprise. "CFO's nephew."

I glanced back at Kevin in time to see him take a long sip of beer before striding over to the group of execs. He clapped one of them on the shoulder and shook the hands of the other three. A couple of them exchanged looks of mild annoyance, but they shuffled around to make room for Kevin in the circle.

"That explains so much," I said.

Dax nodded again but he'd already moved on to eyeing a tall girl in a tight black dress across the room. Clearly this revelation about Kevin didn't bother him as much as it did me. He eventually pulled his eyes away and laughed when he saw my face.

"Lighten up man, who cares how he got his job?"

"We have the same job," I reminded him. "Next time there's an opening, who do you think they're gonna move up?"

"You. Unless he comes up with a more subtle way of sucking up to the execs."

The group didn't look annoyed with Kevin anymore, but they kind of seemed like they were ignoring him. "Maybe. You think you'll move up anytime soon?"

Dax shrugged and looked past me. "Do you know who she is?" He was watching the girl again.

"No, I think she's in HR though." He took a sip of beer and kept looking in her direction. "You seriously don't care?"

Dax dragged his eyes back to me. "Either I move up or I don't. As long as I can still tell the family I'm employed whenever I see them, I'm good."

"You don't think they'll care if you're still working as an entry-level client coordinator in five years?"

He frowned a little, thinking. "I'm not sure they even know I'm *currently* working as an entry-level client coordinator. Normally it's like, 'Hi, Merry Christmas, how's the job? Good. Who wants a glass of Scotch?' The end."

I'd never met Dax's family but based on the type of person he was, I didn't have much trouble believing that. "Okay, that's your family. But what about your own goals?"

He was watching the girl again, barely listening. "I've got a car and I can pay the rent on my house as long as I've got two roommates. I'm pretty much set."

"You don't ever want to be able to *buy* a house? Live without roommates? Support a family?" I couldn't figure out if he was the insane one, or if it was me. Judging by the look he gave, it was me.

"Dude, you need to dial it down a little."

"Yeah, okay." I didn't need life tips from Dax.

"Let's go out this weekend. There's a new bar that opened up, like, one block from my house."

"Maybe."

He started to say something else and stopped, a rarity for the guy who never seemed to have a filter. We sat silently watching the rest of our coworkers talk and drink, mostly just with other people from their respective departments. I saw Bhavesh leaning against the bar top, talking with Tom, the Regional VP of Finance who hired me, and another guy with closely cropped black hair. He looked familiar but I couldn't think of his name or what he did within the company. Bhavesh met my eye across the room and waved me over.

"I'm being summoned."

"Cool. I'm gonna go talk to that girl."

"See you later." I started towards Bhavesh and then added, "I think her name is Caroline."

Dax nodded and ran a hand through his hair, adding to its usual disarray, and headed to the bar where the girl was ordering a drink.

I approached the group and extended a hand to Tom, "Nice to see you." I'd probably talked with him four times in the two years since he hired me. His brown hair had thinned a little and was graying near the temples but he still had the same, commanding presence as always.

"You as well, Daniel," Tom said. I was a little surprise he remembered my name. He turned to the man on his right and said, "Daniel, this is Mark Rhodes, our VP of Asset Management."

"Nice to meet you," I said as we shook hands. That explained why I didn't know him. Bhavesh, Kevin and I fell under Tom's track within the company. Mark Rhodes was at the top of Dax's track.

"Daniel will be with us at the Vegas conference," Bhavesh explained.

"Great," Mark said. "Always nice to be around some new faces."

"Sure beats the hell outta looking at yours all the time," Tom said.

We all laughed even though it wasn't that funny and Tom seemed pleased enough with himself for making the joke. I felt a push on my arm as Kevin appeared, wedging himself next to me.

"Evening gentlemen," he said, extending a hand to Tom and Mark as he greeted them by name.

I watched their faces, expecting for the same annoyed look I'd seen on the other execs earlier, but they didn't appear bothered by him.

"Now we just need Ned over here and we'll have the whole Vegas group," Mark said.

Kevin placed a hand on my shoulder and said, "Ned is the Senior Asset Management Coordinator."

I tensed, as much from the condescension in his tone as the feel of his spindly hand on my shoulder. "I know."

"I'll have to introduce you before Vegas," Kevin continued.

"We've met." I stepped back and his hand fell off my shoulder.

No one else seemed to notice our exchange. The banter about the conference continued until Mark and Tom excused themselves a few minutes later.

"I wanted to make sure you met Mark before we leave tomorrow," Bhavesh said after they'd left. "He can be a tough one to track down."

"He's great once you get a hold of him though," Kevin said before I could reply. "I think he's got a lot of pull with the other execs. You need to get to know him while we're at the conference."

I didn't *need* to do anything Kevin told me. "Thanks, Bhavesh."

It was still a few minutes shy of five o'clock but I went ahead and downed the rest of my beer, set it on the bar top, and reluctantly nodded to Kevin before heading for the door. There was really only so much of that guy I could handle in a twenty-four hour period and I'd reached my limit.

What I *did* need was to do some more work on the doughnut stuff. I knew I wouldn't get much down time in Vegas but Taylor and I couldn't move on until we had a clearly outlined plan of attack. Rachel was going to a movie with some of her friends so I had the rest of the evening to hammer out a business plan.

I arrived home to an empty house. Taylor's car was parked outside but I couldn't find her anywhere. Probably for the better. She'd been so hesitant to commit to the doughnut idea even though I could see that deep down she wanted to. Drafting this business plan would be the last step in getting her on board. Once she saw something concrete and logical I hoped she'd be able to get past how crazy the whole thing sounded. My well-intentioned planning could only take the project so far. Taylor needed to supply the flowery, passionate stuff and an actual doughnut recipe. The trick was not actually saying so in as many words. I'd give her the facts, throw some sort of challenge at her, and then give her time to sort things out with her excessively analytical self.

CHAPTER 13 - TAYLOR

I was more than a little glad for the distraction of going to Lola's after work for my tea making lesson. Anything to stay away from Daniel's deep thinking, life question debates. No answer followed my knock on her door. I waited for nearly a minute and when there was still no answer I tried the door and found it unlocked.

"Hello?" I called as I stepped inside. Nothing. I called a few more times as I walked through the house, poking my head into each of the rooms, before eventually spotting her through a back window. More accurately, I spotted her fuchsia and tangerine colored pants where she knelt weeding in the middle of a green bed of plants.

"Good afternoon," she greeted me when I came out onto the back porch. "I did not hear you arrive without all of the noise."

I really wished we could let that one go, but at least she seemed genuinely amused about it. "Work was a little calmer today."

"Good," she said, standing and brushing the dirt from her knees. "I don't know about you, but I am ready for some tea."

Inside, she began filling a large sauce pan with water and placed it on the stove to boil. She then nudged a step stool in my direction and pointed to a cabinet above the counter. "We need cinnamon, cloves, cardamom, and ginger," she instructed and then turned her attention to slicing several large oranges.

I searched through the shelves, nearly overwhelmed at the vast number of spice jars before me. "Ground cinnamon or cinnamon sticks?"

"Sticks," she replied. The pattern continued for nearly every item as I asked for a ruling on whole cloves or ground, fresh ginger or dried, cardamom pods or ground.

She gave a satisfactory nod when I stepped down with my findings. After passing me a handful of measuring spoons, she pulled the pot of boiling water off of the stove and listed the amounts of each ingredient I needed to toss into the boiling water.

"You love to cook," she said without question as she lowered several oversized tea bags into the sauce pan.

Though true, I wondered what prompted the comment. Anyone who tried her tea would want to know how to make it. "Why do you say that?"

"Your face," she continued. "When you are working in the kitchen, your face is more relaxed."

I wondered what sort of look my face held the other ninety-five percent of the day. She was quiet for a moment while she added the oranges to the water, tea bags, and spices. She stirred them together for a moment before clicking off the stove and pouring the contents of the pan into a tall, glass pitcher. A dense cloud of sweet and spicy steam billowed out of the pitcher and I breathed deeply, trying to pick out the scent of each ingredient.

"Have you considered something with cooking for a job?"

"Never," I said resolutely before remembering the doughnuts. I casually mentioned Daniel's idea, expecting a laugh. Instead, she nodded her head seriously.

"That is a good idea."

"Really?

She looked at me like I was the crazy one. "Why not?"

Why did everyone keep asking that? *Why not.* As if there were nothing else to consider. I could think of lots of reasons why not. "For starters, we already have jobs."

"You are allowed to quit a job," she said.

"We barely have any money."

"There are loans. And," she lowered her chin and gave me an accusing look. "I have seen your brother's car. I think he has a little saved."

"People don't just start a doughnut shop." I felt my argument losing steam.

"Sure they do."

Her easy confidence kind of irritated me. I couldn't be mad at her, but she didn't understand. "I need to hold down a real job, not throw away a bunch of money I don't have. Starting a bakery is what people do when they're, like, old and financially secure."

She shook her head. "That is not how it works."

I didn't know how to respectfully tell her she had no idea what she was talking about.

"I have had a lot of friends with a lot of wonderful dreams," she continued. "Many of them thought they would get to them later, after they saved some money. They found nice jobs and pretty apartments and sat down to wait for a promotion or two so they could have enough money to quit. They got their promotions, and then they thought, *This is very good money. I will wait for one more promotion.* So they waited for another. And then they got married, traded their pretty apartments for pretty houses, and thought, *I will save a little more money, and then I will follow my dreams.* But then they had children and thought, *I need to save money so my children can go to college one day.* Do you understand?"

Immediately I thought, *that's ridiculous and it's not going to happen.* But what if she was right? The idea terrified me. I wasn't one hundred percent sure this doughnut shop was going to be my passion in life, but the possibility of staying with HRG for the rest of my life sounded horrible. "It might not work," I said quietly.

"It might." She smiled at the defeated breath I exhaled. "Come on, let us go feed Balboa while the tea cools."

I almost forgot about him. The sight of the bird as we walked onto the back porch didn't surprise me anymore, but I doubted whether I'd ever get entirely used to seeing him there. Feeling a strange, physical exhaustion from our discussion, I sank onto the steps and let her continue to the pond. I listened while she cooed to Balboa in Spanish and tossed the frozen shrimp at his feet. He ducked his head shyly at her words, but made no movement for the shrimp.

"Why doesn't he eat them?" I asked after Lola returned from stowing the bag of shrimp.

"He eats them," she assured me, sitting down on the step. "But he waits. I am sure it is difficult for him, but the shrimp will certainly taste better thawed." She paused thoughtfully. "I imagine he is able to remember his patience is worth the reward."

I knew what she was doing. I glanced at her and met knowing eyes. It was a little corny and I might have rolled my eyes under any other circumstances but instead I sighed again, tired of all these heavy discussions about life. She squeezed my shoulder affectionately and we watched Balboa until the tea was ready.

I couldn't get what she'd said out of my mind. By the next evening, I came home ready to talk to Daniel. If we were going to entertain the idea of doing this, we needed to plan accordingly. After finding his room empty I checked the garage – no car either. I poked my head in the sun room and found Mom in her usual spot.

"Where's Daniel?"

"On a trip for work," she answered, getting up and walking towards the kitchen.

"When did he leave?"

"This morning," she said from inside the pantry as she started searching for dinner supplies.

"When will he be back?"

"I'm not sure."

She wasn't nearly as concerned about his absence as I was. I left in a huff to go find my cell phone, already formulating the angry text I was about to send him for dropping his bomb of a plan and then leaving town without telling me. Amidst a few colorful phrases, I asked where he was and when he planned on returning. Ever the conversationalist, he replied to my novel-length message with:

`Vegas. Fri.`

Wonderful. He left me with three days to obsess in a state of half-committed anxiety before we could talk any further. Maybe it was a sign to put the brakes on our insane little pipe dream before it even got started. But rather than feeling deterred by having the discussion postponed, I felt oddly defensive. Almost overnight the plan personified itself into *The Plan* - some intangible *thing* in need of my protection and nurturing.

Or maybe I just wanted what I couldn't have. I shook away the internal debate, knowing it wasn't going anywhere. I tried to imagine the extra time might be exactly what I needed to refocus and give work a fair chance but, as if already sensing the betrayal I planned to spring on it, things at HRG progressed even more horribly.

"Hey, wait," Shay said when I walked into the office on Wednesday morning. She lifted a thick stack of papers off the counter of her desk.

"What's this?" I took the stack from her. There were at least fifty pages held together with a binder clip bearing the HRG logo. I didn't even know you could put a logo on a binder clip.

"Employee handbook." Shay's attention was already back on her computer. I studied the acrylic wall panel behind her. I could make out a Facebook page in the reflection.

"Do I need to do anything with it?"

She pulled her eyes off the screen long enough to give me a distasteful look.

"Read it."

"Okay."

"There's some stuff you have to sign too," she said to her computer screen.

"In the handbook?"

Shay's eyes slid back to mine. She blinked. "Yes."

"Right. Okay." I put the handbook in my bag and retreated to my desk. I read through the entire handbook before lunch and didn't find any pages that asked for a signature, but I knew better than to ask Shay again. I put the handbook away in my desk and spent the rest of the afternoon watching HRG ad spots, hoping Bill or Rand or someone would show up with work for me to do. They didn't.

CHAPTER 14 - DANIEL

I hate conferences. I hate attending them. I hate working at them. The Vegas conference was my first time to be on the expo side so I expected it to be better than the handful of conferences I've gone to as an attendee. I was wrong – both sides suck.

In the spirit of efficiency, the team decided to meet at the office on Tuesday morning and shuttle down to the airport together. I was nervous about being late so I got there at six in the morning, a full thirty minutes before we were supposed to meet. I didn't want to waste gas so I turned off the car, got out, and leaned against the hood to wait. Kevin rolled up in his bright blue Prius around six twenty.

"Good morning, Daniel." He got out of the car, straightened his tie, and nodded at me. He wore new glasses, this pair a little more rounded and framed only across the top. "No one else here yet?"

"No."

"How are you feeling?"

"Great." The guy ignores me nine mornings out of ten and suddenly he decides we should be friends.

Kevin walked around to the back of his car and popped the trunk. He pulled out a little shoe shine kit, propped his foot on the car, and started polishing the leather toe of his shoe. I pulled out my phone and started scrolling through emails so I wouldn't have to watch him.

When he finished, he held the polish brush out to me. "Want to do yours?"

"No, thanks."

"Well-shined shoes are the key to making a good first impression."

"Then I guess it's a good thing I've already met everyone." My shoes looked fine.

Kevin put the kit away and pulled his carry-on suitcase out of the trunk. The hard, beveled exterior was fire engine red and looked like he just took the price tag off.

"I think they should be here by now," he said, checking his watch.

I glanced at the time on my phone. It was still a five minutes shy of six thirty. "They've got a few minutes."

He shook his head, looking like a petulant child. "I don't care what your job title is, you should still be on time like everyone else."

"Dude, it's not even six thirty yet." If he didn't dial it back, we were going to have a very long week together.

"Still."

I went back to my phone, determined to ignore him until I had to speak with him again. Thankfully Ned Kennedy pulled up a moment later on the other side of my car.

"Nice to see you, Daniel," he said as he pulled his suitcase out of his car. After Kevin's patronizing offer to introduce me to Ned, I'd actually been a little worried that he wouldn't remember my name. Ned was just one of those stand-up guys though. He didn't talk a lot but he always greeted people by name and seemed like a genuinely happy person. He walked over and greeted Kevin but I felt a little pleased that he'd seen me first. I knew it wasn't a competition or anything but I didn't want Kevin thinking I needed his social aid on this trip. I knew how to work with our directors and VPs just as well as he did.

One after another, Bhavesh, Tom, and Mark pulled into the parking garage. We put our suitcases into the back of Tom's SUV and then piled inside. I took one of the seats in the very back and Kevin followed. I'm not remarkably tall and neither is Kevin but between the two of us there was a lot of leg for the amount of room we had. Bhavesh and Ned took the middle seats and Mark rode shotgun. Once we were all inside with the doors closed, the mixed smell of six guys' aftershaves, deodorants, and colognes was enough to make me want to pass out. When Tom cranked the A/C things got a little better, but the overwhelming smells and the tight space made me a little queasy.

We got to the airport in good time and started through security a full hour and a half before our flight. The whole process always panicked me though. Too many variables could make you late - random traffic delays, a misplaced ID at the security checkpoint, forgotten liquids in your suitcase. I've travelled plenty but there's something about being with better-seasoned travelers that makes me sweat in weird places. But despite my misgivings, we were at the gate with plenty of time to spare. The first flight was on time and we made our connecting flight with no problem. It wasn't until we got to our hotel in Vegas that things headed south.

When we got inside, Bhavesh asked me to go to the events center to check the group in for the conference while everyone else hung back and checked into the hotel. When I returned to the lobby, Kevin was the only one there.

"Where did everyone else go?" I asked.

"Up to their rooms. I said I'd wait for you."

"Great."

We went to the elevators and Kevin pushed the button for the fifth floor.

"Did they say anything about when we should meet back up?"

"I think we're supposed to meet them in the lobby to go to dinner at six," he said.

"You think?"

"Yes."

"You think or you know?"

"I think they said six."

I didn't say anything. If he was right, which I had little faith in at that point, then it would give me a little time to rest before we had to head out again. My shoulder ached intensely from carrying my laptop bag for so long and all I wanted was a few minutes to close my eyes, put on my headphones, listen to some music and ignore Kevin's presence. When the elevator doors open I let Kevin out first and followed him down the hall to our room. After three unsuccessful swipes with the key card, he finally got the door to open.

The light from the hallway illuminated a narrow, carpeted walkway that led past the bathroom and into the rest of the room. The lights were off and the curtains over the window were drawn shut, making it impossible to see, so I fumbled around for a minute, trying to locate the light switch. When I flipped it on, I noted a desk, a couch, a TV and —

"One bed." We'd requested two doubles but there was only one queen size bed.

Kevin crinkled his nose. "I think we should go back down and talk to someone at the front desk."

"Let's just call them." I eased my laptop bag off of my shoulder and sat down on the edge of the bed. On the hotel phone I pressed the button for the front desk and after a long list of general information and extensions, I finally got to speak to an actual human.

A woman's voice came through the phone, "Copley Hotel, this is Krista, how may I help you?"

"Hi, Krista," I said, trying my best to sound cordial. "I just got to my room and there's only a queen size bed, but I believe we requested two double beds on the reservation."

"May I have your name?"

"Daniel Bryant."

"One minute, please." I heard her clicking around for a moment before she came back on the line. "I'm sorry, I'm not seeing that name on the reservation."

"Oh, right." I tried to think of who would have made the reservations. Probably one of the secretaries but surely they would have put the rooms under Tom, Mark or Ned's name? "Is it Tom Hoyt?"

"Yes, that's it," she said. "I do see the request for two double beds, but unfortunately we can't guarantee to honor those requests at the time of booking."

"Oh." I wanted to ask what the point of taking the request was in the first place, but I was still hopeful she could fix this.

"I can go ahead and see if there's anything else available though."

"That would be great."

"One minute, please." She took longer clicking around this time. Kevin took a seat in the desk chair and watched expectantly, which only made me more anxious. "Mr. Bryant?"

"Yes?"

"I'm afraid we don't have any rooms with double beds available."

My heart dropped. "Do you have any other available rooms?" If I had to pay for my own room, I would do it.

"I'm sorry, we don't. We're completely full - there's a conference going on this week and we're at maximum capacity."

I sighed heavily. "Thank you for checking."

"No problem," she chirped. "Enjoy your stay."

The hell I would. I hung up the phone and looked at Kevin. "They don't have any other rooms," I said. His eyes widened. I leaned back on the bed and closed my eyes, thinking. I absolutely would not share a bed with Kevin. The hotel must not have roll away beds or surely the woman on the phone would have suggested that. "Check the couch," I told Kevin after a moment.

"What?"

"Look and see if the couch has a fold out bed."

He got up and pulled off the couch cushions. "Yep."

I sat back up. Sure enough, the handle of a pull out bed was visible. "Great. One of us can take the bed and one of us can take the couch."

"Cool," he said. We stared at each other for a moment and no one said anything.

"I'll take the couch," I said finally. Obviously he wasn't planning to volunteer.

"Okay," he said, replacing the cushions. "I mean, if you're sure."

Suddenly I wasn't tired anymore. I hauled my bag over to the coffee table in front of the couch and dug out my running shoes, a pair of shorts, and a t-shirt. While I was changing, Kevin kicked off his shoes, leaned back on the bed and turned on the TV.

"I'm going to work out," I told him. "I'll be back in an hour."

I realized about halfway down the hall that I'd forgotten to grab one of the key cards. Kevin seemed perfectly happy to lay there and watch TV all afternoon though. He'd let me back in when I returned, I just needed to make sure to put a key in my wallet before we went anywhere else. I didn't plan on being attached to his side for the next three days.

A plaque next to the elevators listed the gym on the Lower Lobby level. I took the elevator all the way down and found the gym just around the corner from the elevators. The space was fairly small but there were about ten cardio machines, a few weight machines, and a big selection of free weights. No one was in there except for a really old guy walking on a treadmill with five pound dumbbells in his hands. I took the treadmill farthest from the guy, walked for a minute while I put on my headphones and got some music playing on my phone, and then I ran.

At first I was running out my frustration with Kevin and then I was running to the beat of the music and then, finally, I was just running. I thought of nothing except for an occasional glance at a clock on the wall to check the time. Some people talk about getting a "runner's high," but to me it felt like depth. My mind sank below the awareness of the wrinkly old guy bouncing a few treadmills down. I tuned out the music pounding through my headphones and forgot about the distance counter on the treadmill display. My thoughts narrowed into nothingness. I ran.

When I stopped, fifty minutes and seven miles had passed. I stretched, grabbed a towel to dab off some of the sweat running down my neck, took a long drink of water from a fountain near the door, and made my way back up to the room. I was ready to deal with Kevin again but knew I'd need some more down time over the next few days. I wouldn't make it otherwise. When I got to the room I knocked on the door and stretched my legs a little more while I waited. A few seconds went by with no answer. I knocked again.

I leaned against the door and called, "Kevin?"

Nothing. I knocked again. I pressed my ear to the door to see if I could hear the shower running or something. No noise came from inside the room. He was probably sleeping. I found his number in my phone and called him. It rang and rang but there was no answer. I pounded my fist against the door. Nothing.

Determined not to let this undo all the peace I'd just gained from my run, I calmly returned to the elevators and went down to the front desk. Good thing I'd left the gym when I did. I still had to shower and change before dinner. If we got all of this sorted out in the next ten minutes, I'd have plenty of time.

"Hi," I said as I approached. There was a young guy with dark-rimmed glasses behind the desk. He was focused intently on the computer behind the desk but looked up and smiled at my greeting.

"Hello, what can I do for you?"

"I'm locked out of my room, can I get another key?"

"Absolutely, no problem. What's the room number?"

"Five twenty-eight."

He typed the numbers into his computer. "Your name?"

"Daniel Bryant."

He frowned. "I'm sorry, that's not the name we have listed here."

I'd forgotten that Tom's name was on the reservation. "Sorry, it's under Tom Hoyt."

"Do you have ID for Tom Hoyt?"

"Um, no."

"I'm sorry," he said. "I can't give you access to the room without ID."

"What about my ID?"

He shook his head. "Not unless your name is on the reservation, which I'm not seeing that it is."

"Can you call the room for me?" Maybe Kevin was still in there.

"Sure," the guy nodded, picked up the receiver on a phone behind his desk, and dialed the number. After a few moments he replaced the receiver. "Sorry, no answer."

My peace was gone. I was going to murder Kevin.

"If you can call Tom Hoyt, I can confirm his information and give you a key," he suggested.

I didn't have Tom's cell number, but I stepped away from the desk and tried Kevin again. On the third ring he picked up.

"Hello?"

"Kevin." I kept my voice calm. "Where are you?"

"In the room."

I took a deep breath and started back for the elevators. "Why didn't you answer the door?"

"I was taking a bath."

"You couldn't have gotten out long enough to let me in?"

"I thought it was housekeeping."

Somehow I had the self-control to hang up the phone without saying any of the thousand, murderous thoughts running through my head. I went back up to the room and when I knocked on the door, Kevin opened it for me. Before I did anything else I shoved one of the room keys in my wallet.

"How was your work out?" He asked cheerfully.

I didn't reply and didn't say anything to him for the rest of the night. Really, it was better for both of us if I didn't. Thankfully he'd been right about the meet-up time. When we went down to the lobby a few minutes before six o'clock, Bhavesh and Ned were waiting.

"How's the room?" Ned asked.

"Great," I answered before Kevin could open his mouth and say something stupid. "How are yours?"

"Good," Ned answered and Bhavesh nodded in agreement.

When Tom and Mark showed up a few minutes later they announced we were going to try an Asian fusion restaurant a few blocks away. We set out on foot down The Strip — already alive with bright lights, gridlocked taxis and rental cars, crowds of tourists, businessmen, and people wearing costumes of varying absurdity. Some people dressed like iconic celebrities offered to take pictures with tourists in exchange for cash tips and others looked like they set out to find the weirdest outfits they could, just for the hell of it.

"Check out those two," Tom said, nudging me with his elbow. I followed his gaze to two men dressed in drag. Their outfits were some sort of sexy cop meets dominatrix type thing. It freaked me out a little bit, but not as much as when my eyes locked with one of the guys and he started towards me.

"Oh god," I muttered. "Walk faster," I said to Tom.

"What?"

Out of the corner of my eye I could see the two guys, girls, whatever they were, pushing through the crowd to get to us.

"Gentlemen, stop right there," one of them called in a shrill falsetto. *"You two are under arrest."*

Tom and I looked over our shoulders to see the guys brandishing riding crops. Mark, Bhavesh and Kevin had stopped to watch, along with a few other people from the crowd.

Tom looked at me accusingly as he started power walking. "What'd you do, Bryant?"

"Nothing, he just looked at me and started yelling."

"Both of you, stop resisting arrest!"

"Should we stop?" I asked Tom. My legs were starting to ache from the awkward walking run we were doing.

"It's possible that we're making it worse," He said, but I didn't notice him slow down at all. A couple of idiots tried to stick out an arm to stop us but we shoved past them.

"*You have the right to remain sexy,*" one of the cops called again.

"The hell," Tom muttered.

They sounded like they were getting closer. I turned to look again and saw that only a few feet separated us now. The one closest to me grinned and waved his riding crop in the air.

"Oh god." I tried to quicken my pace but the sidewalk was becoming even more crowded. Anxiety for whatever was about to happen made my face prickle with sweat. We hit a wall of people standing in a circle and talking with each other and I knew it was over. I started to turn just in time to see the guy's riding crop whack Tom in the butt. He yelled out in pain, which seemed to satisfy the drag cops.

"That'll teach you to evade the police," said the one who'd hit him.

By then, Mark, Ned, and Kevin had caught up and were laughing along with the fifteen or twenty other people who had been watching the whole thing. The drag cops were loving every second of it, swishing back the way they'd come, tipping their hats as people applauded them.

"He hit my ass," Tom said in disbelief. "That guy hit my ass."

I thought it would be poor form to laugh since I was the one who got us into the whole thing, but the rest of our group didn't have the same reservations. Mark laughed so hard tears filled his eyes.

"Get into some trouble with the law?" Mark clapped a hand on Tom's shoulder.

Tom shot an accusing look my direction but almost looked like he was ready to laugh about it. "Bryant over there decides to make eyes at the drag queens and I'm the one who gets the shit beat out of him."

"Shit beat out of you?" Mark asked. "The guy tapped you with a plastic stick."

I hesitated, unsure of whether or not I should make a joke or apologize. "You could take it as a compliment," I suggested. "It probably means you've got the better body."

"Or maybe it means I haven't practiced power walking as much as you have. Learn that from your grandmother?"

I forced a laugh with the rest of the guys, thankful that Tom wasn't legitimately mad at me even though I'd effectively embarrassed the hell out of him in the middle of the Las Vegas Strip. Mark kept laughing about it throughout dinner and every time he brought it up, I felt another knot tighten in my stomach. I barely ate. All I wanted to was go back to the hotel room and not have to worry about saying the right thing anymore.

After the waiter cleared our plates Mark leaned forward and looked around the group with a wide grin on his face. His eyes landed on me. "Who's ready to hit the tables?" I took a sip of my *Kirin* and waited for someone else to say something.

Ned adjusted his glasses and gave Mark a fatherly look. "Night before the conference, Rhodes?"

"Doesn't start until the afternoon," Tom reminded him.

There were a lot of meaningful looks and elbow jostling and jokes until it was decided that we didn't have anything else that needed to be done. Tom paid the bill, stashed the receipt in his wallet for the expense report, and everyone took off for the hotel casino. As soon as we pushed through the huge, brass plated doors, Kevin and Mark split off in the direction of the Texas Hold 'Em tables. Bhavesh and Tom decided on blackjack, and I told them they could find me at the craps tables.

"You sure you don't want to come with us?" Bhavesh asked, raising his voice over the wild clanging of slot machines.

"Yeah, I'm sure. Better odds." Bhavesh raised an eyebrow and I felt a swell of panic that I'd sounded condescending. "I need them," I added. Obviously what I needed was a drink. Bhavesh gave me an amused shake of his head and started towards the blackjack tables with Tom.

I picked out a table with a decent amount of energy and managed to get settled without doing or saying anything else idiotic. I found a place to stand between a stocky, harsh-looking guy dressed in all black and a couple in their mid-thirties, whispering to each other and gesturing at the table. When I tossed fifty dollars on the felt, the guy in all black glanced coldly at me. His eyes, a piercingly light shade of gray-blue, contrasted sharply with his dark hair.

"Chips at three," said the dealer on my left. The boxman did a typical, exaggerated reach for my cash and dropped it through a slot in the table before passing back five ten-dollar chips. To my right, the guy in black turned back towards the table and took a sip of his drink. I felt another knot tighten in my stomach as I racked my brain trying to think of what I could have done wrong in so short an amount of time. I guessed I was about one step away from a stress-induced stomach ulcer at that point, but then the stickman flipped the "On" button, passed two dice to the couple, and called for pass line bets. I tried to ignore the guy and focus on not losing my small handful of chips.

I stood there playing for nearly an hour before the guy on my right acknowledged me again. We were between rounds and I'd been focused on running numbers through my head when he said, "You here for the finance conference?"

He hadn't looked away from the table so it took me a moment to figure out he was talking to me and I stumbled over the 'yes' I managed to mumble back. "Are you?"

"No."

There was an awkward beat of silence and then the stickman passed the dice to him and we went into another round. I didn't know if I should try to pick up the conversation again. I was getting a weird vibe from him so I let it go. A few more rounds passed before he asked, "Who are you with?"

"Colson Caldwell."

He nodded and took a sip of his drink.

"Are you here for business as well?"

He finally looked at me. "Yes."

The stickman pushed the dice at me and our conversation, if you could even call it that, paused for a few more rounds. When another guy joined the table across from us between rounds and the dealer paused the game play to get his chips, I turned to the guy again.

"I'm Daniel, by the way."

I held out my hand and he hesitated, almost unnoticeably, before shaking it. "Steve Mobley."

"Nice to meet you."

He nodded, took a sip of his drink, and turned his attention back to the table. I figured we were done talking for another few rounds or so but he asked, "What do you do for Colson Caldwell?"

"Investment research for potential clients."

His brow raised. "Must be pretty high stakes at a company like that."

I shrugged. "It can be."

We let the round play out and then I asked him what he did.

"Investments."

"Independently?"

He nodded. "I mostly advise and provide recommendations through a little company I started. High pay-off, quick turnaround."

"Sounds kind of similar to my work."

He shot another cold glance my direction before answering, "Similar."

I hadn't meant to discredit his work by putting us on the same level or anything, but clearly that's how he took it. Steve finished off his drink and tapped the felt next to his chips. "Color up," he said to the dealer.

The dealer pulled in his stack of chips and passed them to the boxman, who gave him back a small handful of larger denomination chips. Steve dropped the chips in his pocket and pulled out a business card, holding it out to me between two fingers.

"Give me a call if you need any investment rec's."

I took the card. "Thanks."

He nodded and stalked away like he was late for something. "Weird," I mumbled to myself. I didn't feel like playing anymore but I finished out another two rounds so it wouldn't look like I was leaving just because Steve left. I went back to the room and thanked God, Kevin wasn't back yet. I had the room to myself long enough to get undressed and settle onto the couch. When Kevin eventually banged his way into the room I just kept my eyes closed, rolled to face the back of the couch, and focused on tuning him out until I fell asleep.

We ate a late breakfast the next morning since the conference didn't officially start until the afternoon. Mark dominated most of the conversation with his stories from the night before, occasionally bringing in Kevin's commentary. Every time Mark let him talk, Kevin beamed like a child and worked entirely too hard to deliver whatever line of the story as elaborately as possible. On the bright side, I didn't get more than a cursory ask about my night. My only event, the strange meeting with Steve Mobley, wasn't something I felt like sharing.

The rest of the morning passed slowly until we made it down to the exhibition hall. Four hundred vendors ranging from banks to insurance companies to financial advisors like ourselves filled a massive space on the basement level of the hotel. The bulk of the exhibitors filled a ten-by-ten foot space, but some of the larger companies held fifteen-by-ten or twenty-by-twenty foot areas. All of the exhibitors used the same basic setup - solid backdrop, banner with company name, table with brochures, a container for business cards, and some sort of freebie, like candy or pens with the company's name on them. Once you'd seen five or six, you'd seen them all. The rare exceptions were few and far between which made for a pretty boring afternoon.

Most of the people who visited our booth talked to Mark or Tom, but every so often someone came my way when both of them were busy. Without fail, as soon as we started talking, Kevin appeared by my shoulder and pushed his way into whatever we were talking about. A lot of the people seemed put off by Kevin and immediately started working on excusing themselves from the conversation. Occasionally though, someone came along and hit it off with Kevin, the two of them firing cheesy quips back and forth and laughing their fake laughs. It disgusted me.

On the second day of the expo, I took a break in the afternoon to mill around the exhibition hall and get a break from Kevin. I paused at a booth where some peer-to-peer lending company had set up a roulette wheel with a handful of dinky prizes and one, tiny, sliver of a chance to win an iPad. A pretty big crowd had gathered around the wheel but I stood far enough away to make sure no one would try to draw me into spinning it.

A guy about my height with dark blond hair wandered up beside me. "Ridiculous, the gimmicks they come up with at these conferences."

I looked at him. He was watching the roulette wheel with a passive sort of distaste as a group of men shouldered their way to the front, making a show of flexing their arms and stretching before spinning the wheel. They yelled and groaned as the wheel ticked past the iPad section and came to rest on a five dollar Starbucks gift card.

"But you could win *an iPad*," I said with heavy sarcasm.

The guy narrowed his eyes, studying the wheel. "One in forty chance. Pretty good odds."

"I'm sure the wheel is perfectly balanced."

"Absolutely." He smiled and held out his hand. "Pierce."

"Daniel." I shook his hand.

"What line of work are you in, Daniel?"

"Advising. Specifically investment research."

He nodded. "Do you enjoy it?"

"For the most part." I didn't see any reason to lie to him. "I really enjoy getting to customize portfolios for our clients but lately we've had a lot of repeat business. Kind of takes some of the analysis out of it."

He nodded again. "I could see that."

"What kind of work do you do?"

"Technology services."

That seemed odd. "What brings you to the conference?"

"Always on the lookout for new growth opportunities." His eyes went back to the roulette wheel. "Going to take a spin?"

"Probably going to pass on that one. Takes all of the fun out of it when you know it's weighted."

"There's a chance that it's not."

I shook my head. "If you look at the back of the wheel you can see where they've attached weights to different sections. They didn't do a very good job of painting over them."

The guy's brow knit together and he stepped away to walk around the wheel until he could see the back from a discrete distance. As he studied the back of the wheel I saw his eyebrows lift and he came back with a smirk on his face.

"Nice attention to detail. Guess I'll have to go find other gimicks to entertain myself with." He dug in his pocket. "Got a card on you?"

"Yes, sir." I pulled a business card from my wallet, handed it to him, and took his in return. I held out my hand to shake his again. "Very nice meeting you."

"You as well."

We started off in separate directions and when I was a few feet away I read the card he'd handed me. It was completely blank except for a phone number and his name.

Pierce Fenner.

It took me a second but then it hit me. Pierce Fenner. The CEO of the multi-billion dollar social networking "technology service." I had three minutes face-to-face with one of the most powerful men in business and we talked about *roulette wheels.*

Sometimes I hate myself.

I didn't see Fenner again for the rest of the conference. Apparently he stopped by the booth while I was gone though. When I made it back, Kevin was beside himself with excitement about having talked to him for a few minutes. Not much else happened though. The trip went pretty well overall, but by the end of it I was ready to be done with Kevin. On Friday afternoon, when Tom drove us back to our cars in the parking garage at the office, Kevin still hadn't figured out how little I wanted to do with him.

"I think we should meet on Monday," he said, closing the trunk of his car.

"Why?"

"I think it'd be good to review our work from the conference and plan how to best optimize our efforts going forward."

"I'll look at my calendar." I got in my car and closed the door before he could add anything else. I was exhausted, still puzzling over the strange conversation I had with that Steve Mobley guy at the casino, and kicking myself for the whole Pierce Fenner thing. When I got home I was going to pour myself a glass of Jameson, sip it slowly in the cool darkness of my room, and then sleep for the rest of the weekend.

CHAPTER 15 - TAYLOR

While Daniel bopped around Vegas, I spent most evenings at home trying to force my baking knowledge into doughnut recipes. When that became too frustrating, I went over to Lola's. Somehow pointless activities like reading magazines or watching TV felt less pointless at her house and helped me calm down a little.

On Friday afternoon, while waiting at Lola's for Daniel to return, I surveyed my doughnut notes from the week. They looked pathetic.

"Why do I bother?" I asked Lola.

"It never hurts to try," she offered without looking up from her *Cosmo*.

Everyone says that, but sometimes it actually does hurt. My silence betrayed my dissatisfaction with her answer. Lola set down her magazine and pushed her black, cat-eye reading glasses on top of her head.

"What have you really lost if you try and do not succeed?" My mind began running with answers, but she interrupted to clarify, "Just from this week – what would you lose?"

"Nothing, I guess."

She smiled, satisfied with making her point. "There is more than one way to skin a cat," she said and returned to her magazine.

I thought for a moment, trying to figure out if there was any way for that idiom to make sense within the context of our conversation. I didn't frequently catch Lola making English errors, but when she did, they really stumped me. When I finally determined that figurative cat skinning had nothing to do with our discussion, too much time had passed for my correction to feel relevant, so I let it go.

I couldn't let go of the worry though. Part of me stayed three steps ahead, trying to anticipate and prevent potential failures. I couldn't turn it off. I gave up trying to explain this to Lola, which was just as well. Through the window, Daniel's car came into view as he pulled in the drive, so I thanked Lola, gathered up my things, and left.

"Okay, let's do this," I said, catching up to Daniel in his room.

He took a wary sip of the whiskey he held in his hand. "Do what?"

"Doughnuts."

His face lit up. "Yeah?"

I nodded and he smiled as if he'd known all along. Sitting down at his desk, he removed a leather bound folder from a drawer. Inside rested the charts and notes he'd already shown me. Combined with my notes from the week, we gave every appearance of looking like we knew what we were doing.

"Now what?" I looked at him anxiously.

"We need to work through our business plan," he pulled out one of the papers from his folder, "starting with our purpose." He grabbed a pen, uncapped it, and looked to me.

"What?"

"Our purpose."

"Um, making doughnuts?"

"No, that's what we're going to *do*. Think about our *purpose*. Why do we exist?"

I knew it would piss him off but I said again, "To make doughnuts."

He looked levelly at me, probably trying to figure out if I was messing with him or if I was really as dumb as he imagined. "Think bigger." He started to write, clearly giving up on me. "We exist to provide people with a gourmet doughnut experience." He sat up, read the sentence again, and gave a little satisfactory nod.

"Oh, I'm sorry," I said. "I didn't know you just wanted me to come up with a more flowery way of saying 'making doughnuts.' "

"Providing a gourmet doughnut experience is completely different from just *making* a doughnut."

I still disagreed. "Whatever, let's move on."

"Okay, objectives."

Surely he was kidding. "To *make doughnuts.*"

"Have you really never gone through a basic business plan before?"

"Believe it or not, the labeling and organizing I do at work doesn't require a statement of purpose."

Daniel set down the pen and leaned his forehead into the heel of his hand. "Taylor. I really need you to cooperate right now."

"*Cooperate?*" I hated when he talked to me like I was a child. "What does any of this have to do with starting a doughnut shop?"

"We have to create a well-defined plan so we can know our next steps and stay on track."

"Great, I agree. But let's get specific. Why don't we figure out how we're going to finance this thing? Or how we're going to convince people that we're better than any of the other million doughnut shops around here?"

"We'll get to that, we have to establish our foundation first."

"We have it. Purpose: gourmet doughnut experience. Objective: make enough money to feed ourselves. What's next?"

His mouth tightened in a frown but he picked up the pen and kept going. When we'd worked through enough of a plan to satisfy him, he typed our notes onto the computer and printed out the page.

"Alright," he pulled the page out of the printer. "We're ready to present."

"To who?"

"Mom and Dad."

"For the life of me, I cannot fathom why that would be necessary."

"They'll be a good sounding board."

"What makes you think they're going to support this idea?"

"Why wouldn't they?"

"In sum? It's not practical."

He looked at me darkly. "Are you in this or not?"

"I am," I insisted with feigned confidence. "Doesn't mean Mom and Dad will be."

"They're not going to shoot down something we believe in."

His complete and total conviction about this struck me. Nothing in his expression or tone conveyed his statement was anything but fact. I looked at him evenly, hiding my doubt. "Let's get this over with."

I followed him downstairs to gather Mom and Dad in the sun room. They sat together on the wicker couch with the faded yellow cushions and Daniel and I took seats across from them on the matching chairs. Daniel placed our papers on the coffee table in between us, took a breath, and launched into his spiel with a fervor I'd never seen in him before.

To Mom and Dad's credit, they didn't laugh. They offered every courtesy of listening carefully and nodding along at all the right times before completely tearing our idea apart. Maybe I imagined it, but I swear I watched their expressions move from amusement, *What a fun idea*, to confusion, *They can't be serious*, to dismay, *How did we go so wrong*, as we spoke. At the end of our talk they donned their best conciliatory tones and calmly picked apart the collection of flaws we foolishly called plan.

"The restaurant industry is tough to break into," Dad started.

"And you're both so young," Mom added.

"I'm not understanding how you're going to finance this," Dad continued.

"And restaurants have so much overhead," Mom said. "You could run out of money before you even opened your doors."

Daniel's face tightened with annoyance, but I'd expected their reaction. To be sure, I wanted them to surprise me. I *ached* for them to surprise me, but it didn't happen.

"We both have experience with this sort of thing," Dad reminded us. "Your mom and I tried our hand at quite a few projects like this."

"Really?" Daniel did a poor job of hiding his irritation. "I don't remember hearing about the doughnut shop you tried to start."

"You're right," Mom agreed, her voice calm and placating. "But we did start our own business once or twice."

She and Dad did try their hand at a handful of businesses throughout the early years of their marriage. They spent the bulk of their free time coming up with some new product or service to sell. It started with kitschy eighties jewelry at trade shows and eventually evolved into all sorts of knick-knacks. Their big sellers were these nifty tables Dad made for kids to play with Legos on. The table surfaces were made with the flat "grass" Legos and bordered by a wooden wall of two-by-fours to reign in the chaos and keep stray Lego pieces from underfoot. Not surprisingly, they sold a ton. They dropped their production on everything else and just focused on the tables until a couple of attorneys from Lego came by to "inspect for copyright infringement." After giving Mom and Dad the all-clear, they started churning out their own patented tables a few months later, effectively making it illegal for Mom and Dad to continue production on their own tables. They shifted their focus back to their desk jobs after that.

Mom tried to smile encouragingly. "It can be a lot of fun but a lot more goes into it than you might think."

Daniel stayed quiet while we heard out the rest of their concerns and then retreated back upstairs to his room.

"They're right," I sighed as Daniel fumed about the room, pacing restlessly back and forth.

"Whose side are you on?" He didn't wait for my reply, but continued, "Doesn't matter anyway, we don't need them."

Sitting down at his desk he opened his notes and flipped to a spreadsheet of our finances. I watched over his shoulder as he scratched through the numbers, making notes and adjustments to accommodate our lack of "potential investors." To my eyes, it seemed like we *did* need them. But Daniel already moved onto a different item.

"We need a building," he said, turning to me.

"A building?" I parroted back. He gave me a look on par with the quality of my question. "That's a huge commitment."

He waited for me to continue, not understanding my issue.

"Huge."

"How do you expect to run a doughnut shop without a place to make and sell doughnuts?"

"I don't." His condescension was really starting to piss me off. "But that's not our first step." I snatched the notebook and pen from his hands. Dropping onto the futon I began scribbling as I spoke.

"We need a product. I've never made doughnuts before and you've never made anything." He let the barb pass since it was mostly true. "Once we figure out our recipe we can estimate our ingredient costs and rework this budget."

I frowned at the list I'd made, debating what needed to come next. "We'll have to spend some time getting business permits, commercial food service licenses and *then*," I drew sharp lines under my final item on the list. "We can find a building."

With the smile of a proud parent, he simply said, "Alright," and took the notebook back. Unsure of whether or not he'd somehow orchestrated my sudden surge of participation, I sat quietly for a moment while he typed my notes onto his computer. I refused to believe I'd been manipulated.

"I'm going to find a doughnut recipe," I said and went for my own computer. Tricked into it or not, I enjoyed the sense of purpose.

CHAPTER 16 - DANIEL

It was a productive week, if not one of the more annoying ones I've experienced. It seemed to have been a productive week for Taylor too. I'd been home less than ten minutes when she came bursting into my room all gung-ho about the doughnut project. Even with the praise from Tom, Mark and Ned, I wasn't sure my performance at the conference would lead to a promotion. Until things at work looked more promising, I planned to continue investing in my back-up plan.

Taylor obviously spent a lot of time thinking about the doughnuts while I was in Vegas, which was exactly what I'd anticipated but I tried to seem surprised anyway. Once we talked through things a bit, I sent her on to the second step of my plan - figuring out our doughnut recipe. She'd shut down any talk of finding a building which was fine by me. I could research buildings without her and her energy would be much more effective in the recipe sphere of the project.

After Taylor and I wrapped up, I took my laptop over to Rachel's and sat on the end of her couch. While I stretched my legs across the cushions and situated my computer on my lap, she poured two glasses of red wine for us.

"How was your day?" I asked.

"Not bad. I saw a rat this morning though."

"A rat? Where?"

"In here."

"Rachel, that's disgusting."

"It isn't my fault." She set the glasses on the coffee table. "I called maintenance and they said a couple of other residents have seen one too."

I was horrified. "Why don't they *do* something?"

She shrugged. "They've tried. I think I might need to get a rat trap."

"Geez, you think?" I felt dirty just sitting there, knowing that a rat might have crawled on top of the very place I was sitting.

Rachel, for her part, looked entirely unperturbed. She sat on the other end of the couch, mirroring my position, pulled her laptop onto her lap with one hand and grabbed her wine with the other.

"Aren't cats supposed to keep rats away?" Felix sat watching us from the other side of the room looking half-awake like he always did.

"He tries."

"I doubt it." On my list of favorite animals, cats fall somewhere near the bottom, between snakes and rats. I tolerated Felix because he was in the picture before I was, but if Rachel and I were in it for the long haul, she wouldn't be getting another cat after Felix kicked the bucket. Not a chance.

Rachel ignored my comment about Felix. "How much space are you thinking you guys will need?"

"I'm not entirely sure." I reached for my glass on the coffee table and took a sip. "The best I can tell, we'll need at least fifteen hundred square feet."

She nodded and started typing away on her computer. "Good lord these are expensive," she said a minute later.

"What part of town are you looking in?"

"Um," she squinted at the screen. "Like, Northwest of the loop."

I frowned. It was a decent part of town but definitely not the nicest. "How expensive?"

She looked up from her computer, "One hundred thousand for a year."

I blinked at her.

"I'll try farther east," she said.

"Good idea."

We kept at it for nearly two hours. Somehow I had it in my head that since we needed a space about the size of an apartment, the lease would be comparable to an apartment. Our research proved me wrong. Unless Taylor and I wanted to set up shop in a horribly sketchy part of town, which we didn't, we wouldn't be able to afford our own space. Not without the hypothetical investors I'd already written out of the equation.

"Don't give up," Rachel said. "We'll think of something."

Whenever she dove into my problems and made herself a part of them it kind of made me worried that I wasn't doing the same for her and dredged up the worst kind of insecurity.

"Stop it," she said, interrupting my thoughts.

"What?"

"I know what you're thinking. Stop."

She had an annoying habit of assuming things. "You don't know what I—"

"I want to help you," she interrupted again. "We'll figure this out." She smiled when I didn't reply and went back to her computer.

"Love you," I said, squeezing her foot resting against my leg. Her knee jumped, nearly knocking her computer off her lap.

"You're lucky I wasn't holding my wine." She narrowed her eyes but the hint of a smile showed on her lips. "This is a new shirt."

"I forgot how ticklish you are."

She shook her head, not buying the lie, and reached forward to squeeze my leg right above the kneecap. My knee jolted and my computer slid off my lap. I barely caught it before it hit the floor.

Rachel smiled, "Sorry, I forgot how ticklish you are."

"Alright," I moved my laptop to the safety of the coffee table. "That's enough of that." I took her laptop and put it next to mine. That's about where our building research ended for the night.

CHAPTER 17 - TAYLOR

In typical fashion, my initial optimism quickly faded. If I had to guess, I'd say it happened somewhere between the monotony of waiting hours for dough to rise and the trepidation of staring down six quarts of scalding hot oil sitting deceivingly still on the stove. Nevermind the fact that I'd spent several hours researching doughnuts on Saturday and then most of Sunday morning wrestling with the project entirely by myself. My business partner seemed to feel above this part of the process, which was fine by me for the time being. He'd be in the way more likely than not.

Which left the oil to be dealt with. I desperately wished to skip the frying part of the recipe. Too many childhood experiences of cooking with Mom and getting hit with accidental splashes of boiling water or errant pops of frying pan grease funneled into an admittedly unreasonable fear. With reluctant hands I pinched the very edge of a dough ring and dangled it over the oil for a moment before slowly lowering it down. The smooth surface of oil erupted into tiny bubbles as the dough made contact and I instinctively jerked my hand away. After finding myself unscathed, I continued to lower a second, third, and fourth ring into the oil.

In half an hour I had fourteen puffy, golden brown doughnuts sitting proudly on a wire cooling rack. I moved the hot pan of oil off the burner and started on the glaze. The night before I'd read through dozens of glaze recipes to put together a sort of base so I'd be able to tweak and add variety as I went without having to make large individual batches of glaze. After setting aside a small bowl of the base glaze, suitable for a handful of plain-glazed doughnuts, I divided the remaining amount into two portions for a chocolate and strawberry version.

Cocoa powder sifted through a strainer to get the lumps out created the chocolate glaze. The strawberry required a little more effort and creativity. I couldn't use fresh strawberries without the glaze becoming watery. While digging through the pantry to see if Mom had any strawberry flavoring — I wasn't sure if they even made such a thing — I came across a package of freeze-dried strawberries. Why she owned them I have no idea, but I assumed it wasn't for anything important and tossed the contents of the package into a food processor. Once the strawberries were ground into a fine powder, I added them to the last bowl of plain glaze. I stirred the beautiful swirl of magenta and white until the glaze evened out into a soft shade of pink. The final product had an unbelievable amount of flavor without losing any of the consistency. It was perfect.

I dipped the doughnuts in the glazes and then placed them back on the wire rack to let the excess glaze drip off. I think the general rule of thumb is to let the doughnuts sit until the glaze hardens, but I thought it rude to ignore my empty stomach after all the peril I'd put it through with the oil. I took a bite of chocolate and closed my eyes in appreciation of the light, yeasty dough and the thin layer of fudgey sweetness on top. Sooner than I realized, it was gone. I eyed the rest of the doughnuts. There were thirteen left, which seemed like an unlucky number to leave siting on the counter like that. I reached for a glossy strawberry doughnut and delighted in the punchy change of flavor.

As I finished savoring the last bite, Daniel appeared in the kitchen and I spun around guiltily at his voice.

"How's it going?" He asked, surveying my work.

"Great." I subtly dabbed at the corners of my mouth for runaway glaze.

"That's cool — the recipe made exactly twelve. Gotta be a good sign or something, right?"

"Don't be silly, it's just a recipe." I didn't feel the need to add that the recipe originally made fourteen.

"No," he insisted. "I think it means something." I narrowed my eyes at him, wondering if he'd seen my sample session after all. "Can I try one?"

He went for a strawberry first and seemed to undergo the same transcendental experience. "You made this?" I nodded and he continued incredulously, "This is amazing!"

I beamed humbly under his praise even though I'd given myself the same accolade a few minutes before.

His tone was suddenly all business. "How did you get them to be the right shape?"

I showed him the biscuit cutter I'd used.

"So did you cook the whole sheet of dough and then cut them out?"

After determining that he was, in fact, serious, I tried to patiently describe the process, refusing to dwell on the knowledge that he would know all of this if he'd helped rather than slept in. He nodded thoughtfully while I spoke as if approving the techniques I'd used, but he'd already given himself away and I knew him too well. Daniel didn't understand anything about what I was saying.

"I say we make some more and have a taste testing party this afternoon," he suggested.

I agreed, appreciating that 'we' implied an extra set of hands for the second go around.

"You get started and I'm going to do some more research," he said and, after nabbing one more doughnut, dashed up the stairs.

I watched him go with a wave of disbelief, frustration and, finally, a sigh of resignation. I ate another doughnut for strength and then began measuring the ingredients again. In a couple of hours the second batch was finished and ready to go. I started quartering the doughnuts into a good sample size until Daniel appeared again, demanding I let him take over.

"It's okay, I'm almost done," I said. There were only three left.

"Really," he insisted. "Let me."

I gave up the knife and stepped away. Mom came into the kitchen and wrapped an arm around my waist.

"Should we be blindfolded?" Mom asked with a playful smile.

"I don't know." I turned to Daniel. "Should they?"

"Don't be stupid," he snapped.

I wanted to snap back about his only contribution to the process being to swoop in when I was nearly finished, but I thought I should try to be grateful he'd helped at all.

The doorbell rang and Daniel said, "That's Rachel, will you let her in?"

Mom went to open the door and Daniel looked up casually from his project when Rachel entered the kitchen. He gave her a quick kiss on the cheek while he continued to work. I tried not to gag at the performance. Gone were any attempts at gratitude for his help.

Dad shuffled into the kitchen a little after Rachel, more or less on time for our scheduled taste testing. Our panel of judges complete, we sat them at the breakfast table and presented three plates of quarter-doughnuts, lest they fill up too much on one flavor. In addition to repeating the three from the first batch, I'd scoured the kitchen for new ingredients to create three new flavors. I ended up with a cinnamon sugar, a blood orange and, at a loss for anything semi-normal, a peanut butter and jelly. I thought it'd be a hit, but after being presented with his plate, Dad poked the PB&J doughnut dubiously.

"What happened? Did you drop it?"

I frowned. "The aesthetics might need a little work."

Rather than cutting out the hole, I'd decided to leave the doughnut whole and then fill it with jelly. Unfortunately, the jelly sat too heavily in the doughnut, making it sag pathetically in the middle. The appearance worsened when I tried to add the peanut butter frosting, which had an odd lumpy consistency since Mom insisted on buying natural peanut butter in hopes of the family miraculously beginning to like it. The frosting didn't spread very well, so I had to be satisfied with kind of slopping it on and calling it a day.

Daniel began to guide our judges through trying the doughnuts in some fictitiously precise order. For not being around during any of the cooking, he managed to describe each flavor surprisingly well. After giving them the briefest of moments to chew, he quizzed them on flavor, texture and appearance, absorbing each of their answers. Maybe it's not surprising that my peanut butter concoction fell short in the appearance rankings, but I tasted one of them. Life-changingly delicious.

"There's more to a doughnut than symmetry and smooth glaze," I said.

Four faces blinked at me in polite disagreement. By the end of it all, no flavor pulled ahead of any of the other's. Rachel preferred the plain, Dad liked the chocolate, and Mom refused to vote because she claimed they tasted equally delicious.

"Okay, fine, but are they good?" I demanded.

The panel nodded unenthusiastically and Daniel I shared an exasperated look.

"They're good," Mom offered. "They taste just like a normal doughnut."

"Except the lumpy one," Dad added.

Daniel and I knew enough to understand that normal doughnuts weren't going to put us in business. I let him continue to play the gracious host and dismiss the group while I cleared the plates. Later, going over our notes, he didn't seem to grasp my frustration.

"We'll just try a different recipe or something," he said. A different recipe. Like the perfect doughnut was one of his pretty financial formulas, waiting to be thought of and solved. Even more irritating was how little he'd helped.

"What is 'we?' I was in the kitchen for six hours, where were you?"

"There's more to getting this going than just baking."

I barely agreed. "I'm not doing it again."

"Fine, I'll help you next time."

"Next time? I don't know what else to do, Dan! You wanted doughnuts, I made doughnuts. I have no idea how to make them special. That's like making a pancake special. Sure, some are better than others, but at the end of the day they get doused with syrup and are nothing more than a pancake."

He'd been around long enough to be unfazed by my rant. "I agree," he said calmly. "At the end of the day they'll still be doughnuts, we just need to tweak them a little."

I let out a loud breath. *"How?"*

He didn't answer immediately, but leaned back on the futon, thinking. We sat in contemplative silence and my thoughts drifted back and forth through our problem. Eventually I felt my mind hit a wall and I stood, giving up.

"I've gotta get some sleep before work tomorrow," I told him.

"I thought you were quitting."

"Not until this starts to show a little more promise. We need a product."

"Doughnuts."

I shot him a warning look. I could see he debated arguing but, instead, nodded in agreement. "Keep brainstorming then."

"I will," I promised and thumped his back affectionately as I left. I heard the springs of the futon creak as he reached for a pillow. I quickened my pace to round the corner just in time to let it sail past me into the wall.

I walked into work Monday morning feeling fairly optimistic. Being the believer in unerring universal balance that I was, I'd foolishly convinced myself work at HRG would get better since the doughnut endeavor wasn't panning out so well. The pendulum would swing in favor of the steady career path and the doughnuts could peacefully fall to the wayside.

After giving my theory a few weeks to evidence itself, I began doubting its validity. Neither Daniel nor I managed to come forth with a solution for how to make our doughnuts stand out and, contrary to my theory, work was, well, work. I continued vacillating between hours of inactivity due to too little work and flashes of frantic scrambling to finish occasional assignments largely beyond my understanding. One particularly hellish week was finally nearing a close when I was told I needed to attend a client lunch.

Given my first stunning performance in a client meeting, I couldn't think of a single reason why I might be invited for a round two, much less one downtown at Le Portel. I'd been around long enough to know Bill wasn't a spendthrift and Le Portel wasn't cheap. My attendance would definitely cost them financially, if not socially, but I didn't think it prudent to protest my requested involvement.

Not that I was given much time to protest. Ryan banged on the wall of my cubicle a little after eleven on Friday morning. He smirked at having startled me. "We're going to lunch."

"Who?" If this was his arrogant way of asking me on a date, I was not amused.

"Me, Bill, someone from Fizz, and you."

"Fizz? Like the soda company?"

He nodded. I'd barely heard of Fizz and not at all around the office. The company was trying to make DIY soda a thing. I'd seen them a handful of times at one of those dinky sample booths at the grocery store. Apparently by tossing water and syrup together into their fancy machine, you could make your own soda in a few seconds. I'd yet to figure out why anyone would want to drop a couple hundred bucks on a device that only served to complicate, rather than simplify, one's life. It seemed that others agreed. Fizz had yet to make it past the temporary display shelves.

Which is why Le Portel, one of the swankiest French restaurants in the town, seemed like an unlikely choice. I spent the ride to the restaurant trying to think of a polite way to find an answer without directly asking.

"Nice restaurant." I commented as Ryan handed over the keys to the valet.

"Client's idea."

That explained a little. Bill would never pick this. But then, normally I would say Bill would never *agree* to this either.

Bill and Ryan led the way while I followed a half-step behind, trying to subtly dry my sweaty palms on my pants before I had to shake the client's hand. Bill pushed through the ornate, faux-gold door and, as an afterthought, reached back to hold it open for me.

He gave his name to the hostess as our eyes adjusted to the dim lighting. The restaurant was crowded but remarkably quiet, likely due to the sturdy mahogany half-walls dividing conversations and preventing their sounds from spreading across the room. We followed the hostess to a table tucked away in one of the restaurant's many alcoves.

"Should be here any minute," Bill muttered with an elaborate look at his watch.

We suffered through a few uncomfortable minutes of silence before Bill spoke again.

"Here we are." He stood and I followed his gaze to see a tiny, impossibly thin but pretty woman in a short skirt suit and atrociously high heels making her way toward us.

Revelation dawned and I immediately understood why they were taking this hopeless account, why Bill acquiesced to the restaurant choice, and why I'd been brought along. I had a brother, I knew this trick. Bring along the little sister and not only do you instantly appear vastly more caring and thoughtful for associating with such a lowly creature, but you also put the woman at ease by giving her a buffer of female camaraderie in a potentially intimidating environment. *Well played, boys.*

She introduced herself as Casey Coleman when I stood and shook her hand with Bill and Ryan. I watched unfazed as they awkwardly shared the task of pulling out her chair. I sat, unaided, and did a solo butt scoot up to the table.

A waiter came by to take our drink orders. I asked for iced tea and when he turned to Casey she ordered a water, beaming up at him, "with a twist of lemon."

"You're sure you wouldn't care for a glass of wine?" Bill asked.

She smiled charmingly and declined, "I never drink in the afternoons, it makes me sleepy."

Bill and Ryan matched her light laugh, as if she's just come up with a profoundly adorable quip about alcohol preferences.

We soon learned Fizz was the "brainchild" of Casey and her sister Ashley. I instantly lose a few notches of respect for anyone who uses the word, "brainchild," seriously, but I tried to keep a pleasant look on my face and asked, "Is your sister older or younger?"

"I'm older by two months," she answered and then, seeing my confusion, added, "Ashley's my sorority sister."

The waiter saved me from needing a polite reply. He distributed the drinks and then poised his pen to take our food orders, looking to me first again. I hadn't even looked at the menu and had to scan it frantically while I racked my brain to decide what would be appropriate for a business lunch. I really wanted a salad but didn't want to seem like I was trying to be cheap or health-obsessed. Pasta sounded too heavy and a sandwich would be too messy.

"I'll have the French onion soup," I blurted and then gave myself a mental pat on the back for the quick thinking. Soup – easy, light, perfect for a business lunch.

Casey ordered a salad and, again, Ryan and Bill followed her lead. I decided right then that I kind of hated her.

Ryan asked pleasant questions about how Casey and her 'sister' began their business venture and I nodded along as if I was interested. The whole concept sounded to me like a useless activity two women with too much time on their hands were busying themselves with, but no one asked my opinion.

The food arrived and it took me about three seconds to notice the grave error I'd made. Bar none, French onion soup is the cheesiest monstrosity of all the broth-based soups. I regarded the bowl in front of me. Cheese. Lots of it. Melted on top and stuck to the sides of the bowl. I lifted my eyes and caught Ryan watching me with definite amusement. He knew. Bill, at least, was listening intently to Casey's explanation of the health benefit of dipping salad into dressing rather than pouring it on top.

"How's the soup?" Ryan challenged when Casey took a breath.

"Just giving it a second to cool," I shot back.

Content to wait for my inevitable humiliation, he turned back to Bill and Casey. The conversation shifted to Fizz and all things soda.

"Have you thought about what you're looking for in terms of marketing?" Bill prompted.

Casey launched into a senseless explanation that could have been summarized with, "No." Determining the group sufficiently distracted, I used my spoon to begin assessing the soup situation. A quick poke at the surface confirmed I was dealing with a moderate to thick layer of cheese. One more glance to check for an audience, none at present, and then I set about my task.

"Given our present infrastructure," Casey rambled. *Where did she come up with that stuff?*

I needed to focus. The spoon seemed to have a sharper edge than anticipated and with a little coercion I was able to make a botched cut through the cheese.

"Judging by the auxiliary data..." Bill offered in return.

I wondered if I could sell a dictionary of useless advertising jargon. I gave another quick glance around the table to make sure no one was looking and, thinking the chunk of cheese liberated, I quickly spooned a bite to my mouth. All at once, too fast for my brain to process in which order, the broth, having been insulated by the lid of cheese, hit my tongue with an incinerating slap and, though nearly blinded by the pain of my mouth melting, I saw a long, unsightly cord of cheese stretching from the bowl to my mouth.

Implementing the stop, drop and roll of eating, I opened my mouth and sucked in a gust of air, trying to stop the burning. For all Ryan had been acting interested in the conversation, he managed to turn at that exact moment and ask in a deceivingly neutral voice, "What do you think, Taylor?"

I kept my head down so I could fix the cheese issue while I tried to swallow the scalding hotness, but somehow nearly half the soup managed to escape and dribble down my chin and onto my shirt and pants. My throat, trying to save itself from the half of the bite still in my mouth, closed and I nearly choked as an errant bit trickled into my windpipe. I fought a painful cough while frantically sawing at the cheese with my teeth until it dropped deftly to the bowl.

The show over, I scraped together my remaining shreds of dignity and raised my eyes to meet Ryan's. "Think about what?"

No one said anything. I seemed to have left them speechless. After shedding his look of embarrassed disbelief, Bill attempted a recap of the question while I actively ignored Ryan's shoulders subtly shaking with laughter.

The ride back to the office was silence punctuated by occasional remarks between Bill and Ryan about traffic, weather, and other equally insignificant things. I couldn't figure out whether their lack of comment came from mercy or intense distaste for me as a human, but I felt thankful either way. When we returned, Bill showed me Fizz's pathetic branding elements. Glaring disagreement flared between each item. Their graphic logo, text logo, product label, and print brochures looked as if they each belonged to a separate company. I pointed this out to Bill and he nodded in agreement.

"There needs to be some continuity," I said.

"Think you can handle it?" That might have held a hidden jab at the lunch incident, but I lit up with excitement anyway — I was getting my first real design project.

"I need some direction. What are they going for?"

He shrugged. "Get on the phone with Ms. Coleman."

I eyed the clock. Too much time left in the day to justify putting it off till Monday. I went back to my cube and reluctantly I called Casey and explained the issue.

"You're going to need some brand identity, a theme, if you will."

"Oh, like a party theme," she reasoned.

"Um, yes." Close enough, anyway.

"How about make-your-own soda?"

"More specific," I said gently. "Soda is the product, now you need to describe it. Like, fresh and organic or traditional and classic."

"Fun and ready for a party?"

"You're getting there. Maybe talk it out with your business partner. I can give you guys time to talk and I'll call back on Monday." With any luck, Casey wasn't the brains of the pair and together they'd be able to come up with something substantial.

As I hung up, there was a quick tap on my cubicle wall and Rand leaned into sight.

"Heard about the soup," he said, readjusting his glasses.

"Yeah." What else do you say to that?

"Don't worry about it," he shrugged. "Everyone's had something like that happen before."

I doubted it, but appreciated his attempted comfort anyway.

"What are you working on?" He squinted at the Fizz images on my computer screen.

I gave him a quick synopsis of the theme issue. He laughed when I recounted Casey's suggestions.

With his best valley girl voice he said, "Maybe you should like, make them about, like, fun in the sun. Like a beach party!"

"Perfect," I agreed with mock seriousness.

Starting to leave he added, "If you're still hungry there's some doughnuts in the break room."

Doughnuts were the last thing I wanted to think about — not with this impossibly ridiculous beach-themed soda project in front of me. I told Rand as much and in saying it out loud, I realized this was exactly what I'd been trying to explain to Daniel. Our doughnuts needed a theme, something to give our venture direction, to make our product unique.

Like a final puzzle piece slipping into place it dawned on me - beach soda might not pan out so well, but what if the doughnuts were beach themed? It sounded absurd at first but my mind began racing with ideas. I checked the clock again. What had seemed like a long stretch of time now looked perfect. I had nothing else to finish before Monday so I flipped open my notebook and started sketching.

Late the next morning I dragged Daniel down to the kitchen where a batch of doughnuts waited on the counter, hastily hidden under a kitchen towel.

"Ready for it?" I asked.

"Tell me."

"No, no," I corrected. "Not tell."

I guided him over to the counter where my third round of doughnuts awaited his inspection.

"I give you," I paused dramatically. "Our theme."

Immediate confusion registered on his face. "What is it?"

"Beach. Tropical, summer, exotic, fresh."

He waited, curiosity piqued. I worked my way down the row of doughnuts.

"Piña colada," I pointed to the first one. "Vanilla cake doughnut with pineapple, topped with toasted coconut flakes."

"I came up with that idea," he frowned.

"Yeah, but it didn't work by itself. Now it's part of a collection - key lime, strawberry daiquiri, a beach bonfire s'more. And look," I held up a handful of doughnut holes glazed with alternating red and white sections. "Beach balls!"

Dan smiled. "Taste testing," he declared and went in search of Mom and Dad like a kid anxious to open presents on Christmas morning.

CHAPTER 18 - DANIEL

When Taylor sets her sights on something, she owns it. Seriously. Point her the right way and she'd run forever. With the smallest push in the direction of researching recipes, she'd come back with the kind of idea you retire on.

Mom and Dad were a little underwhelmed with our first batch of doughnuts but they were almost as impressed as I was second time around. Mom got on board as soon as I put a piña colada doughnut in front of her.

She closed her eyes and took a whiff of the doughnut. "Can't you just *hear* the ocean? *Feel* the sand? *Smell* the sunscreen? *Taste* the —"

"Mom," I said. "Just try it."

She took a bite and Dad followed. He looked disbelievingly at the doughnut. "Wow."

Taylor and I passed them key lime, strawberry daiquiri, and s'more doughnuts. They took bites of each, taking their time in between to comment on the flavors. The contrast to last time was unbelievable.

"And look," Taylor held out a plate of the doughnut holes. "Beach balls!"

Mom and Dad blinked at her, not understanding, and Taylor's face sank. I took one of the doughnut holes and held it out for Mom and Dad, turning it back and forth. "See? It's iced —"

"Glazed," Taylor said softly.

"It's glazed to look like a beach ball," I explained. "Get it?"

En masse, the doughnut holes were hard to distinguish between, but once they saw one alone they understood.

"Clever," Dad smiled.

They didn't comment on the business aspect of the project and we knew better than to ask. After they'd sampled all the flavors, Taylor and I went upstairs to my room to look at the business plan we'd written the previous weekend.

"Nice job pulling the doughnut theme together," I told her.

"Thanks." She had a contented smile on her face as she sat on the futon and propped her feet up. I quickly read through the plan, anxious to give her a new assignment while she still felt the high of her victory.

"You mentioned we'll need a business license," I prompted.

"Yeah. I don't know where you get one though."

"Me neither." I waited.

After a few moments pause she said, "I'll find out," and left the room.

She latched onto the new project easier than anticipated. It was a good sign. With a little more time I wouldn't have to hold her hand anymore and then we could really hit our stride.

It was the last Saturday of the month so I balanced my budget and then spent the rest of the afternoon researching real estate. Earlier that day Dax had texted me, asking again if I wanted to go out for drinks. I gave in. He was sort of immature but he was a good guy and kind of my only friend at the office. We'd never hung out outside of work, unless you counted office happy hours, so I had no idea how things were going to go.

He texted me his address and I went over to his house around seven. The house itself didn't look too bad but the neighborhood had a reputation for being pretty rough. To be fair, a block north there's a little strip of bars and restaurants that are pretty popular. But if you head four or five blocks east, most of the businesses have bars on the windows and there's a bunch of pawn shops. Never a good sign in my book. Six blocks south there's a grocery store that I heard has the most armed robberies in the entire state. As I walked to his front door, I pressed the lock button on my key fob twice to make sure my car locked.

Dax answered the door with one of his wide, cheerful grins. "Hey man," he stepped aside to let me in. "Come on in."

I was wearing khaki chinos, a polo, and pair of Sperry's while he wore jeans, a t-shirt, and flip-flops. I hoped he planned on changing but I doubted it. Between that and my could-be-brand-new sports car parked out front, I felt incredibly uncomfortable.

The living room I'd stepped into was really nice looking for a place full of dudes. The hardwood floors were spotless and then beige sofa pushed against the wall didn't have any stains that I could see. The walls were white and also stain-free, and the windows were covered with wooden blinds, except for one. A big sheet of kraft paper was taped across where blinds should have been.

"What happened to your window?"

"Someone threw a rock through it."

"Like, one of your roommates?"

"No, like some random guy."

"Were you here when it happened?"

He shook his head. "It was while we were all at work…" He narrowed his eyes, thinking. "Thursday?" He thought for another moment. "Yeah, Thursday."

"Did they actually break in or just break the window?"

"Broke in. Took, like, three hundred dollars of cash from my room and one of my roommates' stereo. Not our TV though, I can't figure out why they didn't take the TV." He looked at it mounted on the wall. It was a pretty nice TV. "You'd think they would have taken the TV before trashing my entire room for the random cash I had lying around." He shrugged, "Shit happens, I guess."

He was much calmer about it than I would have been. After some weak assurances that my car would be fine, we headed out the front door and up the street. The new bar he'd mentioned stood alone on the corner, bordered by small parking lots on either side. I debated moving my car so at least I could count on the relative safety of having it in a more public place, but as we approached I saw that both the lots were already full. A large sign of weathered wood was mounted to the top of the building with "The Revolver" painted in a Western-style font. Despite the heat, the wooden decked patio out front was already crowded with people.

I followed him onto the deck and we wound through the tables to the front door. Inside, the stools around the bar top and the tables scattered across the room were mostly full as well. Dax headed for the back of the bar top and we found two open seats by some dart boards.

"Are they always this crowded?" Three big guys, trying to claim a dart board, pushed behind me and knocked me into the counter. One of them turned around and called, "Sorry," over his shoulder but the other two didn't even look.

"It's been about like this every time I've been here," Dax said.

"And how many times has that been?"

"Can't remember... five or six I think."

It shouldn't have surprised me. A bartender came by and asked Dax what he wanted. I didn't catch the name of what he ordered, but the beer the guy brought back looked like muddy water.

"Nine percent alcohol," Dax explained with a grin. I ordered a Shiner.

We drank the first beer at the bar and by the time we ordered a second, one of the dart boards had cleared. We took our beers over and started a game. Dax wasn't great which was a nice change from playing with Rachel at the Tavern. She was abnormally good at darts. Usually when we finished a game, she'd practice throwing bullseyes just to see how many she could get in a row. Her record was nine.

Dax and I were about the same skill level though, and once I had a beer in me I started to chill out a little. When I was clearing the scoreboard to start a second game he asked what kind of stuff I did in my free time.

"Rachel and I just hang out most of the time."

"Other than that," he said. "Something interesting."

"I've been looking at starting a little business on the side," I hedged. "Just something for the weekends."

"No way?" He took the darts I handed him. "See, now that's interesting." He threw a dart and missed the board altogether. "My dad keeps telling me I should do something like that since we get so much time off with Colson Caldwell." He frowned. "What are you doing?"

"Just a little project with my sister," I shrugged. "Nothing serious."

"What is it?"

"Uh, a doughnut shop."

He let out a loud, quick laugh. "Dude, that's awesome." He threw another dart and made it on to the board but not onto any of the correct segments. His third one finally hit its target though. That's about how our first game went too. He handed me the darts and I went up to take my turn.

"What kind of doughnut shop?"

"Taylor kind of came up with this beach theme," I said, realizing how dumb it sounded out loud. Dax didn't seem to notice though. "All of the flavors are these gourmet, beach-type flavors. Like piña colada."

"You made a piña colada doughnut?"

"Taylor did."

"Is there rum in it?"

"No. It's just pineapple and coconut and stuff." I poised to throw a dart.

"Do you have a name yet?"

"No." The dart missed the segments and hit the border. I hadn't even thought about names yet.

"You should make it a pun," Dax said.

"What kind of pun?"

"My fraternity used to do this thing where we gave out doughnuts the week of finals. We called it 'Bronuts.'"

"I don't get it."

"Fraternity brothers. Doughnuts. Bronuts."

"Ah." I went to retrieve my darts from the board and handed them back to Dax. "The problem is, my sister isn't a bro, so…"

"I'm not saying you use that name, I'm just saying a pun in general."

"Got it."

We spent a few seconds trying to think of something else, but nothing immediately came to mind so we dropped it and moved onto other less consequential topics for a while. After we'd finished four games of darts and four beers each, we went to tab out. I closed my tab and as Dax pulled out his credit card to close his, four girls came up to the bar and all but threw themselves at him.

They all started screeching at the same time, "*Dax!*" He turned, gave them one of his grins, and hugged them each in turn. My memory may be a little fuzzy but I remember them all being about the same height, with dark tanned skin, and straight dark hair. It kind of freaked me out. They started asking him a bunch of dumb, inane little questions, leaving the bar tab and me momentarily forgotten. I should have left right then.

The next thing I knew he'd put his credit card back in his wallet and was ordering a round of shots for all of us. I don't do shots.

"No thanks, man, I'm good."

He clapped a hand on my shoulder and said, "Live a little, Danny."

"Really, I'm okay. Thanks though."

"Too late, I already ordered you one."

"You take it."

He ducked his chin, fluttered his eyes, and said in a flamboyant voice, "Are you trying to get me drunk?"

I wasn't amused. "I don't want a shot."

"Ladies," Dax turned to the four girls. "My friend Daniel doesn't want to take shots with us."

Their four heads whipped around. All at once they started shouting, "What? Why? Come on! Take a shot!" Dax put a shot of tequila in my hand and I took it to make them stop.

"Great, okay. Let's go," I told Dax.

"We can't leave *now*," he said, putting an arm around the shoulder of the girl closest to him.

"You don't have to leave, but I am."

The girls started twittering again, "Why? Don't leave! You can't leave!"

"Gotta get back to the ol' ball and chain?" Dax asked. The girls made obnoxious *ooh* noises.

"Screw you, Dax." That would have been another good moment to leave.

"I'm just playing man." He moved from the girl to throw an arm around my shoulder. "Tomorrow is Daniel's birthday," he told the girls.

"What? No it's not," I said, but it was too late. One of the girls leaned over to the bartender and came back with another round of shots, doubles, filled with something electric blue. A glass was pushed into my hand and then we were clinking them together and throwing them back. Things got a little fuzzy after that.

CHAPTER 19 - TAYLOR

If you took a poll of the population at large asking where one goes to get a commercial business license, I bet only a handful could tell you. Even Google struggled to dredge up an answer to my variations on the question. I wondered if Daniel passed the task to me only after taking an unsuccessful stab at it. After a week of intermittent research, I came across a suggestion to try the courthouse.

On Saturday, Daniel and I headed downtown. In the car, I tried to get Daniel up to speed on what I'd learned about licenses during my search. Daniel listened intently, asking thoughtful, humble questions as I explained what I'd learned. I felt a little surge of gratitude that he was actually letting me lead the project, until we got to the front desk at the courthouse and he stepped ahead of me to say, "Can you tell me whom I would discuss business licenses with?"

"We," I added quietly as we followed the clerk's directions. "Who *we* would discuss business licenses with."

Daniel ignored me and kept a half-step ahead. We came to a dimly lit fluorescent hallway with a faded plastic wall sign pointing around the corner to the Business Licensing office. The door Daniel pushed open gave a shrill creak and three heads whipped around from their computers. The space, drab and gray, held only three desks with clerks on one side, staring at us expectantly, and empty chairs on the other. Daniel and I paused awkwardly, unsure of whom we should speak with. On the left there was a small man whose balding forehead shone with the glare of the fluorescent lights. In the middle sat an older woman with a sharp nose and angular chin. On the right, a younger, heavy set woman wearing face makeup several shades darker than her neck stared at us with wide, rounded eyes.

"Hello," I greeted the room and Daniel stiffened beside me.

"Can I help you?" The angular-faced woman in the middle asked while the others went back to their computers.

"We're here for a license," I said.

"I figured as much," she said dryly.

I gave a light laugh but her look conveyed she hadn't been attempting humor. I took a seat without invitation and Daniel followed.

"A commercial kitchen license," I added.

The woman, DeeAnna, according to a nameplate on her desk, gave me another charming look before replying, "I assume you mean a Retail Food Operation license."

I felt Daniel's annoyance and knew better than to believe it was aimed at DeeAnna. She heaved open a file cabinet behind her desk and laboriously thumbed through the folders with a remarkable lack of speed. Finally she pulled a folder and set it heavily on the desk, taking her time to pull out a thick packet of papers.

"I'm not going to do this for you," she warned, uncapping a cheap pen and scratching it across a piece of paper to get the ink started. "But I'll get you started. What is the name of your establishment?"

"Uhm," I looked to Daniel. He looked back with an odd combination of panic and anger, as if this was my fault. DeeAnna stared, pen poised with cold amusement on her face.

"Beach Nuts," Daniel blurted.

DeeAnna blinked a few times and then penned the name with a slight shake of her head while I picked my jaw up off the ground. Daniel pointedly refused to meet my stare.

I later discovered that the ten or fifteen questions DeeAnna graciously led us through were the simplest portion of the packet. Nevermind coaching us through the sections on Gross Annual Volume or Partner Proprietorship. Leaving the building though, my concerns were elsewhere.

"Beach Nuts?" I asked, storming across the parking lot after Daniel. "Are you kidding me?"

"You didn't do so hot in there either."

"At least I didn't 'Wow' the room with a semi-suggestive and entirely stupid name."

"First off, Princess, we can change the name. Nothing's permanent until we submit the forms. Second, it's not that bad of a name."

"The hell it's not!"

"Am I yelling?"

I'm still awaiting praise for not slapping him right then.

"You're one to talk with your obnoxious attempt at sounding like an adult and being funny with everyone."

"Someone had to be the adult and do the talking."

We bickered ourselves into an angry silence for the rest of the car ride home until we could separate to our own rooms.

I fell onto my bed, cringing as I recalled the woman's face when Daniel said the name. What kind of place is named, *Beach Nuts?* No one will hear that name and think, *Oh, yum, sounds like a tropical doughnut, I must have one.* And *sound like an adult?* I sat up again, too annoyed to lay down. Who did he think he was?

I tried to do a yoga pose and breathe deeply because I've heard it helps with anger. Unfortunately, Down Dog was the only one I could remember and I felt so stupid trying to do it I resolved to work on the license application instead. *Daniel doesn't deserve me,* I thought as I started in on the paperwork. Half a page in and I felt more clueless than back at the courthouse. During my debate of whether to burn or simply throw away the packet, a knock sounded on my door.

"Come in."

Mom poked her head in. "Are you busy?"

"Not really." I tossed the packet aside.

"What's that?"

A half-hearted reply didn't satisfy her, so I ended up rattling off the whole, detailed story.

"Pretentious crow," she muttered in reference to the clerk. "Can I see the paperwork?"

She pored over the packet, her face gradually moving into a frown.

"She gave you the wrong application."

I mirrored her frown.

"Look," she pointed to a dense paragraph. "The title number correlates to a..." She paused, checking a list at the top of the page. "Mobile Roadside Food Vendor."

I stared.

"You're planning on being neither mobile, nor a vendor. You need this one," she tapped the page. "EF23 - Retail Food Operation."

Just like the clerk said to begin with. I sighed deeply. "I feel like an idiot."

"Don't," she soothed. "These things are complicated."

"Then how did you figure it out?" The question came out meaner than I'd meant it to, but she let it slide.

"You forget I used to have to do this stuff too."

A valid point. I thought back to her Lego table days. "I'll deal with it tomorrow."

"The courthouse is closed on Sundays."

"Fantastic." I needed to deal with it immediately or wait until next Saturday.

"Do you want me to go back with you?"

I could think of few things more pathetic than getting pushed around by a county clerk and then bringing your mom back to fight the battle. But it definitely sounded better than going back alone or with Daniel.

Mom patted my leg and made for the door. "Come on, it won't take more than an hour."

I heaved myself off the bed and followed. Pathetic or not, I just wanted a license and if Mom was willing to help, I'd take it.

Getting the correct paperwork didn't take long. On the way back, in the passenger seat of Mom's car, I held the application carefully on my lap, not wanting them to get dirty or crumpled in my bag. I'd fought too hard for those papers. I closed my eyes to the bright flashes of sun darting through the trees and breathed deeply.

"Thanks for coming," I told her.

"You're welcome. I just hope you're not letting this distract you."

"From what?"

"Work."

I didn't respond.

"These things are fun but they're a weekend project sort of thing. You need to make sure it's not taking time away from your real work," she warned.

"It's fine, Mom," I spat back, annoyed because I actually felt a little guilty for spending time working on the doughnuts. But "weekend project," not "real work?" She'd volunteered to help with the license, how could she say that? What was stopping her from being more supportive? I got enough of this condescending trash at work, I did *not* it need at home in regards to my "weekend project."

Before we made it into the driveway I felt my phone buzz with a text message. I read a short but obviously long-worked on note from Daniel about my needing to be a better "business partner" if we were going to make this work. *Well maybe we won't make this work, Daniel,* I thought bitterly. I shoved the application into my bag and stormed into the house.

CHAPTER 20 - DANIEL

I'd been in a bad mood since my night out with Dax. I have a vague memory of stumbling down the street to Dax's house. I may or may not have thrown my arms around my car when I saw that it was still sitting in the street with all of its windows unbroken and tires on its axles. Dax or one of his roommates, I don't remember seeing their face, shoved a gallon-size jug of water at me. I drank nearly half of it and then woke up on Dax's couch early in the morning. After taking the longest piss of my entire life I found my shoes and keys and got in the car to drive home.

I didn't feel bad for drinking too much but I felt a pang of fear at what the aftermath could have been. The four girls were mostly content to hang all over Dax but a few times one of them had wrapped an arm around my waist or held onto my arm a little too long. It wasn't tempting, that was too strong of a word, but it definitely wasn't a great situation to be in. If I ever did anything to hurt Rachel, drunk or not, I had no idea what I'd do.

The following Saturday I was still kind of beating myself up about it when Taylor came prancing into my room demanding that we go get a business license for the doughnuts. I tried to be pleasant and even offered to drive us down to the courthouse but she spent the entire ride bragging to me about all the random information she'd dredged up about business licenses in the last week.

By the time we got there I was more than ready for her to shut up, but she just kept acting overly cheerful with everyone. For all of her amazing research, she'd managed to overlook the fact that we'd need a business name to put on the license. When the clerk asked her for a name she finally got off her high horse and looked at me all panicked and whatnot. I gave the first name I could think of and then she had the nerve to get all pissy with me about it being a dumb name. After I'd given her some time to calm down, I sent her a nice text message explaining how we could better work through these things in the future since we were planning on being business partners. She never replied.

I'd told Rachel we could hang out after Taylor and I got back from the courthouse. Not long after I got home, she came over wearing running shorts and a tank top with a wild look in her eyes.

"Put on athletic clothes," she said when I opened the door for her.

"Why?"

"It's a surprise."

"No way. You know I hate surprises." We'd had this same conversation every couple of months since we started dating.

"Come on," she smiled, nudging me towards the stairs. "Go change."

"Not until you tell me what we're doing."

"That would ruin the surprise," she said, feigning a serious look. We stared at each other for a few seconds, waiting for the other one to crack. "Go," she said again.

Rachel smiled smugly when I returned downstairs wearing my athletic clothes.

I offered to drive so she'd have to tell me where we were going but she was already out the front door walking towards her car. "It's okay," she called over her shoulder.

"If we're going on a run," I said when I got into her car, "I am going to be really disappointed."

"We're not going on a run."

"Maybe you should just tell me so I'm not disappointed."

"Why would you be disappointed?"

"Because you're not telling me anything," I sighed, trying to sound sad rather than irritated. "Naturally I'm going to think of something really awesome, and then it's just going to be a let down."

"Maybe it'll be really awesome." She looked over and smiled. "You're so cute when your eyebrows get all crinkly and frustrated." She tried to pat my face but I swatted her hand away.

"Focus on driving."

At first, I thought I had it in me to be okay with the whole thing. Rachel knew I hated surprises, that was annoying, but she tried to pull them off because she loved them. In her mind, it was a way of showing love and I appreciated that aspect of it. But when we'd been driving for thirty minutes I wasn't amused anymore.

"Where are we going?"

"I thought we went over this," she said, sounding entirely too much like Taylor earlier that day.

I couldn't keep my voice below a yell anymore. "*Damn it*, Rachel. Tell me where we are going."

Her face darkened. She swerved across two lanes of traffic and pulled into the parking lot of a gas station while my life flashed before my eyes. "What," she threw the car into park, "is your problem?"

"Why can't you freaking tell me where we're going?" I meant to sound stern but it came out sounding whiney and childish.

She leaned an elbow against the steering wheel, her eyes full of fire, and waited for me to say something else.

I thought I was the one who deserved to be mad. "WHAT?"

That set her off with a volume louder than my own. "You don't always have to be in control Daniel. It's okay if you don't know the exact way things are going to go sometimes." She lowered her voice but all of the anger was still there. "I swear you will live if you can't control every single part of your day." She turned to rest her forehead on the steering wheel and closed her eyes.

I clenched my jaw to stop myself from replying the way I wanted to. I watched the clock on the console of her car. We sat in silence for a little over two minutes.

"Hiking," she said quietly.

I looked over, not sure if she'd actually spoken at first. "What?"

"That was the surprise. Hiking."

It would have been a really dumb thing to joke about but she couldn't have been serious. "We live in the flattest part of Texas."

"Hence the driving."

My eyes widened. "We were going to another state?"

"No," she almost smiled. "There's some nature preserve type thing another twenty minutes from here that someone told me about. Apparently you can hike there."

"Well." We had another few moments of silence. I wondered if I should apologize.

"Do you want to go?" She asked.

"Yes," I said, grateful to skip the apology part.

"I mean, it's not like hiking a mountain or anything."

"That's okay."

"It's probably more of a steep hill with trees."

I tried to use a lispy voice that usually made her laugh, "Then I guess we won't have to worry about mountain lions."

She cocked her head to the side.

"Because it's a steep hill," I said. "Not mountains... with mountain lions."

"You do realize that mountain lions don't just live in—"

"Yes," I sighed. "Just drive."

The place really did end up being just a forested hill but I felt a lot better when we drove back home. Something about the combination of nature, Rachel, and the exercise made me feel calmer than I'd been in days. I went into work on Monday still feeling my nature high until all hell broke loose an hour before lunch.

Bhavesh swept back into the room from his management meeting and looked at Kevin and me. "Did one of you talk to Pierce Fenner in Vegas?"

Kevin's panicked eyes darted over to me. I didn't know any better than he did whether the urgency in Bhavesh's tone meant good things or bad things were about to follow. Bhavesh looked between us, impatient for an answer.

"I did," I said, since Kevin was obviously incapable of speaking. "But Kevin probably talked to him longer."

"No I didn't," Kevin said quickly.

"I don't care who talked to him longer," Bhavesh said. "Either of you is fine. His assistant called and wants to discuss his interest in becoming a client. Which one of you can help with that?"

"Shouldn't Dax handle it?" I asked. Talking with clients was in his job description, not mine or Kevin's.

But Bhavesh shook his head. "They want specifics and they're not interested in spending a lot of time on this. Better to talk to one of you directly."

"I can do it," Kevin said looking confident again.

"Okay, let's go," Bhavesh started to turn.

"Wait," Kevin stood awkwardly. "Now?"

"Yes. Now."

Kevin's panic returned. "I, I think I need a few hours, I have to get the right info, I think—"

"His assistant is on the phone now."

Kevin's face reddened and I watched his Adam's apple working up and down. Bhavesh looked to me, eyebrows raised.

"Are they wanting us to develop his investment portfolio during the phone call or something?"

Bhavesh nodded. I shouldn't be surprised, we frequently had high-profile clients coming in wanting preferential treatment. I just wasn't normally the one to deal with it.

"Let me just print some stuff," I said, turning to my computer. After the conference I'd spent some time researching investment options, adding to my personal archive where I saw Pierce Fenner-shaped holes. I'd done it out of boredom really, but I gave myself a fourth mental tally for my overly cautious planning saving everyone's ass again. Out of my peripheral vision I could see Kevin staring as I clicked around on the computer, printing any document of investment info I thought might pertain to Fenner. Kevin was still staring when I stood to get the documents from the printer.

"Ready," I told Bhavesh. I could still feel Kevin watching me as I followed Bhavesh down the hall to the conference room. Mark was talking amiably into the conference phone but looking just as intense as Tom, staring at the phone with his elbows propped on the table and fingers steepled in front of him. Their eyebrows raised when I entered the room and sat down across the table from them.

"Elizabeth," Mark said into the phone. "One of our financial analysts, Daniel Bryant, just stepped in. He and Pierce spoke at the conference."

"Wonderful," a woman's voice crackled back over the speaker. "Hello, Daniel."

"Hi, Elizabeth."

"Shall we continue then?" She asked with a little edge in her voice.

"Absolutely," Mark said. "Daniel — take it away."

"Sure. Elizabeth, can you tell me a little bit about Mr. Fenner's expectations?"

While she spoke I thumbed through my papers, making notes as I went. Gradually I sifted through the different investment options until I narrowed the list down to five items. I gave Elizabeth a brief explanation of each investment opportunity, describing the basic details and how Fenner would be uniquely positioned to take advantage of them. When I finished there was a long pause and the four of us exchanged nervous glances.

"One moment," Elizabeth finally said. "Sorry, just jotting down some notes. These sound like excellent options. We'll be in touch shortly."

"Wonderful," Mark jumped back in. He wrapped up the conversation and punched a button to end the call before standing to shake my hand across the table.

"Well done, Daniel," he grinned.

Tom stood and shook my hand as well. "How'd you pull that together so quickly?"

"I already had the research compiled. Just a matter of sorting through them to find the best fits."

They nodded in approval. "Well done," Tom said again.

Bhavesh followed me out of the conference room and we headed back towards our desks. "That was incredible," he said. "Really nice work."

"Thanks, man."

Dax was already grinning when we got back to our desks. "Did you dazzle them, Danny?"

I laughed because I didn't know how else to respond.

"He sure did," Bhavesh said like a proud parent. In a way, it was a win for all of us though. Fenner's business would definitely put us past our goal for the second quarter, which meant the most to Tom and Mark but affected everyone.

Dax cleared his throat and started on an impression of Will Ferrell's impression of Harry Caray. One of his dumber impressions, to be sure, but you couldn't *not* laugh at it. "It could be, it might be, it is… a home run by Danny Bryant."

I shook my head, determined to ignore him as usual, but then Bhavesh joined in with his own ridiculous announcer voice. "It's safe to say he knocked this one out of the park."

"Straight into the hands of our Lord in heaven."

Bhavesh grinned, trying not to laugh. "How *does* he do it?"

"Bhavi, if I had to make a guess, I would say *all of the hours* he spends saving kittens from trees, *all of the hours* he spends rescuing children from burning buildings has greatly influenced his strength, his focus, his coolness under pressure."

They kept going back and forth, making it impossible to focus on work. I noticed Kevin sitting at his desk, pointedly not looking at any of us. He was an idiot if he couldn't see how this benefitted him too. Dax's and Bhavesh's antics aside, this win helped him too - it helped our whole department. But if he realized it, he didn't care. His eyes flickered up to mine and he looked at me darkly for the briefest of moments before turning back to his computer again.

CHAPTER 21 - TAYLOR

I'd been sitting in silence for an eternity while Bill critically stared at my drawings. Ideally, his silent treatments wouldn't faze me anymore but after a few minutes sweat started prickling my skin. Bill was standing, should I stand? My attempt at Fizz's new branding, a tropical island theme at Casey's request, stood before Bill on a sturdy poster board. The display felt like overkill, but Rand insisted on its necessity.

"It shows your commitment to the idea," Rand explained.

"But I'm not committed to it."

He shook his head and walked away.

Meanwhile Bill had begun slowly nodding his head and it was starting to creep me out.

"This is great." I waited for him to finish with something negative. "This is fantastic," Bill continued. "Really, really nice work."

My chest swelled. I made a mental note to mark the day as the first time Bill complimented my work.

"But I do have a couple of things I'm going to push back on," he added. I'm sure my face visibly fell as he rattled of a short list of 'suggestions.' "I'm assuming you're not finished with the logos?"

Three distinct but similar logos stretched across the board. I'd spent nearly an hour on each of them but somehow, the honest, 'yes' didn't seem like the right answer. "Definitely not, no."

Bill said he was interested in seeing a logo with "less lime" and "more leaf" green hues. Other comparably nitpicky problems followed, leaving me back in my cube wondering why I bothered. Better yet, why did he even hire me? Why didn't he just design the stupid logo himself if he had such particular opinions on it? Or get Ryan to do it. Ryan always came up with something Bill loved immediately.

Rand swung around the wall of the cube, interrupting my increasingly downward spiral of thoughts. "I am not worthy," he said.

"Excuse me?"

"I heard your first run through of the design went well."

"'Not quite." I dispassionately recounted the exchange between Bill and me.

Confusion showed on Rand's face. "Sorry, what exactly are you upset about?"

I couldn't understand where his confusion came from — Bill had picked apart my design from top to bottom, asking for changes on every detail. Rand shook his head, kindly patient in his disagreement.

"Asking you to do another version with some edits doesn't mean he didn't like it," Rand explained. "He would have just told you to start over."

I could kind of see that actually. "Bill thinks you're doing great," he added and left me to work. Warily, I looked at the display board again. Studying my design, I began to see how an earthier green would add a more natural feel to the logo. All of Bill's critiques made sense when I really looked at it. I drew a few redesigns in my sketchbook, noting all of his ideas and incorporating a few improvements of my own.

Later when I told the story to Lola over dinner at her house, selectively leaving out some of my irrational distress about the criticism, she shook her head in annoyance. "Who does that man think he is?"

The conversation paused while she instructed me on where to get plates for the *paella* she pulled off of the stove. The rice, shrimp and peppers had been simmering on the stove with garlic, thyme, and saffron for nearly an hour and the smell was making me hungrier than I had reason to be. Lola instructed me to scoop a helping onto each of our plates and garnish them with a pinch of parsley and a wedge of lemon while she uncorked a bottle of Spanish wine.

"This is from the *Ribera del Duero*," Lola said, pouring a glass for each of us. She looked to the plates of *paella* I was garnishing. "Don't be stingy with the servings. Give us a big scoop."

I moved aside the parsley and added another spoonful to each plate. She lifted a glass of wine and swirled it around before take a small sip, smiling as she did. "The *enologi* age the wine in French oak. It gives it a little hint of vanilla and cinnamon." She passed me a glass. "Can you taste it?"

I took a small sip of the wine. It was delicious but in no way could I taste vanilla, cinnamon, or anything other than just wine. "Yeah," I lied. "It's great."

Lola frowned. "You are a miserable liar." She took her glass and the bottle to the table and then came back to help me with the dishes. We took them to the dining room table we'd already set for two. Lola said a quick prayer of thanks for the food and then asked about the work debacle again.

"It's not that big of a deal," I said dismissively, pushing my *paella* around on my plate. "He actually did like it."

"Then why can he not say so?"

"That's just how he is," I shrugged.

Lola arched an eyebrow but changed the subject. "I have a new doughnut idea for you."

I legitimately hadn't thought of doughnuts since the fight with Daniel. At least not since my anger about the fight subsided which took a reasonable amount of time.

"Cinnamon doughnut," she started, pausing for effect. I nodded. "Warm chocolate drizzled on top." She drizzled imaginary chocolate in the air. "Call it the Spanish Hot Chocolate."

"Isn't the cinnamon chocolate thing Mexican hot chocolate?"

"Where do you think they got it from?" She demanded. "It's like a churro. Which," she quickly added when I opened my mouth to respond, "is also from Spain."

"Got it."

"Now you know," she smiled. "What's next for the doughnuts?"

I admitted that the project was on pause.

"You're quitting," she asked, sincerely confused, "already?"

"It isn't quitting if it wasn't started."

She gave me a look demanding further explanation.

"I just think it might be a good idea to hold down a real job right now."

"What is this 'real job' you think you need?"

"The one I already have. Something with a paycheck."

Lola waited, debating a reply, and finally smiled, "If that's what you want, I support you."

I think she meant it kindly, but I sensed disappointment somewhere behind the statement. *Of course it's not what I want*, I thought immediately. But I caught myself — work hadn't been as bad. Lola took our plates to the sink and began rinsing them. I followed with our glasses and asked her plans for the weekend to stop the crashing thoughts in my head.

"Some good friends are coming over on Friday for dinner. You are welcome to join us if you would like."

As intrigued as I was by the idea of meeting Lola's friends, I'd already made plans with Haleigh for the first time in weeks. I'd barely seen her since she started studying for the LSAT. I knew for a fact she wasn't studying 24/7, even thought that was the excuse she usually claimed, but she was still the only friend I had for the time being. Lola's friends could wait.

"Stop by any time," she said as I slipped on my sandals. "Balboa misses you."

"Somehow, I doubt that," I smiled. "Thanks again for dinner."

The second I was out the door her words came to mind again. *If that's what you want.* I didn't know what I wanted.

At home, Daniel, Rachel, Mom and Dad sat in the sun room, beers in hand.

Daniel cleared his throat to announce with a poorly executed imitation of an epic voice over, "Guess who got promoted?"

I didn't even bother messing with a sarcastic reply, I was genuinely happy for him.

He continued with the epic voice, "And guess how much they're paying him?"

I guessed three thousand up and was wrong.

"Three," he paused dramatically. "Times. That."

I let out a long, slowly building 'woo' and bounced around doing a ridiculous dance until he finally said, back in his normal voice, "Okay, stop. That's weird."

After grabbing a beer from the fridge I flopped down on the couch next to Daniel and we continued talking excitedly. I'd completely forgotten about our fight the previous weekend. His success felt like my own. Surely it couldn't be too long until I was in his shoes, getting my first salary bump and feeling the same satisfaction.

"I am so proud of you two," Mom said during a lull in conversation.

"I'm not the one who got a promotion," I reminded her.

"But you've gotten a wonderful job and are doing so well."

"In spite of your degree," Dad added.

"Yeah," Daniel chimed in. "Congratulations on avoiding the starving artist stereotype."

I frowned, not sharing their amusement.

"Both of you stop," Mom warned.

"What?" Dad laughed. "I think it's great she managed to stumble into a real profession even though she just got an art degree."

"If I'd thought that was possible, I would have picked a blow-off major in college too," Daniel said.

"Like your accounting major was so hard," Rachel interjected from where she sat on the other side of Daniel. She may have been trying to defend me, but only made it worse.

"By itself? No," Daniel agreed. "But on top of the finance major and math minor it a little difficult at times."

I met Rachel's eyes across the room and a look of pity flickered briefly over her face before she looked away.

"Your dad and I only focused on one major." Mom looked at me with sympathy.

"Remind me what they were?" Daniel asked with false innocence.

"Business and economics," Dad said, further underscoring my place on his scoreboard.

"I'm kind of tired," I said, standing from the couch. "I think I'm going to head up."

"Don't be so sensitive, Taylor," Dad said lightly. "We're just having a conversation."

I kept walking to the kitchen, pausing to pour the remains of my beer down the sink.

"Every family needs a black sheep, Taylor," Daniel called from the sunroom.

I chucked the bottle in the recycle bin and pounded up the stairs. I'd just started to brush my teeth when I heard soft footsteps climbing up the stairs.

"Taylor?" Mom said softly through the bathroom door.

I opened it for her but kept brushing.

"You know we're very proud of you."

I looked at her in the mirror, unconvinced.

"Dad and I were very nervous —" she paused as I ducked to spit unceremoniously. "Nervous you wouldn't be able to get a job with your degree, but you did. That's a big accomplishment."

"Thanks," I said hollowly.

She gave the slightest nod and then turned to leave.

"Mom?"

She stopped and turned at the top of the stairs, her hand already on the banister.

"Are you embarrassed of me?"

"Of course not, baby." She came back to wrap me in a hug. "You have a job that anyone could be proud of. And I'm your mom," she pulled back to look me in the eye. "I am always proud of you."

I wanted to take her words at face value but I couldn't ignore her contradiction. 'Always' didn't go with her thinly veiled conditional statement. As long as I held a job to prove that I'd overcome my crippling degree, she would be proud of me.

CHAPTER 22 - DANIEL

As soon as I started researching food distributors, I saw them everywhere — huge eighteen-wheelers barreling down the highway, a guy in a crisp, all white uniform running in and out of the back of the Tavern. According to the Internet, six major distributors handled most of the nations business. Four of them serviced our area but none listed the specifics of their prices on the Internet, so I could only go so far with the research. To reveal their numbers, the distributors required an approved prospective client application, which I couldn't do until we got our business license approved from the state.

In the meantime, I scoured the internet during down hours at work for personal reviews from other restaurants on blogs and forums and things of that nature. Ever since Pierce Fenner's assistant called back to sign on with the company and my consequent promotion, I'd been coasting at work. Bhavesh decided Kevin could handle the investment reports by himself and I got to make the jump to senior financial analyst. Really, I was the new last minute portfolio creator, but the formal title sounded better.

Basically I kept doing a lot of what I'd done for Fenner. Tom or Mark or Ned would come running to me when a client wanted a customized portfolio on the fly. They gave me the highlights of their background, I printed the documents from my computer, got on the call and then let the client talk about themselves until I had my list narrowed down to a handful investment avenues well-suited to their interests. Between the urgent, Pierce Fenner type scenarios, Tom started giving me customized portfolio assignments with more normal deadlines. The work was similar to what I'd been doing before but with a greater sense of purpose and more immediate payoff.

The whole thing pissed Kevin off to no end. He frequently glared at me when I went jogging down the hallway to jump on a call. He didn't talk much to begin with but after the promotion he straight up ignored me.

Most of the clients wanting portfolios were pretty run of the mill, relatively speaking. Pierce Fenner was the largest client we'd had year to date and I expected him to remain in the position until Tom called me into his office one day.

"I've got a big one for you," he said. "Dom Moskovitz."

I had to think about that one for a second. "The social media guy?"

Tom nodded. Moskovitz was one of those who had a lot of money to begin with but lived in relative obscurity until he crawled out of the woodwork with a quirky startup company, sold it for an unbelievable amount of money, and then went back to doing nothing. He sold his social media app a few months ago but still got a ton of media attention for it.

"You've got till end of day tomorrow," Tom said. "His case is kind of similar to Pierce Fenner's, repeat some of the options if they fit, but let's get three unique investment options for him."

"Got it," I said easily, as if it were no big deal. It was a big deal.

"Moskovitz's business alone could put as at our goal for Q3. I need you to impress him."

"Absolutely. I'm on it." I stood to leave. "I'll get those to you as soon as possible."

"Great."

This is fine, I told myself as I went back to my desk. *No big deal.* Tom probably thought two days was more than enough time to put together the portfolio, but I was trying very hard to feel calm about it. I'd made the recommendations for Fenner and the other clients fairly quickly, but that was only because I'd been digging through information I'd accumulated from months of getting my work done early and having time to spare. I'd given the best IT/social marketing options to Fenner. Whatever else I had in my files would be second rate in comparison to the five I already had. If Moskovitz was going to be impressed, I needed to drum up some new options for him.

When I got back to my desk I checked the clock on my computer. It was a little before noon.

"Lunch?" Dax asked.

I shook my head. "Sorry, I'm meeting Rachel." It'd need to be a short lunch, too. I couldn't shake the growing anxiety from the Moskovitz project.

I grabbed my keys and drove to a little cafe, roughly halfway between both of our offices. When we sat down with our food, I gave her the notes I'd made on the food distributors before Tom came calling about Moskovitz. She looked up from a comparison spreadsheet and said, "Are you sure it's a good idea to be doing all of this at work?"

"Why not? I'm getting all of my work done."

"Even so, they just promoted you. Promotions make everyone else hyperaware of your work performance. It's like they want to see for themselves if you really deserved it."

"Maybe women are like that, but guys are different," I said and went back to my french fries. "Tom just gave me a huge project. I don't think he would have done that if he was questioning my work performance."

She took an exasperated breath but went back to looking over the spreadsheet. "This second one sounds like the best so far," she said.

I nodded and took a long sip of beer. "That's what I think too, but it's impossible to tell without having some actual numbers to work with."

"Right," she put the spreadsheet down and thumbed through the other papers. "Any idea what your ingredient costs are going to look like?"

"No I don't think Taylor ever settled on a recipe. She's kind of backed off of the whole project."

"Really?"

"We haven't even talked about it since we went to apply for the business license."

"Why not?"

I shrugged.

"Maybe you should talk to her," Rachel said.

"I don't mind doing all of the research, she kind of sucks at it anyway."

"Hey," she warned. Even when Taylor wasn't around Rachel had some knee-jerk reaction to stick up for her. I generally ignored it because my statements were normally justified.

"There's a reason she studied art," I reminded Rachel. "And if she ends up deciding to stick with her job then I'll just know a lot about starting a doughnut shop."

"It doesn't sound like you're very committed either," she said. When she saw my face she quickly added, "Not that there's anything wrong with that. But I think you're using it as a fun distraction from work. You're coasting at your job and Taylor seems like she's barely keeping her head up."

The confident way she spoke annoyed me. "You've barely been around her, what do you know about her job?"

Rachel just shrugged. "You're right."

She was saying what I wanted to hear. I kept telling myself Taylor was the uncommitted one, but what if it was actually me? Regardless, the research kept me entertained between building portfolios. I'd spent entirely too long trying to anticipate every need at work and do everything in my power to position myself for a promotion, but in the end it was my innate tendency to plan and re-plan that had impressed them. Kind of ironic, really. In a way, there almost wasn't any reason to go above and beyond at your job. Either you had whatever quality your employers needed, meticulous information gathering in my case, or you didn't. The rest was just busy work.

After lunch, I put all thoughts of doughnuts aside. I dug into research for Moskovitz and by the end of the afternoon had three solid picks. I shut down my computer and left the office feeling like I could breathe again. If I could get more than halfway through the project in one day, putting together the other two items would be no big deal. I drove home feeling like I had my life together for the first time in a while. I was still living at home, but now that I'd figured out the trick to the whole job thing, everything else would follow suit. Just a little farther up the ladder at work and I'd finally get the car paid off, and then I could move out and move on to a life with Rachel.

At home, I played a video game for a couple of hours and then went to the kitchen in search of dinner. Taylor sat at the table focused intently on her laptop. Her ears were covered with her big, noise-cancelling headphones and I could hear the faint beat of music, which meant she probably hadn't heard me come downstairs. I stepped quietly behind her chair and bent down so my face was right behind her shoulder, visible in the dark, right corner of the screen if she would just look up…

Her eyes flicked across the screen and caught on my reflection, *"Oh my god,"* she seized in the opposite direction and ripped off her headphones. I could barely hear her say, "I hate you so much," over my laughter.

"What are you doing?" I asked when I finally caught my breath.

"Work."

I looked at the clock. It was past eight. "Why?"

"Stupid branding package," she mumbled, rubbing at her eyes. "It's the second revision and my boss is really particular about details."

"I think all bosses are."

"Maybe you're right." She sounded tired and I regretted not sounding a little more sympathetic. "He didn't like the first one because I used the wrong shade of green."

"That's dumb."

She looked at the design on her computer sadly. "What shade would you say that is?"

I leaned closer and looked at the logo she was working on. "Um," I squinted at the letters. Really they just looked plain green, but I knew that answer wouldn't satisfy her. "Lime?"

She let out a pitiful little moan and put her headphones back on. Clearly she needed to be left alone. I ate a quick dinner and went to find Dad. Light from his office spilled into the hallway. I knocked and stepped inside to find him sitting at his desk. His shoulders were hunched, a break from his normally rigid posture that only happened when he'd been in front of the computer for a really long time.

"Hey," I said.

He took a moment to look up from his computer screen but finally said, "Hey," back.

"How's it going?"

"Good, thanks," he leaned back and stretched his arms behind his head. "How was work?"

"Not bad." I sat down in the dark leather chair across from his desk. "You're not still working are you?"

"Nah, just looking at some side projects."

"Cool." I picked at the nail head trim on the arm of the chair, thinking of my own "side project." One of the rounded pieces of copper was starting to raise from years of being picked at. Dad took off his reading glasses and rubbed his eyes, looking exactly like Taylor. "What kind of project?"

He glanced back at the computer screen. "Looking into a consulting job for a startup."

"You're quitting your job?"

"No, it would just be a part-time, short-term thing." He smiled and leaned back again. "Just to liven things up a bit."

I nodded, breathing easier. Dad started working in corporate sales right out of college and had been doing it ever since, but always with something on the side. I couldn't imagine him at any other type of job. He picked up a miniature rake off his desk, part of a tiny zen garden Taylor had given him for Christmas last year, and start turning it over in his hand. The "garden" was just a little sand box, roughly six inches in either direction, with a rake the size of a pencil and a few polished stones. I thought it was a stupid gift but he seemed to enjoy raking the sand into patterns while he was on the phone or thinking about something.

"It's interesting," he said, starting to rake the sand, "how easily we commit our lives to things."

I took a breath, knowing he was about to get philosophical on me. "What do you mean?"

"Well, look at your job. You started working there before you even graduated and then moved into a full-time position pretty easily."

I wouldn't call it easy by any means, but Dad saw my face and clarified. "I just mean the decision part. Choosing whether or not to work there wasn't very difficult, was it?"

"No."

He picked up the three stones from the garden, brushed the sand off of them, and put them on the desk so he could keep raking. He didn't seem like he planned on saying anything else and I still didn't understand what he was getting at.

"So what's the big deal about the commitment being easy?"

"I just think it's interesting." He put the rake down, replaced the stones, and looked at me. "You'll spend more time at your job than you will anywhere else. You'll be with your coworkers more than you will your friends, your family. Anyone. But we sign on for commitments like that so easily, don't we?"

He looked and sounded calm but he freaked me out. I didn't know if he was having a personal crisis about this or trying to tell me something about my own life or what.

I tried to use my lispy voice. "Someone's being a Negative Nancy."

He vaguely smiled but it didn't reach his eyes. "Did you see how the Rangers did?"

We talked safely in the realm of sports for another few minutes and then I left him to his work. First Rachel accuses of me of fooling around with the doughnut idea because I'm bored and then Dad decides to get all existential about career choices. Nothing he said was untrue though. I counted the hours I worked each week in my head. Definitely more than I could physically spend with anyone else, doing any other thing. I didn't like the idea of that. Work was a part of life, fine, but if I had the option to spend those hours with someone I actually cared about, like Taylor, rather than the Kevins of the world — shouldn't I?

There were a lot of implications to work through. I couldn't think of all of them right then, but I didn't really want to deal with them then anyway. Even if I did, Taylor still needed to work through her own junk. My chest felt a little tight though, like the anxiety was trying to creep back in. *You're fine*, I reminded myself. *The doughnut thing isn't urgent and you'll finish the Moskovitz portfolio tomorrow.*

Despite my efforts to reassure myself, I had trouble sleeping. Halfway through work the next day, I'd only managed to come up with one more investment opportunity and my chest started feeling even tighter. I looked at the clock. I had a little under five hours to find my fifth investment, and it had to be a good one. A perfect one. *You're fine*, I tried to tell myself again, but I couldn't believe it anymore. I was not fine. I needed to find something immediately. What Rachel said about everyone being hyper-aware of my job performance came to mind. What if I failed to get Moskovitz on board? Would they un-promote me? Did companies do that?

Somewhere in the back of my mind a bell went off and I dug out my wallet. I pulled out Steve Mobley's card and studied it. He promised he could get me in with a high pay off investment if I ever needed it. Surely it couldn't hurt to call him. Worst case scenario, he didn't have anything. I put the card in my pocket and took my cell phone to the Reject Room — the smallest conference room at the end of the main hallway. It was the only room that didn't get updated furniture and still looked like it was stuck in the eighties. No one ever used it, which is why everyone called it the Reject Room.

I went inside, closed the door and called Steve. It took an eternity for him to answer but he finally picked up.

"Hi Steve, this is—"

"How did you get this number?"

"Uh, you gave it to me. This is Daniel Bryant. I'm not sure if you remember me, I met you in Vegas a few weeks ago at the casino and—"

"Yeah, yeah," he cut in. "Daniel Bryant. Is this a good number for you?"

"Uhm, yeah—"

"Let me call you right back."

The line clicked off. I looked at my phone, wondering if Steve would actually call back. A moment later the phone rang with a different number.

"Hello?"

"It's Steve."

"Oh—"

"What did you need?"

I glanced toward the door to make sure it was shut and lowered my voice a little, just in case. "Listen, um, you mentioned that you might know of some investment opportunities for me?"

"Yeah. You or a client of yours?"

"A client. A big one."

"How big?"

He wanted a name but I knew I shouldn't give him one. "Like, Forbes 500 big."

Steve let out a low whistle. "You're looking for a pretty serious investment then, huh? Not sure if I have anything."

My heart sank. I didn't know what else to do. I'd never needed information this quickly, it was ridiculous for them to expect me to come up with five solid investments in so little time.

"Actually," Steve interrupted my thoughts. "I may have one for you, but you'd have to act fast. A buddy of mine's got a little biomedical engineering company that's been growing steadily for the last eighteen months. Publically traded but we're talking penny stock. They're under review by the FDA for this big breakthrough in their artificial organ technology. The approval's going to come out any day now and it's going to send their stock through the roof. Your client wants a serious pay off, have him put some money into that."

"You're sure they're going to get approval?"

"Absolutely. There's buzz about it all over the medical journals, you can read all about it. Their penny stock hasn't done much to attract any big investors yet but it will once they get that FDA stamp."

Steve gave me the name and the contact at the company and I thanked him profusely.

"Don't mention it. Your client wins, we all win. I'm just glad the timing worked out. This biomed company's a rare one. You should look at investing a little yourself."

"Would that I had the money," I told him. "Thanks again, Steve."

"Anytime."

We hung up and I exhaled a breath, willing the tightness in my chest to untangle a little. I went back to my computer to finish the portfolio, wondering why I couldn't shake the heaviness.

CHAPTER 23 - TAYLOR

At work on Friday afternoon I took a few minutes to print my updated Fizz branding package for Bill and then made my way to his office. I stopped short, seeing his door partially shut. He'd probably closed it to take a call but by now he might be finished. I moved closer to listen for an indication of whether or not he was busy. I caught a glimpse of Ryan through the door and swung back against the wall to make sure he didn't see me. No sounds came from the office. Were they even talking? Should I go back to my cube?

I started edging back just as Bill's voice rose so I could barely make out, "Don't like the.... Taylor..."

What? Why did he say my name? I stepped a little closer, turning my ear to the door but poising to power walk out of there if needed. Whatever Bill said, Ryan obviously didn't like it. His impatient reply sounded clearly into the hallway. "This is exactly the look Casey wanted."

"She doesn't know what she wants," Bill laughed back. "We'll go with Taylor's design."

Ryan threw open the door and stormed into the hallway before I had time to react, much less move to a less conspicuous place. If he suspected me of eavesdropping though, Ryan didn't show it. With a quick glare he blew past me down the hall.

I knocked tentatively on the open door and stepped into Bill's office, prepared to wade through whatever tense mood Ryan left him with. Instead, Bill greeted me with more than his normal energy. Though possible that he was oblivious to Ryan's frustration, it seemed more likely that he didn't care.

"Let's see round two," he beamed, drumming his hands on the desk excitedly.

I propped my design boards on the easel, his excitement beginning to rub off on me. "What do you think?"

He leaned into hands clasped before his face, his eyes barely crinkling with the hint of a smile. He was sold.

"Can we change the yellow?"

Or not.

"And something's off about that font... is the printer alignment off again?"

"Um, no, I actually hand lettered it."

"Oh. Well, let's fix that yellow and work on those letters a little and then we'll take another look."

I attempted to smile as I nodded and took down my board. "What did you have in mind for the yellow?"

"It's just not working," he said and then added with a warm grin that grated my nerves, "Work your magic."

My magic. Why couldn't he have mentioned not liking the yellow the first time around?

Before reaching my cube I swung into Rand's office. He sat hunched over at his desk, his face inches from the computer screen. Seeing me, he straightened and rubbed his eyes under his glasses. I told him about the yellow.

"Do you need help?"

I lifted an eyebrow, wondering if he was joking. "It's just changing the color, it isn't hard."

"Then what's the problem?"

He wasn't joking, which made me wonder if maybe it wasn't such a big deal after all. I played it off and went back to my cube where I stared rebelliously at the graphic, refusing to change anything. The longer I looked at it though, the less confident I felt. How did I find such a hideous shade of yellow in the first place? And the letters... each one nearly looked like it came from a different font. I squinted at them in disbelief - how had I been so careless?

Ashamed at even showing Bill this version in the first place, I started looking for fonts on the Internet and tried on a hundred shades of yellow. I made countless adjustments for several hours until Rand knocked on the wall of my cube.

"Bill's letting us go early today."

I glanced at the time on my computer screen — *4:38.*

"Twenty-two minutes early," I said. "Wow."

"Hey, it's better than nothing."

They'd already started turning off lights in the office so I quickly shut down my computer and walked out a few paces behind Rand and Ryan. As they passed Bill's office they thanked him warmly. I tried to do the same but couldn't understand why we were getting ready to canonize the guy for letting us go a few minutes early. Bill nodded satisfactorily at the thanks, soaking up the appreciation as if he too believed he was God's gift to his employees.

When I got home I had almost two hours before Haleigh and I were supposed to meet — way more time than I needed to get ready. I remembered I never made her the cupcakes I'd promised when I bought the cupcake book with her a few weeks ago. I found the book and read through the recipe for the pink champagne cupcakes Haleigh requested. I knew Mom and Dad probably had a bottle or two of champagne lying around, but I couldn't imagine trying to explain why I'd used it on cupcakes.

I went upstairs to grab my laptop and see if I could use something else as substitute. I rifled through my work bag then in and around my desk for several minutes before I realized I'd left it at work. I checked the clock. This late on a Friday there wouldn't be anyone in the office, especially since Bill let us go early. My computer was stuck until Monday. I hopped in the car, drove to the grocery store, and found the cheapest bottle of sparkling wine I could find. At the checkout, I gave the cashier the phone number for my parents' reward card and an extra few dollars came off the price. I'd paid more for lattes than that entire bottle.

Back home, I uncorked the wine and measured out a cup for the recipe. I held the cup poised over the batter. Obviously something so cheap wasn't going to be anything remarkable, but what if it tasted *bad?* Would it ruin the cupcakes? I almost took a sip straight from the bottle but reached for a clean coffee mug from the drying rack on the counter instead. I do have some standards, after all. I poured in a tiny splash and took a sip. Not bad. I poured another splash to be sure. On a scale of apple cider vinegar to

Dom Pérignon, the bubbly definitely fell in the lower percentile, but two-thirds of the bottle remained, Bill never seemed satisfied with my work, it was Friday, and Haleigh already promised to drive. I filled the mug to the top and went back to baking.

While the cupcakes baked and cooled I straightened my hair and counted the days, trying to figure out how long it'd been since I'd last gone out. The Chinese food at Haleigh's place a few weeks ago didn't count as going out. With an odd pang in my chest, I realized I hadn't actually gone out since Haleigh's graduation party before I started with HRG.

I stared at my reflection in the mirror, wondering how much I cared. Had I even had any opportunity to go places? I didn't hear much from Haleigh, Daniel spent most of his time with Rachel, and even my parents did things with their friends on most nights. I told myself I was too tired from work, but looking back, I realized I hadn't had any invitations either.

I was fixing it though. I looked for my phone to check the time. Probably sitting downstairs in the kitchen. I finished my hair, drank the last sip of wine, and went to throw on a different outfit.

Flying into the kitchen I whipped up the champagne frosting in record time and took the extra effort to pipe it onto the cupcakes. They looked a little plain. I rifled through a container of baking decorations until I found a little jar of tiny, edible silver sugar balls. After sprinkling a few onto each cupcake, I resumed the search for my phone. Eventually I found it underneath the cupcake book and saw I had two missed calls from Haleigh. Before I could call back, a text came through.

Hi call me back, sad news :(

I took a breath. I called her back. I listened to her explain why she was cancelling. I flicked a silver ball off of a cupcake. Some of the frosting came off with it. She'd forgotten we had plans and committed to a dinner with some people who worked at one of the biggest law firms in the city.

"They're in pretty ground level jobs but they might be able to get me an internship there," she bubbled over the phone, sounding anything but sorry.

I told her it was fine even though it really wasn't. My opinion didn't matter anyway. I hung up and set down my phone, glancing at it before the screen dimmed.

6:07.

Not that it mattered now. No one's cars were in the garage when I'd arrived home so I assumed everyone was out for the evening, giving me the house to myself.

Again.

I refilled the mug with wine.

Mug in hand, I dragged myself out to check the mail. Starting to feel heady from the wine, I set the mug top of the mailbox while I thumbed through the contents, looking for a magazine or something else mildly interesting. Nothing except for bills and a flyer of pizza coupons. Ordering pizza might be fun. Well, not fun but at least it'd be —

"*Ay, Buenas tardes, Marco!*"

I fumbled, trying to catch the mail I'd nearly dropped. I could see Lola through the trees in her front yard, standing on the front porch and hugging a pudgy man at least six inches shorter than her. I guess he'd been waiting for her to answer the door when I walked out. Glancing at the street, I saw a few more cars parked along the curb. They must belong to the friends she told me about inviting over.

Lola ushered the man, Marco, inside and paused to glance back out at the street. She saw me then and yelled out excitedly, "Taylor, did you decide to come after all?"

"Yeah!" I called back with a surprising lack of hesitation. Why did I say that? I tried to subtly pull the mug off the mailbox and out of sight, nearly knocking it off in the process. *Idiot, it's a coffee mug - she's not going to know you have wine inside it.*

"Come on over then!"

"Be there in a minute!" I trotted back inside to ditch the mail on the kitchen counter.

"Guess you'll get some use after all," I said to the cupcakes. I arranged them on a platter, leaving out the one I'd flicked the frosting off of. I held up a hand in front of my mouth and exhaled, trying to see if I could smell the wine on my breath. I could. I brushed my teeth, grabbed a piece of gum, and headed for Lola's, making a mental note not to get too close to anyone for a while. Call me crazy, but pre-gaming for Lola's dinner party seemed wildly inappropriate.

"You did not need to bring anything," Lola exclaimed when she answered the door. She leaned in to hug me and I held my breath until she pulled away. She took the platter and ushered me inside where a group was already gathered in the front room, chatting loudly over Spanish music and holding glasses of deep red wine.

"Everyone," she announced. "This is Taylor."

The group paused their conversations to smile warmly and say hello. Lola poured a glass of wine from a bottle on the coffee table. I couldn't read the label from where I stood but could see it was written in Spanish.

As she handed me the glass, she leaned close and said quietly, "You will have to drink very little until everyone else can catch up."

She pulled away and smiled with knowing eyes. My face reddened as she turned and began nodding to each member of the group, quickly introducing us.

Marco, the man I saw Lola greet outside, was first. He beamed, looking genuinely pleased at my arrival and every bit like the type of person you'd expect to own, as Lola mentioned, a gourmet gift shop — crinkling eyes, an endearingly full face, and warm, olive skin a little lighter than Lola's.

"Our grandparents grew up in the same town in Spain."

"But they never knew each other," Marco added.

Next was Laura, who gave a little wave when Lola said her name. She looked close to my age, no more than three or four years older, but the dim lighting made it hard to tell.

"Laura is my personal accessory guru," Lola said with a theatrical flourish of the bracelets on her wrist and the heavy beaded necklace she wore around her neck. "She made all of these."

The necklace was several strands of chunky, misshapen stones. Most of the stones were a muted, turquoise color, but some looked more gray and some had currents of brown running through them. By contrast, the bracelets looked much more delicate. The stack of five or six bangles were made from small, symmetrical, frosted beads that matched the grayish turquoise stones of her necklace. I never would have picked them out from a store but they looked great put together.

Laura laughed without comment and Lola continued, "This is John, Laura's fiancé."

Sharing the sofa with them were Kelly and Stuart, a couple closer to Lola and Marco's age. "Kelly and Stuart are former students and very dear friends," Lola smiled. "And this is Philip." Leaning against the wall near where we'd entered, stood a tall man with full, silver hair combed back from his smooth, lightly tanned face.

"Lola and I share office space," Philip explained, leaning forward to shake my hand. "Have you taken one of her classes before?"

"No, I haven't," I confessed.

"I haven't either," he admitted with a smirk at Lola.

"Even though it would take him only thirty seconds to get there," she said.

"My art gallery is in the first floor of a building on The Square," Philip told me.

Everyone called our city's modest downtown area The Square because that's all there is. Four streets of boutiques, antique shops, and frilly little restaurants border the city's original courthouse, which now gets used as a theater for local plays and performances. It never occurred to me to wonder where Lola taught her classes, but now that I thought about it, The Square made perfect sense.

"Take the stairs up from the gallery and you're at Lola's," Philip continued. "When she happens to actually teach a class."

Lola took the jab lightly, "I teach the exact amount I want to teach. It is perfect."

"I could probably think of better uses for the second floor of my building."

"You're selling art faster than you can fill the space you already have," Kelly objected, easily sliding into the banter. "We didn't want to say anything to offend you but," she paused, smiling. "It's looking pretty drab in there now."

"A problem, I am sure, Philip is happy to have," Lola said with an amused glance at Philip's scowl.

"You all have such creative professions," I commented.

"Yes, Stuart, how do you muster up all that creativity for the insurance company?" Philip teased, laughing loudly.

I reddened, but Laura caught my eye and shook her head with a slight smile. "Lola seems to be a magnet for certain types of people," she agreed.

"What do you do?" Kelly asked me.

I hesitated. What *did* I do?

"Taylor," Lola answered. "Is a wonderful baker, who happens to be working as a graphic designer right now."

She smiled warmly at me and I let her answer suffice, trying on the feeling of it. Technically it wasn't inaccurate, but the phrase created a sharp contrast to how I normally introduced myself. There didn't seem to be any harm in letting them paint their own picture of me. They didn't know me or my degree or what was expected of me, nor did I get the sense that they would care if they did.

We moved to the modest dining room and shared an incredibly disjointed but delicious meal. Everyone had contributed a dish and the resulting meal was shades of Spain and France and the South in foods that looked like they went together on the outside, but held flavors as unique as the people crowded around the table.

After dinner we returned to the front room where Lola distributed tiny red cups of espresso and passed around my plate of cupcakes. I felt a quick flash of fear that the cupcakes wouldn't taste good but the feeling passed even before the group started raving over them. If there was one thing I could do, it was bake.

The conversation moved into a heated debate of American soccer versus Spanish *fútbol*. I watched quietly, thoroughly amused yet unable to comment, and noticed Laura doing the same. I set my empty plate and espresso cup on the coffee table and turned to her.

"So you make jewelry?" She nodded, finishing a bite, and I added, "Full time?"

"For four years now."

I'd never actually met anyone who did anything artistic full time. Unless you counted the messy handful of professors who'd made valiant but unsuccessful efforts at cementing the history of their respective creative disciplines into my head, urging my understanding of the intangible and abstract qualities of art, while also throwing tangibly ruthless requirements on the projects they assigned. I chose not to count them.

After a sip of espresso, Laura continued, "Of course, I spend surprisingly little time on the actual making of the jewelry."

She detailed her process of designing a piece, explaining that making a few samples didn't take more than a few hours, but then she met with current clients, potential clients and, if the piece proved to be popular enough to exceed her production capabilities, manufacturers.

"And then," she finished, "I need a few hours each week to update my website, my blog, work on invoices and budgets - all of that back-end finance stuff. Unless it's February. The big apparel and accessories market is in March and that's when I get the most purchases from bigger vendors - boutique owners and things like that. It takes me all of February getting ready for it."

"Wow," I replied, for a lack of anything more remarkable to say. I suppose I knew artists did more than just create whatever it is they created, but I definitely did the math wrong. "Doesn't all of the extra stuff get old?" I asked her. "I mean, it's making jewelry you love, right?"

"I might not do the business and marketing side if I didn't have to," she admitted. "At least I wouldn't have in the beginning. But I've kind of come to love it too." She paused, smiling to herself for a moment before she continued. "It's like all of those additional, sometimes tedious things have just become another part of the jewelry making process. I could work for a designer and just make jewelry all the time, but it'd have to be their design, in line with their expectations. Starting my own business has let me follow my art wherever it leads me. If someone doesn't like it, I'll sell it to someone else."

I got it. I completely understood what she was saying, even with my lack of experience. Art, business, all of it. If Daniel and I started the doughnut shop after all... *No.* I stopped myself and tuned back into the conversation with Laura. "I'd love to see your work. Do you have a website?

"I do, but I have a better idea," she said, squeezing my arm lightly. "Why don't you come by my house and I'll show you my studio? It's not terribly exciting but you can poke around, ask questions, give me some motivation to finally get it tidied up."

"I'd love that." I pushed the doughnuts further out of my mind as Lola and Marco started a dramatic waltz across the entryway. I laughed both at the scene they made and myself for the absurdity of sitting with such an odd mix of people on a Friday night, drinking espresso and eating cupcakes. Maybe I should have felt pathetic for not being out with friends my own age, but I couldn't imagine wanting to be anywhere else.

CHAPTER 24 - DANIEL

A warm breeze moved across the balcony of Rachel's apartment. Her A/C wasn't working, an unfortunately frequent occurrence, and opening the windows hadn't done much to cool the apartment. I don't know why she didn't upgrade to a nicer apartment complex, God knows she could afford it. Whenever I suggested she look for a place that could make it more than two weeks without the A/C going out, she just said, "It gets the job done," and that was it.

Warm breeze or not, sitting on the balcony was better than sitting inside with the stagnant, heavy air of her apartment. The sun set hours ago but between the brightness of the moon and the flickering street lamps dotting the parking lot we faced, it was pretty bright outside. We sat in plastic folding chairs with our feet propped on the balcony railing. Other than the faint sound of traffic from the streets surrounding the apartment complex, the night was mostly quiet and peaceful. Our conversation started and stopped with long, comfortable silences in between, both of us drifting in and out of our own thoughts.

My mind kept going back to doughnuts and careers and life purpose. I broke one of the pauses and asked, "Do you think I'm actually supposed to do this doughnut thing or that I'm just drawn to it because it gets my mind off of work?"

"Daniel." Rachel sounded exasperated by the doughnuts more often lately.

"What?"

She rolled her head to look at me. "Have you heard the phrase, 'beating a dead horse?'"

"Oh, okay. Sorry that I value your opinion."

She leaned her head back and stared at the ceiling for a moment before breathing a heavy sigh. "I don't think you're 'supposed' to do anything."

"It's not like making doughnuts is my passion in life."

"Right," Rachel said. "Baking is Taylor's thing."

"But it doesn't have to be something I'm passionate about for it to work."

"Right."

The silence settled in again and Rachel brought her gaze back down from the ceiling. I frowned as another question came to mind. "Am I even ready to start a business?"

Rachel dropped her forehead into her hands.

"I mean, you could argue that Steve Jobs wasn't technically ready to start Apple but he had the whole passion thing going on. But if Taylor and I are working together and she's passionate about it, then that's enough, right? We're like two parts of a whole."

"Daniel."

"I know, it sounds cheesy, but I think it's valid. Jobs had Wozniak, I have Taylor. Or Taylor has me…"

"*Daniel.*"

"What?"

"This is going nowhere."

"I'm processing."

"You're having the same conversation with yourself over and over again."

"I am not."

Her brow raised. "Really? Do you want me to do it? I can now." She straightened in her chair. "Is this doughnut business the right move? I want to do it. But *why* do I want to do it? Taylor is better suited for the doughnut part, I'm better suited for the —"

"Okay, I get it." Somewhere along the way she seemed to have gotten legitimately angry. "Sorry."

Her eyes searched mine. She didn't seem to believe I was really done with the debate, but she said, "It's fine," and we went back to our silence.

I kept thinking about the doughnuts though. I'd need to wait a little while before bringing it up with Rachel again but I couldn't handle keeping everything inside. Talking was the only way to release the pressure building greater with each circle of thought. But in the meantime Rachel seemed content to sit and listen to the hum of traffic and the occasional voices drifting across the parking lot. My mind finally quieted down a little bit and I sat without thinking about anything until a metallic clack sounded from inside her apartment.

"What was that?" I asked Rachel.

She sat up and leaned towards the open window, listening for more noise. She narrowed her eyes as she thought and then they widened in realization. "I think it was my rat trap."

"Your what?"

"My rat trap," she beamed and rushed inside.

I followed and found her crouched on the kitchen floor, peering into a small metal cage. Rachel mentioned seeing a rat a few weeks ago, but I hadn't heard any more about it. I definitely hadn't heard anything about a trap. From where I stood at the entrance to the kitchen, I couldn't see inside.

"Please tell me there is not an actual rat in there."

She turned and looked at me. "As opposed to a fake rat?" She smiled at my irritation and turned her attention back to the cage. "Come look at him."

"Gross, no. Rachel, get away from that thing. Rats have diseases."

"He's in a cage."

"Um, yeah, let's talk about that. A cage isn't really a trap. Traps are supposed to snap or stick or otherwise immobilize the rodent in question."

"Yes it is," she insisted, still looking inside the cage and admiring her work. "It's a humane trap." She stood and looked at me. "We have to set him free."

"Are you serious? What was the point of the trap?"

"To get him out of my apartment."

"Quit calling it a 'him.' If you set it free, it's just going to come back. Rats know how to navigate, like cats."

"Then I guess we're just going to have to go far away to let him out."

"We?"

She folded her arms across her chest and gave me a challenging look.

"Where are you proposing we take it?"

She thought for a moment. "That nature preserve we went hiking at would be a good place."

"The one that was almost an hour away from here? That nature preserve?"

"You said rats can navigate — we have to go far enough so he won't find his way back."

"Not an hour away."

"That's the closest natural habitat. We can't just drop him off in the city." She frowned at the thought.

My patience thinned. "It is a rat. Rats live in sewers and alleys and dumpsters."

"But he could have a happier life in nature," she said, her eyes big and pleading. I couldn't believe we were even having this debate to begin with. When I didn't say anything she added, "We weren't doing anything anyway."

"For the love of..." I pressed my forehead into my palm, feeling a headache coming on. "Fine." I grabbed my keys off the counter and shoved them into my pocket. "Don't," I said as she started to pick up the cage. "I'll get it."

I held the cage out as far as possible so the rat couldn't bite between the bars and infect me with the plague or something. I didn't want to look at it but caught a glimpse of its fat pink tail, slithering across the length of the cage. It made me want to vomit.

"Why didn't you get one of those cages that are solid plastic? Or one that's actually rat sized? This thing could hold a whole family of rats."

"It was on sale. Besides, I thought he might like the extra room."

I didn't have a response for that. When we got out to the parking lot I clicked open the trunk, only to find that the cage wouldn't fit. "You've got to be kidding me," I mumbled as I tried to angle the cage. The height was fine but it was too long. I turned it a little to the side to see if the other way would work better.

"Don't hurt him," Rachel pleaded. I shot her a look. Rotating the cage didn't work so we ended up having to put it in the back seat. I made a mental note to buy Lysol on the way home.

Though quiet until then, the rat started squeaking once the car was in motion. It pissed me off not only because it was an incredibly irritating noise, but it also made it impossible to forget I had a rat sitting in the backseat of my car. I flipped on the radio and turned the volume up loud enough to drown out the noise. Rachel, for her part, seemed entirely pleased, which made me even more annoyed and, admittedly, it showed in my driving. I whipped out of her neighborhood, taking turns a little faster than necessary.

"Easy," Rachel warned after the first couple of turns. We came to a stoplight that I waited until the last possible moment to brake for and when it turned green I punched the gas. The cage rattled with the momentum. Rachel looked worriedly at the back seat but didn't say anything until I took another turn with enough speed to send the cage sliding across the seat and into the car door with a crash.

"Daniel, slow down, you're going to break the cage."

"It's not going to break." I was tired of her delicate, friend-of-the-animals, let's-love-God's-creatures trash.

"The door isn't indestructible. The lock is just a little clicking latch thing."

"It's fine."

The drive felt like it was taking forever. Remarkable, considering the last time I'd been just as irritated because Rachel wouldn't tell me where she was going. It didn't help that I couldn't find anything decent to listen to on the radio. But anything was better than listening to the rat.

We were a little more than halfway there when Rachel said something too quiet to be heard over the radio.

"What?" I asked.

She said it again, something about the rat, but it was still too quiet. I jerked the volume down and asked what she said again.

Her voice was very low and calm. "The rat is on me."

I whipped my head to look at her. She was sitting very still, her back straight and tall against the seat, her shoulders taut. Nothing was on her though. Only her long dark hair, swept down across her neck.

"No it isn't." I turned back to the road.

"I think I would know if there was a rat on me. Which there is. On my shoulder."

I looked at her again. She held her head up, looking forward and not moving at all. I glanced back at the cage. It looked fine. "It's just your hair, Rachel. Touch your shoulder."

Very slowly she lifted her left hand, carefully moving it towards her right shoulder. I didn't believe her but I kept darting glances between the road and her movements. The rest of her body remained motionless and she looked terrified as her hand moved closer. I looked back from the road in time to see her hand disappear on the other side of her neck. Her whole body spasmed as she flung her hand away and let out a scream loud enough to scare the hell out of me even though I watched the whole thing happen.

"*WHAT?*" I yelled once and then again and again in turn with her shrieks while trying to focus on driving. She kept yelling and thrashing around in her seat, shaking out her hair and brushing off her arms. "*WHAT? WHAT IS WRONG?*"

She rolled down the window, as if that would help, undid her seatbelt, and threw herself against the dashboard, trying to create as much distance between herself and the seat as possible. She managed to crawl partially on top of the dashboard, which I would have thought impossible in so small a car. She finally stopped screaming and breathed deep, ragged breaths — one arm stretched across the dash and a leg dangling out the window. How I managed to keep driving and not wreck the car through all of that is still a mystery to me.

"Rat," she said between breaths. "On. My. Shoulder."

I looked around, my skin crawling. I didn't see the rat. "Did you fling him out the window?" I was hopeful.

"No."

I heard a squeak from the backseat. I looked back at the cage. "Rachel, I don't think it got out."

"He. Did."

"Get down," I said.

She pulled her leg back inside the car and nervously eased herself onto the seat again, but she refused to lean back. I turned to glance at the cage again. It was a tough angle but I could see a little shadow in the corner of the cage.

"You probably scared the hell out of - *OH MY GOD*." The sensation of four tiny sets of pinpricks and a brush of fur against my neck was unmistakable. Our screams were deafening as I swerved to the side of the road, desperately punching at the buckle of my seat belt. I punched the brakes and the car ground to a stop in the gravel on the side of the road. I groped for the handle and kicked open the door, yelling and swearing as I flung myself out of the car. Rachel scrambled across the seats and came out on my side of the car, screaming as she went.

I don't know how long that went on until we finally sagged against the car, out of breath and still squirming from the phantom feeling of fur and claws.

"Do you think it's gone?" Rachel asked quietly.

"I hope so."

We edged back toward the car and used our phones as flashlights to search for the rat. We examined the cage and found that the latch on the door had clicked open. Both of us knew the door was my fault but the rat was hers, so neither of us said anything. There was no sign of the rat after a few minutes of tense searching, so we got back in the car with what little dignity we had left and drove back the way we came.

"There's this really cool thing called, Pest Control," I said.

Rachel didn't reply.

"They do all sorts of neat stuff," I continued. "Get rid of insects, rodents..."

"It was a humane trap," she said in her soft stubborn voice.

I looked over, thinking to say something sarcastic again, but stopped. Her hands were folded in her lap, her shoulders slumped and her chin tucked down a little. I can't remember ever seeing her look so sad. I exhaled a frustrated breath and reached for her hand.

"He's further away from the city now," I said, brushing my thumb across the back of her hand. "He can make it the rest of the way to the nature preserve."

"You think so?"

"Yeah."

She smiled faintly and leaned her head against the back of the chair. "I love you."

"I love you too."

She closed her eyes and slept the rest of the way home, but my mind refused to rest now. Without any distraction my thoughts returned to doughnuts and my career. I could almost laugh at how incongruous the two items seemed, how unlikely a pairing they were. Yet they remained to be dealt with and I had no idea what to do or who I could ask for help. I looked over at Rachel sleeping in the passenger seat and remembered her earlier annoyance with the debate. My indecisive rambling would only push her away. I felt a wave of loneliness at the idea.

Maybe the whole idea of doughnuts was beginning to annoy her. She'd said the other day how she thought I was just using them as a distraction from work. I doubted she dreamed about settling down and marrying a guy who ran a doughnut shop.

Besides, work wasn't so bad now. The day after I'd turned in the portfolio for Moskovitz, Tom called be back to his office.

"He signed," Tom beamed as soon as I walked in the door. "He was particularly interested in that biomedical company."

"Really?" I made a mental note to thank Steve Mobley again. "That's great."

Tom nodded. "I didn't think he'd be comfortable with something so fast paced but I guess that's how you younger guys are used to doing business," he grinned warmly. "Keep it up, Daniel. You could go far in this company."

There I was, two days later and the memory of his affirmation still filled me with pride, but the feeling was starting to fade. I couldn't count on Mobley every time I needed a investment recommendation. What would happen when I created a portfolio that didn't win a client over? It took over two years to get this first promotion, how long would it take for the next one?

The tightness in my chest started creeping back again but we were back at Rachel's apartment so I nudged her awake and went back to ignoring the questions I didn't have answers to.

CHAPTER 25 - TAYLOR

"I've got it," Haleigh said, handing the cashier her credit card the next morning. *Someone* felt guilty. I figured as much when she texted me that morning, asking if I wanted to go to brunch. She suggested we eat at Café, which I think should get an award for having the most generic name in the entire world. No adjective or descriptive noun, not even an article. Just, "Café," like no one told the owners they were supposed to come up with a name when opening a restaurant.

Useless name aside, the place held a certain charm. The building was a renovated house from the thirties, a few blocks off The Square. The exterior was painted a warm, muted yellow with white trim and most of the tables were outside, cast around the backyard without any sense or order or pattern. Some of the tables were on a wooden, split-level patio and some were stationed around the garden. It kind of made you feel like you were just having a meal at the house of someone's kind-of-crazy grandmother, who happens to make killer french toast.

We took our coffees to a table on the back patio and I took my time meticulously wedging our number card in the holder, pushing it toward the window, pointedly avoiding eye contact with her.

Haleigh took a sip of her coffee. Checked her phone. I could wait for the apology all day long. Didn't bother me.

"What'd you end up doing last night?" She asked, still looking down at her phone.

I gave up. But she would not win. "Went to a party."

"Really? With who?"

"Some new friends." Not a lie, technically.

I quickly asked about her evening and we navigated away from the party topic before she could dig further. She'd gone to dinner and drinks with the aforementioned handful of lawyers but, she admitted, no actual law or job items were discussed. I listened with a neutral expression, remembering her popping aspirin in the car when I picked her up this morning. I'd pretended not to notice.

"One of them did say they'd give me some LSAT pointers though."

"LSAT pointers. Is that what they're calling it these days?"

She didn't get the joke. I asked her how studying was going, trying really hard to be interested. Her law school happenings weren't very interesting to begin with, but today I'd really hit a wall. Being annoyed about the night before probably wasn't helping.

"It's good, it's just, it doesn't feel like you can actually study for it, you know?"

I nodded, pretending to know.

"You're so lucky you have it all together."

A short laugh burst out of me.

"I'm serious. You've graduated, you got a job, you're using your degree."

She paused as a waiter arrived and set our plates in front of us. When she put my job situation in those terms it sounded a lot more impressive than it felt.

"I mean, I graduated," Haleigh continued sadly. "But I'm about to start all over again with law school. I'm years behind you."

"Nonsense," I said unconvincingly, enjoying the gratification.

"It's true," she stabbed at her french toast. "I guess I have something to look forward to."

I shook my head. If my current situation was something to be looked forward to... talk about a depressing idea. The praise she'd given me felt hollow now. "It's not so great," I told her.

"How so?"

"Don't get me wrong, it's not horrible or anything but..." I tried to find the right way to convey my thoughts. "There's a small handful of things I'm good at in life, right? Baking is probably the thing I enjoy most, but that's not something you go make a career out of. Graphic design is one of them, which is why I took the job at HRG. But I've barely done any design work for them and the projects I get are less like creating and more like following instructions."

"I think that's just how life is," she said. "I mean, I won't graduate from law school and go straight to prosecuting criminals in a courtroom."

"I know, I know." Why couldn't I accurately describe what I meant? "It's not just that. All of it feels pointless. Like, even if I were getting to do more design work, why would it matter? Ryan can do any job I can, would enjoy it way more, and could probably do it better."

"Probably could with that attitude."

I shot her a look. "Maybe I just don't work well with Bill. Or if my dad hadn't been pushing so hard for me to get a job right away —"

"You're the one who decided to take the job." *Not helpful Haleigh.* "And you decided to study art."

I narrowed my eyes at her.

"Don't get mad at me, I'm just saying, you can't blame your boss or your Dad because you're unhappy."

"This isn't about being unhappy."

"That's what it sounds like."

But it wasn't. It was more and somehow I couldn't succeed at articulating what I meant. In the spirit of keeping the peace, I told her she may be right and changed topics again. I finished my french toast and let Haleigh ramble on about the really cute lawyer and the kind-of cute lawyer she met the night before.

"The really cute one has only been there for, like, a year, so he hasn't done much yet but you can totally tell that he's going to like, go really far with the firm. The kind of cute one is who offered to help me with the LSAT."

"Ah."

She managed to carry the topic for the rest of the meal. I waited a few polite seconds for her to finish her last bite before I asked if she was ready to go.

After I dropped her back at her house, I went home, put on a swimsuit, threw a t-shirt and shorts on top, and headed for our pool in the backyard. I stopped in the kitchen long enough to pour a glass of tea and grab a magazine and then shouldered open the screened door from the sunroom, letting it slam shut behind me. At the noise, Mom looked up from where she crouched in the garden, pulling up weeds.

"How was breakfast?"

I walked towards her, wishing I didn't look like the epitome of laziness. She'd created an impressive pile of weeds on the ground next to her but, by the looks of it, she'd only covered half the yard so far.

"Good." I hesitated. "Do you need some help?"

"I'm alright, thank you." She pushed the hair out of her face with the back of her hand. "You're a working girl, you need your time to relax." She smiled and returned to the weeds. I slunk off to my lounge chair feeling a twinge of guilt.

It wasn't even one o'clock yet but it had to be close to a hundred degrees already. The air *smelled* hot. I'd forgotten to grab a towel so I pulled off my t-shirt and tried to use it as a barricade between the hot cushion of the lounge chair and my skin. It still burned but eventually felt tolerable.

I skimmed the contents page of the magazine and at the word 'doughnuts' I stopped. After gagging at the cheesy headline, "Gourmet Doughnuts: Don't Glaze Over These Goodies," I flipped to the page listed. I took in the photo spread of half a dozen doughnuts, coated with richly colored glazes and flecked with chopped nuts. The story described a boutique doughnut shop, located in Charleston, started by four friends from college, now graduated, married, and fathers of adorable families.

I hated them. I tossed the magazine on the table next to my chair. Daniel needed to hear about this. I stalked inside and bounded up the stairs to his room. Empty. I went out front to see if his car was in the garage. The door was open and the spot where his car normally sat was empty, except for Dad poking around in a toolbox.

"Any idea where Daniel is?"

"He left about an hour ago, didn't say where he was going."

I sighed dramatically.

"Did you try him on his cell?"

"No." It seemed better to wait. Down the driveway, the mail truck pulled up, paused in front of our mailbox, and drove off. I glanced that direction, uninterested, and turned to go back inside.

"Why don't you get the mail?" Dad asked without looking up.

I didn't want to get the mail, it probably just had another traitorous magazine waiting inside, but I went. Thumbing through the contents I came to a plain, sterile looking envelope with my name on it. I set the pile on Dad's tool bench and tore into the letter.

"What'd you get?"

"Our business license," I said. "For the doughnuts."

He turned back to the toolbox and was quiet for a moment. "I thought you decided to focus on your job."

"Yeah, well, you never know."

I made for the door before he could reply and returned to my spot by the pool. Condensation had puddled around the glass and waterlogged the magazine I'd left next to it. Not that I cared now. I didn't want to read any more about the stupid doughnut idea-stealers or the magazine that dared to write about them.

I leaned back and closed my eyes, listening to the trickle of the pool fountain. An occasional, *snip snip*, drifted across the yard. Mom must have moved onto pruning. My thoughts circled around Haleigh's remark and doughnuts, even as I tried to ignore them. A doughnut sounded kind of good actually. Not a normal one, but one like I'd made when Daniel and I held our taste-testing session. One like the stupid doughnut shop in Charleston.

I caught a whiff of some herb in the air. Squinting from the too bright sun I looked around, searching for the source. Mom had crossed the yard to crouch in the herb garden. I walked over and watched her methodically pruning a large basil plant, tossing the long stems by the weed pile.

"Aren't you going to do anything with those?"

"No, we have too much as it is."

It seemed silly to waste them. I rescued the handful of discarded stems from the weed pile and took them inside to wash and dry them. The stupid doughnut shop in Charleston had probably never used basil in a doughnut.

I dug out the basic recipe I'd used last time and began mixing the dough. I sliced a handful of thin strips of basil and dropped them into the dough, just enough for a hint of flavor. After the dough had risen, I cut out the rings but hesitated before dropping the rings of dough in the oil - I'd need something sweet to offset the basil.

Scanning the kitchen, my eyes landed on a bowl brimming with peaches. Knowing it was a long shot, I divided the peach into the thinnest slices I could manage, used a beaten egg to secure a few peach slices around the top of the doughnut, and started frying. While they cooled, I followed my recipe for a basic glaze but added in another pinch of basil before pouring onto the doughnuts. Anxious to try them, I attempted to busy myself with doing the dishes while the glaze set, touching one every so often to see if it was ready. Though the glaze still felt a little tacky, I picked up the finger smudged doughnut and took a hesitant bite.

"Mom," I called, poking my head out the back door. "Will you come try this?"

Mom pulled herself to her feet, brushed off her shorts, and slipped off her gardening shoes at the back door. She eyed the doughnuts dubiously while she put her gardening gloves into her pocket and washed her hands.

"What kind are these?"

"Just try one."

She took a tiny, skeptical bite. "Oh, wow." She took another larger bite.

"Good?" I begged, hopeful.

"Really good," Mom replied. "Did you use the basil I trimmed from the garden?"

I nodded proudly and her jaw dropped, eyes wide. "That basil was drenched in pesticide."

My mouth fell open, mirroring her face. Sharp pain stabbed inside my stomach, surely the pesticide beginning to take effect.

"Just kidding," she said, breaking into a smile and popping the rest of the doughnut into her mouth. "Glad you put it to good use."

I swear she has the worst sense of humor of anyone I know. She rinsed the glaze off her fingers and playfully whacked me with her gloves as she went back outside to resume her gardening, smiling proudly to herself.

I set aside a doughnut each for Daniel and Dad to try later and stacked the rest on a plate to take to Lola. Officially giving up on the poolside relaxation project, I changed out of my swimsuit and started down the drive.

"Good afternoon," Lola called from her porch. She held a large tin watering can and moved between the stone pots filled with roses and hydrangeas. She set down the watering can as I climbed the steps and ushered me inside. We went to the kitchen and she poured two glasses of iced tea — she never bothered asking anymore.

"If you keep delivering these desserts, I'm going to have to teach more dance classes. We cannot give Philip the satisfaction. Eat one." She nudged one of the doughnuts towards me and used a fork to section off a bite for herself. I obeyed, not bothering to mention I already ate one.

"My business license came in the mail," I told her between bites.

"For the doughnut shop?"

I nodded, my mouth full again.

"That's wonderful."

"I think I'm going to do it."

"Really?"

The words came without thought yet somehow they almost sounded reasonable. "I think so."

"You absolutely should," Lola said, without surprise.

"Maybe."

She looked at me with an arched brow, not missing that I'd already started to back off the idea again.

"I haven't talked to Daniel about it in a while."

"Do you think he changed his mind?"

I thought about it for a moment. "I honestly don't know. We got into a stupid fight about the business license and then he got promoted at work. It kind of just got swept under the rug."

"Un-sweep it."

I smiled. "Maybe now that I have the license that will get him back on track. I can take him that, one of the doughnuts and, oh—" I'd nearly forgotten the magazine article. "I read the worst article. Some doughnut shop in Charleston is doing almost the exact same thing we're trying to do."

"They are there and you are here," she said dismissively. "And even if they were here, would that really change anything? You may not have anyone directly competing with you here, but it will not be easy to get started. And once you do get started there will be one hundred other obstacles to overcome."

"That's cheerful."

"You can do it," she added. "But do not make the mistake of expecting it to be easy."

"I don't see how it could be any worse than my job right now." I thought of Bill and his constantly changing, never well-explained opinions. "Half the time I don't have anything to do and just have to deal with the monotony of it, or I actually have a project and I can't do it right."

"Do you think your doughnut shop would be more enjoyable?"

"Yes. No question.

"Then it will be harder."

I looked at her dumbly, feeling lost.

"It is not necessarily the actual labor that is more difficult. I would imagine that is sometimes the case, but most of the time it will be just as difficult as any other job. But because not as many people choose the same path, you will feel alone and looked down on, like you are doing less than everyone else. That is one of the prices of following your passion."

"Passion."

Lola nodded. "Whatever it is that pulls at you and wakes you up. The things that make you feel like you're actually living life, not just existing. That is a passion."

Just listening to her made me feel tired. I leaned an elbow onto the counter and propped my chin in my hand.

"What are you thinking?"

I tried to find words for what I felt. "I'm not afraid to work hard," I said after a moment. Lola nodded, encouraging me to continue. "HRG just feels like a dead end."

"Is HRG, or a company like HRG, where you want to be in ten years?"

I shook my head.

"Then it probably is a dead end. You don't have to make a decision right now," she soothed. "Think about it and talk to Daniel. You'll find your answer." She gave a quick, warm smile. "Come on, it is time to feed Balboa."

I slipped off the stool and followed her to the freezer, feeling unreasonably exhausted. Tossing shrimp to Balboa and wandering around the garden proved to be kind of therapeutic though. By the time I left Lola's, I'd gone back to feeling fired up about the prospect of starting this doughnut shop. Daniel's car was back in the garage. Neither of the doughnuts I'd left in the kitchen were missing so I put one on a plate, grabbed the envelope with the business license and the magazine from the counter, and tromped upstairs to Daniel's room. I met him in the hallway at the top of the stairs.

"Have a second?"

"How much of a second?" He checked the time on his cell phone. "I'm supposed to pick up Rachel in half an hour."

"It'll be quick," I promised. "Doughnut?"

Without hesitation he took the doughnut from the plate and bit into it as we walked back towards his room.

"What is this?" He scrutinized the doughnut and took a wary sniff.

"Peach and basil."

"It's weird."

I frowned.

"But I like it." He noticed the envelope and asked through his full mouth, "What's that?"

He flopped onto his futon and took the envelope when I handed it to him. "Our business license."

Daniel pulled out the documents and looked at them. I started ranting about my change of heart, regular life paths and creative, passionate paths while he glanced between me and the license papers. When I finished and he still hadn't said anything, I handed him the magazine and summarized the story about the doughnut shop in Charleston.

"Well?"

He looked at me and ran a hand through his hair, smoothing it back down again as soon as he did. "Are you mad that someone took our idea or are you serious?"

"I'm serious."

He looked at me, doubtful.

"I am," I said again. "I don't know what else you want me to say."

Daniel sighed heavily and looked at the license again before folding it back into the envelope.

"You're ready to go into work on Monday morning and quit your job?"

"There's still a lot we could and *need* to work on before we quit our jobs."

"Yeah," he agreed. "But I don't want to put all that time into it if you're not going to commit."

"I am." I half-heartedly raised a fist in the air and said weakly, "Beach Nuts."

He looked at me challengingly. "Alright," he finally said, rising to his feet. "Start coming up with more recipes."

"Can I borrow your laptop? I left mine at the office."

Daniel sent me off with his laptop and it wasn't until I'd fired it up, opened every dessert recipe I'd ever saved to my cloud drive, and collected enough pens and colored pencils and paper to illustrate a hundred recipes that I began to feel that same wave of annoyance about the division of labor between Daniel and me. Here I was planning out our menu, a significant part of a doughnut shop in my humble opinion, and Daniel was off gallivanting with Rachel. When did he plan on participating in this?

"Start coming up with more recipes," I mumbled, my sketching quickening. The way he'd said it — some obnoxious cross between indulging and demanding. It crossed my mind to be grateful for the evening entertainment but Daniel didn't deserve the credit, especially when a large part of me wished I was out with friends like he was. I wanted to be doing normal things for someone my age not... what was I even doing? I set down my pen and straightened, pushing back from the desk.

I would not quit my job. I would not start a doughnut shop with my brother. I would quit being dreamy and idealistic. I slowly stacked the pages of sketches, closed my laptop, and put my pens away. I carefully placed the sketches in a folder and then slid them into a gap on the shelf above my desk.

By the time Daniel returned home I was already asleep. Avoiding him the next day was easy enough. He didn't bring up anything about the doughnuts and I didn't mention them. On Monday morning, I got dressed and went to work just as I'd been doing for the last couple of months.

"Hey," Rand called from his office as I approached. "How was your weekend?"

"It was alright," I said, leaning against the door frame.

"Just alright?"

Rand was my coworker, not my friend. I reminded myself of that distinction, but he always seemed so calm and steady, like I could confide in him, just a little bit, and he would *get it.* I set down my bag and sat on the little plastic chair against the wall. "Do you ever wish your life were a little more normal?"

His face seemed to convey that either he did not wish his life were more normal, or I'd just spoken in a different language.

I tried again. "Like, everyone else is doing things the right way and you're... not."

"What's your definition of 'the right way?'"

"I don't know. Something different than what I'm doing."

"Why do you say that?"

I hesitated, unsure of how to explain better without mentioning HRG or doughnuts specifically. "What I'm doing now just doesn't feel... right." I searched his face for any sign of understanding. His eyes narrowed a little in thought but he didn't respond. Trying to explain what I meant was still like a word on the tip of my tongue that I couldn't grasp, no matter how hard I thought about it. Daniel and Lola were the only ones who seemed to understand, and it hadn't required any explanation.

"Nevermind," I said.

"Sorry I don't have an answer for you," Rand said.

I stood to leave and had barely stepped into the hallway when I noticed Bill taking quick strides from the direction of my cube.

"There you are," he said. "Do you have the updated graphics for Fizz? Ms. Coleman is coming by at nine o'clock. She's ready to move forward."

I nodded, saying a silent prayer of gratitude that I'd managed to finish everything before I left on Friday. If I hadn't there'd have been no way to finish them in the — I checked my watch, twenty minutes before Casey arrived.

"I'll go print them."

"Great. Bring them down to my office when you're done."

At my cubicle, my laptop was exactly where I'd left it. I turned on the computer and unpacked my bag while I waited for it to boot up. When the home screen appeared, I clicked through the file folders on my hard drive. Graphic... Clients... Fizz... I stopped. The folder for Version 1 was there, but not the folder for Version 2. I clicked on the Version 1 folder to see if I'd dropped it in there by mistake. It was empty. My heart thudded in my chest. I clicked the search button at the top of the screen and typed, '*Version 2.*'

Nothing.

I opened the trash.

Nothing.

Breathing became difficult.

I racked my brain trying to remember saving the files. Of course I saved the files. I opened the program I used to create the graphics. I clicked File... Open Recent... I exhaled a sigh of relief. A list of four Version 2 files cascaded down. I clicked on 'Fizz Logo Version 2.'

`Cannot open the selected item because the file was not found.`

I tried the second file, the text-only logo.

`Cannot open the selected item because the file was not found.`

The third, a graphic-only logo, and the fourth, the package design.

`Cannot open the selected item because the file was not found.`

I ran to Rand's office and dragged him back to my cube. He clicked around in all the same places I had, searched for the file name, checked the trash.

Rand's eyebrows creased with concern. "You're sure you saved the files on Friday?"

"Yes. One hundred percent sure. You came to tell me Bill was letting us go early, I hit 'save,' I closed the program, I went home."

"You didn't do anything to them this weekend?"

"No, I accidentally left my computer here. It's been in the office since Friday."

"How long would it take you to redo them?"

"A couple of hours at least."

He looked grim. I'd already told him Casey would be here at nine o'clock.

"You have to tell Bill," he said.

My mouth felt dry and my chest hurt. I made my way down the hall to Bill's office, trying to swallow. I knocked quietly on his open door, hoping maybe he wouldn't hear me or something.

"Whatcha got?" He asked, brimming with energy.

"Um," I started. "There's um," I scoured my brain, trying to think of the best way to handle this. *Don't make excuses.* "I lost the files. I can recreate them, I remember exactly what I changed, I just need a couple of hours."

He looked at me without saying anything. His jaw tightened a little. I wanted to die. A knock sounded on the door behind me. I stepped to the side and Ryan came in.

"Hey, Bill, sorry to interrupt but I—" he stopped, taking in the scene. "Sorry, is this a bad time?"

'Bad' didn't begin to cover it.

"Taylor," Bill said my name like it was a filthy rag he held at arms length. "Seems to have lost the graphics for our client who will be arriving in the next ten minutes."

"Oh no," Ryan said, his voice full of concern.

"'Oh no,' is right," Bill said without looking at me.

"Well," Ryan scratched his head, thinking. "You know, I've got a design you could look at."

Ryan stepped toward Bill and gave him a flash drive he'd been holding. Bill frowned a little but took the flash drive and put it into his computer. The screen filled with four renditions of the Fizz logo. The images seemed alarmingly similar to mine but a few details looked different. The font on one appeared narrower, the green on another was a few shades darker. I looked at Ryan and he held my gaze, his face expressionless.

"Perfect," Bill said. "This will work. Taylor, you're off the hook. You owe a big thank you to Ryan."

I looked at him again, but this time he wouldn't meet my eye. "I'm just happy I could help," Ryan said, his voice humble.

I needed out of there. I left Bill's office and tried to hold my shoulders normally, focusing on my posture so I wouldn't cry. My face felt hot and fought to keep my eyes open, unblinking, so I wouldn't tear up.

"How'd it go?" Rand called from his office as I walked by.

I didn't stop. I couldn't talk about it. I kept walking to my cube and Rand followed.

"Taylor?"

"I think —" my voice broke and I stopped, took a deep breath, and used my sleeve to touch the corner of my eyes, absorbing the tears that were already forming. I started again, my voice quiet, "I think Ryan did it."

We stood there, neither of us saying a word. I heard Ryan and Bill's voices down the hallway, talking to someone else. Casey must have arrived. I blinked a few times, willing my eyes to dry.

"Why do you say that?" Rand finally asked.

"He came in when I was talking to Bill and gave him a flash drive with some logos. He acted like he just happened to have them but there were four and they were really similar to mine."

"Similar how?"

"Everything was similar. Really there were only a couple of things different."

Rand looked at me for a moment and sighed heavily.

"You think I'm crazy?"

"No," he said carefully. "I don't. But you and Ryan were in all of the development meetings together. He heard the same feedback you did, so it's not impossible that he could create a logo similar to yours."

"Four," I corrected. "He gave Bill four logos, almost exactly like my four."

Rand looked away. He took off his glasses, cleaned them on his shirt, and put them back on before replying. "Look, nothing is one hundred percent original. Everything we do here – the commercials, the ads, the branding – they're a derivative of something. Maybe Ryan used your logos as a basis for the ones he made. But at the end of the day, Ryan had his ready in time and you didn't."

"But I –"

"I know you didn't mean to lose them. I'm not even saying there's something you could have done to prevent it. These things happen."

I glanced at my computer. The error message still covered the screen.

"It'll go better next time," Rand said.

He returned to his office and I sank into my chair, trying to tune out the sounds of Bill and Ryan and Casey's laughter coming from down the hallway. I remember thinking that I hated them and I remember wanting to pack up my bag and walk out right then. I swiveled back towards my desk, closed the folders from my frantic search for the graphics, and checked my email.

CHAPTER 26 - DANIEL

I pride myself for having really excellent intuition. I can walk into a room and sort of sense how everyone is feeling before they even talk. Once you know people, it's pretty easy. Everyone kind of has their own threshold of emotions that they operate within. For example — you come across someone with a neutral expression. If it's Rachel, she could be calmly content or quietly angry. If it's Taylor, she's either tired or depressed. Both of their faces might look the same, but they mean entirely different things.

When Tom came down the hall and called me to his office on Monday afternoon, I only saw a brief glimpse of his face before he turned around, but it was enough to see he was upset. His tone was clipped when he said my name and as I followed him down the hall I saw his steps were short and quick. He was probably erring on the angry side of upset but I couldn't imagine what it would be about.

"Close the door," he said when I stepped into his office. He went to the window and stood with his back to me, hands on his hips. I closed the door. He kept standing there, looking out the window. I didn't know whether to sit or stand. I racked my brain trying to think of what might be wrong. Did we lose a client? Was he leaving the company? Did someone die? He dipped his head and put a hand on the back of his neck. His shoulders raised as he took a deep, heavy breath and then turned around to face me.

"Sit down."

I sat. The tightness in my chest grew. It didn't seem to go away anymore, it just tightened and loosened in varying amounts throughout the day. Tom finally sat in his chair and leaned forward onto the desk, his shoulders tight and his face set in firm rigid lines. Normally he looked young for his middle-aged years but the creases on his forehead and beside his eyes seemed more pronounced, making him look as old as Dad or Ned.

"We got a call from Moskovitz this morning," he said.

My first guess was right then – he must be pulling his business. I didn't know what to say though.

"He made a move on one of the investment options we suggested."

My chest cinched tighter.

"The biomedical company."

My ears throbbed with the beat of something. *My heart? My pulse? What is beating?*

"According to your recommendation it was a..." He picked up a paper from his desk, and scanned the page until he found my words. "Low risk, high rate of return. Multiple avenues of growth, stable, recurring cash flow, and low capital expenditure requirements." He put down the paper and looked at me.

"It was, is–" I cleared my throat. "It's all of that." Talking was difficult. I'd taken Steve Mobley's lead but I did all of my usual research on the company's market position, their historical performance, the industry trends. Everything I found supported Mobley's claim. "I did the due diligence, you can look through my notes."

Tom's jaw worked back and forth. "I went through and verified the information myself, it holds up." He leaned back a little and drummed his fingers on the desk. His eyes bore into mine. "Curious, then, that Moskovitz would purchase half a million shares only to see the stock not just fall below your projected value, but to plummet below what he purchased it for."

Right about then is when I started wondering if I was having a heart attack.

"Daniel," Tom sighed heavily. "You've heard of pump and dump schemes? Microcap stock fraud?"

I think I managed to nod.

"Look, I don't care who you talked to, I don't want to know. I've seen some really smart guys fall into company with someone throwing a bunch of false hype about a stock, making it sound like you'd be an idiot not to purchase it. Once the guys running the scheme get enough people on board, they dump their overpriced shares, the stock falls, and the investors lose all their money. They're good at misleading people or these things wouldn't happen. You've been here long enough for me to know you wouldn't have knowingly walked into this sort of thing, not after all the great stuff you've been doing around here."

"Thank you, sir," I said quietly.

"But that's not it."

I don't know if it was the adrenaline or what, but things start getting cloudy after that. Tom said something about my web browsing history, how I might have been more watchful or something if I wasn't distracted. I thought he was referencing Rachel at first.

"Sir?"

Tom picked up a paper and placed it on the desk in front of me. It was some sort of spreadsheet with IP addresses, URLs, dates, times. "Over the last three weeks, thirty-five percent of your time has been attributed to non-work related web browsing. Does any of that seem incorrect?"

I pretended to scan the page but I couldn't get my eyes to focus on the small print. "No."

Tom studied my face, searching for something. His tone changed. He sounded softer, but desperately confused as if he couldn't understand how someone he'd hired had screwed up so badly. "What is all of this?" He picked up the spreadsheet and started picking through the URLs. "Food sourcing, restaurant supplies, commercial baking equipment?" Tom lowered the spreadsheet again and looked at me. "A bakery?"

"Um. A doughnut shop actually."

The corner of his mouth twitched. "Ah."

That one seemed to have thrown him for a minute. He studied his hands, shook his head, and then looked back to me. "Neither of these incidents would be so bad by themselves, but we've been getting pressure to trim some fat around the office. I could think of a lot of people I'd give the boot before you Daniel but Arthur James is the one who brought this issue to my attention."

"James?" I was sure I'd heard him wrong, but he nodded soberly. Arthur James, the CFO of Colson Caldwell. Kevin's uncle.

"You've been a great asset to the company."

Been. I probably nodded again, I don't really remember. I do remember the way he looked at me — not with anger, just pity. Tom said something about his hands being tied, something about waiting a day to make a final decision. I stood and numbly returned to my desk to shut down my computer.

"Where ya going?" Dax asked.

"Doctors appointment," I said without looking at him.

My heart rate was through the roof. When I first met Steve Mobley my internal alarms went off – why did I ignore them? I went down to the parking garage and drove halfway to Rachel's before realizing she would still be at work. I pulled a U-turn at a stoplight and started heading towards the Tavern, thinking I could meet her there after she got off work. I made it most of the way there before deciding I didn't want to talk to her right then. I couldn't.

I changed directions again and headed for home, stopping first for a couple of six-packs from the liquor store. When I got home I stashed one in the fridge and took the other one up to my room. I drank a third of the first bottle in one swig, desperate for something to calm myself down. Trusting Mobley would go at the top of my mental list of the worst decisions I'd ever made, right above buying that damn car. This would be my downfall. This was the end. I finished the first beer and started on a second. I tried to play a video game to distract myself but couldn't focus.

I turned off the TV and pulled a third beer out of the pack. I couldn't blame Mobley – he was doing what he did and I was doing what I did. He was sharp and cunning, I was incompetent and now I was going to be fired over it. It was only fair. I didn't deserve a real job. Even if they gave me another chance, it would surely only be a matter of time before I screwed up again. I started pacing the room. The movement helped. Movement was good.

Would they give me severance pay? How long would it take to find another job? What if I couldn't find another job? I had credit card bills, another ten months of those damn car payments. God knows how long it would be before I could move out now, and this would put a definite halt on moving forward with Rachel.

Oh my God, Rachel. What would she say? She'd always been supportive and understanding about my pitiful income but what about *no income?* The third beer disappeared and I started in on a fourth. I sat at my desk and closed my eyes. I needed a plan. I needed something fast and good. Rachel needed to know she could trust me, that I could provide for her.

The doughnuts. Of course – everything pointed to the doughnuts. Taylor and I already made *some* progress, we weren't starting from scratch. We still hadn't found a place for our business though. We needed retail space. I powered on my laptop and started a frantic search for commercial real estate in the area. Forget leasing – we could buy the space. If we put in a bid before I officially lost my job we could apply for a loan, we'd get the business going, we'd pay it off in no time. If the business didn't work, we'd sell the property again and get our money back.

I tossed the fourth empty bottle of beer in the trash can and hurriedly swept through online auction sites. I didn't care what the damn thing looked like in person, we were on a time crunch. I found a compact little place – eight hundred square feet and already outfitted with an oven, some counter space, and a commercial dishwasher. It sounded sufficient. What we were lacking we could have put in. Prime location. The bid was at four hundred thousand and only had two hours left to go. I started to do the math, trying to compare what some of the other properties we looked at leasing cost and how that compared to the price of this space. I couldn't remember an exact price and the numbers jumbled in my head. *Forget it.* I registered with the website, filled out my personal information, entered in my bid amount, and pressed 'Submit.' A notification filled the computer screen:

Your bid has been submitted.

I straightened in my chair. I had an odd, quiet moment. The best I can compare it to is when I played baseball in high school. The first time I hit a ball out of the park, there was the most beautiful, solid crack of the bat and I started sprinting for first. I rounded second and was almost to third when I realized my team was going crazy – yelling, jumping up and down. I couldn't figure out why at first. I was still running and all I could think about was running until I put all the pieces together and noticed the outfielders staring past the fence, the other team just standing there, looking pissed off and not at all ready to field any incoming throws.

No one on their team has the ball. The ball is not in the park. I hit the ball out the park. By then I was over home plate and I don't remember anything else, there was too much adrenaline and yelling and my teammates jumping at me and clapping my on the back.

That's kind of where I was after submitting the bid, except the slow, realization that settled in wasn't happiness. *There's a notification that says I submitted a bid. I placed a bid on a property. I do not have the money to pay for a property.*

"Oh my god," I said quietly. "No. Shit. Oh my god."

I slammed my laptop closed, as if that could undo what I'd just done.

CHAPTER 27 - TAYLOR

I came home from work and went to my room to drop off my laptop bag. I found the article about the gourmet doughnut shop in Charleston torn from the magazine and laying on my desk beneath a sticky note with my name. Even from a few feet away I could recognize Dad's blocky and severe handwriting.

Seeing the article after the whole missing graphics debacle, I was ready for murder. I stormed down the stairs to Dad's office, article in hand. He'd just stood to switch off his desk lamp when I barged in, demanding to know why he'd left the article in my room.

"Isn't that neat?" He asked cheerfully. "I didn't know if you'd seen it."

"I saw it."

"Their business model is all wrong though."

I could not be less interested in hearing more reasons why he thought owning a doughnut shop was a bad idea.

"They've made a decent attempt at building customer loyalty but they're a little off on the intricacies of owning and managing a consumer driven business." He held out his hand for the article and started on another diatribe, losing me for a few minutes in all of his business jargon. "And then there's the menu," he sighed. "They're not doing anything to help themselves there."

I narrowed my eyes. "How so?"

"Well for starters," Dad sat back down and turned on the lamp again. I went to look over his shoulder as he brought up the doughnut shop's menu on his computer. "They serve the same five doughnuts day in and day out, with one additional flavor each month."

Venom, Taylor. Say it with venom. You are curious, but you are pissed off.
"Why is that bad?"

He tried to explain and, after mentally filtering out the unnecessary technical language, I think he said something along the lines of the model not allowing the shop to build a customer following.

"If a particular niche of people love February's flavor…" he paused to find the flavor on their menu. "Cherry Chocolate. If a certain group of people decide they like the Cherry Chocolate doughnuts better than anything else, the owners probably think the people will buy all they can during February, since it'll be another year before they can have it again. In reality, your average individual is only going to eat so many doughnuts during a month anyway, and they'll likely have forgotten their beloved Cherry Chocolate doughnut by the following February."

He leaned back in his chair, touching his fingertips together in front of his chest, pausing to make sure I was tracking with him. I was still skeptical about where he was going with all of this. "What's the alternative then?"

"A similar idea – keep the rotating flavors, but rather than changing them out on a monthly basis, narrow it down to a weekly calendar. So you've got your basic flavors but then on Monday, your customers know they can also get Flavors A, B, and C. On Tuesday they'll be able to get Flavors D and E, and so on."

"Sounds like you end up having to do a lot more flavors that way."

"Maybe," he agreed. "But then you get customers who are building a doughnut into their weekly schedule. They know their favorite flavor is available only on Wednesdays so they allow themselves the indulgence of a mid-week treat at your shop. Your business builds slowly and consistently, rather than having drastic peaks that may or may not lead to long-term, returning customers. They call that the Life Time Value of a customer."

It sounded reasonable. But then I caught myself wondering why he'd gone on this tangent anyway. "I thought you weren't pro doughnut shop."

He shrugged noncommittally. "Just sharing some business tips." As he turned to switch off his computer again I caught the smallest hint of a smile on his face.

"Got it."

I thought to tell him about what happened at work, wanting to know if he had any 'business tips' on that particular trauma, but I didn't want to ruin our moment. Plus, I'd told Laura I could be at her house by six and I didn't think it'd be a great idea to make her wait, given the fact that she was sacrificing part of her evening to show me her studio. When she'd called yesterday to follow up on the offer she'd made at Lola's, I hadn't known how perfect the timing it would be. I felt deeply thankful for the distraction as I went back out to my car and typed the address Laura had given me into the GPS on my phone.

Laura lived closer to the city in a neighborhood with a spray of modest-sized homes, many of them wooden and painted in light, pastel colors. I drove down streets heavily shaded by ancient oak trees stretching up from their yards and above the road to twist branches with the trees on the other side. Nestled unassumingly between two larger houses, I found Laura's home – a cottage in comparison to the others. A short sidewalk cut through the lawn to the front door of the small, blue wooden house.

Laura answered the door, her auburn hair in a wild bun, a hammer tucked under her arm and some nails cupped in her hand.

"Hi friend," she said, giving me a hug with her free arm.

Laura stepped aside to let me walk past her into the living room. The house was fairly dated but Laura clearly had a knack for decorating. She'd contrasted the hardwood floors with cream colored walls and furniture to make the room feel larger than it was. A few pieces of art hung on the wall near the door and one larger painting sat on the floor against the opposite wall, evidently waiting to be hung. Following my gaze to the painting, Laura told me it was an early wedding present from Philip. Remembering his sarcasm and the edgy demeanor he held, I could hardly believe he'd painted the piece - a light, ethereal landscape of the ocean. Light blue waves crested into foamy tips and faded into the sky to create a seamless scape of blues and whites and grays.

"Great, huh?"

I nodded in agreement. Despite its size, the piece wouldn't overcrowd the small room but instead seemed like it added a window of light. I felt calmer, standing there looking at it, though it could have been Laura's house in general. Absorbing the feel of a new space, clean and uncluttered, made my mind feel like it could be the same.

A sudden, heavy thud sounded in the other room, and I jumped a little. Laura made a slight frown, calling towards the sound, "You alright, babe?"

She started toward the direction of the sound and explained over her shoulder, "John's working on the guest bedroom."

Around the corner from the living room, Laura stepped into a doorway and handed the hammer to John, who stood on a ladder, holding a curtain rod in one hand. He'd already attached a large, decorative mount to hold the rod against the wall, but the other one was on the ground beneath the ladder. Laura retrieved the piece and handed it back to John.

He noticed me standing in the doorway and lifted the hand with the hammer in a half wave. "Hey, Taylor."

"Hey, how's it going?"

He surveyed his work so far. "Slower than expected."

"Do you need any help?" Laura asked.

John gave a hearty, theatrical laugh. Laura waited, holding back a smile.

He cleared his throat. "I'm great thanks."

"Taylor and I will be out in the studio."

"Have fun. I'll let you know if I fall to my death or something," he said, grinning as Laura turned away, shaking her head.

I followed her down the shortest of hallways and out a door to the backyard. We crossed a wooden deck and made our way to a back house with large, paned windows. Laura unlocked the door, its white paint peeling away near the doorknob, along the bottom and around the window. She led the way inside, not bothering to turn on a light. The windows let in enough sunlight to perfectly illuminate the space with the warm and comforting glow of the early evening sun.

The studio couldn't have been more then twenty feet long and fifteen feet wide but, like the living room, she'd laid out the space perfectly to make it seem larger than it was. In the center of the room's dark stained concrete floors stood a heavy slabbed wood table. Along the two walls without windows was a stretch of L-shaped desk made from the same, thick wood as the table, and several floor to ceiling bookshelves filled with canvas-lined wire baskets, a few books, and a handful of odds and ends. The room was all at once industrial and inviting, humming with invention and creativity. It made a drastic contrast to my cubicle at work.

I brushed my hand along the wooden table top, gazing at the view back at the house. Laura gave me a moment to walk the length of the studio, taking in the details of the space. The books on the shelves intrigued me. I tilted my head to better read the titles on the spines. A couple were related to jewelry or jewelry making, but most covered other subjects — travel, nature, food, architecture.

"Are these for inspiration?" I guessed, thinking of how I'd used other dessert recipes to create the doughnuts. It wasn't quite the same, but similar enough. "Or did you just need the storage space?"

She laughed, "A little of both, but mostly the inspiration."

I came to the L-shaped desk. Above the desk, a cord was stretched between two hooks nailed into the wall. At various places along the cord she'd used small metal clips to hold partially colored sketches of jewelry pieces. "What are these?"

"Just some of my latest ideas. Usually I can send a completed design on paper to the manufacturer, but sometimes I have to get my hands on the materials to finish working it out in my head. Which is what these are for." She went over to the bookshelf and began pulling some of the wire and canvas baskets off of the shelves and placing them on the table. "For the crazier stuff, I'll just make a few of a design myself to see how well it's received."

I joined her at table and saw the baskets were filled with beads, stones, wires, cords, and metals. For every material I could think of that might be used to make jewelry, Laura had it in every color.

"What's this for?" I asked, pulling out a thin carabiner clip holding five metal posts about the length of my pinky finger and in a variety of widths.

"They're metal stamps of my initials." She tilted the bottom of a post up at me. A tiny 'LR' raised from the surface at the end of the post. I looked at the others and saw they all had the same 'LR' but in different sizes.

"The smallest one I use for rings and necklace clasps and things like that," she explained. "I don't use them as much as I used to. But before I was established I needed a way to put my signature on my work to make sure someone else couldn't say it was theirs."

I thought of the Fizz files. "Did you ever have anyone try to steal your work? Like, copy one of your designs?"

"Thank, God, no," she shook her head. "I can't imagine how horrible that would have been."

I could have told her just how horrible it was but I didn't want the pity. Her reply felt sympathetic enough and I realized that someone stealing one of her jewelry designs seemed a lot different than Ryan stealing my work for HRG. You didn't have to know Laura for long to see how she put part of herself into her work. I'd worked hard on my designs for Fizz and I was still walking a fine line between despair and murderous anger about the ordeal, but they weren't a *part* of me. I'd just followed instructions and designed some graphics.

"I've been working on a new ring," Laura said, pulling me back to the present.

The box she was picking through held at least seven different pairs of pliers and wire cutters. She removed a pair with a flat, clamp-like end and then stepped over to the desk again. From the drawer of the desk she pulled out two wooden boxes, one brimming with rough, pale blue stones, the other containing short copper sticks.

"It's one of the designs I decided to make a few by hand before sending to a manufacturer for mass production," she explained, pulling another item from the drawer — a small rounded cone with lines drawn around it at intervals. I assumed it was a mold for rings but didn't interrupt to ask. She pinched a few of the metal sticks from the box and handed one to me to inspect. Looking closer, I could see it was a copper twig.

"John and I were on a hike one day and stopped at a bench to take a break. I was kind of kicking the dirt absentmindedly when I saw a little twig. I picked it up and, as crazy as it sounds, I remember thinking it was the perfect twig. I didn't know what I'd do with it at first, but I brought it back here and eventually began wondering what it'd be like as a ring. So I created a mold and cast these," she nodded at the bronze twigs. "And this," she held up a ring. "Is eventually what I came up with."

I took the ring from her and looked closer. She'd shaped the bronze twig to almost a complete circle but left one end a little higher than the other. Between them she'd placed one of the pale blue stones. The ring looked raw and elegant all at once.

"Do you want to make one?" Laura asked.

"Really?"

She nodded, seeming amused by my surprise.

"I'll show you," she grinned. "You can give me a baking lesson in return."

"I'm really not an expert at baking."

She lowered her chin and gave me a look. "I don't believe that for a second."

I guess I did know a fair amount about baking, but I never thought of myself as proficient enough to teach it. Without another word, Laura began with a ring sizer, showing me how to use it on my own finger as an example. She told me how to shape the bronze twig using the cone I'd correctly guessed was a mold. She demonstrated each step on her piece of copper and then gave me the tools, patiently talking me through how to do what she'd just done. When we finished, she dropped her completed ring in the box with the other's she completed, but shook her head when I moved to drop mine in.

"Keep it."

"Really?"

She nodded and I understood why she used the ring sizer on my hand. I thought it was just for the sake of demonstration, but the ring slipped on perfectly.

Laura smiled. "Isn't it wonderful to create something with your hands?"

"Yeah." The familiar liveliness brought doughnuts to mind for the briefest of moments before I pushed the thought away.

"Thanks for taking the time to show me all of this."

"I'm happy to," Laura said as she started replacing the materials we used. "I don't think I'd be where I am if so many people hadn't done the same for me."

"What? Let you tour their studios?"

She laughed and handed me a basket to return to the bookshelf. "Well, yes, that, but also taking the time to teach and encourage me about art and business. Creative jobs can be lonely ones."

"It doesn't seem so bad."

"It's not horrible but it has its moments. I think expecting the loneliness helps. Lola taught me a lot about that."

"Really?"

"I met her at an art fair where I was doing one of my first jewelry showcases. She bought a bracelet and the next thing I knew we were having this deep conversation about art and creativity. She wanted to know who 'my people' were and where I was getting creative support and encouragement — neither of which I had at the time."

"She does tend to get right to the point."

Laura smiled. "One of my favorite qualities about her."

She handed me the last basket to shelve and then I followed her out of the studio. The sun was beginning to set as she locked the door behind us and I felt reluctant to head home. Inside, John had finished hanging the drapes and was packing up the tools when we walked past. I waved goodbye and hugged Laura at the door. "Come over any time," she said.

"Careful. I'll take you up on it." I crossed the lawn to my car, wishing I could live her life for a little bit longer.

CHAPTER 28 - DANIEL

"Damn hives," I said to my reflection in the bathroom mirror. Tiny red bumps flamed across my chest and shoulders, around my back and down the insides of my arms. They appeared about half an hour after my genius idea to put a bid on a property worth more than my life. Thank God someone ended up outbidding me but the hives remained and they itched like hell.

I went back into my bedroom and turned the ceiling fan up another notch, hoping the cool air would help. Not that it mattered anymore. I'd given up on sleep. I first got in bed a little after midnight, feeling exhausted from the panic of the online real estate auction, the itching hives, and the invisible chokehold on my chest, squeezing tighter with every thought of work, Dom Moskovitz, Steve Mobley, and all of the horrible things that followed. Four hours later I still hadn't seen any sleep.

Rachel called earlier in the evening, probably just wanting to talk about the day, but I didn't answer. She would know something was wrong in less than five minutes. She always knew. I sent her a text saying I was working on doughnut stuff with Taylor. She sent something back full of smiles and exclamation points, wishing us a good time. I felt even worse about myself.

By five in the morning, I couldn't stand being in my room any longer. I threw on a pair of running shorts and a t-shirt, slipped quietly outside so I wouldn't wake anyone else in the house, and took off jogging down the street. Even at such an early hour the air wasn't cool. It'd be a few more weeks, the beginning of September at the earliest, before the temperature started to chill at night.

I focused on the sound of my steps, hoping to lull myself into the familiar, calming rhythm of running. My chest still hurt and I couldn't tell whether or not running made it worse. What if all of the sudden I just gave out and hit the pavement? Was I old enough to have a heart attack? I hadn't brought my phone and it'd probably be a long time before anyone driving by saw me. By the time they found my body it'd be too late to resuscitate me. I turned around and started jogging back towards the house.

When I got to the office, I didn't know what to do with myself. It seemed quiet, but probably wasn't any quieter than normal. Should I sit down and start working? Go straight to Tom's office? I knew Tom frequently had meetings first thing in the morning – would he want to talk to me before or after?

Tom *did* say I was a valuable asset to the company. Maybe all of this would blow over and six months from now, no one would even remember it. I turned on my computer and started work as if everything were normal. Footsteps sounded from the hallway leading from the elevator and I looked up in time to see Kevin round the corner, visibly surprised as he met my eye.

"What?" I asked.

His eyes avoided mine and he shook his head. "Nothing."

I watched him meticulously unpack his things and knock over a cup of pens with his bag. His eyes flicked up to mine and then darted away as he scrambled to pick up the pens. He sat down and adjusted his tie.

"Acting a little odd there, buddy."

He became intensely focused on his computer screen.

I didn't have much to lose at that point so I went out on a limb. "Surprised to see me?"

He looked up with panicked eyes and his mouth opened and closed like a fish. Before he could reply Dax came bounding in. "Danny, you're alive!"

Had Tom already started telling people about what happened?

"What'd you have?" Dax asked, and then I realized he was only referencing my lie about a doctors appointment. He had no idea about Moskovitz or the doughnut research during work. He leaned on my desk and looked at me seriously. "Heartworms?"

"Only dogs get that you idiot."

"Right," he agreed, barely dodging the punch I aimed at his arm as he went back to his desk, laughing at his own joke.

Kevin was zoned back in on his computer screen but I still felt like he was watching me. Nothing to be done about that though. He was easy enough to ignore with Dax around. I started in on my usual routine, half-listening as Dax told a story he'd heard at the gym last night. Bhavesh came in, nodded to all three of us, and we settled into our rhythms. I never realized how much I appreciated our pattern – my arrival at the office, always followed by Kevin, Bhavesh, and then Dax. Dax's stories and the way Bhavesh kind of acted like he was above all of us without being a jerk about it. Even Kevin's lurking presence added to the whole scene and I felt genuinely appreciative for it.

Maybe the whole ordeal with Steve Mobley happened so I'd have a wake up call and realize how good I had it. Rachel might be leaps and bounds ahead of me in her career but I was doing okay. I had a place at the company, Dax and Bhavesh were kind of my friends, and Kevin added color to the day, if nothing else. My mind dialed down to a calmer level than I'd experienced in days. I breathed deeply and almost smiled to myself until a well aimed stress ball hit me in the chin. I flinched like a girl, which caused Dax no end of amusement, but I couldn't even feel angry about it. I probably wouldn't have picked these guys as the three people I wanted to spend fifty odd hours a week with, but I was stuck with them for now. In a way, they were kind of like family and that counted for something.

CHAPTER 29 - TAYLOR

At work the next morning, I idly stared at the little stone on the ring I'd made at Laura's, willing it to bring back the peace and contentment I'd felt making it in the studio. I'd barely slept the night before, trying to anticipate what the day would hold. For the life of me, I couldn't imagine what Ryan would do or how I should act. The last thing I'd expected was to be ignored, but that was exactly what happened. Two hours into the morning and I still hadn't seen Ryan, Bill, or even Rand for that matter. I hadn't looked for any of them, but normally someone passed by or could be heard down the hall. A couple of times I rolled my chair to the opening of my cube so I could glance around somewhat inconspicuously, but I didn't see anything.

Without the Fizz account I was back to not having anything to work on. When I couldn't stand trying to look busy any longer, I decided to look for Bill. I couldn't just sit around and wait for another project to come knocking. When I didn't find him in his office, the conference room, or Ryan's office, I shuffled down the hall to Shay's desk.

"Um, hi, do you know where Bill is?"

"He's out today," she said without looking up from her phone. "So is Ryan."

"Really? Where?"

"Meetings."

Normally I could deal with Shay's attitude just fine but for some reason it really set me off right then. I gritted my teeth together and had only a passing thought that maybe I should keep my mouth shut. "Did anyone ever tell you that you're supposed to actually *look* at someone when you talk to them?"

Her eyes slid off her phone and met mine with a resentment I'd never seen from her. She let her phone clatter to the desk and looked at me expectantly.

"Please," I held up a hand. "Don't let me distract you from your thrilling text messages." She opened her mouth to talk but I kept going. "No, no. I'm good. Just thought I'd share that tidbit with you in case you ever decided to become a well-mannered person."

I took off down the hall before she could respond, my heart hammering in my chest. I called her a name under my breath and went back to my computer. I wasted the next hour reading through blogs and other useless websites. When it finally reached a socially acceptable hour for lunch, I grabbed my bag and headed for the car, exiting from a side door to avoid Shay. I was crossing the office parking lot, already radiating with the late summer heat, when a thought dawned on me — *I could leave. I could just not go back.* I glanced in the rear view mirror, half expecting Shay to be watching me. Through the glass of the front window, I could see she wasn't even at her desk anymore.

I pulled out of the parking lot and drove straight towards home. I parked on the far side of Lola's house so my parents wouldn't be able to see my car. Lola welcomed me in without any visible surprise, which made me appreciate her even more than usual in that moment. She knew nothing about why I was there, yet she was all smiles and no judgment.

"To what do I owe this wonderful visit?" I waited as she handed me a glass of tea and we settled into the chairs in the front room before I let my words start tumbling out. I told her how I suspected Ryan of sabotaging my computer. Somehow that led into the story of Haleigh ditching me, which brought on a lengthy explanation of how I had no friends and then, tears rolling down my face, I finished with a long-winded bit about Laura's studio. Lola was silent for a moment after I finished.

"I mean, have you seen her studio?" I wiped pathetically at my eyes.

"No." The corner of her mouth lifted a little.

"It's beautiful," I said sadly.

"I'm sure it is." She thought for a moment before asking, "If you had a doughnut shop, what would it look like?"

"I don't know, I haven't thought about it."

Lola waited for an answer so I let my gaze drift to the window and tried to imagine what it would be like. The name on our license was still

Beach Nuts, thanks to Daniel. I didn't doubt that it was possible to change but I didn't want to tango with the people at the licensing office again.

"Our name is Beach Nuts," I started.

"What is a beach nut?"

"I don't know, a beachy doughnut, I guess. Daniel came up with it."

She raised an eyebrow but said nothing, so I continued. "A beach thing might not be entirely bad from a simple design standpoint. That's kind of what I've been working on for Fizz. I still think their product is pretty stupid but the branding sort of appeals to me. The green and yellow would have to go. That would be too bold for a doughnut."

"The walls could be the color of sand and we could do wooden floors like a boardwalk and lots of natural light. You would step inside and everything would feel clean and fresh and you could smell the toasted coconut of our piña colada doughnuts wafting from the kitchen."

Lola smiled, shaking her head slightly, "You've got something."

"Maybe," I sighed. At the very least the doughnuts were fun to dream about.

I glanced at the clock on her wall. It took me a little less than ten minutes to get to the office and I'd already been at Lola's for nearly thirty. If I was going back, I needed to go. I said goodbye and snuck carefully to my car, keeping an eye out for either of my parents. Through the bushes I saw our garage door open and Daniel's car parked inside.

I glanced at my phone to make sure I had the time right. I couldn't imagine why he'd be home this early. Curiosity winning out, I cut across the driveway, tentatively went inside the garage door, and inched through the house, half expecting to catch Daniel running by, only at home to retrieve something he'd forgotten before heading back to work.

I finally found him outside, stretched on a lounge chair beside the pool, taking a long sip of a beer as I approached. Some sort of rash or abnormally speckled sunburn spread across his bare arms and chest. Three empty bottles sat on the other side of the chair. He wore sunglasses and hadn't said anything yet, making it impossible for me to know if he'd heard or seen me come outside. I made sure to stand out of punching distance in case I startled him.

"Hey," I said.

"Sup," he replied, unperturbed. Either he'd seen me or he'd downed just enough beer to lull himself into a remarkable state of Zen.

"You do this often?"

"Nope."

I could see that his eyes were closed beneath his sunglasses and I wondered if he wanted me to leave him alone.

"What's the occasion?"

He sighed heavily. Finally he answered, "I'm ushering in unemployed life."

"Did you quit?" I asked, nervous for the implications of either answer.

"Nope."

"Oh," I said.

"Yep."

I bit my lip. We were on thin ice, that much I knew. "Why?"

He took another sip of beer and didn't say anything for a minute. I waited, careful not push him.

"Do you want the long answer or the short answer?"

"Um. Whichever you feel like telling, I guess."

"We'll hit the highlights," he said in a light tone that freaked me out a little bit. "I met a guy in Vegas, he told me he could help me find investments if I needed some good leads, my ass was on the line for a big client, I panicked, called the guy, and ended up screwing over our client which, in turn, screwed Colson Caldwell over and, in turn, screwed me over."

"Wow."

He took another long sip, finishing the beer, and tossed the bottle to the side with the other three.

"Surely you guys recommend investments that don't work out sometimes though, right? That happens?"

"Yes," he agreed. "It does. According to my boss, it's not so much the 'what' of the matter, it's more so the 'how' and the 'why.' It also didn't help that the CFO's nephew made a complaint about my Internet browsing history."

"Oh," I said, uncomfortable for what I thought was coming.

"Doughnut stuff," he said. "Get your mind out of the gutter."

"Oh." I stared at my feet. "Coworkers suck," I said, thinking of Ryan.

His jaw tightened and his fists clenched, but I didn't say anything. The last thing I wanted was to give him a reason to direct his anger at me. I didn't know what else to say though. I didn't know how to be his friend or offer consolation without sounding trite. Anything I could think of was more likely to annoy rather than comfort him.

"Forget them," he said eventually. He sat up and pulled off his sunglasses to look at me. "Are you still serious about doing Beach Nuts?"

"Can we not say, 'doing' beach nuts?" I smiled but he just looked at me, waiting for a real response. We'd had this basic conversation more times than I could count but now it was serious in a terrifyingly real sort of way. "Are you sure you shouldn't keep working until we get further along?"

"I just lost my job."

"Yeah, but you could get another one, just for a little while."

"All that would do is slow us down. Why wait when we have a plan?"

I *wanted* to dive in head first. I *wanted* to quit my job, start a business with Daniel, and do something I loved. But I wanted someone to tell me it was okay. I wanted something or someone to validate our plan.

"I need to think." I turned and started for the house.

"Will you bring me another beer?" He called after me.

"No." If we were going to do this, I needed him sober.

CHAPTER 30 - DANIEL

My phone buzzed with a text from Rachel.

You. Answer the door.

Odd. I went downstairs and opened the front door to Rachel standing with her arms crossed and an impatient look on her face.

"Did you knock?" I asked her, stepping aside to let her in.

"Yes."

"Sorry, I didn't hear." Not too surprising. I'd been kind of out of it since I'd come in from the pool, probably from too much sun and beer.

She pushed past me and I followed her up the stairs to my room. She stood in the middle of the room with her arms crossed over her chest while I sank down onto the futon. "Do you want to sit?"

She looked like she didn't but, after debating it for a second, dropped her purse down on the ground and took a seat on the far end of the futon. "Want to tell me what's going on?"

I took a breath. "Okay." The sun was setting blindingly through the window, right above her shoulder. I got up to close the blinds so I could see her without squinting. "We need to talk," I said when I sat back down.

She raised an eyebrow. "I gathered that. You've been ignoring my texts and calls."

"Something happened."

Her eyes widened. "What?"

I took a breath. I didn't know where to start. I guess the beginning. The beginning would be good.

"Daniel, just say it. You're freaking me out."

203

Another breath. "Okay. I met this guy at the conference and—"

"The one in Las Vegas?"

"How many other conferences have I been to in the last six months?"

"I'm just making sure we're on the same page."

I hated when she asked unnecessary questions. I told her about meeting Steve Mobley, my initial skepticism about his offer, and the details she'd already heard about Pierce Fenner but seemed important to recap. I explained how big of a deal the Moskovitz account was, how Kevin had been acting like even more of an asshole lately and what Dax told me about him being the nephew of our CFO. I confessed that I panicked about not being able to dredge up enough investments for Moskovitz, how I took up Steve Mobley on his offer, which seemed great until the investment fell through. I told her about Tom calling me into his office, how he knew I'd been wrangled into a microcap scheme, and that they looked at my web history after a tip off from Kevin.

"And then he called me in this morning and told me they were letting me go."

"Okay," Rachel said after a moment. "That's not that bad."

"*Not that bad?*"

"Don't get mad at me," she warned. "The way you start stories is horrible."

I glared at her. It wasn't the time for nitpicking about the way I told stories.

"It's okay though," she said gently, putting a hand on my knee. "This isn't catastrophic."

"I got *fired* from my *job*, Rachel. I have car payments and insurance and a million other expenses."

"You'll get another job."

"Who's going to offer me a job after I got fired? Obviously I'm inadequate and incapable of even the most normal, bottom of the barrel work tasks."

She shook her head. "You're not inadequate."

"Pretty sure Tom would say differently. If I was worth anything they would have kept me on."

Her mouth tightened into a firm line but then her expression softened. "I hate when you talk about yourself like that. From the way you tell it, I don't think Tom really wanted to fire you, but his hands were tied. These things happen. You can either see it as an opportunity to go do something better or you can whine about how you don't think you're good enough."

I wanted to get on board with what she was saying. I wanted to believe it was just an unfortunate series of circumstances. I also wanted to her to say that she didn't think less of me for all of this, that she still believed I was great somehow. I propped my elbows on my knees and dropped my head in my hands. "I'm an idiot. I could have done better."

"Probably," she agreed. "But you're not an idiot."

I shifted a hand away from my eye to look at her. She tried not to smile.

"Would a compliment kill you every now and then?" I asked.

"You wouldn't believe me even if I did compliment you."

"Yeah I would."

She straightened her face and tried to sound meaningful and serious. "Daniel," she said, leaning forward. "I think you're an incredible person and I deeply respect you." She watched my face for a moment and then laughed. "See? You don't believe me."

"Not when you use that tone, no." I sighed heavily and leaned back. "So now what?"

"Go do something else," she said.

I closed my eyes, resisting the urge to tell her how annoying it was when she made things sound more simple than they were.

"Here's a crazy idea," she continued. "You could start a doughnut shop."

I kept my eyes closed.

"Way out of left field, I know."

When I opened my eyes to see she wasn't smiling anymore. "Are you serious?"

She shrugged. "Why not?"

Because there's not a great chance it'll work, I thought. *And if I fail again then how many years would it take me to earn back what I'd lost? Would you even stick around that long?*

"Stop it," Rachel said. "Quit beating yourself up. Take a chance."

"Get out of my head."

"You're horrible at hiding your emotions."

Not much point in arguing with her. "You really think it's worth a shot?"

She nodded. "I do."

"Okay." I took a deep breath. "Yeah. Okay. I can totally do this."

Rachel kept nodding with an amused look on her face. Taylor and I could do it, we just needed to start moving forward.

"I did something really dumb the other day," I told Rachel.

"Uh oh. What?"

"I kind of placed a four hundred thousand dollar bid on some retail space."

"I take back what I said earlier. You are an idiot."

I frowned.

"Kidding. I think that's your next step though. You guys need to find a place."

"There's no way we'll get approved for a loan. Not without my job."

"No, probably not," she said, leaning back and tilting her head to look towards the ceiling. The fact that she even wanted to help after I shut her out was more than I deserved. I didn't expect her to come up with a solution too, but leave it to Rachel try to find one anyway.

"You've talked to your parents?" Rachel asked.

"Enough to know it's not an option."

She closed her eyes in thought. "Don't they have, like, collaborative kitchens or something?"

"Doubt it. Not for retail use, at least. It doesn't need to be figured out right now, why don't we go get dinner or–"

"Hush. I'm thinking."

I went to the closet to grab a pair of shoes. Let her puzzle it out. She'd throw out a few more ideas and then give it up for a while. I sat on the edge of the bed with my back to her while I slipped on my shoes. The futon creaked as she sat up suddenly.

"Wait, I've got it."

"Hm?"

"I have an idea."

I turned around to look at her. "What?"

She grabbed her purse and bounded out of the room. "Come on," she called, already halfway down the hallway.

I followed her to her car at my own pace. When I climbed into the passenger seat, she already had the engine going and the car in drive.

She handed me her phone while she pulled away from the curb. "Can you text my brother?"

"Robert?" I assumed she was referring to her youngest brother, the only one who still lived in town.

"Yeah, see if he's home."

I texted him and fiddled with the radio while we waited for a reply. Her phone buzzed before I managed to settle on a station.

"He's home."

"Tell him we're coming by. And not to tell Mom."

I tapped out her reply. "Why are we going there?"

"Robert and I had lunch last week and he told me about the pizza place he's been working at all summer to save up for college. Just a summer job, nothing remarkable, but he said he really likes the owner. The guy's around a lot, likable, pitches in with the grunt work, gets to know the employees."

"Great." I waited for the point.

"Robert can introduce us to the owner."

"And?"

She looked at me expectantly.

"Eyes on the road."

She kept looking at me for another defiant moment before sliding her eyes forward again. "Pizza places have commercial kitchens and they aren't open on Saturday or Sunday mornings. If this owner is as cool as Robert says he is, maybe he'd be willing to make a deal and let you guys use the space on the weekends."

I thought about the logistics for a moment. "Oh my god. That's brilliant."

The corners of her mouth turned up a little. When we got to her parents' house, she pulled up to the curb and parked. We sat inside her car waiting for Robert to come outside. After ten minutes and no sign of him I suggested we just go inside.

"No," she said firmly.

"Why?"

She gave a wary look at the house. "My mom is probably home and she'll just want to talk."

"Why is that so bad?"

"Lately she's been watching a lot of reality TV shows about weddings." She slid a glance at me. "Now she wants to discuss it every time I see her."

"The shows?"

"Weddings. Hypothetical ones."

"Oh."

Finally the front porch light flicked on and her brother Robert came loping outside. Whenever I went a while without seeing him, it shocked me all over again to see how gangly he was. Seriously, the kid is all limbs and knobby joints. Rachel and her mom claimed he'd fill out in college like her older brothers, but he was a few weeks away from starting his freshman year and he looked the same as he always had.

Rachel rolled down her window as Robert approached. He looked up and down the street before bending down next to the car and leaning in the open window. He lowered his voice and asked, "You got the goods?" His eyes darted down the street again, as if someone might be watching.

Rachel unlocked the doors. "Robert, get in the car."

He stood and got in the back seat. I glanced in the rear view mirror. "How it's going?" I asked him, trying to be pleasant.

"Sup."

The guy has the conversation skills of a twelve year old. He tossed his head back in a useless attempt to get his long hair out of his eyes.

"Where are we going?" Rachel asked.

I glanced back again. Robert's face was illuminated by the blue glow of his phone. "Um," he hesitated, distracted by whatever he was looking at on the phone. "Work."

Rachel glared at the rear view mirror. "I realize that, Genius."

"Um." Robert leaned forward onto the center console. "It's kind of by the high school." He attempted to flip his hair back again. "Just drive in that general direction."

"Is it before or after you get to the school?"

"After." He leaned back and pulled out his phone again.

"How far?"

"Not very."

She pressed her lips together. "Can you be a little more specific?"

"Um." He took a moment to pull his attention away from the phone. "I'll tell you when we're close."

Rachel tightened her grip on the steering wheel.

"It's like a surprise," I said with mock cheerfulness. She gave me a murderous look.

While we drove, Rachel briefly explained why we wanted to talk to Robert's boss. "Right or left?" She asked when we came to a stop sign near the high school.

"Either," Robert said without looking up from his phone.

Rachel took a deep breath and turned right.

"Left is probably faster though."

Rachel looked at me, irritated and expecting me to say or do something. I just shrugged. Her hands clenched and unclenched on the steering wheel.

Robert got us there eventually. The pizza place sat on the corner of a run down little shopping center next to a dollar store. Only a few cars filled the surrounding parking spaces and I could only see one person through the tinted window with *Louie's Pizza Parlor* painted across it. We seemed to have missed the dinner crowd, assuming that there even was one.

I tried to imagine people flocking here for Saturday morning doughnut. "This is it?"

Robert tossed his hair. "Yeah." He unbuckled his seatbelt and slid out of the back seat. Rachel and I followed him to the door that sounded a faint, crackly bell tone as we stepped inside.

A kid behind the cash register with long hair like Robert's nodded his head in greeting. He had a name tag labeled, Mark, pinned to the front of his uniform – a red t-shirt and plain black pants.

"Sup, man." Robert approached the counter. "Joe here?"

Mark shook his head. "Nah, he left about an hour ago."

Robert looked back at Rachel and me. "Sorry," he shrugged. Rachel and I glanced at each other.

"He's normally here," Mark said. "If you call and ask for him, someone can pass you along." Mark reached below the counter. "Here," he offered a takeout menu. "Number's on the back."

I took the menu from him. "Thanks." I kind of liked the guy. He seemed like a more competent person than Robert.

We got back in the car and took Robert home. Rachel and I watched from the car as he disappeared inside the house and flicked the porch light off.

"It could have been worse," I said as she pulled away from the house. She let out an exasperated breath. I turned the takeout menu over in my hand. "It's too bad the owner wasn't there though. I was hoping Robert could introduce us."

"Robert probably wouldn't have been much help."

"I guess."

She shook her head. "Seriously. I think it would have done more damage than good."

It wasn't too hard to imagine Robert finding a way to botch the thing. Maybe she was right. "Okay, I'll talk to Taylor about it."

"Is she on board with things now?"

"I'm working on it, but she hasn't quit her job or anything yet."

"You think she will though?"

"I hope so."

Rachel nodded encouragingly. "I'm sure she will."

There was no telling what Taylor would do though. Realizing how much I needed her brought back the anxious chest pangs I'd grown familiar with over the past few weeks. In a way, I was dependent on her now. It didn't sit well.

"It'll be okay," Rachel said again, patting my arm. I told myself to believe she was right.

CHAPTER 31 - TAYLOR

I wanted someone else's opinion on what to do about the doughnuts. Against my better judgment I went to Dad for advice.

"I think you know where I stand on the issue," he said, frowning from behind his desk.

"Can you try to be more unbiased?" I asked. "Pretend I'm not the daughter that you wanted to have a better degree and a better job and just tell me if you really think it's a horrible idea?"

The crease between his brow deepened. "Who said I wanted you to have a better degree or job?"

"Are you denying it?"

He shrugged his shoulders. "It's your life," he said. "You're the one who has to live with the decisions you make."

I looked at my feet. "I still care about your opinion."

"I can't tell you what to do."

"I don't *need* you to tell me what to *do*," I insisted. My voice wavered, caught between wanting to scream and cry at the same time. "I just want to know what you *think*. Tell me what you think." I wanted him to walk with me through it and tell me it'd be okay if I failed. I wanted him to say he believed in me. I also really wanted him to hug me.

He sighed and I could see the internal debate going on behind his eyes, but he was unyielding. "You need to figure this one out on your own."

I stormed out of his office, too mad to say anything else. That conversation ended my search for advice. I knew what everyone else would say. In my mind I could easily picture the dividing line between those in favor and those opposed. What was the point in asking for advice when I already knew what people would say? All of their opinions would be shaped by *their* circumstances and their attempts at putting *themselves* in my shoes. There wasn't anyone who fully knew me or understood my situation well enough to offer guidance.

I still believed Ryan was behind my missing Fizz images, and it didn't help to know that quitting my job would make him think he'd won. Rand would think the same and I wanted them to understand it was bigger than that. I debated holding off, just to put some distance between the events, but ultimately that seemed pointless, just like Daniel said. Either I was quitting or I wasn't. It didn't make sense to postpone the inevitable.

My mind wasn't entirely made up when I went into the office, when I waved hello to Rand, or when I sat down to my desk, wondering if it'd be one of my last times to do so. The morning began as all the recent ones had and the monotony settled over me like usual. I lapsed into a daze while reorganizing the files on my computer when Ryan's voice startled me back into reality.

"Boss wants you," he said curtly and continued down the hallway.

The only time Ryan ever seemed annoyed was when he'd been slighted by Bill. Could Bill be bringing me back on the Fizz account? I stood and smoothed my dress. Maybe Bill had found out about Ryan stealing my work. As I approached Rand's office, I wondered if he had believed me after all and told Bill my suspicions. I smiled warmly to him as I passed. He'd come to my rescue after all. Outside Bill's office, I paused to take a breath, and then tapped on the door as I walked inside.

"Ryan said you wanted to see me?"

"Yes," Bill said, focused on his computer.

He pulled slowly away, finding a stopping place in whatever he was doing. I wondered whether it was the graphics themselves or a tell-all email from Rand. Either way, I needed to focus on remaining calm and not letting the emotion of the conflict with Ryan show.

"Yes," Bill said again, pushing back from the desk.

I steeled myself to humbly and coolly accept his apology. It wasn't the time to gloat or play games.

"I need your help with something."

"Alright," I said, wondering if I'd have to do another version of the branding after all. Or maybe the meeting with Casey had gone well and we were moving forward?

"Two things. One, Ryan and I will be meeting with Casey and her business partner on Thursday. Can you find a place for lunch and make a reservation? Something girly, whatever. Your call. Two, we're working on a new client who is interested in seeing some of our work. The owner is about to be off the grid for a few weeks and wants hard copies of our reels. I need you to send the DVD's over to him. I'll forward you his address."

Bill switched back to the computer, presumably to forward the address, while I worked on picking my jaw up off the floor. Scheduling lunch and a mail errand.

"Got it?" He asked, looking back to me.

"Yes, sir."

I quit, I thought as left his office. The words repeated over and over in my head as I called a restaurant to make lunch reservations for Thursday. I'm surprised I didn't accidentally type them as I sent an email to Bill, relaying the restaurant location and reservation time. *I quit*. I stalked to the supply closet and pulled bubble mailers off of the top shelf for the DVD's. *I quit*. I scribbled the address Bill had given me on the mailers. *I quit*. In one short exchange, Bill managed to demote me to secretarial duties. I started to drop the DVD packages into our outgoing mail bin when Bill's voice caught me.

"Will you take those to the post office? I need them on their way ASAP."

"I have a doctors appointment in an hour. I may not be able to make it back to the office in between."

"That's fine," he said, already turned away, tapping at his phone as he returned to his office.

The quickness and ease of the lie startled me, but it gave me an odd sense of pride as well. Getting to the post office and mailing the packages took less than fifteen minutes which I reasoned left me with roughly two hours before I needed to be back at work. I drove to Lola's practically in autopilot.

When I got there, Lola ushered me inside only moments after I'd knocked, as if already expecting my impromptu visit. I followed her into the kitchen where she was making tea and arranging flowers cut from her garden, just as she had been on that first day I'd come over. I smiled a little thinking of how far we'd come. But what was our relationship really founded on? How much of our time had I spent whining about my job and endlessly debating this doughnut stuff? I'd been needy and unstable and I hated myself for it.

I settled onto a stool at the counter and dropped my chin onto my folded arms. I tried to think of what to say but not a single thing came to mind that hadn't already been said. I closed my eyes. I wanted to go home, get in bed, and not wake up for a very long time. I heard the click of the stove burner switch off and the pot of tea slide to a cool burner. The faucet turned on and off and then there was the tinkling of metal as the bracelets on Lola's wrists shook dry. Footsteps moved softly closer and then the stool next to me pushed back.

"What are you thinking?"

I kept my head down. "I don't want to do it anymore," I said weakly.

Lola put an arm around my shoulders and we sat quietly for a moment. "I wish you could see how much freedom you have," she said softly, her voice full of emotion.

For the life of me, I couldn't imagine what freedom she was talking about. I'd never felt more trapped in my entire life.

"Think of your talents and your dreams and imagine where they lead you. Put them together and what do they add to?"

It was a rhetorical question. "I think we both know the answer to that."

"Then go do it."

"It's not that easy."

"Is anything worth having ever easy?"

"No, but, *damn it.*" I pushed off the stool and her arm fell from my shoulders. I'd never sworn in front of Lola before. I felt like I'd just sworn in front of my grandmother, but she kept looking at me with her calm, watchful eyes. I paced away from her. "I have no idea what I'm doing. I don't know what's right." I swatted at a lock of hair that fell into my eyes, unreasonably annoyed by it. "I've barely been at HRG for three months. My parents won't tell me what they think, Dan keeps pressuring me to quit because he's unemployed and now it really matters. Haleigh just sits there *judging* me and acting like she knows what this is like, and all of the sudden I'm at this high stakes crossroad and have to make a decision and I don't know what to choose."

I took a deep breath, went back to the stool, and sat down again. I propped my elbows on the counter and dropped my head in my hands. "I don't know what's right. I just want to do what's right."

"There is not a right or wrong in this, darling. Look at the big picture. You have a job. If you quit, no one is going to die. People quit jobs all the time. You're going to try something else and if it does not work out, you can go get another job."

I noticed she'd stop talking about the doughnuts hypothetically. All I could say was, "Okay." She patted my shoulder and then stood to finish the tea. She didn't give it time to cool, the tea was still warm when she filled our glasses, but I didn't care.

"You are going to be fine," she said while we drank our tea.

I nodded and mostly believed her, but found myself thinking of my parents. Fine that they didn't want to sway me one way or another with their opinions, but would it have been so hard for them to say Lola's same words? *You are going to be fine.*

On my way back to the office, my heart started crawling into my throat, lodging itself there with no indication of going away. I stopped by Rand's office first, trying to delay the inevitable.

"What's going on?" He asked as I sat in the chair next to his desk.

My heart thudded in my chest. *Did he know?* "Nothing," I said, trying to sound casual.

"Cool." His eyes went back to his computer. He didn't know. I was being paranoid. My presence didn't seem to bother him so I stayed, trying to work up the nerve to go talk to Bill.

"That's a cool ring," Rand said, interrupting my thoughts.

I looked down at my hand. I hadn't realized I'd been fidgeting with the ring I'd made with Laura.

"Is it new?"

"Kind of. I made it actually."

"Wow. That's awesome."

"Yeah." I remembered the satisfaction I'd felt after making it and it was like a final puzzle piece slipping into place. *This is worth struggling for — to create and connect with people and let all of it intertwine with passion and purpose, meaning and depth.*

I took a deep breath, stood, and started down the hall. I sort of prayed Bill wouldn't be in his office but, of course, he was. I gave my usual tentative knock and stepped inside when he acknowledged me.

"Do you have a moment?"

"Sure," he said, giving me his attention immediately. The directness unsettled me.

"Um. Well." I clasped my hands together. They were already sweating. "I've decided to leave HRG."

The briefest flicker of surprise showed in Bill's eyes before his neutral expression returned.

"I've really enjoyed getting to be a part of the company," I added quickly. "But I've spent a lot of time working through this decision and I don't believe I'll be a good fit with HRG long term."

Bill blinked at me a few times, his face void of emotion. "When will your last day be?"

I hadn't thought about that. "Next Friday," I said, but it sounded like a question. Two weeks seemed safe enough but I wasn't really up to speed on quitting protocol.

He looked at me a moment, his jaw tight. Finally he said, "Don't worry about it."

"Sorry?"

"You can go ahead and pack up your things."

"Right now?"

"Yes."

"But the two weeks?"

"No need," he shrugged. "You don't have any projects going on right now, do you?"

"No," I agreed hesitantly. His cold, calmness alarmed me a little bit. I hadn't expected him to yell or anything but normally he was all fire and energy.

"Not much point in dragging it out then," he said.

Lest I had any lingering feelings of guilt for leaving them short-staffed, I had my confirmation. I was not needed. I shook Bill's reluctant hand and went to Rand's office.

"Hey, so, I'm leaving HRG."

He looked at me for a long moment and then dropped his gaze to his computer. His eyes closed as he pinched the bridge of his nose, underneath his glasses.

"Rand?"

He let out a breath and looked at me again. "How come?"

I hesitated. I had a diplomatic answer ready if Bill wanted a reason, but it didn't seem right to use vague half-truths on Rand. I wouldn't necessarily call him my friend but he'd been a kind of friend to me at HRG. He wouldn't understand though. "It's just not a good fit," I told him.

His mouth opened as he started to say something and stopped. "You'll be missed," he said simply.

"Thanks."

I'd never brought much into my cubicle so there wasn't much to pack. I threw a few pens into my laptop bag and tossed a handful of papers in the trash. I nervously made for the door, hoping not to run into Bill or Ryan. Neither was in sight.

When I neared Shay's desk I paused. We hadn't spoken since I went off on her. I cleared my throat. "So, um, I'm leaving HRG."

She didn't look up from her computer. "'Kay."

"Is there anything I, like, need to sign or something?"

Her eyes dully flickered up to mine. "No."

"Okay."

She went back to her computer and I walked past her, shaking my head. I walked out the front door. *For the last time*, I told myself, thinking it would make it feel more real. It didn't. I dropped my bag onto the passenger seat of my car and glanced back at the building before climbing in. I felt nothing. No regret, no excitement. All I felt was a quiet grimness, as if what I'd just done was small and insignificant and the truly hard part was still to come.

When I told Mom and Dad at dinner that night, there was the briefest moment before they said anything, they just looked at me, their faces carefully set in neutral expressions.

"So what are you going to do instead?" Mom asked calmly.

I met Daniel's eyes across the table and willed him to help. When he turned to speak I felt a rush of grateful affection for him.

"We're going to do Beach Nuts," he grinned.

My confidence died a quick death. In response to Mom and Dad's widened eyes, Daniel explained the name.

"Do you have any idea what kind of hours that's going to take?" Dad asked.

"Or how little money those things make?" Mom added.

Daniel and I exchanged a glance again. It'd be useless to counter their arguments.

"Yes," I said simply.

They looked at us again with that mildly sad look and returned to eating. The conversation shifted topics but their disappointment hung heavy in the room. After dinner, Daniel and I retreated upstairs to my room.

"We need to narrow down our menu," Daniel said, eyeing our collection of doughnut ideas we'd laid out on the floor. I sort of admired him for his lack of caring about Mom and Dad's opinions. I felt like a little sick to my stomach but he looked and sounded perfectly fine.

"I know we can't know for sure which ones are going to work yet," he said. "But we can sift through the flavors that are too similar to each other and ditch any repeats."

I nodded. "Let's also ditch the ones that don't fit into our beach theme in some way or another." In a few minutes we'd worked the list down to ten options, knowing we'd probably lose three or four more once we started testing them out.

"Let's go try some of these," I suggested.

He picked up his phone and focused on the screen. "Okay, you go get started and I'll check in a little later." He stood, his eyes still glued to his phone.

He was probably texting Rachel. Long-stored anger flared as I watched him stand up to leave. Yet again he was leaving me with the brunt of the work while he ran off to do God-knows-what. It was one thing when we were playing around, toying with the idea and having doughnut tasting parties, but it was serious now. I quit my job for this and if he wasn't going to help we had a problem.

"Seriously?" I said, standing from where I'd been sitting on the floor.

"What?" He glared at me, instantly defensive from my tone.

"You can't just leave, we have work to do."

"Recipes are your thing."

"Last time I checked, both our names are on the business license. That means it's our thing."

He looked like he would have smacked me if I wasn't a girl.

"I quit my job for this," I continued, really getting going. "Unlike you, I had a choice, and I'd appreciate it if you could have enough respect for me as your new business to partner to do even close to half of the work."

His jaw tightened as his eyes locked on mine. He took a deep inhale and let it out in a short, heavy breath.

"Where are you going to buy supplies from?" He asked coolly.

I didn't say anything, unsure of where this was going.

"Flour? Eggs? Milk? You'll need those in pretty large quantities, huh?"

I didn't reply.

"And how are you going to get the word out? Where are you going to sell these? Surely you weren't thinking we could just move right into a store and start selling doughnuts?"

I bit the inside of my cheek, already realizing the point he was going to make. He stepped forward and lowered his voice.

"I've been shopping food suppliers and narrowed it down to the guys with the best quality for the best price. Once you nail down which recipes we want to use, we can get exact figures for the supply costs, which means we can figure out the price point we need to use for the doughnuts."

He turned and left, not interested in whatever weak reply I might try to make. Even after he'd gone down the stairs and I'd heard the garage door close, I remained where I stood for a moment, trying to process his words. Clearly I underestimated the time he'd put into the doughnuts, but he couldn't expect me not to get mad when he kept all of his work hidden from me. I refused to let him make me feel bad.

I began with the familiar spread of ingredients for the basic dough and debated whether I'd need a double or triple batch to cover the variety of flavors Daniel and I had decided to try. After a little deliberating I decided on a double batch but when it came time to start needing the dough, it seemed too wet. I skimmed back through the list, trying to figure out if I'd made a mistake. The dry ingredients looked right, I'd done the right amount of vanilla… one egg for a normal batch, two for the double.

"Check," I said to myself. I'd done everything correctly. I must have copied the recipe wrong before printing it off my computer. I went to the trash can to throw it away. When I lifted the lid, my heart sank. Sitting in the top of the trash can I counted three broken egg shells. I was only supposed to use two. Mom walked in the room and saw me looking pathetically at the trash can.

"What's the matter?"

"Just destroying some doughnuts. I added too many eggs."

"Let me see." She held out her hand for the recipe and read through it quickly. "Let's just make it a triple batch." She went to the mixing bowl started measuring out another cup of flour.

I narrowed my eyes. "I'd hate for you to have a moral crisis over this." It sounded dumb as soon as I said it but I wanted the sentiment conveyed.

She arched an eyebrow at me, not understanding the sarcasm.

"You made it abundantly clear how opposed you are to this doughnut stuff."

"I'm just worried you acted a little rashly quitting your job," she said. "I understand how fun these little projects can be but that doesn't mean you have to make a career out of them."

"You tried the same thing, didn't you? Back when you and Dad made all of that stuff?"

"It was just a hobby," she said without looking at me.

I studied her, debating whether or not to push the issue further. "Is that why you and Dad won't support this? Because it didn't work out for you?"

She shook her head. "That was an entirely different scenario. We had a little side business selling handmade stuff."

I noticed she didn't answer my question.

"What's next?" Mom asked.

She had finished fixing the dough. I let the question of her support go for the time being. Together, we examined the list of flavors and got to work making each sketch come to life. It was late by the time we'd finished and I was ready to go to bed.

"You'll clean up?" She asked

"Yeah." I hated that she had to ask. Just because I lived at home didn't mean I'd regressed to being a teenager. She went off to bed while I wiped down the counters, put away ingredients, washed and dried the dishes. Right when I finished Daniel came in.

"Those look awesome," he said, depositing his keys on the counter and going for the plate of doughnuts.

Right on cue, I thought coldly. "So how was your evening?"

"Fine." He scrutinized my face while he ate. "What's your deal?"

"Either we're in this together or we're not."

He rolled his eyes in response.

"I don't care if you've thought through some logistics about setting up shop – I feel like I'm doing all the work."

"I forget that you haven't had the chance to know what actual work is like."

"I had an 'actual' job, with 'actual' work, that I *quit* for us."

"You quit because you're entitled and didn't like having to do the office's bitch work. At least I can commit to something." His fists clenched and unclenched, working as he fought for control of his anger. He saw my eyes start to water and finally he let out a deep, slow breath.

"I didn't mean that," he said quietly. Lowering his voice seemed to curb his anger. His face softened as he took another breath, but I knew better than to speak yet.

"Taylor, you know I'm not good at cooking. The kitchen's always been your thing. I'm happy to help with ideas and try to learn the recipes, but I don't think it's such a bad idea for us to use our own strengths here. Do you?"

"No," I said softly.

"Okay." He nodded as if to convince himself as well. He looked at me for a moment and then pulled me into a hug. I couldn't remember the last time he'd hugged me. It was jarring and caught me off guard, but I needed us to be a team. I couldn't afford to push him away, literally or figuratively.

"We've got some stuff to work through," he said. "We need a place to sell these."

He'd mentioned that earlier. Until he'd brought it up, I'd thought we'd find a store and open up shop. "The cost never even crossed my mind."

"The lease on even the smallest, most basic building is at least a year long commitment and worth almost as much as I have saved up right now, which I'm guessing," he raised an eyebrow at me. "Is definitely more than you have saved."

He had me there.

"I have an idea though." He reached into his pocket, pulled out a takeout menu and passed it to me. Bright, glaring shades of red and green and white depicted a cartoon of a round-bellied man with a dark mustache standing in front of a brick oven.

"Louie's Pizza Parlor," I read aloud. I looked up to see if he was joking.

"Rachel's younger brother worked there this summer. He knows the owner."

"And?"

"He's going to tell the owner about us and then we're going to talk with him." When the blank look remained on my face he continued, "Think about it. If you needed to make one hundred doughnuts here, in this kitchen, how long would that take?"

I glanced at the pan I used to fry the doughnuts resting on the counter. I did well to maneuver four at a time in there.

"Louie's has a commercial fryer," he explained.

"Don't they need it to make their own food?" I asked, thinking I was pointing out the obvious.

"Not on Saturday mornings."

I got it then. "That's brilliant."

"Well," he admitted. "It's not brilliant if the owner doesn't agree to it. I'm supposed to get a call tomorrow morning. I'll let you know when I hear from him."

"Sounds good," I said, and began pulling out plastic containers to house the remaining doughnuts. I was too tired to sit down and analyze which flavors worked and why the others didn't. That would have to wait for morning too.

"Let me," Daniel said, taking a container and starting to place the doughnuts inside. He was taking more care with them than necessary, only fitting four per container when six would have done with a little negotiating, but I resisted the urge to say anything. He was trying.

"Thanks," I said. "And I guess tell Rachel thanks for setting this up."

"Isn't she amazing?"

I would have said it was more surprising than anything. To be fair, I didn't see much of her, but I hadn't witnessed her say a single encouraging thing about the doughnut project.

"She's been really supportive during all of this," he said.

"How so?"

"I don't know, I guess just being really understanding and encouraging. Part of me expected her to want to break up when I lost my job, especially since she was already doing better than I was."

"But she didn't care?"

"She cared but she didn't, like, count it against me, you know?"

I nodded, thinking of how Lola had viewed my job and quitting so objectively.

"She's excited for us that we're doing this," he continued.

"Really?" He must have been adding 'us' for my benefit. Rachel hadn't shown any interest or feeling toward me in the entire time that they'd been dating.

"Yeah. I've told her how good you are at baking and she already knows what my skill set is," he paused to break off another piece of doughnut. Between bites he added, "She thinks we'll make a great team."

I hoped she was right. "Make sure to save some of those," I told Daniel.

He gave me a thumbs up as he downed the other half of the doughnut.

"At least one of every flavor."

"Mmhm," he replied, his words muffled by a full mouth.

***

The doughnuts may have won over Daniel, but Haleigh remained unimpressed when we met for coffee a couple of weeks later. I'd brought her a couple from another trial batch but she only eyed them suspiciously on the table in front of us.

"They're not going to hurt you."

"I'm worried about you."

"Why?" I asked, more annoyed than touched by her concern.

"You don't go out anymore, you've been spending all this time baking, and now you quit your job." She took a sip of her latte and looked at me with a sad shake of her head.

"I don't have people to go out with." I neglected to remind her that she ignored most of my texts. "And when did that become a requirement for mental health?"

"It just isn't normal."

I didn't want to argue with her. "What *is* normal?" I smiled, trying to keep things light.

"What you were doing before you freaked out and quit your job," she insisted. "Why can't you go back and talk to your boss? Tell him you were upset and you made a mistake. Maybe he'll give you your job back."

"I don't want my job back."

"Do you know how bad that's going to look on your resume, that you didn't even make it six months with them?

I studied my cup of coffee. I hadn't even made it four months.

"Tay, we all make mistakes. It's okay to admit that."

The amount of condescension coming out of her mouth truly astounded me. "You think I've made a mistake?"

Her eyes were wide and confused. "Can't you see that?"

"No."

"You're being so selfish," she hissed. "Everyone has to work after they graduate. I'm going to be in the exact same boat as soon as I get out of law school. But *now* - just because you think you're some kind of exception, I'm going to have to pay more to rent an apartment by myself." She paused to take an irritated breath. "And you're stuck with your parents for God knows how long. Have fun with that."

"I couldn't afford to live with you even if I kept the freaking job and we all know your parents are paying your rent so whenever you're ready to drop the poor law student act, let me know." Out of the corner of my eye I caught a couple at a neighboring table looking at us. "Believe it or not," I said in a lower voice. "Quitting my job wasn't about you."

"Obviously," she said darkly. "I should go."

She dropped her unfinished latte in the trash can and left without another word. I gave her a minute to get to her car and then stood to leave, shooting a look at the couple who had been way too interested in our conversation.

When I returned home, I stomped inside the house and slammed the door behind me to let the entire family know I had returned and not to mess with me. Just to the right of the entryway, Dad's office door opened and he leaned out.

"Got a moment?" I paused for too long, unsure of how to answer. "Come see me for a minute."

I followed, sank heavily into a chair opposite his desk, and dropped my purse on the ground.

"Yes?" I asked.

He looked at me for a moment without saying anything, slowly swiveling his desk chair back and forth. He clicked a pen cap open and closed in his hand. Finally he said, "Do you think we should talk about your job?"

"You mean my old job? The one I no longer I have?" I thought of Haleigh, *Tell your boss you made a mistake, maybe he'll give you your job back.* "The one I completely and irrevocably quit?"

"Nothing is completely irrevocable," Dad said.

I glared at him.

"You still haven't told me why you quit."

"To do the doughnut thing, Dad. We've been through this."

"I understand that, but clearly something wasn't right with the job or you wouldn't have been looking for something else to do."

"There were lots of things. It's just not what I wanted to be doing long term."

"Tell me some of the specific things."

I exhaled heavily. "I mean, Bill had all but made me into his secretary. I was doing mail runs and scheduling lunches. When I quit he made it pretty clear that I wouldn't be missed."

"I thought you were working on a pretty big project for some new client of theirs?"

"Well, yes. I was."

"What came of that?"

"Um, well, there was an unfortunate incident with some of the files for the branding package I was working on."

He looked at me levelly. "What happened?"

"The files randomly disappeared from my computer some time between when I went home one Friday and the following Monday morning when Bill wanted me to present them."

"Did you not save them?"

"I saved them," I said coldly.

"What did Bill say?"

"He didn't really say anything," I said, frowning at the memory of that day in his office. "I told him what happened and before he could really respond, Ryan came in with a flash drive of some graphics he just happened to be working on."

"Who's Ryan?"

"The other graphic designer, the one who was there before me."

Dad thought for a moment. He took off his reading glasses, twirled them around by the arm for moment and then asked, "What did Ryan's graphics look like?"

"Oddly similar to mine," I said simply, wondering if he would come to my same conclusion.

"He wouldn't have been able to access your laptop, would he?"

"He might have. I accidentally left it at the office over the weekend."

"But you have a password?"

I bit my lip.

"*Taylor.*"

"I've never needed one before! Who's going to be on my laptop anyway?"

"Your coworkers, apparently." He put his glasses back on. I watched his disappointment settle into a deep frown. His jaw clenched and he went back to fiddling with the pen cap.

"Dad?"

Abruptly he stood and went to the cabinet behind his desk, opening it's tall glass door and digging around inside.

"Um, Dad?"

He took at a box and began shaking something into his hand.

"What are you doing?" He turned and I saw him holding a box of ammo. "Dad!"

"Gonna teach that goddamn weasel a lesson," he muttered. He saw my look of horror and waved one of the bullets in the air. "It's a rubber buck, I'm not gonna kill him. Just buzz him a little."

"Tell me you are kidding. This is a really good time to reassure me that you are kidding."

He lowered his chin and looked at me over his glasses. "Do I look like I am kidding?"

"Unfortunately, no."

He nodded to himself. "Good. Still got it." He proceeded to drop all but one of the rubber bullets back into the box with perfect calm. I realized I'd been holding my breath.

I didn't know if he was actually mad or just trying to make me laugh. Either way, I immediately ranked it as one of his dumbest antics to date. "Maybe we should, like, not joke about murdering people," I said.

"Rubber bullet, Taylor," he said again, and tossed me the bullet. It hit his desk before I could catch it and I felt his amusement as I fumbled for it.

"Still." I should have known better though. He'd done a similar charade when a boyfriend in high school broke up with me the week before homecoming. I fell for it that time too.

"You're right," he conceded, sitting back down. "Rubber or not, it'd hurt like hell to get hit with it. You can keep that to remember who's got your back."

"Gee, thanks." I turned the bullet over in my hand. Half of the shell was bright green, making it look a little less lethal than a real bullet, but I still wouldn't want to be on the receiving end of one. I set it down on the desk.

"Jokes aside," Dad said. "I wish you would have told me. We could have figured out a way to handle it."

I shrugged, and flicked the bullet on the desk, sending it spinning in place. "That wasn't the only reason I quit. Besides, I wasn't sure you'd care."

"I always care. Just because you're all grown up doesn't mean you can't still come to your Mom or me for help."

I looked at him, a little surprised that he'd said I was grown up. It may have been a first at that point. "You guys haven't really been on board with the whole doughnut thing."

"Whole doughnut. Kind of an oxymoron, isn't it?"

I looked at him.

"You know," he said. "Cause they've got holes and —"

"I got it."

He smiled at my impatience. "Well, I guess you and Daniel are as likely as anyone to succeed in starting a doughnut shop. And if you fail, you fail. You guys can always go try something else."

On the surface, it was just a mild vote of confidence, but his words resonated deeply with me. "Thanks, Dad."

I stood to leave and grabbed my purse from the floor.

"Don't forget," he said, nodding to the bullet I'd left on the desk.

I shook my head, unwilling to admit my amusement with his joke. But I took the bullet and dropped it into my pocket, smiling just a little after I turned away from him.

CHAPTER 32 – DANIEL

I woke up early, before Taylor's alarm even went off. I'd made a plan the night before and I intended to accomplish it before noon. I was going to figure out how to run a doughnut shop.

In the car, I pulled up the list I created on my phone of all the doughnut shops within a five mile radius of the house. There were four. Anyone else might have been discouraged by the number of competitors so close but Taylor and I were working on a far superior product. Until we were ready to unveil it though, I planned on learning from the others.

First on my list was Happy Donut. The place was one of your standard, strip center doughnut shops with linoleum floors and fluorescent lights. A bell jingled against door when I pushed it open and behind the counter a cheerful, round-faced Asian guy reached for a square of wax paper in anticipation of my order.

His accent was thick but he had a disarming ability to smile the entire time he spoke. "What would like for you?"

"I have some questions," I said, pulling my list out of my pocket. The man looked confused. "Can I ask you some questions?"

His head bobbed up and down. "Sure, sure."

"Great, um." I pulled out my phone and poised to type his responses. "Let's see. How long have you been in business?"

The man's smile fell a little. "Sorry?"

"Um, how long have you been open?"

The smile returned. "Six-oh-oh."

"Six hundred?"

He pointed behind me. "Six-oh-oh."

I turned to look over my shoulder. On the door, the shop's hours were printed in peeling vinyl letters. They opened at six a.m. I decided we should move to the next question.

"Do you make all of your doughnuts in-house?"

"No, no, no." He looked wounded. "Make fresh in kitchen."

I pointed at the door leading to the kitchen. "In there?"

"Yes," he beamed.

"Who is your supplier?"

His face went slack.

"God. Um. Where do you get the ingredients?"

More blankness. I pointed at a doughnut. "Where from?"

"Make in kitchen."

I put my phone back in my pocket. "Thanks for your time."

Things went about the same at the second shop and I gave up on three and four before I even got there. Taylor and I weren't even a full day into our commitment to the doughnuts and I could already see I'd dragged us in way over our heads.

I went back home and took a cup of coffee up to my room. On the computer I tried searching for other resources, anything that might provide some insight on what we were doing. The closest I came was the New Restaurant Financial and Accounting seminar downtown the following weekend. Unfortunately, or maybe fortunately, I had the finances down already. Mostly down, anyway.

Almost as soon as I opened up my email, a chat message dinged in from Dax.

Hey man what's going on?

Not much. Working.

It was only a partial lie.

Kev-O is hawking again.

I actually laughed out loud. Whenever someone was watching or listening in on a conversation from afar, Dax called it 'hawking.' The term got used a lot in reference to Kevin. I could vividly picture Kevin leering from behind his computer. I didn't miss that environment at all. It had only been a couple of days, sure, but I doubted my feelings would change. Dax and Bhavesh were great coworkers but Kevin made up twenty-five percent of our immediate team. Not only did he constantly bring the mood down, but they guy had ratted me out for no reason at all. As long as his uncle remained as the CFO, did he really think his job was in jeopardy? I hoped the rest of them eventually figured out the kind of person he was. What's the point of working with someone if you can't trust them?

Which reminded me – Taylor trusted me. I'd made plenty of promises about our inevitable success, swearing that she mostly needed to handle the baking and I could sort out the rest. But I had nothing sorted out.

I went back to the chat with Dax.

Know any small business/marketing guys?

His reply appeared almost immediately.

`Yeah.`

That surprised me. I waited for the punch line. Nothing came.

Really?

`Yeah.`

Go figure.

Want to meet for a beer tonight?

`Sure.`

**One beer.

I intended for it to be a joke.

`OK, Mom.`

I would have thrown a stress ball at him if we'd been back at the office. A soft knock sounded on the door and I looked up to see Taylor leaning in the doorway.

"Whatcha doing?" She asked.

"Working." I decided to keep going with that story.

"Cool." She came in and sat down on the edge of the bed, facing me. "I had a thought. I know I wasn't at HRG very long but I learned a fair amount about branding and I figured our business needs some." She frowned. "Our business. Doesn't that sound weird? I don't know what else you call it though. Our shop? The doughnuts?"

"Beach Nuts," I reminded her.

"Right." She crossed her arms over her chest. "You still want to roll with that?"

She picked the dumbest things to get hung up on. "Did you have a better idea?"

"No," she sighed. "I guess it's memorable."

"And clever. You have to admit, it's clever."

Her eyes blinked a few times. "Anyway. Branding. We'll need a logo and something to get the word out, like you said." Her eyebrows knit together in a look of mild worry. "I guess that means we'll need a website. Any idea how to do those?"

She admitted I came up with an idea. She remembered that I thought of needing a way to get the word out. "Yeah, I can do websites," I said, because confidence seemed like the best way to thank her for finally acknowledging my efforts. "No problem." I didn't intend for it to be a problem for much longer anyway.

Her face relaxed. "Oh, good. That helps a lot. I'll go figure out a logo then." She stood from the bed. "Maybe some tangible form of branding too, like a sign or something. What do you think?"

"Great idea."

"Do you still have that business plan you put together? With all of our objectives and theme ideas and stuff?"

"Um, yeah, somewhere." I dug around in my desk until I found the folder with all of my initial research and the business plan. I passed it to her and she took the paper carefully, like she might damage it or something.

"Thanks," she smiled. "Let me know if you think of anything else I need to work on." She closed the door softly behind her.

I wasn't exactly sure what just happened. Taylor wasn't always flat out belligerent, but I could count on one hand the number of times she'd deferred to me about anything. On no occasion could I remember her asking for my direction on something.

I went back to the computer and asked Dax to meet me at the Tavern when he got off work. I doubted how much he'd be able to help, but on the off chance he wasn't just screwing around, I needed to make sure I prepared for our meeting. If Dax's guy really knew about marketing, I wanted to pick his brain on getting the word out to the community, cross-promotion opportunities, and anything else we might need. I knew enough about the subject to understand there were a thousand ways we could get the job done, but I wanted to know the best way.

After writing myself a list of questions, I spent an hour doing as much personal research as possible about the topics, and then set aside the notes for later.

Next on the list was a payment solution. Joe's cash register was programmed for Louie's, which meant we were on our own in that department. I toyed with the idea of just accepting cash but that would be inconvenient for customers and for Taylor and me.

I did a web search for cash registers, expecting to be led to some restaurant supplier or something to that effect. The first few hits were basic office supply retailers in the area. I clicked on a link in disbelief but, sure enough, they had them. For a couple hundred dollars. Not ideal.

Footsteps creaked from the hallway and I looked up to see Taylor appear in the doorway again.

She studied my face. "What's the matter?"

I closed my laptop. "Cash registers are expensive."

Her nose crinkled. "Are they?"

I nodded.

She thought for a moment and then asked, "Have you looked into that app?" I had no idea what app she was referring to. "You know the one that lets you take credit or debit card payments? You set it up through a tablet."

"What's it called?"

"Not sure. You'd have to look it up."

I opened my laptop again, did a search for 'credit card payment app,' and clicked on the first hit.

"It's free," I read to her. "They just take three percent off of each transaction." I looked up. "That's not bad, is it?"

"No, I think it's reasonable."

"Where did you hear about this?" How I managed to overlook such a perfect solution in all of my research was beyond me.

"I've seen it places," she shrugged. "Coffee shops and things like that."

"So you just set up your tablet and go? That's it?"

She nodded. "They have stands you can buy for your tablet that prop it up and let it swivel around."

"Will you buy one? Save the receipt and I'll file it with our other business expenses so you can get reimbursed if we ever turn a profit." She nodded and I finally noticed the stack of papers Taylor held in her hands. "Whatcha got?"

She crossed the room to the futon and laid out four pages of sketches she'd been working on. I guessed she was still working out a few different ideas, trying to hone in on one of them, but even in their early stages they looked great.

"I like it."

She seemed skeptical. "Really?"

I nodded.

"Huh."

"Why does that surprise you?" She'd been doing art in some form another for her entire life. There would have been something seriously wrong with her if she wasn't good at it by this point.

She shrugged. "I don't know. Glad you like it though."

We talked through the different designs for a few more minutes and then she left again. I placed the order for the app's card reader and then kept at my research until it was time to go meet Dax.

When I walked inside the Tavern he was already seated at a barstool with a beer in front of him.

He turned as I approached. "Hey buddy." He pointedly looked over my jeans and t-shirt before reaching to loosen his tie.

"Nice tie," I said.

"Board meeting today. You got out just in time."

Work was the last thing I wanted to talk about. I cut straight to the point. "Tell me about your guy."

"Oh." He took a sip of his beer. "I was just kidding about the guy."

It crossed my mind to get up and walk right back out of the bar. Dax cast a sideways glance and smirked at my face. "As it so happens, I have some experience with marketing."

"Go on."

"It's what I got my degree in, anyway."

"Really?" How had that never come up in any of our conversations? I went ahead and ordered a beer.

"This about your doughnut enterprise?"

"Yeah." I pushed a hand through my hair. Might as well shoot him straight. He was probably the least likely person to judge for any of this. "I have no idea what I'm doing."

He nodded thoughtfully. "What marketing outlets have you already looked into?"

I pulled out my list and for once he didn't make fun of me for being OCD. For a full hour he managed to be serious and thoughtful, patiently explaining his thought process and suggestions. I kind of couldn't believe it was him. At times I caught myself losing focus on what he was saying because I was so taken aback by how much he knew.

"Why the hell did you decide to do finance?" I asked when we were wrapping up our conversation.

He smiled a little as he swirled his beer around in the glass. "I ask myself that same question every time I catch Kevin's beady little eyes watching me from behind his computer."

"Seriously though. You're good at this stuff and it seems like you like it."

He shrugged. "Sometimes you just go where the money is."

"You could make money in marketing."

"Maybe."

We left it at that and I paid for our beers. As we were walking out to the parking lot, I realized I'd forgot to ask him about websites. "Any chance you know about those?"

"I know they're important," he said. "You might be able to make one yourself. There's some web apps that make site building pretty easy. I don't remember the names off the top of my head but I'll find them and send you a list."

"Okay. Thanks, man. For everything."

"No problem. I expect a doughnut when this gets off the ground."

"I'll think about it."

When I got into my car I checked my phone and saw I had a missed call and a text from Rachel. I put my phone back in my pocket and drove out of the lot. I had too much work to do. Hanging out with her would have to wait. For every item I'd set out to address with Dax, he'd come up with two more I hadn't thought of. He provided a little clarity and I felt reassured about what needed to be done, but now I needed to go do it. Normally I wouldn't put work ahead of Rachel but, in the long run, this was for her. For us. Everything else could wait.

CHAPTER 33 - TAYLOR

I expected the meeting with the owner of Louie's to go about as well as the meeting with the county clerk for our business license. His name was, Joe, not Louie, confusingly enough. His tousled blond hair and deep set tan made him look about as authentically Italian as the takeout menu Daniel gave me did. We met at a coffee shop and Joe, dressed in dark designer jeans and a black fitted t-shirt, ordered a cup of coffee with a shot of espresso. As we sat down, Daniel asked Joe about his heritage and he told us his parents had been born and raised in Italy.

"My dad came to America with his parents when he was twelve, but my mom didn't make the move until right before she married my dad when she was twenty-two."

"Which of your parents taught you to make pizza?" I asked.

"My mom." He scratched at the stubble on his jawline. "Not sure she ever expected me to do it for a living though."

"But your parents support it?"

"My mom passed away before I got started. I used to talk to her about opening up a pizza place someday and she was always encouraging about it, but after she died I quit cooking for a long time."

"What made you pick it back up?" Daniel asked.

Joe smiled, laughing a little as he said, "My dad. I'd been moping around for a few months and one day he walks into my room, I was still living at home, and says," Joe paused, making his face serious. "Giotto, *non fare il salame.*"

Daniel and I glanced at each other and then back at Joe.

"It basically means, 'don't be an idiot.' He thought I was wasting my life, which I was, and more importantly," he grinned, "I was wasting my culinary talents."

"That's awesome," Daniel said. Joe had won him over but the problem was, we needed to win him over.

"Now," Joe said, folding his arms and leaning onto the table. "Talk to me about doughnuts."

I glanced at Daniel again and when I saw his hesitation to launch into the explanation, I took the wheel. "We're trying to start a doughnut shop. We both just quit our jobs," I said charitably, with a small smile at Daniel. "Most of our menu is nailed down and we've got the bones of the business put together, but we're a long way from being able to afford leasing our own space."

"Taylor's been using our kitchen in the meantime," Daniel explained, and I appreciated that he didn't try to take credit for the cooking. "But, obviously, that won't work if we're trying to mass produce these."

Joe nodded thoughtfully. "You have a name?"

We gave our usual pause, still trying to put confidence behind our name.

"Beach Nuts."

"Sorry?"

"Beach Nuts," I sighed. "It's like a really loose beach theme with doughnuts... Beach Nuts."

Unabashedly, Joe let out a loud, hearty laugh. "Right," he smiled. "So what all do you need? The fryer, I'm assuming."

"That's basically it," Daniel said. "Fryer and some counter space."

"Refrigerator space?"

"I guess that too," Daniel answered. He looked at me with a little frown. "Hadn't thought of that."

Joe told us how much he paid on his lease per month and what the cost broke down to per day. "Technically you'd only need the space for about half a day," he reasoned.

The half day cost came in way lower than we'd anticipated. Even if we only broke even on doughnut sales, we could still cover renting the space for a few months.

Joe scratched at his jawline again, thinking. "Do I get a landlord discount or something on the doughnuts?"

"Absolutely," I said without hesitation.

"Will you name one after me?"

"Definitely," Daniel said.

Joe grinned, looking between the two of us. "I like you guys," he reached out to shake our hands.

Joe laughed again and Daniel and I joined him, even though we didn't know why we were laughing. I'm guessing Joe was laughing simply from the hilarity that he'd just doled out one-sixtieth of his lease to two kids trying to start a beach-themed doughnut shop. I couldn't blame him.

Before parting, we arranged a time later that afternoon to go by Louie's so Joe could show us around. Things were moving, but I felt overwhelmed at the magnitude of what remained to be done. We needed to finalize the menu items, order supplies, convert the dozen-yield recipes to larger batches, and learn how to use the commercial fryer. At home, Daniel sat anxiously in front of his laptop at the kitchen table, working on our website.

"Maybe you're overthinking it," I suggested.

He shot me a deathly look, arguing the contrary. We needed to get the word out to as many people as possible about where we'd be and when. The plan for now was to open for business on Saturday mornings at Louie's until we established a reasonable customer base and accrued enough cash flow to justify leasing our own place. It seemed like a fairly safe plan, but it also meant that our Saturday mornings had to run as close to perfect as possible.

We decided to aim for an even spread of each flavor for our first day, but as time went on we wanted to be able to communicate with customers and create an easy way for them to request specific flavors. We needed a website to meet all of those needs and, ideally, offer the functionality for people to pre-order larger quantities if they wanted. The problem was neither of us knew the first thing about websites.

"I don't even know what distinguishes a good, functional website from a bad one," he said.

"I don't either. I think we're probably just going to have to trust our eye and go with what feels right."

He looked at me caustically again. I knew he wasn't a fan of taking steps without concrete reason, but I didn't see another option available. Moreover, the design of the website was entirely irrelevant if we weren't able to get people to visit the site in the first place. Daniel kept pushing for a social media campaign while I held that we needed another, more tangible way of getting the word out too.

"I'm open to it, but you're not actually suggesting anything," Daniel complained.

"Help me come up with something then."

"Not until we nail down a social strategy," he insisted. "And a website."

I closed my eyes, resisting the temptation to continue the argument. I left him to battle it out with the interwebs and returned to my room, where I'd spent most of the morning making futile attempts at our branding. At the end of the day, it was our doughnuts that we're going to be the key factor to our success, but the months I spent at HRG made it impossible for me to ignore branding altogether. I'd sketched out a few options and could name a few merits in each but none felt entirely complete. I needed another creative opinion.

I texted Laura and she replied almost immediately. Grabbing my purse I bounded down the stairs back to the kitchen.

"I'm running an errand," I told Daniel.

"You'll be back in time to go to Louie's?"

I glanced at my watch. We had a little under two hours before our meet-up. "I'll meet you there."

"Don't be late," he warned unnecessarily, as if I had any faith he could learn the ropes of the commercial kitchen without me.

When I got to Laura's, I followed her straight through the house, explaining the branding and marketing conundrum as we walked back to her studio. Inside, I pulled the sketches out of my bag and we leaned over the large center table to examine them.

"I see what you mean," she said. "They're three very different looks."

"I feel like it's better to go with the simpler one," I said, nodding at one of the two she was holding in her hands. "But then I feel like a simpler design creates the need for a more complex marketing campaign."

"Not necessarily," she said, continuing to examine the sketches seriously. After a moment she set them down, crossed the room to the bookcase and pulled down two containers. "You've made business cards before?"

"A few times." If memory served, I'd made them once.

From one container she pulled out a piece of card stock and cut a piece roughly the size of a business card. She held it up for my inspection. "That's about the size, right? Close enough?"

"I think so."

With a felt tip pen, she began drawing a circle on the card. "What if you took that design," she nodded to the simple one as she continued a rough imitation of it. "Printed it on the card like this, and then wrote your info on the back?"

She took a black marker and began writing on the reverse side of the doughnut, following the outline of the shape. From the other container, she took out two circular, die-cut lever punches. She used the larger one first and cut the doughnut she'd drawn from the business card and then the second to cut out the middle of the doughnut. She passed me a perfect cardstock doughnut. One side featured the colored drawing of a doughnut and the other side held the business info.

"You should be able to fit all the info you need on the back there. I know the cutting is more labor intensive than just printing the cards but it might be worth it. You could do stacks of fifty or so and leave them various places, give them to your friends to hand out, whatever."

"This is perfect," I said, turning it over in my hands. It was everything I'd tried to articulate to Daniel about needing a tangible piece of material.

"I promise, I won't be offended if you don't use it."

"No," I told her. "I love it. Thank you."

I showed the doughnut card to Daniel at Louie's and he hesitated, unsure about the idea. Joe took the card and laughed warmly as he inspected it.

"This is perfect," he marveled. "Did you come up with this?"

"I had some help," I admitted.

"Really, really great," he said and handed the card back to Daniel. "You're lucky to have such a creative business partner."

Daniel raised an eyebrow. "Yeah." He put the doughnut card in his pocket.

"Ready to get started?" Joe asked.

We'd been standing behind Louie's in the overflow parking lot. It was a weekday afternoon, not their busiest time of day, so most of the spots were empty.

"We'll go in the back just to be safe," Joe said, opening the door. "I don't need customers thinking we regularly give tours of the kitchen."

He ushered Daniel and me in ahead of him and we paused inside, letting our eyes adjust to the dimness of the storage area we were now in.

"If you guys have any dry goods – flour, sugar, whatever – you can store them here," Joe used his foot to point at an empty shelf on the bottom. "Have you found a supplier yet?"

I looked to Daniel. "We're looking at a couple," he answered. "Always open to suggestions though."

Daniel and Joe lapsed into a discussion about the merits of various suppliers, something I'd paid a pitiful amount of attention to so far. While they debated I took in the rest of the room. To the left of the door we'd just come in there were two imposing metal doors with small windows in the center. I guessed one was a refrigerator and the other a freezer, but couldn't tell which was which. Opposite the exit was a door that could only lead to the kitchen. The circular window in the door was at just the right angle to prevent me from seeing anything inside, but the bright fluorescent light and the smell of pizza wafting from that direction seemed like a reasonable clue.

One door remained on the right, which Joe and Daniel walked through. Joe flipped on a light, revealing a small office with a mostly neat desk, two chairs, an ancient computer, and a cluttered bookshelf.

"It's your decision, of course," Joe said, handing Daniel a stack of papers he'd pulled from a desk drawer. "But take a look at the numbers before you decide."

"Great, will do."

Daniel handed me the papers and I dutifully put them in my purse.

"Back on track," Joe said, clapping his hands and looking around the room. "Not much else back here. Fridge and freezer over there," he pointed at the metal doors. "My office," he nodded back to the room he'd pulled the papers from. "And kitchen," he finished, leading the way to the final door.

We followed him inside and found two guys wearing the Louie's red and black t-shirt uniform, standing on opposite sides of the kitchen. The older of the two, a heavy set guy with stringy, thinning hair, tossed a marble-sized ball of dough at the other employee, a kid with long, shaggy hair who couldn't have been more than sixteen. The kid caught the dough ball in his mouth before the two noticed our entrance.

"I see we're having a productive day," Joe said. My stomach turned at the idea of eating raw pizza dough, much less a piece handled by the guy with the greasy hair.

The kid who'd been catching the dough balls ducked his head and shuffled out a door to the front of the restaurant, mumbling a 'sorry' as he passed Joe. The older guy shrugged unapologetically and tossed his remaining handful of dough balls in a trash can. Joe shook his head and sighed before continuing through the kitchen.

"Here are your new best friends," he said, indicating two large vats of sizzling oil built into the counter. I may have overcome my fear of scalding oil back home, but this raised the stakes considerably.

"You just drop your doughnuts into the oil and use the basket to lift them out. "Hey," he called to the older guy, who now stood across the kitchen, leaning against the counter. "Toss me some dough."

The guy broke off a piece a little larger than he and the kid had been playing target practice with and threw it across the room. Joe caught it easily and worked it into the shape of a doughnut. "Might as well attempt an accurate demonstration."

He tossed the pizza dough ring into the grease and we watched as it sank a moment before returning to the surface in a eruption of bubbles. While it cooked, he went to find a fork and then returned to flip it on the other side.

"I'm sure you have better utensils to work with than salad forks," he smiled at me. I didn't admit that I used a fork at home. After another minute he lifted the handle on the basket to lift the doughnut out of the grease and then flip it onto the counter.

"That's it."

Daniel and I continued to follow him around the kitchen as he pointed out where they stored various utensils, pots and pans. He showed us how to work the stoves and ovens, though most of it was self explanatory. None of the mechanics seemed very different – just larger and more intense.

"You guys wanna come in for a trial run?" Joe asked.

I looked around the kitchen and imagined baking in here with Daniel. I felt a little dismay at the thought. By no means was this the doughnut shop I'd dreamed about with Lola, but it would have to do for now. I needed to keep reminding myself that this was nothing more than a stepping stone necessary to get to where we wanted to be.

"Sure," Daniel answered for us.

"Great. You guys are welcome to come in around twelve and stay till five, give or take an hour on the back end.

"P.M.?" Daniel asked.

"A.M.," he replied evenly.

"Um."

"What time do you think doughnut shops normally fire up the kitchen?" Joe asked.

Given that most doughnut shops around town opened at six in the morning, I knew he couldn't be far off. But we were still quite a few weeks away from opening. There wasn't any need to make doughnuts all through the night just for kicks.

"I'm helping you," Joe insisted when I shared my thoughts. "It'll get you in the swing of things."

I sincerely doubted that and, from the look on Daniel's face, he did too. Yet there we were a week later, pulling up behind Louie's a few minutes after midnight, Daniel driving while I downed a cup of coffee in the passenger seat. When we parked, Daniel popped the trunk and I hefted an industrial size bag of flour against my chest. Leaving the other items to Daniel, I kicked at the door to the supply room, hoping someone was close enough to hear and open it for me.

"Morning," Joe greeted us cheerfully, propping open the door.

I muttered a sleepy reply and pushed past him, feeling the bag start to slip from my arms. Barreling into the kitchen I managed to get the flour onto a counter before my arms gave out. Looking around, I saw the kitchen was already spotless, less than an hour after their closing. One of the employees was busy locking up the register but, other than that, the place was empty.

"Not there," Joe said coming into the kitchen. He nodded back toward the supply room. With more animosity than the situation probably warranted, I slung the flour bag off the counter and followed Joe back into the supply room. Daniel knelt on the floor, shoving our stuff onto the bottom shelf. From another shelf, Joe pulled a ten gallon plastic bucket, the kind normally used for paint or mixing other industrial items, off of a stack and handed it to Daniel.

"It's for mixing," Joe said, adding, "Don't worry, it's clean."

Daniel handed me the bucket and I hesitated, unsure of where to set it down while we mixed the ingredients.

"Throw in all of your wet ingredients and then add the dry," Joe said.

Daniel nodded thoughtfully but I bristled at the unnecessary instruction. I knew the correct order to mix ingredients in and wanted to say so.

"Do you have your recipe?" Daniel asked, distracting me just as I'd started to open my mouth.

I dug in my pocket for the two pieces of paper I'd jotted down our recipe on. One was the original we'd used at home and one had been multiplied and rewritten in a much larger portion.

"How many will this make?" Daniel asked.

"Ten dozen."

He looked at me with wide eyes. "Ten?"

"That's still a small batch by most standards," I said. "We needed to try them on a larger scale at some point."

"I guess you're right," he said, cracking eggs into the bucket. "Do you know how much the ingredients for will end up costing per batch?"

"No, and I don't want to," I said with more force than necessary. "Calculate it, write it down – fine, but this isn't something we can cut costs on."

"She's right," Joe said.

Daniel and I glanced at each other in mild annoyance at the interjection. I hadn't anticipated Joe staying the entire time, but he settled against the wall with no apparent intention of moving while Daniel and I hauled the bucket across the supply room to the various locations of our ingredients. When Daniel took the bucket of finished dough into the kitchen, I followed with a small container of flour to sprinkle on the counter. Joe followed closely behind and settled comfortably against another wall to continue watching. Daniel emptied the dough on the counter, took a small step back, and then looked to me expectantly.

"Start heating the oil," I told Daniel. I carefully sprinkled another handful of flour on the dough and then dusted my hands with the extra, stalling a little. I found myself taking extra care to be precise, as if Joe was sitting there judging my technique and my use of his kitchen and tools.

When I finally dared a glance in his direction he was texting on his phone. I refused to look again, wanting to make myself believe he really wasn't paying attention after all. I kneaded, rolled and cut the rings and set a timer for them to rise. We tidied up what we could, hyperaware of Joe watching us, and then I gave Daniel the go-ahead to toss into the fryer.

"Aren't they supposed to puff up?" Daniel asked after turning over a few to cook on the other side.

I looked up from my rolling and cutting. The rings were the same height as when I'd cut them. Normally they rose to nearly two inches tall.

"How hot is the oil?"

He read the thermometer. Right on the dot where it was supposed to be.

"Did you flip them too soon?" I asked, knowing that wasn't the problem. The already cooked side was a perfect golden brown.

Daniel lifted the basket to dump them out and I poked one tentatively with a fork. Cutting it open, I could see it was dense and still a little undercooked in the middle.

"Are you sure you got the recipe right?" Joe asked.

I seethed inwardly. *Yes I got the recipe right.* To humor him I pulled out the recipe and began reading down the list, confirming we'd added each one.

"Eggs, milk, vanilla, flour, sugar, salt, baking so—" I stopped and thought hard. "We forgot the baking soda."

It was quiet for a moment. Daniel didn't say anything and my mind raced, desperate for any solution to save the pounds of dough we had left. I wished Mom were there to fix it like she had the other day when I'd messed up the recipe.

"We have to start over," I said.

"Can't you just add it now?"

"Not with everything already mixed and kneaded together, no."

He looked at me like he was using every bit of self restraint he possessed not to yell at me.

"*Non tutte le ciambelle riescono col buco,*" Joe said with a shrug.

I glared at him, no longer able to hide my annoyance that he was here, much less saying stupid Italian things at us.

247

"Do tell," I said with heavy sarcasm. "What *ever* does that mean?"

"Not all doughnuts come out with a hole."

I looked at him. Was he really that dumb? "The doughnuts have holes, they just haven't risen."

"It means things don't always turn out like expected," he clarified.

Wonderful. Not only was our pseudo landlord going to insist on looking over our shoulders the entire time, but now he'd decided to be our resident Italian fortune cookie. I'm sure he knew exactly how irritated we were but he just sat there, looking at us expectantly. No one moved or said anything for a few moments.

"Try again," he smiled.

I looked at Daniel, hoping he'd cooled down a bit.

"Excellent use of resources," he said.

I had no reply. It couldn't have been that much money, but every bit counted right now.

He shook his head at me and grabbed the dough bucket. I tossed our failed dough into the trash can and followed him back into the supply room.

CHAPTER 34 - DANIEL

"I don't like this," I told Dax. We were at his apartment in front of the computer, looking at the payment page for some freelance web designer.

"Dude, it's fine. People use this site to hire freelancers all the time."

"What people?"

He shrugged. "I don't know. People."

Not exactly the stunning reference I was hoping for. The site allowed freelancers from every field imaginable to post their portfolios and put in bids for jobs as they were posted. After a week of no progress on creating a website myself, Dax talked me into posting a query about it on the site.

"Just to see," he said. "You never know."

Twelve people replied within three days, but only one of them proposed a bid under a thousand dollars. Using the site's internal email system, I messaged back and forth with the guy to reiterate exactly what we were looking for. At any given time I expected him to take issue with one of my requirements and raise the bid, but all he did was type back an 'O.K.' for every item on the list. It all looked good on paper, but I was incredibly nervous about pressing the 'Accept' button on the job, and effectively signing over nearly a thousand dollars to someone I'd never met.

"They have a way you can end the project if he ends up being sketchy," Dax reminded me.

"I'm still out most of the money though."

"You worry too much."

He sounded like Rachel and Taylor. I wanted to punch him.

"Come on," he continued. "Take a chance on..." he squinted at the screen, looking for the name of the freelancer, "Fazil from Sri Lanka. And then wrap it up." He checked his watch. "I'm meeting my trainer in twenty minutes."

"Okay, fine." I pulled my wallet out of my pocket, whipped out a credit card, and started punching in the numbers with sweating hands. The site would store the information and charge the first thirty percent but hold the remaining seventy percent until the project was completed, hopefully to my satisfaction.

"Proud of you, buddy." Dax clapped my shoulder. "That was a big step."

"Shut up."

He laughed and got up to put on a pair of running shoes. "Want to come? You're looking a little soft. When was the last time you lifted?"

"Can't," I said, ignoring the last question. "Going to see Rachel."

"Work out and then go see Rachel after."

I shook my head. "I've been so busy with the doughnut stuff, I've barely seen her all week. You know how it is."

"I don't actually."

I didn't know what to say to that. He sounded kind of bitter, but the way he usually talked about girls didn't make it seem like he was interested in anything resembling commitment. He finished tying his shoe and stood. "It's cool though. Keep me posted on the website stuff."

"Alright man." I left Dax's and called Rachel when I got in my car. She sounded tired when she answered the phone. "Have you eaten yet?" I asked.

"No."

"Want to go grab a bite then? I'll pick you up."

"Sure."

Her shortness unsettled me, but it was nearly the end of the week. She was probably just tired from work. "I'll be there in ten," I told her and hung up. I decided to take her to Adeline's. We hadn't been since the beginning of the summer and we'd been seeing a lot less of each other since I started digging into the doughnut work. A nice evening out was just what we needed.

When I got to Rachel's apartment I went up the stairs and knocked on her door. She answered wearing running shorts and a t-shirt to my jeans and a button down.

"Is that what you're wearing?" I asked.

She looked down over her clothes. "Should I not be?"

"I thought we'd go to Adeline's."

She sighed heavily. "Could have told me that on the phone."

"I didn't think you'd be wearing workout clothes."

Her eyes narrowed. "I went to the gym after work. What was I going to do, change back into work clothes?"

"You don't need to get all pissy about it, just go change."

Her back straightened and she crossed her arms over her chest. I was trying to be nice and take her to her favorite restaurant.

"What?" I asked.

She just rolled her eyes, dropped her purse on the floor, and turned to go back inside. I nudged her purse out of the walkway with my foot and stepped inside in time to see her bedroom door slam closed. At least that meant she was changing clothes.

I sat at her kitchen table and checked my email on my phone while I waited. An automated reply from the freelancing site confirmed my acceptance of Fazil's bid and a second email, directly from Fazil via the site's email system, contained his own confirmation in his cheerful, overly formal, and kind of broken English. He seemed to have a lot of confidence about getting the site done the way we needed within the week, but I still didn't feel great about the whole ordeal. Optimism is a lot easier when you don't have so much on the line.

Rachel stalked out of her room a minute later wearing a dress. "Better?"

"You look beautiful." I smiled, trying to smooth over whatever mood she'd worked herself into. "That's a great dress on you."

She gave a thin smile that didn't quite reach her eyes and went to grab her purse. "Let's go." She held open the door and waited with a hand on her hip until I exited. I heard her sigh again as she locked it behind us and stepped past me to go down the stairs.

I couldn't handle it anymore. "What," I started trudging down the stairs after her, "is your problem?"

She stopped walking and whirled around to face me. "*My* problem?"

"You've been acting weird ever since I started working on this doughnut stuff and I could really use your support right now."

"You think I'm the one who's acting weird?"

"If it's because I got fired from my job, just say it now. I'm trying to make this work. I get that it's not the sexiest career path, but it's all I have right now."

"Unbelievable." Her hands moved to her hips. "You're the one who's been all but ignoring me for the past two weeks. You were happy to talk through things and let me help you before this became your main project, but now you're shutting me out. Why do you always think I don't respect what you're doing?"

"I don't—"

"Yes you do," she cut in. "You were insecure about what I thought of your old job almost the entire time you worked there. You seemed fine about the doughnuts until you actually started doing it full time and now you're doing it again. You pigeon-hole me into this 'girlfriend' category of your life, and then you go about your work and whatever else. I get a call when you finally want to grace me with your presence and then you come over here expecting me to have anticipated your plans for a nice dinner. What the hell is that about?"

"You're mad because I forgot to mention where I planned to take you to dinner?"

"*NO*. Are you even listening to what I'm saying?" She took a deep breathe and lowered her voice. "We've talked about getting married someday – how is that going to work if you keep pushing me into a corner every time life gets stressful?"

"I don't push you into a corner."

"Yes, you do. When things started going badly with your job, you didn't tell me. You didn't tell me anything until after it was all over. Now you're starting to do the same thing with the doughnuts."

"Have you ever stopped to consider that maybe I don't want to tell you every single time I screw up?"

"You have to. You have to tell me what's going on with you, that's how this works."

"Why? So you can have more reasons to feel like the better, more successful part of this relationship?"

Her volume escalated again, *"Daniel,* where are you getting this from? What have I ever done to make you feel stupid or inadequate when you fail? Everyone messes up." She quieted again. "You make yourself feel small."

Neither of us said anything for a moment until she spoke again. "Nothing I say or do is going to be louder than the voice in your head. But if you keep holding back these huge parts of your life and don't communicate with me, we're never going to make it." She sighed and dug her keys back out of her purse. "I think I'm just going to stay home tonight. Call me later."

She went back upstairs and closed the door softly behind her, leaving me there to process what just happened. I got in the car and drove. I'm not sure where I went or how long I was gone, but it was nearly dark by the time I got home.

I'd mostly lost my appetite but I went to the kitchen for lack of anything better to do with myself. On the kitchen table sat a pile of the supplies Taylor used to make the doughnut business cards – huge stacks of heavy paper with the doughnut design and two die-cut punches to cut the outer and inner parts circles of the doughnut. The idea was clever enough but why she'd picked a design we needed to make by hand was beyond me.

For three days the supplies had been sitting out on the table with a short note asking me to pitch in and giving instructions on how to cut the cards she'd already printed. She'd divided the paper into two stacks, one for each of us. I'd watched hers progressively diminish as her stack of completed doughnut cards grew while mine remained untouched. That night when I approached the table to find her stack, as well as mine, completed. Five hundred hand-cut business cards, ready and waiting.

"Excellent," I said to no one. I felt like crap. She'd been a lot less demanding lately, mostly content to let me work on my areas of expertise while she kept to her own stuff. This was the one project she'd asked for my help on, and she'd ended up doing the whole thing herself. I let her down, just like I'd let Rachel down.

I couldn't even pretend to be hungry any more. I got a beer from the fridge and went up to my room to work on the marketing plan because, clearly, I was incapable of anything else.

CHAPTER 35 - TAYLOR

"I thought I talked to you about bringing desserts over here," Lola said when she opened the door to find me holding a container with a dozen doughnuts.

"Technically this is breakfast."

She raised an eyebrow but extended a hand to accept the doughnuts. "How is your work?" She asked as she led the way to the kitchen. I loved that she referred to the doughnuts as my work. They were, of course, but to call them so made things seem established and respectable, which was the exact opposite of how they felt.

"Exhausting," I admitted. "Still doing a lot of work on the marketing materials. Thankfully we finished making our business cards. I had the brilliant idea of coming up with a design that required hand-cutting."

"You cut the business cards by yourself?"

I nodded. "We used die-cut punches, but it was still a lot of work. Daniel did a ton though." I shook my head a little, still surprised by his effort on the project. "I asked him to do half of them and he did nothing for like, two or three days. I didn't think he was going to do anything but then I came home one night and *all* of them were done, including half of the stack I'd set aside for myself."

"You have a good brother," Lola smiled.

A few months ago I probably wouldn't have agreed with her, not out loud anyway, but I had to then. "I still need to work on some branding stuff, but Daniel and I have been at Louie's every night for a week now."

"Making doughnuts?"

I nodded. "The owner, Joe, is letting us take all the prep time we need without charging us any extra, as long as we're not in there during their business hours. I thought we should just work until we had one successful batch, but Dan wanted more."

"I see that." She opened the lid on the doughnuts. "What flavor are these?"

"Raspberry lemonade."

"Hm." She leaned in to smell them. "The scent is good." She pulled a fork from a drawer and sectioned off a bite. "The taste is good too. Will Daniel let you quit making the test batches now?"

"I hope so. I've made at least three batches of each and haven't botched any like the first go around with the baking soda." She nodded, remembering the story. "We've had so many little snags though. It's making me constantly anxious for the opening day."

"What day will that be?" Lola asked.

"First Saturday of September." I handed her one of the tiny cardstock doughnuts. The front looked the same as my original drawing but on the back, in addition to the address of Louie's, we'd added the scheduled day of our first run — less than two weeks away. It felt unreal.

"How are you feeling?" Lola asked, seeing my anxiety.

"Excited. And terrified."

"Of what?"

"I wish I knew."

"You may fail," Lola said firmly. I looked at her with mild alarm. "I don't think you will," she continued. "But you might."

Deflated, I sank onto my usual kitchen stool.

"Darling." I could hear the ache in her voice, wanting me to understand what she was saying. "It is never too late to back out. But I think you need to do this."

I felt acutely aware of my eyes starting to water. I was tired of crying in front of her. I blinked a few times, willing the tears to stop before they fell.

"You are so young," she said.

She didn't mean it harshly, but I wanted something to throw my frustration at. "So I'm already set up for failure?"

"Set up to bounce back if you fall," she insisted. "Tell me, what happens if you fail? What will you have lost?"

I thought of all the work Daniel and I had done – the paperwork, the late nights baking, the money we'd spent on supplies. He'd even caved and paid someone more than we'd budgeted to build us a website.

"A little over a month of your time?" Lola asked, interrupting my thoughts. "A little bit of money?"

"Yeah," I agreed. When she put it that way, the potential loss felt less weighty.

"And if you succeed?"

The image of the bakery I'd once described to her came to mind. My heart lifted at the thought but stopped the daydream from continuing. She made her point.

"You know the risk is worth what your reward could be. Now stop worrying about it."

"I'm not worrying," I argued. Worrying was my mom still wanting me to send a text letting her know when I'd be home. I was being cautious.

"Any of those negative preoccupations you hold onto are worry."

I looked at her helplessly. Surely she knew she was making it sound far easier than it was?

"I've missed out on a lot of todays by being in tomorrows. What is on your to-do list today?"

I recalled my mental list and rattled off the six or seven items Daniel and I needed to complete.

"Okay, do those. Plan for tomorrow, but do not *live* in tomorrow."

I nodded, almost willing to admit that I made things more complicated than necessary. I didn't enjoy feeling crushed by our project, but so much was on the line. I understood what she was saying. Technically we could fail and it would be "okay," but I didn't know if I actually had it in me to bounce back.

"Would you like something to drink?"

I smiled, grateful at how easily she concluded our talks. "Yes, please." A glass of Lola's tea was exactly what I needed. She turned to get the glasses as my phone buzzed. I pulled it from my pocket and found an enormously long message from Daniel. He wanted my opinion on formatting for the website. There were some screenshots I couldn't really make sense of and the onslaught of information was stressing me out. I put my phone away as Lola placed two glasses of dark pink wine in front of me.

"Wine?" I asked.

"Rosé."

I glanced at the clock on her oven. "It's one o'clock."

She shrugged. "It is common to have a glass of wine with your lunch in Spain."

"But we're in Texas."

"It is a day for wine," she said, pulling one of the glasses towards her.

I had to smile again. "Cheers," I said lifting my glass to her.

"*Salud.*"

We clinked our glasses and Lola took a seat on the stool next to me. She flipped open an issue of *Cosmopolitan* she'd left on the counter and we sat in silence sipping our rosé, letting me slip into the processing time I needed.

***

We were at Louie's in the earliest hours of the morning when I caught a strange whiff of something in the air. I stood crouched over a handful of cooling doughnuts, trying to streamline the process of frosting them with marshmallow cream and drizzling chocolate over the top. They were our attempt at a s'mores doughnut and no matter what I did, it still took entirely too long to make them. I'd focused so tightly in on the doughnuts that nothing else entered my mind until the unusual scent of something disrupted my thoughts.

"Daniel," I said without looking up. "What's that smell?"

I continued drizzling chocolate, wanting to finish the doughnuts in front of me before coming to a stop.

"Daniel?"

I set down the pastry bag of chocolate and straightened, feeling my back kink a little at the change in position. I couldn't see Daniel. Smoke began clouding the air, pouring from the fryer. *Did I leave doughnuts in there?* I leapt towards the fryer but it was too much movement after bending over the doughnuts for so long. My back seized up, immobilizing me as pain shot down my spine. The fryer burst into flames. Terrifying licks of orange fire shot out from beneath the smoke while I clutched at the counter, trying to stand while my back felt like it was crumbling in on itself. I screamed for Daniel but my voice cracked from the smoke starting to fill the kitchen and my lungs.

And then I woke up. It was my fourth nightmare in the days leading up to our opening. I dreamed of no customers showing up and Daniel and myself becoming inexplicably bankrupt from the one failed run. I dreamed of our doughnuts making our customers so violently sick that, without exception, they all needed to be hospitalized. I even dreamed that Joe had backed out of our deal last minute and hordes of people had shown up to Louie's on Saturday morning, only to find locked doors and the lingering smell of pizza.

When I told Daniel he looked at me with wide eyes from across the kitchen table.

"Maybe because I've dreamed about it, none of those things will happen now."

He looked skeptical at the suggestion.

"Like metaphysical insurance."

Daniel shook his head and continued working through the inventory list he held in his hands. I'd counted all of materials we'd received in today's shipment, our final before Saturday, and added to what we'd had leftover from the nights of trial runs. Now it was Daniel's turn to count, double checking my work to make sure we wouldn't need any frantic, last minute grocery runs.

We'd been sitting across from each other at the table for hours trying to think of those last minute details when Mom and Dad came shuffling into the room, Dad carrying a large cardboard box.

"What's that?" I asked, looking up from our work.

They looked at each other and grinned. "Guess," Mom said.

"I don't know," Daniel said. Mom and Dad looked to me.

"A puppy."

"No," she said, and moved to open the box, taking a painful amount of time lifting the flaps and grabbing hold of whatever was inside, before finally pulling it out in a dramatic flourish. She shook the wrinkles out of a sky blue t-shirt and held it out for us to read. 'Beach Nuts' was screen printed on the front with a graphic of one of those tropical drink umbrellas sticking out of a doughnut.

"Your uniforms," she said excitedly, handing Daniel and me a t-shirt before pulling out two more.

"Who are those for?" I asked.

"Us," Dad answered.

Daniel and I exchanged a glance.

"We thought you guys might need some help tomorrow," Mom said.

"Technically it's tonight, isn't it?" Dad asked. "What time do you guys get started?"

I met Daniel's eyes again before answering. He looked as confused as I did. "We've been averaging about five hours of prep time from when we get in to having a full batch of each flavor completed. We're opening at seven so we'll need to start working around two."

They nodded thoughtfully, not looking the least bit concerned.

"Are you really going to help us?" Daniel asked.

"We thought we'd try," Mom shrugged. "You never know when an extra pair of hands will come in handy."

"Handy," Dad repeated with a grin. "Get it?"

Mom was the only one who laughed at the pun.

"We'll need to leave around one thirty," Daniel said.

"Do you two need help with anything before then?" Mom asked.

Honestly, we didn't. At that point we were just obsessively checking our work.

"I'm going to go take a nap then," she said.

"Okay," I said. "Thanks."

"Sure," Dad said easily, toting the cardboard box out of the room as he left with Mom.

Daniel and I looked at each other, neither of us really believing the exchange that had just taken place.

"They made it seem like it was nothing," I said.

Daniel nodded, silently agreeing. It was the exact opposite. It was everything. We went through our check lists one more time and then agreed to put them away.

I handed Daniel the papers to file and pushed my chair back from the table. "I'm going to go pick up our signs and stop by Laura's, do you need anything while I'm out?"

"I don't think so." His forehead creased. "Are we forgetting anything?"

We'd been asking each other different versions of that question for weeks. I opened my mouth to speak but he saw my face and quickly added, "I'll text you if I think of something. What are you doing at Laura's?"

"She's helping me with a little last minute project."

"Doughnut project?"

"Kind of."

He nodded, content to let it go. I went to the printer first to make sure I caught them before they closed. Only one employee was working which normally meant a painfully long wait, but no one else was in the shop.

The woman behind the counter was a tiny, mousy woman with long, gray hair pushed back from her face with a fabric headband straight out of the nineties. "Hello," she called as I approached. The counter was almost as tall as she was so when she crossed her arms to lean against it, they rested just below her collarbone.

"Hi there." I almost felt like I needed to stoop down to talk to her. "I'm here to pick up an order."

"Wonderful," she smiled, as if it really was the most wonderful thing she'd heard all day. "What's your name?"

"Taylor Bryant."

"Let me go check the back." She disappeared through a doorway behind the counter. I wondered how she would fare with the signs. One of them was just a small piece of plastic, about the size of a notebook, meant to hang on the door. That one wouldn't be a problem, but the other was a huge rectangle of vinyl intended to stretch across the window where *Louie's* was painted in huge, cursive letters. Our sign measured six feet across and four feet tall and should be able to hang right over the window, according to the employee I'd originally spoken with over the phone.

A mechanical bell chimed as the front door opened and I turned to see Rand, of all people, come inside. His eyes swept the space before finally seeing me at the counter.

"Hey, there," I said as he did a double take.

"Taylor." He crossed the room and put an arm around my shoulders. "How are you?"

"Great, thanks. What are you doing here?"

"Printer's broken at work." He pulled a flash drive from his pocket and placed it on the counter. "Is anyone here?"

"Yeah, she's in the back getting my stuff."

"Ah." He adjusted his glasses, a nervous habit I'd noticed at HRG. The woman came back with the smaller sign tucked under her elbow and her arms wrapped awkwardly around a cardboard canister, towering above her head and probably twelve inches in diameter. She shuffled to the counter and carefully set down the canister while trying to keep the one arm pressed against her side to hold the little sign. It looked painful but with the counter between us, all I could do was watch.

She finally got the canister on the ground and leaned against the counter so it wouldn't fall. "Whew," she said, flipping her long hair over her shoulder. "Big sign you got there."

"Yeah," I agreed apologetically. I slid my credit card through the reader and stuffed the smaller sign into my purse.

"What are those for?" Rand asked.

"Um, well, my brother and I are kind of starting this doughnut shop."

"A doughnut shop?"

I nodded, acutely aware of how ridiculous it must sound to him.

"That's interesting," he said. It was almost like the idea of me going from a B-rate graphic designer to opening a doughnut shop was beyond his scope of understanding. "When do you start?"

"Tomorrow, actually." I fished one of the doughnut business cards out of my purse and passed it to him. "Feel free to come by if you've got a sugar craving."

He took the card and smiled faintly at the design. "Clever."

The woman behind the counter gave me my receipt and tipped the canister over the counter like a seesaw and then pushed it forward until it slid down on my side. "Do you need help getting that to your car?"

"I've got it." I couldn't imagine that she would be much help. "Thanks though."

"You sure?" Rand asked.

"No, no, it's okay," I said as he started to reach for the canister. "You've got to get your stuff printed and get back to the office."

"Alright. Good seeing you."

"You too." I settled for dragging the canister across the store and out to my car. After leaning the passenger seat down, scooting it as far forward as it would go, and lowering the window, I managed to slide in the canister and only block half the view out of the rear window. When I pulled up to Laura's, she was outside getting the mail.

"Whatcha got there?" She asked as I got out of the car, seeing the canister protruding from the window.

I glanced back at the car. Through the window, it kind of looked like I chopped down a tree and stuffed it in my car. "It's a sign for the window at the pizza place."

Her eyes lit up. "You're so close! How are you feeling?"

Everyone seemed to be wondering the same thing. What else would you ask someone in our positions though? Like with every other momentous occasion in life, there were only so many questions you could ask to make conversation. *How are you feeling? Are you nervous? Are you excited?*

"I'm okay," I told her. At that precise moment, following her through the house to the studio, I was okay. As long as I kept moving, things felt manageable.

She paused in front of the studio to unlock the door. "John and I are coming by," she said. "I'm debating running a few miles beforehand though."

I laughed. "One doughnut won't hurt you."

"Oh, I don't intend to eat *one*," she said seriously. "I want to try them all."

"All eight of them?"

She paused. "If John and I split them…"

"So, four doughnuts each."

She looked at me. "Maybe half this weekend and half next weekend."

I smiled. "Good plan."

I set my purse down on the work table in the center of the studio and Laura went to the shelves of supplies. "We're making a necklace, right?"

"Correct."

She surveyed the shelves and pulled down a container. "A pendant necklace?"

I didn't know what that meant. "Um?"

She turned around and lifted the necklace she wore around her neck. "Like this. Where you have something - a gem, a stone, a charm, hanging from a chain."

"Right, yes. Pendant."

She grabbed one more container and brought them to the table. "Let's see it."

I dug around in my purse until I found my only contribution to this necklace making project and placed it in her hand.

She laughed when she saw it, holding it up to the light to see it better. "This is great."

"I think so too," I smiled. Laura placed a pair of wire cutters in my hands and we got to work.

CHAPTER 36 - DANIEL

Shortly after Taylor left to go run her errands, I went upstairs to change and then headed to Rachel's to pick her up for dinner, just as I had the other night. The motions were the same, but I was on a very different page mentally. Rachel and I went two full days without talking before we ended up rescheduling the dinner at Adeline's. It was the longest silence in the entirety of our relationship and I sincerely hoped it never happened again.

We hadn't talked about our fight yet. We rescheduled the dinner with the unspoken agreement to talk when we saw each other in person. Rachel set a time and I called ahead to make a reservation. Apprehension knotted my stomach as I climbed the stairs to her apartment. I was smart enough to know I'd have to do most of the talking. The fault was mine, I could admit it, but I still didn't understand how Rachel expected me to fix it.

She pushed me to tell her everything but, really, it was better if she didn't know some things. I told her the things that mattered in the context of our relationship and kept the rest of it to myself. What was wrong with that?

I knocked on the door and Rachel answered wearing a dark green dress that matched the color of her eyes. Her hair fell in the long, loose curls I always told her were my favorite.

"Hey there," she said with a faint smile. She opened the door to let me inside and I noticed her eyes look tired. Had she worried about this conversation as much as I had? Her shoulders looked tense as she took slow, precise steps to go turn off the TV in the living room. I deserved to be kept awake at night worrying about all of this, but she didn't. Something stirred in my chest, some type of deep, aching sadness.

"I don't know —" my voice cracked like a eleven year old boy. "Damn it." I cleared my throat and tried again. "I don't know what to say Rachel."

She replaced the TV control and looked at me from the other side of the living room. Her mouth opened and closed as she started to say something, but she just shook her head and sank down onto the couch. "It's not that difficult," she said after a moment. "I just want you to be open with me."

I sighed and crossed the room to sit next to her. "I *am* open with you."

She raised her chin. "We went through this part already."

"Look." I held one of her hands between mine and took a deep breath. "I am more open with you than I am with anyone else. You understand me better than anyone else. These past two days whenever I've tried to talk to Taylor about things I'm thinking, she looks at me like I'm crazy. I understand what you're saying. I get that there's this little void between us and I know that I'm probably mostly to blame for it, but I *don't* get why it's so bad that we keep some distance." Her eyes darkened and I quickly added, "Not distance. Poor word choice. Um," I searched for what I actually meant. Clearly I still stood on thin ice. "I don't get why it's so bad that we keep part of ourselves separate?"

"It's not," she said. "That's not the problem."

I gave up. I didn't understand her, or women, or what the hell they wanted.

She took her hand back and stretched her arm over the back of the couch. "There are always going to be separate parts of ourselves and maybe even parts that we don't understand about each other."

I nodded. That was good, that made sense.

"But," she continued. "That doesn't mean you can't tell me about big life things like losing your job or what's going on with your new job." Her eyes searched mine. "Do you think I think your doughnut business is dumb?"

"Kind of, yeah." She really was very perceptive.

"I've been supportive about the doughnuts this entire time."

"When they were an idea. Now they're a reality."

"Still supportive."

"What if they fail?"

"Still supportive."

I looked for some sign that she was lying, but her face still looked calm and determined. A little lock of hair had fallen out of place at some point during our conversation. I reached out to sweep it back from her face and then kept my hand there. I brushed my thumb across her cheek, down the smooth line of her jaw.

"If I screw this up, I'm letting everyone down."

"You're not letting me down," she said quietly. "And I don't think you're going to screw it up."

I traced my fingers to her chin and back to the side of her neck. "Why?"

"Because you're brilliant. You're resourceful. You anticipate needs and find solutions before most people even notice they exist. And you don't give up."

"You really do believe in me."

"Yes."

I pushed my fingers through her hair and brought her face closer. She pressed her lips against mine and that was the end of our conversation.

We ended up missing our reservation at Adeline's and ate a late dinner at the Tavern instead, which was perfectly fine with me. I felt okay again. I mostly believed that Rachel would support me even if I botched everything with the doughnuts, and that felt like enough.

When I got back home that night, most of the lights were off in the house even though it was barely past nine o'clock. I figured Mom and Dad were sleeping but when I went into the kitchen, I could see a lamp on inside the sunroom. I kept walking and saw Mom in her usual chair with her feet tucked up under her. She balanced a book on her lap and a cup of coffee in her hand, looking like she did almost every morning. Except it was nighttime.

"Mom?" She looked up from her book. "What are you doing up?"

"I couldn't sleep any longer."

I frowned. "We've got a lot of time before we need to leave, shouldn't you at least try to sleep more?" I eyed the cup of coffee, realizing the unlikelihood of that scenario.

She raised her coffee cup and smiled in confirmation. "I'm okay," she insisted. "Want to come sit for a minute?"

I sat down on the worn wicker couch across from her. The yellow cushions were faded and showing their age, but just as comfortable as they'd always been. I stretched my leg towards the matching wicker ottoman and pulled it closer with my foot so I could prop my legs on it.

"Did you and Rachel go to dinner tonight?"

"Yeah, just at the Tavern."

"Fun." To anyone else it may have sounded sarcastic, but Mom frequently made comments about how cute she thought it was that we went to the Tavern. It reminded her of some place she and Dad used to go to when they were dating back in college.

She took a sip of her coffee and asked, "Are y'all still friends?"

"Friends?"

"You know," she bobbed her head a little in the way she did when she was trying to make something sound cool. "Still getting along?"

I held in a laugh. "Yes, we're still friends."

"Has she been helping with the doughnuts?"

"She was at the beginning. I guess I haven't really given her much chance lately."

"Why not?"

I pushed a hand through my hair. *Here we go again.* "I don't know. I guess I kind of want to do this on my own."

"You'll never get anywhere if you try to figure everything out by yourself."

"I know that." I *did* know that, Rachel had all but beaten me over the head with that truth lately, but I realized part of the issue was still unresolved. "This is supposed to be my... career, my livelihood." I hesitated, debating how real I wanted to get with Mom. "If I'm supposed to provide for her and for a family someday, it kind of defeats the purpose for her to be overly involved in it."

Mom's forehead creased, either in worry or disagreement. I tried again. "If she's having to work at something with me, if I can't handle this business on my own, then I'm not providing for her, I'm burdening her."

Mom frowned a little and shook her head gently. "That's not how it works."

"How what works?"

"Relationships. Love." She tilted her chin and gave me a meaningful look, "Marriage."

I looked away. How had we managed to go from doughnuts to marriage in the less than five minutes?

"Your heart is in the right spot," Mom said. "But you're not supposed to carry every responsibility by yourself. Definitely not in marriage, but not in other relationships either. You can lead, you're a natural leader, but that doesn't mean you do everything alone without consulting other people. The best leaders are the ones who look to the people they trust for help, advice, input." She took another sip of coffee. "Cut yourself some slack."

It freaked me out how well she knew me. I know she's my Mom and she's supposed to but, really, I hadn't told her much about what had been going on with Rachel, and work, and the doughnuts. She just *knew*. Combined with the conversation I'd had with Rachel, I felt some deep, powerful calmness that I hadn't experienced in a long time. I was known and loved in spite of it, or maybe because of it.

"Thanks, Mom." I left her to her coffee and went upstairs to go to bed. On the way to my room I noticed Taylor's light was still on. I tapped softly on her door and heard a small crash from inside the room. I eased the door open and saw her on the ground, gathering up a scattered pile of pens and pencils.

"You scared the crap out of me," she said.

"Sorry." I didn't feel like I was to blame though. If she wasn't so high strung and deep in thought all the time then every little disturbance wouldn't scare the hell out of her. I bent down to help with the rest of the pens and shoved them back into the container she'd knocked onto the floor. On her desk were sketches of signs, outlines of doughnuts and scribbled notes that looked like the beginnings of recipes.

"What are you doing?"

"Planning."

"Shouldn't you be sleeping?"

She gave me a stubborn look and picked up a pen. "I'm not tired." She went back to a drawing of a sign with *Beach Nuts* written across it in big, blocky letters.

"We already have a sign." I had a moment of panic. "You did pick it up from the printer, didn't you?"

"Yes." She looked offended at the question. "It could probably be better though."

"It looks great." I hadn't seen the final product yet, but we'd debated the design in excruciating detail before she'd sent it to the printer.

"It could be better," she said again. We certainly had the perfectionism thing in common. I began to understand what it was like for people to deal with me on a daily basis.

"Taylor. Put down the pens, go to sleep. We've planned every detail we could think of, now we just need to go with it." Listening to myself, I could barely believe I was coming up with that stuff. It was like I'd changed in a matter of hours. I was on a roll and kept going. "Nothing you come up with tonight is going to make any difference with what happens tomorrow. All we can do now is get some rest."

She narrowed her eyes at me. "Are you high?"

Maybe I deserved that. "No."

I was trying to pass on a little of the calmness I felt, and she was being difficult. She stared at me another moment and then capped the pen and put it back in the container with others. "Okay. I'll see you in a few hours then."

"See you then," I nodded and started to leave. She still didn't look like she felt even remotely peaceful though. I paused at the door. "Whatever happens tomorrow, I love you."

She seemed doubtful but so was I at first. I didn't hold it against her. "Thanks," she finally said. "You too."

I closed the door behind me and headed for my room, still surprised at myself. I half expected my familiar anxiety to come crashing in at any moment, but the calm remained even as I turned out the lights, got into bed, laid down alone with my thoughts, and drifted off to sleep.

CHAPTER 37 - TAYLOR

The whole family piled into the car to drive to Louie's together. Everything about the experience was strange — Mom and Dad riding in the back seat — for the opening day of the doughnut business Daniel and I were starting — at two o'clock in the morning. None of those things went together in my mind and the whole drive felt like one of the dreams I'd been having all week.

Daniel unlocked the back door with the keys Joe had made for him. Toting in all of our supplies took a lot less time with four pairs of hands, as did the rest of the prep work. We were done and ready to go an hour earlier than normal.

Daniel and I went to the front of the store to hang the large sign I picked up from the printer the day before. The floor to ceiling windows on either side of the door were painted with the Louie's logo and the same tacky red, white, and green Italian man from the brochure. The paint took up most of the window from the waist up, which is why Daniel and I had opted for such a large sign.

"What did you get to hang it?" Daniel asked.

I fished out two suction cups with hooks from my pocket. "These came inside the canister with the sign."

Daniel frowned. The sign was about five feet long and three feet high. The suction cups were a little larger than a quarter. "Those are supposed to hold it?"

"We'll find out."

We drug two chairs outside and stood on them to place the suction cups. Each of us grabbed one end of the sign and eased the two hole punch-sized holes over the little hooks. Surprisingly, it held. Daniel hopped of his chair and stood back to look at the sign.

"It's uneven," he said. "You placed your suction cup too low."

"How do you know you didn't hang yours too high?"

He gave me a look. I sighed and unhooked the sign to nudge my suction cup a little higher. "Better?"

"Yeah."

I hopped off the chair and started to drag it back inside.

"Wait," Daniel said. "Come look at it."

"Why? Is it still uneven?"

"No, just come look."

I just knew he was going to say it was crooked or nitpick at the quality of the sign. I went and stood next to him and looked at the sign. Crisp, white letters spelled, "Beach Nuts," and a doughnut with tangerine frosting contrasted with the cheerful, sky blue of the background.

"You did a really great job with the logo," Daniel said.

"Really?" I was kind of pleased with it but it surprised me that Daniel was too.

"Really." He gazed at the sign, smiling, and then turned to me. "Come on, let's go back in."

We put the chairs inside and went back into the kitchen. Mom pulled out a big thermos of coffee I hadn't seen her bring in earlier and filled four mugs she brought from home. Dad found some folding chairs in the back by Joe's office and brought them in for us to sit on while sipped our coffee. We chatted a little bit about how the prep had gone but mostly we sat in silence, conserving our energy and mentally preparing for whatever was about to happen.

When I went to unlock the front door at six fifty-eight, I saw a car door open in the parking lot. I squinted through the dark glass and saw Haleigh walking up. Unsure of what to do, I walked back behind the counter and bent down to straighten the doughnuts in the cases.

"Hey," she said when she walked in the door.

I stood from behind the case. "Hey."

Neither of us knew what to say to each other. I couldn't decide if I felt cool or embarrassed in my Beach Nuts t-shirt. After an awkward moment she bent to peer through the glass.

"How many different types do you have?"

"Eight," I answered. "Nine if you include beach balls."

"Sorry?"

"Doughnut holes," I explained. I held one up so she could see how we'd glazed them to look like beach balls.

"That's awesome."

"Thanks."

"Well," she said, starting to dig for her wallet. "How about two of each and a dozen beach balls?" I must have looked surprise because she added, "I've got an LSAT study group in half an hour."

"Right," I said and started filling a box for her.

She waited quietly while I went down the display case, picking out the doughnuts and putting them in a box.

"I love your necklace," she said after a moment.

"Thanks," I said, touching the chain I'd cut in Laura's studio the day before.

She squinted, as if just then looking at it. "What is it?"

"A bullet," I said. "Just a rubber one."

"Oh." I smiled a little as she tried to sound interested. "That's so cool."

She thought it was weird. Her reaction amused me more than it offended me though. Even if she'd asked why I wore it, I didn't think I'd be able to tell the story of Dad giving me the bullet with the meaning it deserved. It wasn't just a reminder of a funny time where Dad was being Dad. The bullet symbolized everything he normally left unsaid – his love, his support. Talking about the meaning to someone who wouldn't understand would only cheapen it.

I rang up the order, she swiped her credit card using the reader I'd fixed to my tablet and signed the electronic receipt with her fingertip.

"Thanks for coming by," I told her as I handed her the box.

"Of course," she said cheerfully. "Good luck."

"Thanks." We looked at each other awkwardly for a moment. "That means a lot," I added. It sounded trite, but I meant it. I finally understood Haleigh and I were very different people. That we were friends at all was kind of remarkable in its own way.

"Bye, Daniel," Haleigh called as she headed towards the door. He had been watching our conversation off to the side and offered a smile and a wave as she exited. The smile disappeared the second the door closed.

"What's her deal?" He asked.

"What do you mean?"

"She seemed all standoffish and cold."

I shrugged, "Nothing new there."

"Probably jealous," he muttered. "You just started your own business and she comes in here like she's better than you." He shook his head bitterly. "What's she even doing with her life?"

"Going to law school."

"Oh," he said. He thought for a moment and then smiled at me, "Who needs lawyers?"

It was a nice attempt to make me feel better but I was surprised to realize I didn't need to feel better, I felt fine. The ever-present insecurity following me around for the past few months was gone. I looked at Daniel, idly scratching at the neckline of his t-shirt, and tried to cement the moment in my mind, knowing that whatever happened with Beach Nuts, every detail of the day would be worth remembering.

"Daniel?"

"Yeah?"

"Your shirt is on backwards."

He stopped scratching and looked at the shirt. He held it away from his neck and found the tag in front, where it had been causing the itching. He sighed heavily and pulled his arms in to turn the shirt around just as the door pushed open and Lola came barreling in, a huge group of ten or fifteen people following her.

"*Buenos días*, Taylor!"

"Good morning," I smiled back. "Lola, you've met Daniel?"

Daniel struggled to free his arms, now stuck inside the sleeves of his t-shirt. She smiled, waiting to shake his hand until he forced his right arm out. The left one was still stuck in the sleeve like a T-Rex arm.

"Nice to meet you," he said, his face flushed.

"I brought my salsa students," she said, gesturing to the group behind her. "I made promises of a Spanish doughnut to compliment their Spanish dancing."

"They won't be disappointed," I assured her, and reached into the case to pull out a cinnamon sugar doughnut with chocolate drizzled on top. "I give to you the only doughnut not even remotely related to our beach theme. Per your suggestion, the Spanish Hot Chocolate doughnut."

"Not related to your beach theme?" She put a hand on her hip. "What do you think seventy percent of Spain's border is made of?"

It was a stretch but I let her have it. Her students crowded around the case and began pointing at all of the doughnuts, asking about the flavors and the toppings.

"Go. Work," Lola said with a smile.

Daniel and I began rattling off answers to all of their questions and ringing up orders as fast as we could. Before we attended to even half of the group, another wave of five or six people came through the door. Every time I managed a glance at the clock it seemed another hour had flown by. A little after nine o'clock, Joe came through the front door and straight to the counter, past three people already in line. They glanced at him with a hint of annoyance.

"It's okay." Joe flashed one of his wide, charming grins. "I own the place."

Somehow that proved sufficient to appease the other people. "You've got them?" I asked Daniel.

He nodded and I moved to the end of the counter to talk to Joe.

"How are my doughnuteers doing?" He bent and inspected the doughnuts inside the case.

"Pretty sure we just fall into the 'baker' category."

"No," he shook his head. "I like doughnuteer." He straightened and leaned an elbow on the top of the case. "I'm here to collect the rent."

My eyes widened. We didn't have much cash on hand. I could write a check but I hadn't brought my checkbook – who even carries one around anymore? Did we discuss paying the rent? Maybe Mom had her checkbook and I could pay her back?

"Doughnuts," Joe said, seeing my face. "I haven't had breakfast."

"Oh. Right, of course." My face flushed but, really, it was a miracle I was even functioning on so little sleep over the past week. I felt no shame. "What sounds good?"

"Surprise me."

"May I," I pulled out a wax paper square with a flourish, "interest you..." I stretched down to the bottom shelf of the case to retrieve a doughnut, "in a Joe-nut?"

His face went slack. "You didn't." A genuine smile, not his routine, charming grin, lit up his features. "What's it called?"

"A Joe-nut," I repeated, unable to say it without smiling.

Joe laughed so hard and loud that the other customers in line whipped around to see what he was laughing at. All they saw was Joe doubled over laughing and me holding a doughnut. Dan smiled knowingly and went back to filling orders.

Eventually Joe stopped laughing long enough to take the doughnut from me. "What kind is it?"

"Vanilla cake doughnut, mascarpone frosting, and espresso ganache. Kind of a tiramisu sort of thing," I explained. "Because you're—"

"Italian," he said with me. "This is amazing."

"Daniel came up with the name."

"And you came up with the recipe?" I nodded and he added, "You two make a good team."

"Well, the day is young."

"Hey," Joe reached into his pocket for his cell phone, "Will you take my picture with the Joe-nut?"

"Sure," I laughed. I took the phone and snapped a picture.

"*Grazie.* Now go deal with your actual customers," he waved me off. "I'll be over here." He took a seat at a table in the corner and kicked up his feet on a neighboring chair. I watched him take a bite of the doughnut and then yell loud enough to be heard over the conversation of the other customers, "*This is the best doughnut I've ever had.*"

Daniel looked at me with wide eyes, embarrassed by the outburst. "Just laugh," I told him. Someone sitting near Joe had already struck up a conversation with him and a moment later was at the counter ordering a Joe-nut.

As we started to run out of certain flavors, Daniel and I called back to Mom and Dad to start frosting more of them. By eleven, we'd sold out of everything – nearly three hundred doughnuts and just as many doughnut holes.

Daniel flipped the Louie's sign to closed and he looked at me. "Did that just happen?"

"I hope so."

We stood there quietly, absorbing the moment. You always expect times like those to feel monumental and powerful, but somehow they don't. Any attempts to wrap your mind around the gravity of what happened come up short.

Mom and Dad came out from the kitchen. "What's with the glazed looks?" Mom asked.

"Get it?" Dad asked, playfully swatting my arm.

"I've been waiting for a chance to use that all day," Mom said.

I shook my head at them.

Dad smiled and slung an arm around my shoulder. "You did good today."

"We couldn't have done it without you guys," Daniel said seriously.

Mom and Dad shrugged off the praise. "We've got most of the kitchen cleaned up," Mom said. "Do you two want to wrap up out here and we'll go grab a bite to eat?"

"That sounds good," I said.

Mom and Dad went back through the kitchen doors. I looked at Daniel and his expression looked undeniably peaceful and satisfied in a strong, quiet sort of way. It was everything I was feeling too. We'd sold more doughnuts than we dared hope, but there was more than to it than the plain joy of success. There was purpose and meaning, intertwining to shape a type of satisfaction with a feeling all its own.

Maybe finding our purpose in a ragtag doughnut shop seemed silly on the surface, but there was a depth I couldn't articulate yet. Doughnuts weren't the purpose in and of themselves, they were our medium, and they were a first, large step in the right direction.

"I think this is going to work," Daniel said.

I raised a fist in the air and said quietly, "Beach Nuts."

He smiled. "Beach Nuts."

ACKNOWLEDGEMENTS

They say it takes a village to raise a child. I think the same sentiment can be applied to writing a book. Indirectly, I've been preparing to write for my entire life and a whole cast of characters played integral roles to the process.

Mom and Dad – my coaches, my cheerleaders, my truest fans. Your commitment to cultivate creativity in me, to open every door and push me to explore every opportunity made it possible for me to believe in myself. Thank you for every dance lesson you let me take and every golf tournament you refused to let me withdraw from. You guys get more credit than anyone for helping me become the person I am.

This book would never have happened without the brother who dreamed up the crazy idea of a beach-themed doughnut shop. Moreover, you've shown me what it is to love deeply, fight hard, and still be a best friend at the end of the day. David, did you ever imagine our secret Pinterest board would turn into a book?

Dreams don't really seem to count for a whole lot unless you're pursuing them. I spent a lot of months anguishing over my dreams rather than pursuing them until Michael Belk appeared on the scene and called me out (within five minutes of meeting me, for the record). The metaphorical ball of my writing pursuits may have already been rolling by that point, but Michael definitely gave the ball a swift kick in the pants.

Of course, there were still hours spent debating sensibility, practicality, and my sanity. Without Lucinda Martens, my Lola, bombarding me with wisdom and encouragement, I'm not sure if I would have ever made the jump. Following God is kind of a crazy thing sometimes, but you've shown me the best picture of what that looks like.

Sticking with the theme of Pushes in the Right Direction, Claire Hogan gave me a powerful example of what it is to feel the tug of purpose and then follow it with a huge leap of faith. Thank you for reassuring me I wasn't crazy.

Claire also connected me with my first editor Tucker McCormack. When we first started our editing meetings, I likened it to something like having your soul ripped out and thrown into a washing machine. In more normal terms – it was painful, but you challenged me to keep developing the story until it looked like an actual novel.

After the almost-finished story laid dormant for a few months, Megan McConnell swooped in and brought it home. I will never be able to thank you enough for giving such a huge portion of your time and expertise to finish editing the book, developing all the collateral no one ever thinks about (press releases – what?), and pushing me to complete every aspect of the publishing process with excellence.

I joined the writers group at Art House Dallas right when I picked up writing full-time. Our Thursday mornings were incredibly inspiring and life giving, especially on the days when I just sat back and listened. Thanks to all of you for creating a space of creative community and encouragement.

I know everyone has moments of doubt along their journey, but I don't know if they all have a Joel Zandstra to bring them coffee (and queso, and wine, and massages at appropriate intervals), speak truth into their lives, and then push them back into the office, as it were, with strict instructions to stay in there until they finished a novel.

To everyone who wrote or spoke a word of encouragement, who believed in me and told me I could do it — thank you.

ABOUT THE AUTHOR

Kate Petty's storytelling humbly began at the age of three with a mystical scroll of stories (i.e., a bamboo sushi mat) and an awe-stricken, captivated audience (i.e., two very amused parents). Eventually she traded the sushi mat for a notebook and then a computer, but she likes to think she's maintained the same spirit for invention and creativity.

In college, Kate studying filmmaking and screenwriting. Her background includes documentary production, corporate videography, photography, and editorial writing.

The variety of her experiences opened the door to work as the director of marketing for a technology company in Dallas. She worked with the company until she decided to craft a life better suited to her passions and talents. Kate now focuses on encouraging others to pursue their own passions while maintaining her commitment to live intentionally and with purpose.

Made in the USA
Lexington, KY
20 September 2015